Praise for Priscilla Oliveras's Keys to Love Series

"A big-hearted, beautiful book about first love, second chances, and finding one's place in the world. Oliveras writes with a rare warmth that not only brings her characters to life but also lets her readers sink into the gorgeous Key West sunrises she so lovingly describes. An exceptional getaway of a book!" —**Emily Henry, New York Times bestselling author of Beach Read**

"*Anchored Hearts* has it all: undeniable chemistry between its irresistible leads; believable roadblocks to their happy ending; a heartwarming world filled with familia and comunidad; and a lush Key West setting that leaps off the page. Alejandro and Anamaría's love story is not to be missed!" —**Mia Sosa, USA Today bestselling author of The Worst Best Man**

"I finished *Island Affair* with a big smile on my face. I can't decide what I adored more: Luis and Sara's love story, their relationships with their complicated and difficult and loving families, or the setting of Key West, which sounded so beautiful I wanted to jump on a plane. I can't wait to read more by Priscilla Oliveras!" —*New York Times* **bestselling author Jasmine Guillory**

"Rich with emotion and breathtaking prose, *Island Affair* delivers a captivating love story that demonstrates the power of forgiveness and strong family bonds." —**Farrah Rochon, USA Today bestselling author**

Praise for Priscilla Oliveras's Matched to Perfection Series

"Oliveras's tangled, topical conflicts between multidimensional characters blend with lovingly portrayed family life and an intricate, realistic plot, enmeshing the reader in her created world." —*Publishers Weekly,* **STARRED REVIEW**

T0026465

Her Perfect Affair

Also by Priscilla Oliveras

Anchored Hearts
*Summer in the City**
*A Season to Celebrate**
Their Perfect Melody
Her Perfect Affair
His Perfect Partner

*Anthology collection

Her Perfect Affair

Priscilla Oliveras

ZEBRA BOOKS
Kensington Publishing Corp.
www.kensingtonbooks.com

Acknowledgments

Latinos are known for our comunidades—our strong communities. Bueno, this Latina thankfully has a strong community of people who love and support her, and there are some in particular who deserve a shout-out for helping me bring Rosa and Jeremy's story to life for my readers.

My heartfelt gracias to:

My parents—Joe and Migdalia—for the never-ending love and support and cheerleading. Words alone cannot express how much I admire, cherish, and love you, and that doesn't happen often to an author. ¡Los quiero mucho!

My first and, so far, only beta reader, who happens to also be my lovable big sis—Jackie, you are a constant ray of sunshine in all of our lives and I am so lucky to have you not only as my sister, but as my best friend.

My second sister, by choice if not by blood—Melissa, gracias, for being my partner in crime in pretty much all things memorable and fun.

Charlee Allden, write-in partner extraordinaire—those hot afternoons quietly writing in my backyard together helped me meet my Book 2 deadline, which we both know wasn't easy. Thanks for not minding my salsa dancing when I used my standing desk.

My AMAZING agent, Rebecca Strauss—you talked me off the debut author Book 2 self-doubt ledge; I truly appreciate your guidance and insight.

My beach getaway, happy hour, tailgate posse—Jen, Heather, Steph, Tammy, Kristy, Kathie, Paula, Kathleen, Leslie—thanks for the laughs, good memories and sisterhood.

My fellow Latinx romance authors, especially Mia, Sabrina & Alexis—may our stories continue to be told, shared, and celebrated. #LatinxRom ¡Sí se puede!

Most importantly, my three incredible, awe-inspiring daughters—Alexa, Gabby, and Belle. You three are the light of my life, my greatest joy. Achieving my goal of becoming a published author wouldn't mean half as much without you here to share in the excitement. ¡Las quiero . . . as Rosa and Jeremy say . . . para siempre!

Chapter One

Rosa Fernandez stared at the sea of wedding guests whirling on the dance floor. Her toe tapped to the beat of the salsa music, but she didn't join in the revelry. Not when it was her responsibility to make sure everything was running smoothly.

Scooting around a potted palm, she made a beeline for the buffet tables and wedding planner, relieved that so far all had gone according to schedule. Her big sister and her new husband had departed over an hour ago amidst kisses and well wishes. With huge grins on their faces and love for each other in their eyes, they'd headed upstairs to one of the finest suites the downtown historic Chicago hotel boasted.

Now, with the clock close to striking 1 AM, the party would be ending soon.

Without Rosa having worked up the nerve to ask a particular someone to dance. Her gaze scanned the crowd, looking for—

"It was a beautiful September wedding, mija."

Rosa turned her attention to her neighbor, bending to accept the elderly woman's hug. "Gracias, Señora Vega."

Señora Vega smiled, the wrinkles on her face deepening.

"You did a fabulous job. Just like the church senior social you organized last month."

"I'm glad you enjoyed them."

"Bueno, no one doubted tonight would come together beautifully in your capable hands," Señora Vega said. "You're always on
top of things. That's your specialty, verdad, nena?"

Right.

Or maybe it was her affliction.

Rosa kept the errant thought to herself, returning Señora Vega's
smile with a tremulous one of her own. "Yazmine and Tomás deserve the best."

"Que nena buena eres." The older woman patted Rosa's cheek,
a wistful sheen in her eyes. "Your parents would have loved this,"
she said, leaning in for a good-bye hug.

Rosa nodded mutely, melancholy wrapping around her heart at
the thought of her parents and how much she missed them. They
should have been here. Sure, there was nothing any of them could
have done to stop Papi's cancer, but her mother's car accident all
those years ago . . . that should never have happened.

For now, Rosa pushed aside the memories and guilt. Today was
her big sister's special day, so Rosa would do her best to channel their
mom and her knack for organizing the best parties anyone could
throw.

As Rosa wove through guests, the reception music changed to
the heavy bass of a popular reggaeton song and the crowd on the
dance floor let out a cheer.

"Hey, Rosa, come join us!" Arms raised overhead, her younger
sister waved at her.

Surrounded by a crowd of her old high school friends, Lilí
shimmied her hips and shoulders in reckless abandon to the Spanish rap music. Thanks to her sweaty gyrations throughout the
night, her pixie haircut had lost some of its spike, but Lilí's playful
grin had only grown bigger.

One of the guys snaked his arm around her lower back, and Lilí
plastered her lithe body against his. They moved to the music as
one, simulating an act that more likely belonged in the bedroom
than on the dance floor.

Rosa shook her head in bemusement. Lilí puckered up and
made a show of blowing her a kiss.

Ay, the little brat. A cocktail dress and heels could not a properly behaved young lady make.

Lilí yelled another catcall in her direction.

Rosa waved her off. Mosh-pit-style dancing wasn't really her cup of café con leche. Lilí knew that.

Lilí stuck out her tongue, then went back to her fun.

With a resigned sigh, Rosa turned away. Lilí might not understand that there were responsibilities to attend to, but *she* certainly did. With Papi's passing earlier this year, Rosa felt compelled to take charge. Even more so than after Mami's death almost ten years ago, when Rosa and Yaz had been in high school.

Be responsible. Do the right thing. It was what she did best. Even if the "good girl" reputation Señora Vega had referred to sometimes made Rosa itch to break out of the mold.

Shaking off the lingering melancholy, she continued moving through the crowd, stopping now and then to chat with friends and guests, thanking them for their attendance, reminiscing about her parents.

She was halfway across the ballroom when a thick arm encircled her waist from behind.

"Red Rosie, you've been avoiding me."

Recognizing her former classmate's voice, Rosa bit back a groan.

"Héctor!" She turned, leaning away from him, barely stopping herself from stomping on his foot with her heel. It would serve him right after grabbing her butt earlier in the buffet line!

"No seas mala!" he complained.

"I'm not being mean. I'm busy."

"One dance. A slow one. Come on, Red Rosie."

The embarrassing high school nickname grated on her already frayed nerves.

"Héctor, I have to check in with the wedding planner."

"All work and no play—"

"I know, I know. But this party is all about Yaz and Tomás. How about you go play a little harder for the both of us, okay?" Rosa schooled her face into her understanding-yet-I'm-not-giving-in expression. She might only be seven weeks into her job as the librarian at Queen of Peace Academy, but she'd been practicing this look in the mirror for months. "Marisol is sitting by herself. I'm sure she'd love to dance with you."

Rosa pointed at their mutual friend.

When Héctor gave her a sad-eyed pout, Rosa arched a brow to make her point, but softened it with a teasing smile.

"Está bien," he finally moaned.

She watched him trudge away, part of her wanting to join him and the crowd having fun. Yet, she held back. Her job wasn't done.

Moments later, after a short discussion with the wedding planner, Rosa learned all was in order. She wasn't needed anymore. Just like at home now that Papi was gone and Lilí was off to college.

Uncertainty weighed heavy in her chest.

She glanced from her peers, excitedly dancing, to the older couples chatting at the circular tables. Most people here would say she fit in better with the older, more reserved crowd. Not that she could blame them. It's where she typically gravitated. She heaved a sigh weighty with resignation.

No one knew about the increasing number of times lately that she wondered how it might feel to shake up the status quo. Do something just because it felt good, without worrying about the consequences.

Although, shaking things up might not be what the Catholic diocesan school board at Queen of Peace Academy in their quiet Chicago suburb of Oakmont, Illinois, wanted from their new librarian. She'd worked hard to finish her MLS on time so she could take over when Mrs. Patterson had retired this past summer. Now was Rosa's chance to carve her own niche amongst the staff, moving from former student to colleague. Allowing her to work on becoming a mentor to her students.

So what if she felt something was missing. It would pass.

Feeling out of sorts, Rosa edged her way toward the back of the ballroom near one of the portable drink stations.

"One ginger ale with a lime twist for the señorita, coming right up," the bartender said as she approached.

"You remembered!"

The grey-haired man filled a cup with ice and smiled at her. "Why aren't you enjoying yourself with the other young people?"

"I was just about to ask her the same question."

Rosa started at the deep voice coming from behind her. She glanced over her shoulder, thrilled to find Jeremy Taylor standing close by. His broad shoulders and footballplayer physique filled out his navy pinstriped suit to perfection. Even though her heels added a good four inches to her five-foot-six height, Jeremy still towered over her. He smiled, his blue eyes crinkling at the corners. A thrill shivered down her spine.

"I'll have what she's having, please," Jeremy said.

"Ginger ale?" the old bartender asked.

Jeremy blinked in surprise before he slowly shook his head. "Rosa, Rosa, Rosa. How can you celebrate your sister's marriage without enjoying some champagne? C'mon, share a glass with me?"

Longing seared through her, fast and hot. Ay, little did he know that she'd share pretty much *anything* with him.

Jeremy tilted his head toward her, urging her to say yes. But not pushing.

Ever since Yaz had introduced the two of them almost four years ago, Jeremy had been nothing but friendly, almost brotherly. After Papi's death back in January, Jeremy had been amazingly supportive. A perfect gentleman.

Just not *her* perfect gentleman.

Now he waited for her answer, an expectant gleam in his blue eyes.

Technically she was off the clock. The wedding planner had said she'd wrap things up and touch base on Monday.

What could one glass of champagne amongst friends hurt?

Before she could change her mind, Rosa nodded, pleased by the way Jeremy's grin widened at her response. He held up two fingers at the bartender, who winked at Rosa.

"Buen provecho," the old man murmured.

She gave him a shy smile of thanks as she reached for the proffered champagne flute, then sidled away from the bar.

Jeremy fell into step alongside her and her heart rate blipped with glee.

"What did he say when he handed you your drink?" he asked. "Good something, right?"

She nodded, remembering Jeremy's recent decision to start learning Spanish. "Literally it means, 'enjoy your meal,' but in this sense, it's more like, 'enjoy.'"

"Well then"—leaning closer to her, he clinked his flute against hers—"buen pro-pro—"

"Provecho," she finished, her belly flip-flopping at his chagrined smile.

They walked a few more steps before she worked up the courage to ask, "So, um, where's your date?"

The tall blonde who'd been his plus-one was the epitome of old money and high class, a glaring reminder that Jeremy came from a wealthy, established Chicago family. Rosa, on the other hand, came from a small town on the Island, her parents having transplanted from Puerto Rico to the Humboldt Park area of Chicago when they were first married, then later to Oakton in the suburbs.

She and Jeremy, not to mention his date, weren't quite the same pedigree.

"Cecile?"

"Uh-huh. Is she your . . . ?" Rosa let her voice trail off, wondering what his response might be.

"Family friend. I mean, we dated years ago, but decided we're better as friends."

Rosa breathed a soft sigh of relief.

"Anyway, she ditched me a while ago." Jeremy brushed it off like his date leaving him behind didn't bother him. "Her parents are hosting a charity event over on Michigan Avenue and she wanted to put in an appearance."

"You didn't want to go?"

"And miss this fun?" He jutted his chin out at the people dancing to a well-known merengue hit. Couples packed the floor, some more seasoned and coordinated than others, but all having a great time.

They reached an empty table and Jeremy pulled out a chair for her.

"I haven't seen you out there," he said. "How come?"

He sat down to join her, his muscular thigh inadvertently brushing against hers. Tingles of awareness danced a cha-cha down her leg.

"Um, well." Hyper-attuned to his nearness, it took Rosa a second to find her words. "This is more Yazmine and Lilí's scene. I guess I tend to be a much better party planner than a partygoer."

"I wouldn't necessarily say that." Jeremy's lips quirked as he slid her a teasing glance. "I seem to recall you play a mean game of charades."

Rosa laughed, remembering Lilí's birthday this past spring. It'd been their first family celebration since Papi's death, so Lilí had kept it an intimate affair at home with the three sisters; Tomás; his six-year-old daughter, Maria; Jeremy; and a few other close friends.

She and Jeremy had wound up on the same charades team. That night, they'd been on a similar wavelength or something, quickly guessing each other's clues before anyone else.

Lilí had cried foul play.

Yaz had dubbed them the dynamic duo.

Rosa had soaked up the shared moment, their uncanny connection. Later, she'd composed a few verses about it in her private poetry journal.

"By the way, Yaz mentioned how you stepped in to help so she wouldn't stress as much today. Everything turned out great." The pleasure in his bright smile, directed right at her, made Rosa's pulse skip.

She ducked her head, embarrassed by his praise. "It wasn't that much."

"Right," Jeremy answered, his tone dripping with disbelief.

She peeked at him from under her lashes. At some point in the evening, he'd shed his suit jacket and rolled up his shirtsleeves, revealing his muscular forearms. As always, she was drawn by his ruffled dark blond hair and square jaw. But even more so by his friendly eyes and the easy camaraderie they shared.

He took a swig of his champagne, eyeing her over the rim.

What did he see when he looked at her?

Anxiety fluttered in her chest at the thought.

No way did she measure up to Cecile, or any of the other women who traveled in his family's social circle. Cecile's diamonds had been real. Rosa wore costume jewelry she'd found on sale. Her red taffeta bridesmaid dress, bought off the rack, was far from designer label.

She tugged at her hem, uncomfortable with the short style Lilí had preferred. Hating the fact that even among her sisters she sometimes felt like she didn't measure up.

They were movers and shakers, life-of-the-party people.

She was the low-key Fernandez sister.

For a long time, she'd preferred it that way, especially after . . .

It was simply safer.

The thing was, safer often also meant lonely.

"How come you didn't bring your own plus-one tonight?" Jeremy angled toward her to be heard over the music, his shoulder bumping into hers. His earthy cologne teased her senses.

She shrugged, her bare shoulder rubbing against the cool material of his shirtsleeve. "Pretty much everyone I know was already coming. Plus, I thought it'd be rude to leave a date alone if the caterer or someone needed help."

Besides, the only man she would have liked to ask was already on the invite list. With his own plus-one. And probably way out of her league.

Not that Jeremy had any inkling of her major crush on him.

"Always thinking of others, huh? You're pretty amazing, Rosa Fernandez." Jeremy raised his glass in salute with a playful wink.

"Thanks," she murmured. His flattery and sincere tone caused heat to flood her cheeks, reminding her of Héctor's earlier Red Rosie comment. She despised the nickname that dated back to her freshman public-speaking class and the vicious blushing episodes she'd suffered.

Rather than press her flute to her warm face, Rosa settled for a gulp of the cold champagne.

"Mis amigos, it's almost closing time." The DJ's rich baritone elicited a groan of disapproval from the partiers. "We'll play our last slow song, then finish the night with a bang. Gracias por venir esta noche! For you gringos, that means 'thanks for coming tonight' to celebrate Yazmine and Tomás's wedding! Now, here's one for all you couples out there."

The beginning strains of an old Spanish love song drifted from the speakers. Regret and loss tightened Rosa's throat when she recognized the tune as one Papi and his trío had often played at their gigs throughout the years.

Around the ballroom, dancers quickly paired up. Rosa watched a young teen work up the nerve to ask a pretty girl from their church to join him. The girl hesitated, hands clasped behind her back. Rosa waited, anxiously hoping the poor boy's spirits weren't about to be crushed.

Dios, her adolescent memories were pockmarked with similar self-esteem-diminishing moments. Waiting for this cute boy or that smart one to invite her to a school dance, or out for ice cream. Or even for a library study date. The one time she'd tried taking the initiative, she'd bungled it. Badly. Eventually, she'd given up wishing for a date. Books were far safer companions.

Finally, the girl gave a shy nod and the young couple moved to join the others. Out of the corner of her eye, Rosa noticed Jeremy pushing his seat back. She turned to say good-bye, only to find him holding out a hand to her.

"You're not going to let the night end without allowing me one dance, are you?" His blue eyes warmed with a plea for her to say yes.

Surprised anticipation hummed in her chest.

She'd wanted an invite from him all night, but figured his date wouldn't appreciate it. Now that the statuesque socialite was out of the picture. . . .

Behind him, Rosa caught Lilí laughing with her partner, enjoying herself, having done very little tonight to help behind the scenes.

Diviértete, Lilí had chided her earlier during the wedding party dance.

Her little sister was right. It *was* time for her to have a little fun. The thought had Rosa's pulse pounding like she'd already started dancing a salsa.

Rising to her feet, she set her hand in Jeremy's larger one.

His fingers closed around hers, the tight grip welcome, reassuring. He led the way to the edge of the dance floor, where he pulled her close to him.

Arms draped around his neck, Rosa laid her head against the front of his shoulder, savoring the feel of his strength under her cheek. She took a deep breath to steady herself, his subtle musky scent mixing with the warm, sweat-laden air from the bodies surrounding them.

Dios mío, she'd dreamt of a moment like this with him so many times over the months of wedding preparations. The number of poetry stanzas she'd written about it was actually a bit embarrassing. That's partly why her work was for her eyes only, never shared with anyone.

Jeremy's hands pressed against the small of her back sent waves of heat pulsating through her as they swayed to the music. Their thighs brushed together, the intimate contact weakening her knees with desire.

"It's been an incredible evening." Jeremy bent his head closer to hers, his breath warming her ear.

"Mmm-hmm," she murmured. And definitely more incredible now.

"I wish Rey could have been here. I don't think there was a dry eye in the church when Pablo read your dad's letter."

The shock of hearing Papi's words had definitely brought the prick of tears to Rosa's eyes. At that point of the ceremony, plenty of men had reached for their handkerchiefs, too.

"He was an amazing man," Jeremy continued.

Knowing Jeremy understood how much Papi had meant to her and her sisters endeared him to her even more. Papi had always said that a good man recognized another. Jeremy and her father had shared that awareness. She'd been lucky enough to witness it.

Rosa tilted her head to look up at Jeremy. The white disco lights above them turned his dark blond hair to burnished gold, leaving his handsome face a mix of shadows. But this close to him, she couldn't miss the depth of tenderness in his eyes.

"Papi would have loved being here," she said. "He'd have been so proud of Yaz."

"He would have been proud of all three of his girls. Especially you."

"Pues, I appreciate that, but I don't know. . . ." she demurred.

"*Well*, nothing." Jeremy brushed his knuckle across her cheek, continuing the path lower to trace the edge of her mouth. His gaze shifted down to her lips and back up again. Desire curled through her. "You amaze me, Rosa. Always downplaying your talents, but I know better. I've seen you in action."

His finger brushed her lips ever so softly. Once. Twice. Slowly he bent toward her and she rose up on her toes, aching for his kiss.

Someone bumped into her side, knocking her off balance.

"Ooooh!" she gasped, stumbling in her stilettos.

Jeremy tightened his hold to steady her.

"Perdóname," the older man, one of Tomás's cousins from Texas, apologized. His matronly partner reiterated the sentiment. Rosa waved off their concern with a smile and the couple resumed dancing.

"You okay?" Jeremy asked, stepping back a bit to look her over.

Rosa nodded, swallowing her disappointment. Ave Maria purísima, had their potential first kiss just been dashed? Now she'd never know.

Thankfully, the song hadn't finished and Jeremy gathered her in his arms again, gently pressing her head to his shoulder.

His hand skimmed down her back, stopping at the curve of her hip. Tendrils of desire floated through her like wisps of sensuous smoke from a fire banked too long. She let her lids drift closed, lost in the thrill of his touch. The rush of pleasure at what might have just happened.

For some strange reason the image of Cecile, his date for the evening, flashed through her mind. Guilt quickly followed, but Rosa squashed it. The woman must be crazy to have left early; obviously she wasn't really interested in him.

"Let's enjoy the last of the night while we can," Jeremy said in her ear. "When I'm sitting in my office in Japan, missing home, I'll think of tonight and smile."

His words filtered through the desire fogging her brain and Rosa jerked in surprise. Japan? What was he—?

She stutter-stepped, accidentally catching Jeremy's toes. "Ay, perdóname."

"That's okay." Jeremy eased them back into step with the music.

"Um, Japan? What do you mean?"

Her question brought his gaze to hers. A confused frown creased his brow. "You didn't hear?"

"Hear what?"

"My company landed a new project in Japan and they appointed me to lead the team. I told Yaz a few days ago. She didn't mention it?"

Rosa shook her head.

"It happened pretty fast, actually. I leave in two weeks and will be gone anywhere from four to six months. It's a really great opportunity." Excitement rang in his voice, his expression brightening like that of a boy who'd just hit his first Little League home run.

Six months overseas?

Dread crept over her, threatening to ruin the best part of her evening.

The stunning news of his imminent departure, on the heels of what she'd thought was their heart-stopping almost kiss, left her feeling deflated.

"I'm . . . wow . . . congratulations." She forced her lips into a smile, then quickly laid her head against his chest, afraid he might see the regret in her eyes.

The song came to an end and the DJ cranked up the volume for one final bass-thumping, beat-pumping fast song that had the others whooping. As Rosa and Jeremy slowly broke apart, Lilí slid into the space between them. Her head bobbed and weaved to the beat, her hips swaying in tempo.

"Hey, Jer!" Lilí tossed over her shoulder at him. "Give me a sec with my sister, will you?"

Jeremy glanced at Rosa as if to gauge her reaction before he tipped his head and moved away.

Lilí reached for Rosa's hands, giving them a squeeze. "Me and some of the gang are going clubbing downtown. I thought I'd see if you wanted to join us."

"Excuse me?" Her head still reeling from Jeremy's news, Rosa was certain she'd misheard her sister.

"Come on, party with us."

"Ay, I don't think that's a good idea."

Lilí rolled her eyes. "You haven't had any fun tonight."

"That's not true, I was just . . ." Rosa slid her gaze over Lilí's shoulder, relieved to see Jeremy seated at their table.

Lilí stepped closer to her, pivoting to follow Rosa's gaze. Her sister's eyes widened and she quickly turned back around.

An impish smirk on her lips, Lilí dragged Rosa to the opposite edge of the dance floor, away from the crush of dancers, but also out of Jeremy's sight.

"Is something up with you and Jeremy?" Lilí asked. She clapped her hands with glee, excitement lighting her face.

"I—I don't—" Mortified that she may have let her crush be known, Rosa waved off her sister's question. "It's nothing."

"But it could be!"

Rosa shook her head, her face growing hot with embarrassment.

"Hey, girl, news flash, you're only a librarian at Queen of Peace, not one of the nuns." Lilí grabbed her shoulders. "Take off your control-top panty hose and let loose for once."

"I'm not wearing—" Rosa bit off the rebuttal when she caught the flash of humor in her sister's eyes. "Ay, por favor, quit messing around."

Lilí pulled her in for a quick hug. "Jeremy's a good guy. And he just transferred to the Chicago office so now he's back in town, too. What could it hurt to ask him to hang out for a bit once this all winds down? See what . . . develops."

Rosa opened her mouth to argue, but Lilí cut her off before she could.

"Don't answer that, just promise me you'll think about it," Lilí said. "I'm heading out, and I'll plan to crash in Trish's room so I don't wake you up when I get in."

"Ha, more like so I don't bother you when I wake up at a decent hour tomorrow morning," Rosa countered.

"Bueno, que será, será. But I say, go for it! Either way, you got the hotel room to yourself tonight. Don't do anything I wouldn't do!"

With a saucy waggle of her eyebrows, Lilí melted back into the crowd. Rosa couldn't hear what her sister said to her group of friends, but they let out a roar of raucous excitement and upped the intensity on their mosh-pit moves.

Skirting the edge of the dance floor to avoid being trampled, Rosa headed back to the table where Jeremy waited. He tugged at his tie to loosen it, and Lilí's "see what develops" taunt echoed in Rosa's head.

If only . . .

"Everything okay?" Jeremy asked when she reached him. He stood to pull out her chair, sinking back beside her when she sat.

"It's fine. Lilí's heading out to continue the celebration else-where."

"Oh, to be that young and carefree again," he said, his words laced with amusement. His lips quirked in a sexy grin.

Rosa's mind jumped back to their near kiss on the dance floor. His intent gaze as his knuckle caressed her cheek and the edge of her mouth.

Dios mío, was it possible? Could Jeremy really be interested in her?

A nervous shudder shimmied her shoulders.

She bit her bottom lip, considering. Yaz was up in the honeymoon suite, off to frolic in Cozumel with Tomás in the morning. Lilí was hitting the town, ready to party all night, damn the consequences, or hangover, tomorrow.

Why couldn't she have her own fun? Instead of always playing it safe to avoid getting hurt or rejected.

"Hey, what's wrong?" Jeremy hooked his fingers through hers on top of the table, giving her hand a little shake.

His touch was like a defibrillator shooting an electric current up her arm and straight to her heart, sparking her to life.

"Are you tired?" she asked. Nervous energy pulsed through her at the idea formulating in her mind.

Jeremy shook his head slowly, eyeing her with interest.

"What do you say we grab some bubbly to share? Maybe hang out a bit? If you don't have anything else—"

"I'll take care of the drinks. You sit tight." Jeremy was up and out of his chair before she even finished.

She watched him stride away, all six-foot plus of gorgeous maleness.

Over the years she'd mostly watched him from a distance since he lived near Yaz in NYC and Rosa had been at school in Champaign. Of course, there'd been the occasional get-together when they'd both been home in Chicago over the holidays or if she visited Yaz.

It wasn't until this past spring, her last semester at U of I, with Jeremy on campus for a co-op between his IT company and the school's College of Computer Science, that they'd spent more time together. Without Jeremy there, a connection to home after the devastation of Papi's death, Rosa didn't know how she would have fared.

Still, inviting him for a nightcap was a bold move. Especially for her.

Across the room, their friendly bartender handed Jeremy two bottles of champagne. Jeremy turned, holding them aloft, and flashed her a triumphant grin.

Just like that, all her doubts faded.

Forget her usual need for planning and pro-con list making. In two weeks, Jeremy would be gone for six months. Six months! Any chance of capitalizing on their "almost kiss" on the dance floor might fade.

¡Es ahora o nunca! Her father's old adage whispered in her ear.

It's now or never—words he always told her and her sisters when they talked of dreams, but doubted themselves.

She, ever the conservative one, had rarely dreamed anything extraordinary. Never felt that ahora o nunca necessity.

Until tonight.

Now it was time for her to take a page out of her sisters' book and "go for it"!

Later, when Jeremy and she said good night, she'd do so with a kiss that let him know she certainly didn't think of him like a brother. Then they'd see, as Lilí put it, "*what developed.*"

Desire and fear coalesced inside Rosa, two opposing forces crashing against each other like the ocean waves against the rocks at the base of El Morro in Old San Juan. She grabbed onto the first with both hands. Strived hard to squelch the latter.

Jeremy strode toward her, his gaze locked with hers. She grinned back at him, itching with excitement.

Sí, tonight Rosa Fernandez had finally decided to break away from the wallflowers and take a walk on the wild side.

Chapter Two

Jeremy pushed the cork out of the champagne bottle with his thumbs, the resounding *POP* still not enough to knock some sense into him.

He should probably not be in a hotel room, alone, with this sexy Rosa Fernandez look-alike. The same one who had an uncharacteristically playful glint in her caramel eyes.

Agreeing to a nightcap with her had been a no-brainer. They hadn't seen each other much since her graduation in May. She'd been busy transitioning from college to her new job. His own schedule had been pretty crazy, splitting his time between the New York and Chicago offices while finding and moving into a place downtown. Then the Japan project had come up.

He couldn't deny that he'd missed her company though. Especially the calmness he felt when he was around her. Stealing a few quiet moments for them to catch up sounded like the perfect way to end the evening.

After he'd snagged the champagne from the bar earlier, the two of them had started out at a back table in the ballroom. That plan was quickly vetoed to avoid getting in the way of the hotel clean-up staff.

Next, they'd nixed sneaking into the closed hotel bar area. Rosa, ever the rule-follower, had balked at that suggestion.

They'd moved to the hotel lobby seating area, but even at this late hour there'd been a lot of foot traffic making it less conducive for private conversation.

Never, not in a million years, would he have anticipated Rosa's next idea: heading up to her room.

With any other woman, he would have assumed it was an invite for something more than simple drinks among friends. With Rosa, no way would she play the coquette.

Still, when he found himself alone inside the elevator with her, the demure tilt of her head juxtaposed with the come-hither smile curving the edges of her full mouth set his blood pressure sky-rocketing. And his brain power plummeting.

For months, he'd been wondering if Rosa could ever see him as more than her older sister's good friend. Over the spring semester, with her finishing her master's program and him working in the university's computer engineering department as part of his company's co-op, they'd spent more time together than the previous few years of their friendship. Time he had come to value.

Rey's passing had devastated all three of his girls, but the quiet pain that radiated from Rosa's dark eyes had struck a chord inside him. Even without Yaz asking him to, he'd gone out of his way to make sure Rosa was okay.

They'd shared quiet walks across the snow-covered campus talking about their favorites—movies, music, food, vacation places, books, whatever. God, the debates they'd had over his preference for Hemingway's minimalism and hers for the romantic words of Jane Austen and the Brontë sisters.

He'd met her for lunch or dinner several times a week, at first because he wanted to make sure she was taking care of herself. Later, because he found himself both relaxed and energized when he was with her. Normally quiet and shy around others, Rosa opened up in private. She was smart, opinionated, and witty, and when she felt strongly about a topic, like funding for the arts and education, her passion was a palpable force seen in her flushed cheeks and fiery eyes.

Before Jeremy knew it, he was making early-evening coffee runs across town to her favorite café con leche joint when he knew she'd be up late working on her thesis. He told himself it was all in the name of helping her ace her final requirements.

But deep inside, he knew better.

Sometimes, alone at night, he'd close his eyes and picture her face when they shared a joke or she teased him about some goofball thing he said or did. Her smile widened. Her eyes sparkled. Her normally reserved demeanor melted away. Hell, lying there in the dark, he even heard her melodic voice or throaty laughter in his head.

By the time her graduation rolled around, Jeremy was forced to admit that what had started out as his intent to help a good friend through a heart-wrenching loss had morphed into something more. Something he wasn't quite sure he should pursue.

His moving back to Chicago would come with certain family obligations and expectations. The same ones that had driven him to take a job in New York right out of college. Rosa was a quiet person. She'd probably hate the hoopla that surrounded his family on a regular basis. And with him now heading to Japan for the next six months, he had no business thinking about where things with Rosa could lead.

Then he'd held her in his arms on the dance floor tonight. Smelled the sweet vanilla scent of the lotion he knew she kept in her purse. Stared into her eyes. Come *thiiiiis* close to kissing her.

So, yeah, saying yes to her invitation had definitely been a no-brainer for him.

He cast a quick glance at her now, perched on the edge of the hotel room's king-size bed.

She looked more like a sexy siren than a shy librarian in her red bridesmaid dress with her dark hair pulled up in a fancy twist. A few delicate tendrils curled around her neck, enticing a man to lean closer, sample a taste of her tanned skin.

His body hummed with anticipation.

Jeremy gulped.

His wayward thoughts made his hands a little unsteady as he poured champagne into a flute, then handed it to Rosa. "Here you go. Buen pro-provecho."

Her sweet smile brightened at his bumbling attempt at Spanish.

"Gracias. Wanna sit?" She patted the space beside her, scooting over to make room.

"That's okay," he mumbled.

Glass in hand, he pulled out the leather desk chair, forgoing the bed, and temptation.

She took a sip, then slid back until her legs were straight out in front of her. Kicking off her silver stilettos, she wiggled her toes with a groan. "Ay, it feels divine to get these torture devices off!"

"They make your legs look great, but I don't know how women wear them." Jeremy's gaze strayed from her pink-painted toenails, up her shapely calves to where the edge of her red, figure-skimming dress had crept up to midthigh.

"You answered your own question."

"Hmm?" He pulled his gaze away from the appealing view of her legs. "What do you mean?"

"Women wear heels so men will admire our . . . I guess you might say, attributes." Her champagne glass pressed to her lips, Rosa stared at him intently. Damn if she wasn't giving him signals his body had no trouble interpreting.

But he had to be mistaken. This was Rosa. Modest, usually re-served Rosa.

Sure, she was beautiful. What guy wouldn't be attracted by her curvy figure, soft doe eyes and kissable lips?

For him, though, it was her charm that appealed to him even more.

When he was with her, it was like she saw the real him. Not the dollar signs or connections his family name triggered in the minds of so many others. She was the first woman in a long time who didn't look at him and consider what his family name could do for her.

"So you girls lure us in with your wiles. And your . . . attributes, as you call them. Then you have your way with us?" he teased.

"If the shoe fits." She lifted a dainty bare shoulder in a half shrug, the shiny material of her dress tightening across her breasts.

Jeremy nearly swallowed his tongue.

Rosa laughed, the sound light and rich. Sexy.

Damn, he liked it when she let her guard down and allowed the playful side of her personality to take the reins. It didn't happen often, or with many people, so he always felt a little special when she did with him.

Her eyes sparkled with a teasing glint.

Yeah, he liked it. A lot.

Leaning back in his chair, he took a deep breath, working to calm his racing pulse. He jerked his tie loose, leaving it to hang open around his neck as he waited for her next move.

Rosa reached her free hand up to push against the elaborate twist she and the other bridesmaids had worn. "This up-do is so tight. I swear it's giving me a headache."

"Take it down. The evening's almost over."

He liked it better when her hair was loose anyway, the dark curly waves brushing her shoulders.

Rosa bit her lip. A habit of hers that clued him in to the fact that she was contemplating his suggestion.

Rarely did she act without thinking things through. Even something as simple as a meal choice might invite the nibbling on her lower lip while she deliberated over her options. In his weaker moments, he wondered what it might be like to nibble on that lip himself.

He wouldn't give in to that urge though. Not without a clear sign it was what she wanted, too. Before tonight, she hadn't given him one, and even now he cautioned himself to be sure. He'd never force a woman into anything she wasn't ready for. He wasn't like—

"Do you mind if I change out of my dress? Put on some comfy clothes?"

Jeremy did a mental double take at Rosa's unexpected question. Would a starving man turn down a cheeseburger?

"Uh, no. Go for it," he said instead, striving for casual when he felt anything but.

She nodded, then slid off the bed and stepped to the dresser, where she pulled out a pair of shiny black sleeping pants and a matching long-sleeved button-down shirt. When the bathroom door closed behind her, Jeremy drained his champagne glass and quickly poured himself another.

Man, he must be misreading her signals. It had to be wishful thinking on his part.

One side of his brain warned he should leave. Now. Before he did anything foolish. Like throw her down on the bed and satisfy this need for her that had been slowly simmering to a boil for months now.

The other side of his brain told him to stay calm, take a breath. No need to get ahead of himself. He and Rosa had shared countless conversations over drinks before.

Though not in a hotel room. With champagne. And one of them slipping into "something more comfortable."

He tugged at his collar, deftly undoing the top button of his dress shirt.

Then he changed his mind, deciding it might be better to keep himself buttoned up tight.

The bathroom door opened and Rosa stuck her head out.

"Um, Jeremy, could you help me with something?" The timid note in her voice drew him over faster than any come-and-get-me call would have.

"Sure, what do you need?"

Rosa pushed the door open further and he saw she still wore her dress.

"I—I think the zipper's stuck," she said, turning her back to him.

The smooth expanse of her tanned shoulders beckoned him.

She craned her neck to look at him. The nervous frown between her brows told him this wasn't some coy move on her part.

She reached behind her with one arm to swat at the zipper pull. "Would you . . . would you give it a try, please?"

Ha, the irony. He wanted nothing more than to help her out of that dress.

Instead, he reminded himself to slow his roll. If he ever wanted a chance with Rosa, he'd have to keep taking his cues from her. Let her take the lead so she didn't feel rushed into anything.

"Oh-kay," he answered. "Let me see what we have here."

Rosa moved farther into the bathroom, allowing him to step in behind her.

His fingers fumbled with the metal zipper tab, then finally grasped it and gave a tug. The darn thing wouldn't budge. He leaned his head closer, Rosa's subtle vanilla scent filling his lungs.

"Hold on, the material's jammed." He dipped a hand inside the back of her dress to get a better grip, and Rosa jumped like he'd jolted her with a taser.

"Sorry," he mumbled. "My hand's probably cold."

Though not for much longer, what with the heat from her back burning his skin.

"You just caught me by surprise, that's all."

The quaver in her voice made him pause.

He looked up to catch Rosa's gaze in the bathroom mirror. She was only about five-foot-six, so at six-four he towered over her, making her look tiny as she stood in front of him, her head barely reaching his shoulder. The intricate twist hung a little loose on her nape, like she'd already removed some of the pins from her hair. It gave her a mussed, bed-tousled appeal his body readily responded to.

"Do you still want me to try and get it undone, or . . ." he trailed off.

Or what? Lilí was out for the night. No way Rosa wanted to sleep in her gown.

"Yes, please. I'd appreciate it."

His gaze remained locked with hers for several heartbeats. Then, fingers trembling, he tugged hard on the material. It released from the zipper's teeth allowing him to slowly pull the zipper down.

The dress hung open, exposing the expanse of her back, revealing the fact that she'd gone braless. Pressing both hands to her chest, Rosa held the material against her.

Without stopping to consider whether he should or not, Jeremy skimmed the back of his hand up her spine. Across her shoulder blades to the smooth column of her elegant neck. Her head lolled to the side, as if inviting him to taste her.

He couldn't resist. Just one little nibble to satisfy his craving for her.

Leaning down, he pressed his lips to the warmth of her neck, breathing in her sweet smell.

Rosa moaned with pleasure.

The low, guttural sound shot desire straight to a part of his body he couldn't control. He trailed his lips up her neck to the edge of her ear, where he gently blew on her skin. Her body trembled. Need pulsed through him.

His tongue snuck a quick taste of her, and all he could think of was one thing—honey. She tasted as sweet as honey. Like a bee to a hive, he thrummed to be inside her.

She leaned back against him with a sigh, her butt pressing against his arousal. The reflection of their bodies melded together caught his eye. One more minute and he'd be a goner. Beyond control.

"Rosa, we have to stop," he whispered raggedly in her ear, struggling to remain the gentleman she deserved.

"Mmmm," she answered, her heavy-lidded eyes gazing back at him in the mirror. "Why?"

"Because . . ." He couldn't think straight with her pressed so intimately against him. "Because you're . . ."

Suddenly she spun around, her face a mix of frustration and despair. "Because I'm the good girl? Because everyone expects me to always make the right decision?"

He reared back, surprised at her uncharacteristic vehemence.

"What if I want to have a little fun for once?" she cried.

Her dress slipped, giving him a peek at the curve of her breasts. A blush of emotion—embarrassment, anger, desire?—flooded her cheeks.

"Don't you?" she demanded.

His mouth opened and closed, but for the life of him he couldn't form a coherent response.

As fast as it had boiled over, her anger dissipated. She sagged back against the counter behind her, her expression confused.

"Was I wrong?" she whispered. "Downstairs I thought . . . Bueno, it seemed like . . ." Her brows furrowed, creating a tiny V between them as if she was trying to figure something out. Then she shook her head and looked him straight in the eye as she asked, "Are you not interested in me?"

Not interested? The question barely computed in his lust-fogged mind.

He was so damn hard with wanting her he thought he might explode.

"Is it—" She paused, the dismay and hurt in her voice ensnaring him. "Is it because I'm not—"

He swooped down and kissed her to stop her from saying anything foolish about herself.

He expected Rosa to resist. To tell him he was moving too fast.

She proved him wrong, sliding her arms along his waist to curve around his back.

His hands were in her hair, and he was vaguely aware of the tinny sound of pins falling to the ceramic counter as he deepened the kiss.

She opened her mouth to him, her tongue meeting his in a sensual caress. He groaned with pleasure. His quiet little mouse had morphed into a tigress, her fingers kneading the muscles along his back, pulling him closer.

He wanted more, needed more of her.

But, damn it, he shouldn't, not like this. Not this fast. He knew she wasn't one to sleep around and he didn't want to do something she'd regret.

The last vestige of common sense had him breaking their kiss, pulling back to rest his forehead against hers. They both gasped for air, the warmth of their breath mingling in the tiny space separating them.

"We need to . . . we should . . ." He strained to form the right words. His mind, his senses consumed with the sight of her—swollen lips, hair mussed, chest heaving.

"Move to the bed?" she whispered, her voice pitching higher on the last word.

He closed his eyes, trying but losing the battle with temptation.

Rosa backed away.

He watched, entranced, as she let her dress drop to the floor at her feet.

She stood before him wearing nothing but a flimsy pair of black lace panties, her round breasts the perfect size to fill his palms. Her hands fluttered at her sides, revealing her nervousness.

"I know what I want, Jeremy. If it's, if it's what you want, too, then . . ."

Her sincerity, her bravery in what he felt certain was not a proposition she offered lightly, nudged Jeremy over the edge.

Bending down, he scooped her up in his arms, laughing with elation at her yelp of surprise. A man on a mission, set to erase any doubts about whether or not he wanted her, Jeremy strode out of the bathroom and headed straight toward the king-size bed.

Chapter Three

Eight weeks later

One. Little. Pink. Line.

Relief tsunamied through Rosa, swiping her legs out from under her. She sank onto the tile floor in her upstairs hall bathroom. Forehead resting on her bent knees, she sent up a prayer of thanks.

"Gracias a Dios," she murmured. The threat was gone.

Everything could go back to normal.

Her shoulders slackened on a soul-cleansing sigh. Turning her head, she peeked her eyes open, needing the confirmation of that one little—wait, two?

She frowned, then blinked rapidly to clear her vision.

Nothing changed. Two intersecting lines still formed a perfect plus sign.

Her stomach plummeted, threatening to bring up the Export Soda crackers she'd barely choked down earlier. The pregnancy test wand trembled in her hand as if laughing at her disbelief, its pink symbol ensnaring her gaze like a magic talisman.

"No puede ser verdad," she murmured. Panic tightened her chest, stealing her breath. Dios no, no, no no. It couldn't be true.

She gave the stick a quick, frantic shake.

A lo mejor, yeah, maybe, like a thermometer, she was supposed to force the fluid down to the bottom for it to work properly.

Only . . . her hand stilled . . . the mercury was *in* the thermometer, and you shook it *before* you stuck it in your mouth to get the reading. More importantly, you definitely *didn't* pee on it.

Besides, she'd read the freaking packet insert from front to back. Three times. Could probably recite the information from memory. The most important point had been emblazoned on her brain. *One line signifies negative. Two intersecting lines signify positive.*

She hadn't failed a test in her entire life! How could she possibly start now?

Tears stung her eyes. She blinked rapidly, trying to keep the tears at bay, but the idea that she and Jeremy—

Dios mío, Jeremy!

Just thinking about him sent anxiety rippling through her.

¡Esto no puede estar pasando! The denial ricocheted in her head. Unfortunately, repeating it over and over didn't matter because this *was* happening!

The proof was right in front of her in the form of an obnoxious pink plus sign.

With a muffled curse, Rosa dropped her chin to her chest, resting her forehead on her knees.

It'd been nearly eight weeks since Yaz and Tomás's wedding.

Eight weeks since she'd rushed Jeremy out of her hotel room that awkward morning after, his halting apology and stricken expression letting her know he regretted their intimacy. She'd cut him off before he could finish, ashamed that she'd practically thrown herself at him the night before. Her main thoughts had been on saving face, keeping her pride intact. Getting him out of there in case Lilí decided to show up after all.

That was the last thing she needed, her younger sister catching her in the most humiliating situation of her life. Especially after all the lectures she'd given Lilí about "proper behavior."

Afterwards, Rosa had avoided his attempts to see her in the two weeks before he'd left for Japan.

It'd been fairly easy to use her commitments to school activities as an excuse.

Once he'd left though, being halfway across the globe hadn't stopped Jeremy from trying to reach her. She'd screened her calls and replied to him via text with short, innocuous responses.

Hope the jet lag has passed. Good luck with the project.
Sorry I missed your call, super busy.

In reality, she'd simply wanted to avoid hearing another soul-crushing, awkward apology from him. She just couldn't face the idea that their friendship might be irrevocably damaged because of their night together.

She'd spent the past two months praying that what she'd first considered to have been an incredible night hadn't in actuality been an irreversible blunder on her part.

Ha! You couldn't get more irreversible than this.

The thought of breaking the news to Jeremy, over the phone no less since he was in Japan, left her clammy with mortification.

And what about her sisters? Tía Dolores and Tío Pablo? Dios mío, what would they all say?

Not to mention her students and principal at Queen of Peace?

The slew of panicked thoughts hit her like a barrage of bullets.

Her thoughts flew back to the night of the wedding, when she'd decided to do something because it felt good. Maybe shake things up a little.

¡Ave Maria purísima!

A hysterical giggle bubbled up in her throat, and Rosa clapped a hand over her mouth in dismay. The testing wand clattered to the floor. Her head spinning, she lay down in front of the bathtub, pressing her heated cheek against the cool tile.

Cálmate, cálmate.

She willed her pulse to calm, her thoughts to slow as she sucked in a deep breath.

The smell of the pine-scented cleaner she used to mop the floor filled her lungs, turning her stomach. Another wave of nausea crested as her gaze caught on the pregnancy test wand a few feet away. Mocking her.

Her eyelids fluttered closed, blocking out the offensive object.

Buying the damn kit had been a whim. She'd honestly thought she'd been battling the flu the past few weeks. If not for the random comment she'd overheard from a pregnant teacher in the break room the other day, she'd never have counted back the days.

Even then, she'd been so sure the results would be negative. For goodness sake, they had used protection. Still . . .

A baby.

She pressed a hand to her roiling stomach.

When she'd prayed for something of her own, a sense of belonging, a role in which she felt confident, this wasn't really what she'd had in mind.

Dios no te da lo que no puedes manejar.

Mami's favorite mantra drifted through Rosa's jumbled thoughts. Her mom had usually been right. God didn't give you what you couldn't handle.

The words provided comfort, a chance for her to reevaluate. This wasn't the end of the world. Actually, it was the beginning of something new.

As much as Rosa hated change, it was coming at her now. Big time.

Years ago, Mami's death had forced her to learn how to deal with the ramifications of her choices. Like then and every day since, Rosa had been determined to make things right. This time, it couldn't be any different.

First, she needed to draft a to-do list. At the top, as scary as it might be, was figuring out how to let Jeremy and her sisters know.

Pushing herself to her feet on shaky legs, Rosa snatched up all evidence of the test, then shoved it back into the plastic drugstore bag. She'd have to dispose of it on her way to work tomorrow. Lilí was still away at school and wouldn't be home until next week for Thanksgiving, but who knew when Yazmine might drop by the house. No need to leave proof lying around before she was ready to share her secret with her sisters.

That wouldn't happen until she'd spoken with Jeremy. He deserved to know first.

Her cell phone vibrated on the bathroom's granite counter, and Rosa jerked in surprise. Warily, she reached for it.

Jeremy Taylor flashed on the screen.

She froze, her finger hovering over the green icon that would answer the call.

Her insides quivered, and she said a quick prayer before tapping the screen.

Ready or not, she was much closer than she'd anticipated to checking off item number one on her to-do list.

Jeremy fiddled with the wineglasses on the breakfast bar separating his kitchen from the dining area in his condo. Two glasses for the bottle of pinot noir beside them, two different ones for the Riesling chilling in the fridge. His gaze strayed to the coffee mugs next to the fresh pot he'd brewed. Not sure what Rosa would prefer, he'd tried covering his bases.

After weeks of only communicating via brief text messages, the fact that she'd finally picked up his call was a step in the right direction.

She had turned down his dinner invitation—no surprise— but asked instead if she could stop by his new place—huge surprise.

Before calling he had reminded himself to keep things casual, go back to his previous game plan and take baby steps with her. She wasn't one to be pushed or move too fast when it came to letting people get close. Well, except for the night of Yazmine and Tomás's wedding.

That had been an amazing night he would never forget.

Unfortunately, it had been followed by a train wreck of a morning after he hated remembering.

He winced every time he pictured the mortification on Rosa's face when she woke up to find him beside her. The guilt filling her expressive eyes had him fumbling to find the right words to ease her obvious remorse. Emphasis on the fumbling.

Damn, he'd never been given the heave-ho as fast. When that woman set her mind to something, like shoving him out her hotel room door, there was no stopping her.

His doorbell chimed, bringing him back to the present and signaling Rosa's arrival. Anticipation at seeing her again after nearly two months hurried his steps into the foyer.

Out of habit, he checked the door's peephole, knowing full

well Bill Ryan and his team at the security desk wouldn't let anyone through without prior approval, or a quick phone call requesting clearance if Jeremy hadn't alerted them of a visitor. Rosa's
image appeared oddly misshapen through the tiny lens, but no
way could he miss the telltale speck of white teeth as she worried
her lower lip.

Looked like he wasn't the only one who was nervous.

He quickly turned the bolt and swung the door open.

"Hey, you! It's good to see you," he greeted her, striving for a
laid-back tone.

Her lips curved in a hesitant smile, but her brown eyes flashed
with unease.

Jeremy's apprehension hitched up a notch.

"Hi. Um, thanks for letting me come over."

If the slight tremor in her voice hadn't given away her discomfort, the fact that her fingers twisted her leather purse strap in a
death grip certainly did.

Still, he soaked in the sight of her, surprised by the relief en-
veloping him now that she was here.

Her mid-thigh-length black winter coat hung open, revealing
black, slim-fitting slacks and an emerald sweater. Her dark hair fell
in loose waves to her shoulders, framing a face that, as he looked
more closely, seemed a little pale. Definitely thinner. Even so, to
him, she was beautiful.

Knowing her, she'd been focused on starting off her first year at
Queen of Peace on the right foot and was working long hours. Not
taking care of herself, like she'd been prone to do in her last semester
at school.

"Of course, I'd let you come over," he answered. "You're welcome anytime. I'm glad you suggested meeting here. Come in." He
stepped aside so she could enter. "Here, let me."

He reached to take her coat, his hand inadvertently catching
hers. Rosa pulled back, her gaze sliding away.

Disappointment at her reticence dampened his pleasure over finally seeing her.

Apparently, despite all those months of friendship and sharing
private confidences that had led him to think she might be ready to
move their relationship to a deeper level, they were now back to

square one. Maybe even worse, based on the way her gaze bounced around to every corner of the foyer like she couldn't bring herself to make eye contact with him. Rosa seemed less comfortable with him today than when they'd first met.

Frustrated, but not wanting her to notice, Jeremy moved to hang Rosa's jacket in the foyer closet.

Patience. He got paid well for his problem-solving and trouble-shooting skills. Why not put them to good use now?

That awkward morning after had turned into an awkward two months later. He'd have to tiptoe carefully through this minefield if he wanted to get them to the other side together. Which he did.

"Make yourself at home." He gestured toward the combination living-dining room. "I think I'm finally settled in. Yaz has stopped by a couple of times with Tomás and Maria. Lilí crashed here with a friend over Columbus Day weekend when I was gone, but I think this is your first time seeing the place since I moved in, right?"

He knew it was, despite his attempts to get together with her, especially before he'd left for Japan.

Over the summer, there'd been several casual invites to the sisters as a whole. Each time one or the other had a conflict.

After his night with Rosa, he'd left her a voice message, a personal invite to join him here for a drink before heading to the ballet when his dad had given Jeremy their family box seats. A few days later, he'd sent a text asking if she was open for dinner and a foreign film at one of the smaller cinemas in the city. She'd declined each invite via polite texts citing "previous plans."

He'd spent the past six weeks in Japan, thinking about her back home. Wishing like hell she'd answer her phone so he could hear her voice.

Yesterday, as soon as he'd landed at O'Hare, she'd been the first person he called. Nearly dropping his phone in surprise when she answered.

As he reached for a coat hanger, he noticed Rosa moving down the hallway into his open living area. Now that she was finally here, he considered his condo through her eyes.

Compared to the Fernandez home with its rich colors, touches of their Puerto Rican culture, and numerous family pictures, the modern black and cream décor his mom's interior decorator had gone with here might seem a bit cold and bland. With his move so rushed, he'd mostly gone with her recommendations. The space itself is what had appealed to him. He liked the clean lines and open feel to the rooms, but he especially loved the—

"Oh, wow!"

Rosa's cry of surprise was right on cue. She must have discovered his balcony view of Lake Michigan. Everyone claimed it was the best selling point.

Jeremy closed the foyer closet door and headed her way, thinking he'd find Rosa at the wide glass balcony doors. Instead, she stood in front of his small but worthy book collection next to the fireplace along the far right wall.

Of course. He should have known the lake view didn't stand a chance in Rosa's estimation.

"May I?" she asked, pointing to the row of first-edition novels he'd amassed during his travels, starting with his first study abroad trip in college. The barely contained delight on her face relaxed his discomfort over whether or not she'd like his place. Whether or not he'd be able to convince her to visit him again.

This was the Rosa he knew. The one he missed. Sincere and smart. Charmed by the little pleasures in life.

"By all means"—he waved an arm to encompass the shelves, happy to oblige her—"enjoy."

She grinned like a little girl standing at the gates of Disney World as they opened. He remembered her telling him over coffee one afternoon that part of the appeal of books was how they let her escape from her world for a bit when needed. Took her to places beyond her imagination.

Kind of how he'd describe their night together.

Carefully, Rosa tugged out his leather-bound copy of *The Adventures of Tom Sawyer*, definitely a finder's coup for him. He watched her gently open the book, her fingers caressing the aged pages.

A memory flashed like a bolt of lightning, powerful and bright. Her fingers digging into the muscles along his back, pulling him closer, her breath warm on his neck as she cried out in passion.

"Jeremy, these are amazing." Rosa slid the book back into its place on the shelf, then ran a hand along the spines of a few other classics. "Que maravilla."

He may not know Spanish too well, but he figured out that word pretty easily. If you asked him, he'd say *she* was pretty marvelous.

He should have known that his minilibrary would be the trick with Rosa. Once, when they'd been talking about their favorite classic novels, he had mentioned his collection, but hadn't thought to remind her about it once he'd gotten moved in. That might have lured her to come over sooner.

As it was, whatever reason had led her to want to stop by today, he could only be grateful for it.

"Peruse to your heart's content," he said. "My personal library is yours. May I pour you a glass of wine while you're browsing?"

"Oh, uh, n-no thanks." A panicked expression flit across her face before she glanced back at the bookshelf, her hand stopping near his copy of *The Old Man and the Sea*. "I shouldn't, um, I'm driving."

"Cup of coffee?"

She gulped, and he'd swear her face turned a slight shade of green. "I'm fine, thanks."

"Are you sure?"

She paused, frown lines marring her brow. "Maybe a glass of water, if you don't mind?"

Her joy from moments ago had dimmed considerably. Something, he wasn't sure what, had drawn her back into her reserved shell.

"No problem," he answered, striving to keep his voice light. Free of his growing concern. "I'll be right back."

He strode to the kitchen, feeling like, frankly, he could use a glass of pinot noir himself. Instead, he settled for water along with her.

"Do you mind if I use the bathroom?" Rosa called softly.

"Not at all. It's the first door on the right down the hallway."

"Thanks."

Moments later, he heard the door close behind her. His shoulders relaxed, but the tension between them made him antsy.

Man, it felt like he and Rosa were tiptoeing around a purple-striped elephant sprawled on his designer couch. Both afraid to poke it, fearing the potential fallout.

It didn't seem like Rosa was going to broach the topic of their night together. He probably should have known better than to think his normally reserved, if sometimes surprising librarian would do so.

That left it up to him.

They had to find a way to move forward, whether as friends or, even better, as two adults willing to explore where the chemistry between them might lead. Now that the Japan project had been put on hold and he was back home indefinitely, he hoped to spend more time with her.

She couldn't leave without them trying to come to some sort of consensus on where they stood with each other.

God forbid their night together made it uncomfortable for him to spend time with her, or her family. Being able to get away from the hoopla and circus-like atmosphere that tended to envelop his family, knowing there was a place close by where the people—one in particular—cared more about him as a person than the wallet he carried in his back pocket . . . he didn't want to lose that simply because he and Rosa had leapt when maybe they should have taken a ministep.

He loved his family, but their expectations weighed heavily on him. Hanging with the Fernandez sisters at their house, even just a short forty-five-minute drive away from downtown Chicago, felt like an entirely different world—in a good way.

He couldn't lose that. Couldn't lose the easy friendship he and Rosa shared. He refused to lose *her*.

Their waters in hand, Jeremy strode back to the living room, where he placed her drink on the glass coffee table. Easing down onto the black and grey patterned sofa to wait, he considered the right way to start the conversation without scaring her off.

Moments later, Rosa emerged from the bathroom. She'd pulled her hair into a loose ponytail low on her nape. Her face glistened, her skin even paler than when she'd first arrived.

Worry had him rising to his feet. "Are you feeling okay?"

She patted the back of her neck with a tissue, then wiped her brow before replying with a small nod.

"Are you sure? You don't look so good." He cringed. Okay, that had not come out right. "I mean, you—"

"I'm pregnant."

Every molecule, every sensation, every brain function inside Jeremy froze.

For several moments, he lost all ability to think or react. Then his water glass slipped from his fingers, hit the tile floor, and shattered.

Rosa gasped, her brown eyes wide with shock. Seconds later, abject despair swooped over her face before she turned, racing for the front door.

"Wait!" He ran to catch up with her in the foyer, his hand snagging the crook of her arm. "Rosa, hold on a minute!"

"I—I shouldn't have-shouldn't have come." She pulled out of his grasp, shaking her head back and forth so hard her hair tie slipped off, leaving her loose curls undulating around her shoulders. Tears shimmered in her eyes, but determination hardened her jaw. "I wasn't ready. And I don't think—I don't belong here."

What? Fear squeezed his chest at her words.

As night fell and the city lights twinkled on, she was the one person he imagined sharing a glass of wine with out on the balcony. It was her he thought about when he sat alone on his couch, watching one of her favorite old black-and-white classic films.

Of course she belonged here.

He dragged a hand through his hair, grasping for a way to make sense of everything, for some way to reach her. "You can't—"

"I have to go."

Panic mushroomed inside him. "Rosa, you cannot blurt out news like this and then take off."

She flinched at his gruff tone.

"Just . . ." Jeremy held his hands out in supplication. "Just give me a minute to process this. Please."

His entreaty came out on a ragged rush of jumbled emotions, but it seemed to do the trick because Rosa sagged back against the door rather than opening it.

A tense silence filled the foyer for several seconds.

"I am so sorry," she finally whispered.

"You don't have to apologize."

She shook her head, misery stamping her pale face.

His chest tightened, his own uncertainty and the need to soothe her consuming him. God, what he wouldn't give right now to wrap his arms around her and promise that everything would be okay. But he didn't know that for sure. Worse, she probably wouldn't even welcome his embrace.

"I had a plan," she continued. "I did, really. I practiced what to say a million different ways on the drive over. Not a single one was like that." She jabbed a hand toward his living room as if their disastrous scene from moments ago was still pictured there.

"Believe me, that is not how I envisioned telling you. And—and I know it's the last . . ." Her voice shook as it trailed off. Her dark eyes glistened, her fingers nervously fiddling with the gold crucifix on her necklace. ". . . the last thing you wanted to hear. Just like, just like—"

Two tears streaked down her cheeks to drip off her quivering chin. "Just like sleeping with me was probably the last thing you thought about doing that night."

"Hold on now. Don't go putting words in my mouth." He took a step closer, desperate to touch her, to show her how wrong she was about him.

She shrank back against the door and his frustration skyrocketed.

"This was a mistake. I should go," she repeated.

Sparks of anger shot through him. "No, you shouldn't."

Wariness flared in her brown eyes.

He clamped his mouth shut, annoyed with his inability— again!— to find the right words to calm her. Like the morning after Yaz's wedding. Only, this time, Rosa was intent on walking out the door herself.

He couldn't let her. Not now. Not knowing that she was carrying his baby.

Because yeah, there was no doubt in his mind that this child was his.

His only doubt at the moment involved whether he could convince her to stay. Or how exactly to proceed from here.

Rosa was having *his* baby. The words filtered through his shock-fogged brain.

Suddenly, like someone jerking open the curtains and allowing the morning sunshine to fill a darkened room, Jeremy understood what this meant. What he needed to do.

"Come on, let's go back and sit down." Dazed but certain, he made a conscious effort to keep his voice level and calm as he held out his hand, willing her to take it. "We need to talk about this."

Rosa stared at him uncertainly. Her gaze darted from his proffered hand to his eyes. When she started worrying her bottom lip, the pressure in his chest eased the slightest bit.

That was a good sign. At least it meant she was considering his plea. No longer ready to race out the door.

Because, no matter what, walking away was not an option for him. If Rosa gave birth to his child, whether she wanted him to or not, he'd be a part of that kid's life. Maybe he carried Roger Wilson's deadbeat father genes; there was nothing Jeremy could do about that. But he'd been raised by Sherman Taylor since the age of six. Adopted by Sherman at the age of seven when he had married Jeremy's mom. The man was a great father figure and role model.

Sure, when Jeremy's loser dad had come around trying to extort money by threatening to sell his sordid tale to the tabloids, Jeremy may have gotten a little spooked. What kid wouldn't if you were the spitting image of a scumbag like Roger. Jeremy had heard the maid and cook gossiping about his resemblance. Still, looks could be deceiving, and blood alone did not make a father.

"I didn't come here expecting anything from you," Rosa said, interrupting his thoughts. Her voice trembled, but she held her head high, her shoulders proud. "I can handle this on my own."

Her spurt of gumption in the midst of what he knew had to be a scary situation for her filled him with admiration.

As shell-shocked as he was right now, he could only imagine how Rosa, demure and devout, must be reeling.

"I'm sure you didn't. Expect anything, I mean," he explained when her expression crinkled with confusion. "You're probably the least conniving person I know, Rosa. That's part of your charm."

She blushed, bringing a deep pink to her otherwise chalky complexion.

Now he realized the cause of her pallor, the reason why she'd refused his offer of wine and coffee earlier. She'd already begun considering the needs of their child.

Their child.

The phrase brought anxious anticipation whipping through him at tornado speed.

He was going to be a father.

Rosa was going to be a mother.

Together, they had created a bond between them that would never be broken. Not if he had anything to say about it.

Unlike Roger Wilson, Jeremy was man enough to respect the mother of his child, refusing to make her feel alone or defenseless.

Instead, he'd be the kind of father Sherman Taylor would be proud of. The kind of man who brought honor to the Taylor name by doing the right thing. And that meant . . .

"I think we should get married," he announced.

Rosa's head reared back, thumping against the front door behind her. Her arms went slack at her sides. Her purse dropped onto the floor, something inside hitting the tile with a *clank*.

That weird shade of green slowly crept into her face again before she slapped a hand over her mouth, pushed past him, and ran down the hall.

Seconds later, he heard her vomiting in the bathroom.

Chapter Four

"I am *not* going to discuss this right now," Rosa whispered, desperate for Jeremy to drop the topic before one of her sisters walked in on them arguing in the kitchen. She shot a nervous glance over her shoulder at the archway leading to the family dining room.

Por favor, Dios, let them stay out there.

"We have to figure out—"

"Yes, I know that. But not today." She shook her head, taking out her frustrations on the boiled potatoes she was mashing. "I'm still processing everything. Please, you have to back off."

She spun around, a dollop of potatoes dropping off the masher and splattering onto the worn linoleum floor. She glared at Jeremy, her annoyance mounting when he merely shrugged his shoulders, his expression calm.

Through the archway, she caught sight of Lilí and Yaz, along with Tomás and his daughter, Maria, setting the table for the Thanksgiving meal. Maria chattered away, probably sharing another story about her dance class with Yaz or something that had happened at school. The sounds of a football game on the television in the family room drowned out Rosa's conversation with Jeremy in here—she hoped. Like she'd told him several times since his surprise arrival, this was neither the time nor the place to discuss their situation.

She hadn't figured out yet how to tell her sisters. Was dreading it, actually.

At the moment, her plan was to take a page out of Scarlett O'Hara's how-to manual and leave this conversation with Jeremy until "tomorrow." When her sisters weren't within earshot and after her first appointment with Dr. Jiménez.

"I thought you were going skiing with your family in Aspen for the holiday?" She ripped a paper towel off the rack, then crouched down to swipe at the potatoes before someone stepped in them.

"Yaz invited me to join you guys. I can go skiing anytime," Jeremy answered, apparently nonplussed by Rosa's less than effusive greeting. She, on the other hand, was still reeling from the shock of opening the front door to find him standing on the porch earlier.

Talk about a Thanksgiving surprise.

"And of course you jumped at her offer. Great." Rosa surged to her feet, giving her indignation full throttle. Ignoring her conscience reminding her to stop overreacting and start being the good hostess her mami had taught her to be. "Even though I told you I'd call when I was rea—"

She broke off, belatedly realizing her mistake in moving too fast as the blood rushed out of her head. The edges of her vision greyed. Jeremy's face blurred and she swayed to the side.

He grabbed a hold of her arms to steady her before she faceplanted next to the splattered potatoes. "Easy. I got you."

For as long as she'd known him, Jeremy had been a good person to lean on. As a friend. All week, he'd been pressing for more.

Before, she would have welcomed his advances. Had even pined for his attention, penning countless lovesick verses about her secret crush.

Now, things were different.

Now that he finally sought her out, it was only because of his sense of obligation.

Disappointment churned in her belly, adding to the nausea she'd been fighting all day.

Tiny white spots filled her vision, the greyed edges growing until all she saw was a pinprick of light.

"Everything okay in here?" Lilí poked her head in the kitchen archway just as Rosa's entire body went slack.

Jeremy scooped her up in his arms like she weighed no more than a rag doll. The metal masher utensil slipped from her grasp to clatter on the floor, making the mess even bigger. At this point, she was too weak to care.

Her limbs felt heavy, like someone had injected her veins with lead. Eyes closed to ward off the dizziness, she pressed her cheek against Jeremy's chest and his soft cableknit sweater.

"What the hell happened?" Lilí cried.

"Nada. Por favor, don't worry," Rosa murmured. "It's no big deal."

Jeremy muttered something she couldn't make out, but thankfully he didn't argue.

Instead, he carried her out of the kitchen, past the dining room and the cacophony of voices asking what was wrong. Once in the living room, he gently laid her on the coffee-colored microfiber sofa, his cool hand smoothing the hair off her forehead.

"Qué pasa? Is Tía Rosa gonna be all right?" Maria's squeaky little girl voice was pitched higher than usual, her concern evident.

"I'm okay, nena," Rosa answered, not wanting to alarm the six-year-old. "I just got a little dizzy. Give me a minute and I'll be ready to serve the food."

"Uh, no, I don't think so. Between the rest of us, we can do it," Jeremy countered.

"Yeah!"

"Of course!"

"I'm a good helper!"

"Tell me what you need."

Her sisters, Maria, and Tomás all joined in the chorus of helping-hands volunteers. Rosa's frustration escalated. She was not about to spend their first Thanksgiving without either of their parents lying on the couch, feeling useless when it came to helping her family. Just like when Papi had made her stay at school to finish her master's degree, so Yaz had come home from New York to care for him when he got sick.

"No, es nada. Estoy bien," she argued, struggling to push up to a seated position. Her stomach complained, and she grimaced at the rising nausea.

Jeremy nudged her shoulder until she lay back down. Then he knelt on the carpet beside her. "It's not 'nothing.' You practically fainted."

"What?" Yaz rushed forward. She bent over the back of the sofa, her face scrunched with worry as she scrutinized Rosa. "Are you feeling sick again? I told you the other day you didn't seem like yourself."

Rosa brushed aside Yaz's hand when her sister reached out to check her temperature. "I said I'm fine."

The room had stopped spinning. The vertigo had passed. Embarrassment over being the focus of everyone's attention sent a heated blush creeping up her neck and into her face.

"I was wiping the floor and stood up too fast, that's all. There's nothing wrong."

Jeremy started to say something and Rosa sent him a pointed "hush up" glare.

"Estás segura?" Yaz pressed.

"Yes, I'm sure." Rosa wanted to be annoyed at the henpecking, but she had to admire how easily Yaz had stepped into the worried parent role. Being a stepmom agreed with her sister.

Unlike pregnancy apparently did with Rosa.

The past few weeks, she'd spent more time crouched in front of the toilet bowl than anywhere else. Gracias a Dios she had a private restroom in the library's office at Queen of Peace. That's the only way she'd been able to stay at work.

"Maria, come along and get Rosa a glass of water. Lilí and I can see what still needs to be done in the kitchen. Tomás, will you carry the turkey to the table, por favor?" Yaz rattled off the instructions, then turned back to Jeremy. "You—"

"I'll sit tight with Rosa for a minute, make sure she's good to go."

"I don't need a babysit—"

"Good." With a brisk nod, Yaz spun around and headed to the kitchen. Maria skipped along beside her.

"You don't need to hover. I'm fine," Rosa groused. She despised her petulant tone, but Jeremy's pushiness was driving her to it.

Already today he'd brought up the idea of marriage again. It made her heart race, and not in a good way.

"I'll believe you're fine when you start looking a little less like Kermit the Frog. Green isn't really your best color." Still kneeling beside the couch, Jeremy peered down at her. "I'm worried about how much weight you've lost. Have you seen an obstetrician yet?"

"Shhh!" She pressed her fingertips against his lips to silence him. "Por favor."

Heat flared in his blue eyes, sparking an answering heat within her. Quickly she dropped her hand, curling her fingers on her lap.

Her gaze darted toward the dining room, where Tomás was busy setting the stuffed turkey in the center of the table, oblivious to what was going on between her and Jeremy.

Rosa took another breath through her mouth rather than her nose. It was the only way she'd been able to stand being in the kitchen surrounded by all the Thanksgiving dinner smells while her stomach revolted at the idea of eating anything. Until a few minutes ago she'd been doing okay.

Lilí bustled in to place the plantain tortilla on the table. She glanced over, and Rosa tried to give her sister a reassuring smile.

"Fine," Jeremy mumbled. He lifted Rosa's legs so he could sit at the end of the couch, then laid her feet on his lap.

She watched the muscle work in his jaw. More than likely, he was fighting the urge to voice the arguments about why his idea was "for the best." Though she'd heard them already.

She prayed he wouldn't go there again. Not now.

His proposal—if you could even call it that—had replayed over and over in her head in the days since she'd visited his condo. Certainly by her romantic-heart standards it left much to be desired.

Having him say those words to her was something she'd dreamt of before. Silly dreams. Her poet's heart spinning romantic lines in her journal. But the reality of it was, he'd only asked her to marry him because of the baby. Not because he loved her.

Regret pierced her chest with a swift, burning pang. Having a strong sense of responsibility was an admirable trait, but not a reason to propose to someone.

"I'm *commm-iiing*," Maria singsonged. She walked carefully toward them, carrying a tall glass of water filled to the top in one hand, and a bowl of her favorite bite-sized wafer cookies with flower-shaped frosting in the other. Her eyes were focused on the glass's rim, as if she could will the liquid not to spill.

Love for her niece swelled in Rosa. What a blessing the little girl was to their family. Her youthful spunk and excitement over having a new stepmom and two new tías had eased them all during the dark months since Papi's passing. Rosa could only hope her sisters would feel the same about her unexpected little one.

"Tía Lilí and Mamá were busy with hot food, so I broughted your drink." Maria carefully handed Rosa the water. "And some of my Florecitas. Cookies always make me feel better."

"Gracias." Rosa nearly corrected the child's grammar, but Maria's pleased smile was too bright to risk dimming.

Jeremy listened to Rosa chat with her niece, frustration simmering beneath the surface of the cool façade he was struggling to maintain in front of her family. After a few minutes, Maria thankfully skipped back to the kitchen, leaving him and Rosa alone.

He reached for the television remote on the wooden coffee table, increasing the volume on the Chicago Bears football game. It wasn't the ideal solution, but the noise would offer them a measure of privacy.

"You didn't answer my question," he said, pitching his voice low.

Rosa's full lips twisted with a grimace. She sat up slowly and swung her feet off his lap, dislodging one of her black slippers in the process. It landed on the couch beside them. He picked it up, marveling at the tiny size stamped on the cushioned insole. *Six.* Another new fact he filed away in the ever-growing corner of his mind reserved for Rosa Fernandez.

"You've asked a lot of questions today. Which one do you mean?"

"Have you seen a doctor yet?"

She shook her head, her gaze trained on the television despite the fact he knew she didn't care a fig about sports. Stubbornness was a Fernandez trait the girls and their dad used to joke about. Jeremy had seen it in Yazmine during the years they'd lived in the same apartment building in New York when she was working as a dancer on and off Broadway, but he'd rarely witnessed that Fernandez stubbornness in Rosa. Until recently.

In fact, Rosa's calm, genuine personality had appealed to him from the get-go. With Rosa, he normally felt at ease. She was different from the socialites he'd dated in the past. Women like Cecile who lived for the fancy dinners and charity balls where they'd see and be seen. The types of events that a Taylor was expected to attend and support.

The need to get away from that pressure, from the questions about why he'd chosen not to go to law school and eventually to work at Sherman's firm and the whispers about how the "Taylor adopted son" was thumbing his nose at the family business, was the main reason he'd taken the job with his company's New York office after earning his master's.

After six years away, he'd been ready to come back home. He missed his family and his city. He was at peace with his career choice and determined he could find another way to make the Taylor name proud. Part of ensuring that meant doing what was best for his child.

"You can't just ignore the situation, you know," Jeremy said. "Sooner or later, people will figure it out."

Rosa shot him a you-don't-say glare he figured he deserved.

Though he was right. Sooner or later, her pregnancy would begin to show, because one thing they *had* agreed upon back at his condo was that Rosa was having this baby.

Admittedly, at first, listening to her tossing her cookies in his guest bathroom, he'd been worried about what she might decide. Sure, he would have made himself go along with whatever Rosa felt was best, but the idea of her not wanting his child had scared him more than pretty much anything else in his life.

He'd known that her Catholic upbringing might sway her. Knew her family's devotion to each other and the sanctity of life were important values to her. But he hadn't been one hundred percent sure what she would do until she'd spelled it out.

Right before refusing his marriage proposal. Again.

Now Rosa's eyes drifted closed, her dark lashes creating a soft shadow on her pale cheeks. A rush of breath blew from her parted lips. "Yes, I agree we need to talk. Right now, I . . . I just can't."

Her hands trembled in her lap, her obvious distress making him feel like a jerk for pressing her to pacify his own concerns. Needing to feel a connection with her again, he placed a hand over hers.

A slow heartbeat later, she twisted her hand so they were palm to palm. Their fingers laced, the small sign of unity giving him a measure of hope.

"I don't mean to put you off," she said. "I get that we have to make some decisions together. But I won't be rushed into something that might not be right. For either of us."

Her "might not" kept him from arguing his point. It was the first time that she hadn't totally written off his proposal. He'd take it. For now.

"My first appointment with Dr. Jiménez is tomorrow," Rosa continued.

"It is?"

A spurt of relief perked him up even more when she nodded.

"Would you—" He broke off, uncertain if she'd feel comfortable with his request, but figuring she should know how committed he was to her. "Would you mind if I went with you?"

She gave him a side-eye glance, doubt stamping her features. "You'd want to do that?"

"Yeah. I'm with you in this, Rosa. One hundred percent." He squeezed her hand lightly, grateful for the Mona Lisa smile she gave him.

"Everything's ready!" Lilí called, her quick steps thudding on the carpet as she hurried toward them.

Rosa slipped her hand out from under his, breaking their connection before her sister arrived.

"Why's the TV so loud? You probably can't even hear each other talk." Lilí leaned on her stomach along the back of the couch between them, teetering forward to reach for the remote on the coffee table. "The darn Bears are losing anyway. Who wants to watch that? Te sientes mejor?"

"Yeah," Rosa murmured, "I'm feeling better."

She craned her neck, peering over Lilí's back to snag Jeremy's gaze. The guarded frustration she'd flashed at him all day was finally gone, replaced by a plea for him to understand her need for time. At least she wasn't pushing him away anymore. That had to be a good sign.

"Don't let this big lug bother you." Lilí mussed his hair, like he'd done to her when he'd greeted her earlier. "He takes his big-brother role with us a little too seriously sometimes."

Rosa blanched, her gaze still caught on his.

Jeremy swallowed a laugh. The absolute last thing he felt for her was "brotherly." She had to know that by now.

Before he or Rosa could respond, Lilí pushed off the sofa and headed back to the dining room with a cackling laugh.

Rosa's mouth opened and closed a few times like she wasn't sure what to say.

"Hey, what do you always tell me? Ignore her teasing, she doesn't know what she's talking about," Jeremy said, hoping his smile would allay Rosa's discomfort. The youngest Fernandez daughter had a well-earned reputation for being a jokester. "Quit stressing. It's not good, for you or—"

Or the baby.

He didn't say the words, but Rosa seemed to follow his thinking.

"I know," she answered, reaching for her glass of water. She took a couple small sips before continuing. "I appreciate you understanding about my decision to not . . . to keep . . . well, thanks."

Had she really doubted that he would? He figured she knew about his background. His worthless dad. His mom raising Jeremy alone. It wasn't something he shared easily. Or, ever really. But, all anyone had to do was search his and his mom's names on the Internet and any number of old news articles would tell the sordid tale.

Now he wondered if Rosa hadn't bothered to look. If not, was that a sign that she didn't care about his past, or about him in general?

Rosa braced herself on the armrest and pushed herself to a stand, interrupting Jeremy's mental meanderings. He stood as well, accidentally bumping into her with his shoulder.

"Sorry." He grabbed hold of her elbow to help steady her, surprised by the spark the simple touch ignited. "Look, I fully support your decision. I just ask you to understand mine, too. I'm not going anywhere, Rosa. We're in this together."

"In what together?"

Rosa and Jeremy jumped apart at Yazmine's question.

"Dominoes!" Rosa cried.

"Dishes!" Jeremy answered.

Yaz frowned, her gaze going back and forth between them.

Rosa ducked her head. He caught the flash of her teeth as she worried her bottom lip, more than likely trying to think of how to cover up their blunder.

"We mean, after I help with the dishes," he improvised, "we're pairing up for dominoes. Didn't you say we were playing a few rounds in honor of your dad?"

Suddenly everyone grew quiet. Even Lilí, who'd been rattling off some story to Tomás at the table, stopped talking. Her normally animated expression sobered.

Jeremy swallowed a curse. Dumb move on his part. In trying to keep one can of worms from bursting open, he'd inadvertently popped the top off another by reminding the girls about their father. Talk about being on a roll today.

"I think playing dominoes is a great idea," Tomás finally answered.

Jeremy shot him a relieved look of thanks. Tomás dipped his head in a much appreciated I-got-your-back nod.

"Me, too." Her eyes misty, Yaz smiled at him and Rosa. "Come on, let's celebrate."

Rosa linked arms with her sister, letting Yaz lead the way to the table.

Jeremy followed, waiting to take his cue from the girls and Tomás. This was their first major holiday without Reynaldo. It was strange to see Tomás seated at the head of the table, though it was now his rightful place. The sisters and Maria chose seats along the two sides. That left Jeremy as the head at the opposite end, directly across from Tomás.

"Would you like to say grace, Maria?" Yazmine asked.

They all joined hands, Jeremy with Rosa on his right and Lilí on his left. Lilí gave his hand a quick squeeze, tossing him an impish smile. He returned it, encouraged that the feisty troublemaker was trying to lighten his mood. Little did she know what else weighed on his mind besides the loss of the girls' father.

Jeremy glanced at Rosa. Head bowed, she waited for Maria to begin. He gently rubbed his thumb across Rosa's knuckles, wanting to reassure her—hell, both of them— that they'd figure things out.

He didn't know how, but he knew he'd do everything in his power to make sure they were okay. That their child knew he or she was loved, and wanted. By both of them.

Rosa tilted her head to look at him sideways, a question looming in her eyes. He winked, pleased to see the gentle curve of her lips before she ducked her head back down in preparation for the prayer.

Maria started with gusto, thanking God for everything from her family to her baby doll's new dress, to the class pet hamster.

"And thank you for my new tías and especially for my new mamá!" Maria's closing earned an "Awww" from her aunts and a blown kiss from Yazmine. Soon, they were going around the table, each sharing something for which they were thankful.

This was a new tradition for him. His family, while close, wasn't as open with their private thoughts as Rosa's. Hell, he hadn't even told his mom about the pregnancy yet. He hoped she'd be excited for him. And he expected she would understand his rationale in asking Rosa to marry him. At the same time, he did worry about dredging up painful memories his mom had worked hard to move past. Put behind her.

Waiting for his turn, a list of trite responses to the "what are you thankful for" question flitted through Jeremy's mind. Finally, only he and Rosa were left.

"For new beginnings, even unexpected ones," Rosa answered, her words slow and measured, as if she weighed each one before she spoke.

"It's great things are going so well for you at Queen of Peace," Yaz said, spreading her napkin across her lap.

Rosa nodded as she took a sip of her water, evidently content to let her sisters continue believing her job was the only "new beginning" she faced.

Knowing how close the sisters were, he was surprised that Rosa hadn't confided in them yet.

All eyes turned to him now. Apprehension skittered across Rosa's face.

Jeremy caressed the top of her hand with his thumb again, intending the gesture to give her some reassurance. Her secret was safe with him. She had nothing to worry about.

The warmth of their palms pressed together brought a sense of belonging he'd never felt before. One he didn't want to deny.

He cleared his throat, surprised by the lump of emotion suddenly clogging it. "Let's see. I'm thankful for the invitation to join in this special day with all of you."

"Aw, you're such a sweet-talker," Lilí joked.

He shot her a playful glare and the rest of the family laughed. Rosa's shoulders visibly relaxed.

"I'll also add," Jeremy continued, "I'm thankful for new challenges in the near future that bring meaning to my life."

There was a beat of silence, like the others expected him to elaborate. Then Tomás gave a hearty cry of "Here, here!" and raised his wineglass in salute.

While everyone else started loading their plates with food, Jeremy sought Rosa's gaze. He hoped she'd caught the underlying meaning of his words. The fact that he was ready to do anything to prove himself worthy of her and their child. Prove himself a better man than his biological dad, in every way possible.

That was his goal in everything he did.

Rosa smiled at him with her expressive brown eyes. It was that same look of hers that inevitably made longing steal through him, seeping into the shadows of doubt he kept hidden from outsiders.

"What happened with your project in Japan?" Yaz asked as she slid a slice of the plantain, cheese, and egg tortilla dish onto her plate.

"Turns out the other company is in the midst of acquiring a smaller entity." Jeremy served himself a spoonful of mashed potatoes, then passed the bowl to Lilí on his left. "We decided it was best to wait until the merger goes through so we can include all their offices in the IT upgrades."

"Cool!" Lilí said. "So you're home for now, then you'll go back?"

"That's the plan."

Or it had been a week ago. Now he was considering asking to be moved to another project. It'd be less prestigious, but local.

He wanted to be closer to Rosa and the baby.

Out of the corner of his eye, he saw Maria reach for one of the large turkey legs. "Here, Tía, my mamá said this was your favorite piece. You can have it if you want."

The little girl swung the leg in Rosa's direction, nearly smacking her on the nose with it.

"Oye, cuidado, nena!" Tomás cautioned.

"Yes, careful, you're going to hit Tía Rosa." Yaz waved for Maria to put down the turkey leg.

Lilí snorted with laughter.

Rosa turned her face away, her skin slowly morphing to that same shade of pukey pale green it had the other day in his condo foyer. Hand pressed to her stomach, she pushed away from the table, her chair legs scraping against the hardwood floor.

"Permiso," she excused herself before hurrying toward the downstairs hall restroom.

Jeremy was up and out of his chair before the door slammed shut. Yazmine followed close behind him.

"What the hell?" Lilí called out.

The sound of Rosa throwing up drove Jeremy to try the doorknob. He muttered a curse when he found it locked.

Yaz pushed him out of the way to bang on the wood frame. "Rosa, let me in."

"Go away," Rosa answered, her feeble voice barely audible from the other side. "I'm fine."

"Quit saying that. You're not fine," Jeremy argued. "Last Sunday, you said you'd been throwing up all—"

"What do you mean she's not fine?" Yaz frowned at him over her shoulder. Worry pinched her features as she tucked her long black hair behind her ears. "What do you know that I don't?"

Hands on her hips, she spun around to face him, staring him down in prime big-sister mode.

Damn, this was getting more complicated by the minute. Jeremy shoved his hands in his back jeans pockets and clamped his mouth closed. His frustration with keeping their news a secret mounted.

"Yeah, what were you two whispering about over on the couch earlier?" Lilí came around the corner to join them in the hallway.

"Jeremy," Yaz drew out his name as if she were speaking to a recalcitrant child.

He barely held an eye roll in check.

Arms crossed in front of their chests, the two sisters stared him down. Yaz's black high heel and Lilí's brown ankle boot tapped against the wood floor, the sound like a clock ticking off the time he had to respond before all hell broke loose.

Jeremy squirmed under their combined pressure. Man, when the Fernandez sisters teamed up, they were a force to be reckoned with. But this wasn't really his secret to tell. And he had made a promise.

"Rosa's just . . . well, she's not *just*," he stammered, struggling to come up with a feasible explanation. "Honestly, I think she'd rather . . ."

The sound of the toilet flushing, followed by the faucet running had Rosa's sisters shoving him aside and clamoring toward the door. A welcome reprieve from their Spanish inquisition.

After several moments, the bathroom door opened and Rosa stepped out. She held onto the wall for support with one hand. The other splayed across her belly. She still looked a little peaked, her beautiful face slightly dewy with sweat.

Lilí rushed closer. "Are you okay?"

"Why didn't you say anything about not feeling good?" Yaz asked. "Is it that flu you've had that keeps lingering?"

Rosa sagged against the door frame, tipped her head against it, and closed her eyes.

"I'm not sick," she murmured.

"Qué?" Yaz and Lilí asked in unison.

"The vomiting and nausea. It's not because I'm *sick* sick." Rosa looked pointedly at her older sister, her expression serious. "Not in the sense you think, anyway."

"What? I don't get it." Lilí scratched her head, mussing her pixie haircut.

Rosa and Yaz stared at each other, an unspoken conversation

going on between them. Jeremy remained quiet, loath to interrupt. More loath about what would happen when Yaz put two and two together. Or rather, one and one, and how it made three.

Finally, understanding dawned in Yaz's dark eyes. Surprise, followed quickly by resolve flashed across her face. "What Rosa is trying to say is that she doesn't have the flu or any other kind of bug, right?" Yazmine waited for Rosa's nod, before continuing. "Our dear sister is pregnant."

Lilí's outraged gasp was horror-film classic.

"And somehow, I doubt it'll take us three guesses as to whom the father might be," Yazmine added.

The oldest and youngest Fernandez sisters turned to him in unison, accusation zinging at him with arrow sharp precision.

"It's not what you think," Jeremy said. He held his hands up, as if it would help placate the two sisters. "It wasn't exactly planned."

"Obviously," Yaz muttered, her mouth twisted with derision.

"But I've asked Rosa to marry me."

Lilí and Yaz's jaws dropped, their shock so intense you'd think he'd told them he had asked Rosa to join him on a trip to Mars.

"You proposed already?" Lilí's voice rose on a screech. "Pero, papi, you need to, like, hit the brakes a bit!"

"This isn't a joke." Yaz elbowed Lilí in the ribs, keeping her sharp gaze on him the whole time. "Have you two discussed a date yet?"

If only they'd gotten that far.

Jeremy glanced at Rosa, hoping to find even the tiniest of signs that she might be changing her mind. Instead, despite her pallor and the tired lines creasing her face, she gave him a firm shake of her head.

Damn it. Maybe she wasn't sure, but it was important to him that her sisters know his intentions. "*I* was hoping maybe over the Christmas holidays."

Rosa's mouth pursed, her annoyance obvious by her scowl, but he was only speaking the truth. Hell, he'd marry her tomorrow if she'd just say yes.

"Or," Jeremy continued, refusing to be put off anymore. Rosa should know how much he'd been thinking about this. How serious he was. "Maybe around Valentine's Day if she wants more time to plan, but—"

"But I turned him down." Rosa's softly spoken yet firm response sucked the wind out of his sails.

In fact, it silenced all of them. Well, except for Maria.

While Yaz and Lilí gaped in stunned confusion at their sister, Maria's excited voice carried to them from the dining room. "Papá, if Tía Rosa gets married, do I get to be her flower girl, too?"

Yes! The word shot through Jeremy's head, barely stopping on the tip of his tongue. At least one other person in the house seemed excited about the possibility of a wedding.

Now he simply needed to figure out how to get Rosa to agree.

Based on the pissed-off glower she shot his way, that wasn't going to be easy.

Chapter Five

Sitting propped up in her bed, Rosa leaned her head against the pillow sandwiched between her back and the headboard. Her limbs heavy, her stomach aching after the dry heaves, she closed her eyes on a tired sigh, longing to give in to the sleep tugging her under.

"Are you comfortable?" Yaz asked, her voice heavy with concern.

Rosa nodded, too weary to do much else. She hadn't expected the "big reveal" to go down quite like it had moments ago. Interrupting everyone's Thanksgiving dinner. An impromptu family meeting in the hallway with an impressionable Maria in the next room overhearing Rosa's confession.

Then again, lately little was happening according to any plan she'd concocted.

Yaz tucked the covers around Rosa's legs, creating a comfy cocoon, and an elusive sense of peace wove through her, easing the tension tightening Rosa's muscles.

The mattress shifted on either side of her, a sign that Yaz and Lilí were joining her on the queen-size bed. The last time that had happened, it'd been a couple days after Papi's funeral.

That night, Rosa had lain awake in the dark, silently crying tears of grief and pain.

The emptiness that came from not having Papi as her anchor anymore had consumed her. When he'd been alive, her life choices had been so clear-cut. Finish her degree, come home to work at Queen of Peace and take care of him, continue in Mami's footsteps as Rosa tried to atone for a mistake she would never forgive herself for.

With Papi gone, nothing had felt certain anymore.

Lost in the dark emotions, she hadn't heard her door open, hadn't been aware anyone else was in the room, until Yaz whispered her name in a raspy voice. Rosa had taken one look at her sister's pain-filled face, then scooted over to make room for Yaz. They'd clung to each other and cried, eventually falling asleep side by side.

At some point in the night, Lilí had come in and crawled into the bed, too.

They'd awoken in a cramped jumble of arms and legs, with tired and tear-swollen eyes, quietly thankful to have each other.

Now, the comfort her sisters offered was a welcome balm to Rosa's burdened soul. Ever since the pregnancy test, fear had been driving her, its foot pressing hard on the gas pedal while life as she'd known it was left behind in the dust.

She knew what she wanted to do. What her heart felt was best.

Like she'd told Jeremy several times already, her decision had been made, and as scared as she might be about it, she couldn't back down.

At the same time, she was cognizant of the turmoil her choices would bring to her and Jeremy. And probably her sisters too, knowing how their community would react once the news of her pregnancy hit the gossip wires.

The pressure tightened her chest, and Rosa took a deep breath, slowly releasing it while repeating Mami's mantra in her head. Dios no te da lo que no puedes manejar.

Oh, how she needed those words to be true. She simply had to trust that God hadn't given her something she couldn't manage. Another life was in the balance because of her. She couldn't make a mistake again. That guilt would devastate her.

Yaz reached for one of Rosa's hands, squeezing it between both of hers. "Do you need anything? Maybe some water?"

Rosa's eyes fluttered open. She met Yazmine's troubled gaze and gave a little shake of her head.

"No lo puedo creer," Lilí whispered, her expression still shell-shocked.

"Tell me about it," Rosa murmured. She couldn't believe it either.

"Never in my wildest dreams," Lilí went on, hugging one of the orange throw pillows from Rosa's bed against her chest. Lilí crossed her legs tailor-style, her left knee poking out of the hole in her faded jeans. "I mean, Rosa, the good girl, is the one of us who got knocked up!"

Rosa cringed at her sister's crass statement.

Yaz reached across Rosa's legs to smack Lilí on the back of the head.

"Ow!" Lilí yelped.

"Callate la boca," Yaz admonished.

Lilí glared at their older sister, but followed her reprimand and grudgingly closed her mouth.

Tears burned Rosa's eyes. She blinked them away, craning her neck to stare up at her ceiling fan.

Guilt and shame pecked at her conscience. This was why she hadn't said anything to her sisters earlier. The fear of facing their disappointment in her. The worry that she might let herself get talked into "doing the right thing" like she always had before.

"What Lilí meant to say is," Yaz grumbled, "qué está pasando?"

Yaz tightened her grip on Rosa's hand, drawing her gaze away from the dark brown patterns in the wooden ceiling fan blades.

"Pues," Rosa said slowly, stalling for time. "What's going on is . . . I'm pregnant."

"Yeah, we got that much already," Lilí said, then she huffed in frustration when Yaz glared at her.

"And Jeremy is the father," Yaz added for her.

Rosa nodded, her insides quivering, whether from nausea or nerves, or both.

The thing was, as long as this had been her secret—well, hers and Jeremy's—she'd been able to remain in a strange sort of limbo. Vacillating between excited and frightened about the idea of having a baby and being a single mom, the changes that meant for her life.

Change usually brought strife or pain. After Mami's death, it had even brought guilt.

Dios mío, the guilt was the worst.

Rosa had lived with it every day since then, an oppressive weight she hadn't been able to shed or share with anyone, not even her sisters. Especially not them.

Guilt had shaped her life. Though no one else knew.

If she hadn't begged Mami to come pick her up from school that afternoon, too embarrassed to face her classmates after her foolish behavior in the lunchroom, the car accident wouldn't have happened. Mami might still be alive.

After that, Rosa had stepped in, determined to fill the void, do everything in her power to follow Mami's lead and become the caretaker in their home, ensuring everyone else's needs were met.

With Papi gone and her sisters making their own paths, she'd been praying for a way to find a role of her own. Maybe this new challenge was a sign. Like Mami telling her to follow Papi's advice and start writing her own story, instead of always helping others write theirs.

A tear slipped from the corner of her eye to trail a warm path down her cheek.

"Hey, qué pasa?" Yaz asked. She tucked Rosa's hair behind her ear, something Papi had often done before pressing a good-night kiss to her forehead when he tucked her in as a child.

"We're here for you, Rosa, really. I was kidding before." Lilí scooted closer on the bed, laying a comforting hand on Rosa's shoulder. "We all know if there's anyone who's going to be a wonderful mamá, it's you. No offense, Yaz." Lilí tossed the last part over to Yaz with a jerk of her chin.

Yazmine's lips twisted in a smirk. She pushed her long black hair over her shoulder, a dark brow arched in a haughty angle as she muttered, "Whatever."

Rosa chuckled, comforted by their typical sister banter. Appropriate or not, Lilí always knew how to break the tension in a room.

"Personally, I've enjoyed seeing this new motherly side of you with Maria." Rosa gave her older sister's hand a love squeeze.

"Gracias," Yaz said, then her expression grew serious again. "But you still haven't explained much. How did this happen? No sex-ed wise cracks out of you, Lilí."

Their younger sister flashed her mischievous Cheshire cat grin, but wisely remained quiet.

"When did you and Jeremy, uh, start dating?"

Rosa winced at Yaz's question. Of course they'd assume she and Jeremy were an item. It would never occur to them that she might be a one-night stand.

She bit her lip, vacillating between how much to share and how much was too embarrassing to admit.

"I hadn't realized you two were even together," Yaz continued. "I mean, over the summer you moved back home and he bought his place downtown, but you never mentioned meeting up with him in the city. After your graduation, I thought you hadn't seen each other until my wedding. Even then, Jeremy brought that snooty girl as his plus-one."

True, but that snooty girl had left early, and he'd stuck around.

Lilí's dark eyes widened like a cartoon character who'd figured out an important clue. Her grip on Rosa's shoulder tightened, her fingers digging through Rosa's sweater.

Rosa gulped. Meeting her little sister's gaze, she noticed the same shock and awe she'd been grappling with since seeing that pink little plus sign.

"No me digas," Lilí whispered.

"Sí," Rosa answered.

"Don't tell me, what?" Yaz demanded.

"Increíble." Lilí's shock gave way to her awe and she leaned in to envelope Rosa in a tight hug. "As strange as this sounds, I am so freaking proud of you."

Rosa smiled, touched by Lilí's words.

"Will someone please tell me what the *hell* is going on here?" Yaz complained, her voice rising with frustration. "What secret are you two keeping from me? And how did that even happen? You're never on the same page together!"

Yaz was right; Rosa and her little sister tended to butt heads more often than not. Hearing Lilí's praise, feeling the love in her embrace, offered a comfort Rosa hadn't expected to find from her. Overwhelmed, Rosa tightened their hug.

"Gracias," she murmured, holding her sister close a few more seconds.

Fingers strumming on her crossed legs, Yaz wiggled impatiently on the bed. "Well? I'm waiting."

Rosa actually laughed. For the first time in weeks, fear no longer clawed at her chest.

Reaching out to both her sisters, she grasped their hands. Her earlier trepidation over revealing the "how" she and Jeremy had gotten into this predicament faded in the strength of her sisters' love.

"The night of your wedding," Rosa began, "Jeremy and I kinda . . . bueno, we were sharing some champagne, and, *ay* I guess you could say that we . . . hooked up."

Yaz blinked, her face going slack in surprise.

Heat crawled up Rosa's throat and onto her cheeks. "I invited him up to my room for drinks after the reception. And—"

"Wait a minute." Yaz held up a hand to stop her. "Please tell me you weren't tipsy and things got out of hand. He knows better. Lo mato! I mean it, I will kill him!"

Yaz swung her legs off the bed like she was ready to go tearing after Jeremy right now.

"No! Wait, por favor!" Rosa cried. She grabbed Yaz's wrist, tugging her sister to a stop. "It wasn't like that at all. Can you just let me get this out? It's embarrassing enough as it is without you freaking out on him."

Her lips pursed, Yaz jabbed a fist onto her hip. She held her tall dancer's body stiff, her expression fuming.

Ave Maria purísima, getting married and becoming a stepmom had really pushed her older sister into protective mode in a way Rosa had rarely seen.

"Come on, you know Jer. He'd never hurt Rosa. Any of us," Lilí said, a surprising voice of reason in the room.

Gracias, Rosa mouthed to Lilí with a grateful look.

"Hey, I've done some pretty stupid shit in my life," her younger sister admitted. She rubbed Rosa's thigh through the comforter. "Despite your nagging, I've always known you had my back."

Tears blurred Rosa's vision again. She swiped a knuckle under her right eye, smearing a drop of moisture.

"Fine." Yaz plopped back down on the bed and pushed up the

sleeves of her maroon sweater. "And when did you get so smart, huh? You're making me feel old."

Lilí smirked back at Yaz. "College life, fun but eye-opening. The stuff I deal with as the RA on my dorm floor? Unbelievable."

With Yaz settled back on the bed, Rosa took a deep breath, then continued with her confession. "What happened with Jeremy and me was consensual. Actually—" She broke off, self-conscious about admitting the truth. "I'd have to say that I was the instigator."

"No me digas!"

Heat flaming in her cheeks at Lilí's "you don't say" exclamation, Rosa smothered her laugh with a hand. "Uh-huh. Honestly, I can't believe I did it."

"You and me both, girl." Lilí nudged Rosa's shoulder with a conspiratorial chuckle. "When I encouraged you to go for it with Jeremy, I never thought you'd—"

"You encouraged her?" Yaz sputtered. "Are you crazy? Qué estabas pensando?"

"I was thinking it was time for her to have some fun," Lilí fired back. "What's wrong with that?"

The two of them glared at each other in a staring contest battle of wills. The tension between them ratcheted up, bringing Rosa's stress level with it.

She was about to step in and try to broker peace when Lilí flung one of the round orange throw pillows at Yaz, hitting her in the chest.

"Get off my case," Lilí complained. "What's wrong with you?"

"Basta, por favor. Enough," Rosa repeated, putting her hand on top of the pillow where it had landed on Yaz's lap, intent on keeping Yaz from throwing it back. It had been years since she'd broken up a pillow fight between her sisters. She had no desire to do so now. "What happened is on me. No one else."

"And Jeremy!" Yaz's ire darkened her tanned cheeks. Her brown eyes flashed with anger and betrayal. "I can't believe he would do this to you!"

"Jeremy didn't *do* anything to me, Yazmine!" Anger boiled up inside Rosa. She wasn't a helpless innocent to be protected, needing others to take the blame for her actions. "If anything, I seduced him. Is that so hard for you to believe?"

"Frankly, yes."

Rosa jerked back as if Yaz had slapped her. The idea that her sister believed her incapable of drawing Jeremy's attention jabbed at one of Rosa's deepest fears. She'd never been good enough to get the guy she wanted before. What made her think now was any different?

Tears of shame and aggravation filled her eyes. Damn these hormones. All she seemed to do lately was cry or throw up.

Hurt consuming her, she sagged back against the pillow. "That's a hateful thing to say," Lilí ground out, practically spitting the words at Yaz. "What is wrong with you?"

"What?" Yaz looked back and forth between the two of them. Confusion creased her normally smooth forehead. It took her a minute, but Rosa watched Yaz replay their conversation in her head, dismay quickly replacing her confused frown. "Oh, Rosa, I didn't mean anything against you."

"It's okay," Rosa mumbled.

"No, it's not," Lilí argued. "Don't give her a pass for saying something so bitchy to you."

The fact that Yaz didn't argue with Lilí's assessment told Rosa how ashamed her older sister must feel.

Adding credence to Rosa's thoughts, Yaz reached out to gently wipe a tear from Rosa's cheeks. "I'm sorry for how that sounded. Anyone would be lucky to be with you. I know that. I guess, with Papi gone, somehow I feel more protective of you two. Even when you're being a little brat." She exchanged a playful scowl with Lilí, then turned back to Rosa with a remorseful expression. "You and Jeremy getting together, I just didn't see it coming. That's all. I'm, I guess I'm shocked."

"You've been in wedding-prep fog for months," Lilí said. "But I noticed how Rosa kept tabs on Jeremy at her graduation dinner. Goo-goo eyes and all."

"You did?" Rosa and Yaz spoke in unison.

Lilí's face beamed with a cat-who-ate-the-canary grin. "You two don't give me enough credit. Why do you think I told you to take a shot at the reception?" She nudged Rosa. "Though, I gotta admit, girl, I totally didn't expect *this* at all."

"You and me both," Rosa admitted.

She and Lilí shared a soft chuckle, then the three of them grew silent as the gravity of the situation descended on them.

Rosa picked nervously at the orange and red design stitched into her comforter. The emotional highs and lows had her feeling like an unmoored boat tossing back and forth upon the waves.

"So, Jeremy proposed, but you said no?" Yaz finally asked.

Chin ducked, Rosa nodded.

"¿Por qué?" Yaz pressed.

This answer was easy. "Because I will not force him into a marriage of convenience. He deserves better than that. *I* deserve better than that."

Rosa pressed a hand to her churning stomach. The thought of single parenting scared her, but the thought of always being the one Jeremy settled for was much worse. She could do this. Lots of women and men were single parents. Look at Tomás. He'd been a single dad until Yaz came into the picture last year.

"It's not that simple." Yaz shook her head, worry painting her features once again. "Your baby will be a Taylor. That's big around here. Jeremy's family has influence in the city—they come with lots of strings attached. That's one of the reasons why he moved to New York after college. To get away from the craziness."

Jeremy had shared a little bit about how he didn't always enjoy the limelight that shone on his family because of his dad's high-profile cases and the fact that he'd co-founded one of the most highly sought-after boutique law firms in Chicago.

"The local media will have a field day with the news that he's fathering a child out of wedlock," Yazmine continued. "I'm sure they'll hound you once they find out who you are. Can you deal with that?"

Rosa gulped at the question. The difference in the social circles she and Jeremy traveled in was one of the reasons she'd been hesitant about the possibility of a relationship with him in the past, not that he'd given any indication that he was interested. At least, not before they'd jumped the gun by jumping into bed.

Yaz was the one used to paparazzi and the spotlight after years of dancing on Broadway. Rosa felt more comfortable in the shadows, behind the scenes. But for her baby, she'd face anything.

"I'll learn to deal if need be," Rosa answered. But inside, her trepidation grew at the prospect of having her one night of indiscretion detailed in the *Tribune*'s society pages.

"And how about Queen of Peace?" Yaz asked, poking at another potential sore spot Rosa's pregnancy created.

"What about it?" Lilí picked up another throw pillow and set it on her lap, hands clasped on top of it. "I don't see how the school has anything to do with this."

"Actually, they kind of do," Rosa answered.

Telling Principal Meyer and confessing to Father Yosef, her family's and the school's priest, was going to be exceedingly difficult. She anticipated, and deserved, their disappointment.

Guilt burned in her chest. Failing to meet expectations or responsibilities went against every instinct she'd honed in the years since Mami's death. The need to please others and do what was right had become second nature. Her penance, though she had never shared this truth with anyone.

Yet, a voice inside her kept whispering it was time she stop second-guessing herself and listen to her heart.

"I don't get it. What does the school care if Rosa's pregnant?" Lilí asked, drawing Rosa out of her spiraling thoughts.

"The diocese added a morality statement to the teacher manual this year," Rosa explained, meeting Lilí's confused gaze. She had already mentioned the statement in passing to Yaz at the beginning of the school year. Back then, neither one had any inkling that the clause would matter to her at some point. "It's not in our contract, but they plan on adding it next year. I'm not sure if they can hold me to it at the moment."

"What does that mean?" Lilí pressed.

Rosa scrubbed her hands over her face, overwhelmed by the mounting complications. "An unwed, pregnant librarian isn't really high on their list of acceptable role models for their students, especially when it comes to faculty or staff. It might be more difficult to fire me than if the clause was actually in my contract, but I'm sure there's still the possibility that the school council could recommend my dismissal."

"That's bullshit!" Lilí punched her fist into the pillow in her lap.

"Yeah, but it's a reality," Yaz countered. Stretching out across the bottom half of Rosa's legs, Yaz propped her elbow on the bed, resting her head in the palm of her hand. Her black hair pooled around her, a stark contrast to the cream-colored background material of the comforter. She stared intently at Rosa, her brow furrowed with concern. "The school, the church, our community. Not to mention Tío Pablo and Tía Dolores."

"Ay, ay, ay, Tía Dolores! She's gonna freak!" Lilí's pained look mirrored Rosa's reaction every time she thought of her godmother and how the woman who was like a second mother to all three of them was going to take the news.

"I know!" Yaz pursed her lips as she nodded. "I can't even imagine that conversation. But it should happen, soon! Once word gets out, everyone, especially the viejitas at church will have an opinion. We all know those old ladies don't hold their tongue."

The ever-widening ripple effect her actions had created set Rosa's queasy stomach to complaining again.

She closed her eyes, listening to her sisters as they commiserated over the maddening way gossip burnt up the airwaves within their community. Each one upping the other with stories of times past when one or the other had been the topic of choice. It was no surprise that most of the gossip fodder featured Lilí.

Strangely, having Yaz and Lilí voice the same concerns she'd been anguishing over on her own for the past week made them less daunting than before. She drew strength from her sisters. That strength in turn fed this new sense of determination that had taken root deep inside of her. Steadily growing along with the tiny baby in her belly.

"You're right," Rosa interrupted. "About all of it."

"What do you mean?" Lilí asked.

"Todo esto es una realidad," Rosa repeated Yaz's declaration from moments ago, because there was no hiding from the reality of it all. "But, that doesn't change my mind. I'll face whatever newspaper gossip, hold my head high at mass on Sundays, and listen respectfully to Tía Dolores's lecture."

"Girl, there'll be more than one of those. Believe me, I know." Having been the recipient of countless Tía Dolores's lectures in the past, Lilí pressed a hand to her chest, her expression dire. "I love you, but let me know when you plan to tell her. I want to make sure I'm not there."

"I don't care what she says," Rosa asserted. "It won't change my mind. Jeremy thinks he needs to do the right thing and marry me. That's not enough. Not for me, or for this baby."

Calling on every ounce of grit within her, she sat up straighter. "He's a good guy. You know that. So I trust we'll figure things out. Maybe some type of co-parenting, I don't know. Only, not a quickie wedding for the wrong reasons."

Her hands fluttered nervously and she clasped them on her lap to steady the trembling building inside of her. Anxiety urged her to play it safe. Follow conventional advice.

A new sense of desperation screamed at her not to listen.

Scared but determined, she met Yaz and Lilí's gazes. "If that means I have to leave Queen of Peace and find a new job, so be it."

The slack-jawed shock on her sisters' faces was almost comical. Rosa would have laughed, if she wasn't afraid her laughter might morph into tears. These days, it was hard to tell, thanks to the hormonal emotion roller coaster.

"I mean it. No one is going to force me to do what I don't think is right for me or my baby. I'm not settling. I want to be strong enough to not do that anymore in my life." Rosa stopped, hope and trepidation clashing inside as she asked, "Can I count on the two of you to stand with me?"

The bed jostled as Yaz pushed herself to a seated position, tucking her legs underneath her.

Without missing a beat, her sisters held out their hands to her and each other, creating an unbreakable circle of trust.

"I'm with you, whatever you decide," Lilí asserted, her grip tightening around Rosa's.

"Gracias," Rosa answered, her throat clogging with unshed tears.

"Me, too. And I'm sure Tomás feels the same," Yaz added.

Hearing her brother-in-law's name reminded Rosa that the rest of the family waited downstairs. Their Thanksgiving meal growing cold on the dining room table.

"I'm sorry I ruined dinner. You two should go back, make sure Maria's okay."

"They're good—"

"I'm sure it's—"

"No," Rosa interrupted her sisters. "I'll get some sleep. Or maybe work on my poetry for a bit. You know it soothes me when my thoughts are jumbled."

"You and your writing. I'll never get it. Give me a dance-off any time I need to get rid of stress!" Lilí shimmied her shoulders to some music inside her fun-filled head.

"Whatever." Yaz chucked their younger sister on the shoulder and rose. "Come on, let's give her some space."

After quick hugs, Yaz and Lilí left, and the room grew quiet.

Rosa reached for her Moleskine journal and favorite ink pen on her nightstand. She rubbed her fingers over the smooth surface, flicked her nail at the letter from Papi that marked her place. There was comfort in the familiar talismans.

Leaning back against the headboard, she closed her eyes. Fear, anxiety, and determination swarmed through her in a frenzy. She was too worked up to put pen to paper right now.

Taking a deep breath, she focused on centering herself. Allowing her emotions to settle around her so she could better translate them to the page.

Only then did she realize that hovering above them all was relief.

Dios mío! She'd been so worried Yaz and Lilí wouldn't get behind her unconventional idea. How foolish.

Sí, this wasn't going to be easy. She'd have to stand strong in the face of busybodies here in Oakmont, not to mention what would inevitably come from those in Jeremy's circle. Add to it the uncertainty of what might happen with her position at Queen of Peace.

But when it came down to it, none of that mattered.

For her child's sake, for their future, she was intent on standing her ground.

Her one hope was that Jeremy would see things her way. If not, the road ahead would be even bumpier than it appeared right now.

Chapter Six

It didn't take Jeremy long to remember that part of the beauty of living in a small suburb all your life was the close relationships you developed over the years with friends, neighbors, and, apparently, even your doctors. Less than five minutes after he and Rosa had checked in with the receptionist, they were quietly ushered into an exam room.

The nurse made quick work of taking Rosa's temperature—normal—pulse and blood pressure—higher than usual—and weight—down ten pounds since her annual check-up only four months ago. The older woman didn't say anything, but Jeremy noted the assessing once-over look she gave Rosa before typing more notes in the online medical chart.

The nurse shot him a perfunctory glance, then told them the doctor would be in shortly.

As soon as the door closed behind the nurse, Jeremy moved his chair closer to the examination table where Rosa lay partially reclined. Eyes closed, she held a death grip on a throw-up tray the receptionist had given her. Once again, her face had that drab olive color that descended moments before she got sick.

Dark circles shaded the skin under her eyes and her lips

pinched with her discomfort. Unable to resist his need to comfort her, he gently brushed her silky hair off her forehead, tucking it behind her ear.

"You're being a real trooper," he told her.

The edges of Rosa's lips curved the tiniest bit. "Funny, I don't feel like a trooper. More like a party pooper."

He smiled, relieved by her attempt to make a joke. "You do know how to bring a dinner party to a close, don't you? Must be one of your hidden talents."

She started to laugh, then winced and pressed a hand to her stomach.

Poor thing, she'd been throwing up or dry heaving so much lately, her stomach muscles had to be sore.

"Hey," he said, tugging a lock of her black hair to gain her attention. "Thanks for letting me come with you. This means a lot."

Her eyes fluttered open and she turned her head to look at him. "It's only fair," she murmured.

He hoped her need to do the right thing wasn't the only reason she'd asked if he wanted to drive her to the appointment, but he'd take it for now. "I meant what I said. I'm all in."

"Jeremy, please don't start—"

"In for whatever you're comfortable with," he added, not wanting to upset her. Besides, her doctor's office wasn't the place to discuss their plans for the future. Not unless she intended to accept his proposal. If that were the case, he'd take a yes anytime, anywhere. "It's enough that you know I want to be here. With you."

She gave a tiny nod in response, but her full mouth curved in the opposite direction of her shy smile. The uncertain hesitance in her brown eyes, something new since their night together, worried him.

He swallowed a frustrated curse, despising the wariness he sensed from her.

Several moments ticked past with nothing but the sound of voices in the hall interrupting their strained silence.

"Is it true that Yazmine and Lilí read you the riot act after dinner yesterday?" Rosa eventually asked.

"Yeah. Your sisters aren't too happy with me. Especially Yazmine.

But at least they waited to vent until Tomás had left to take Maria home."

Rosa's gaze dropped to the plastic hospital bowl in her lap. "They're being protective, that's all."

"Understandable. Tomás surprised me, though." Jeremy leaned back in his plastic chair, tugging at his jeans legs to make himself more comfortable, then splaying his hands on his knees. "I'm pretty sure he wanted to stick around and join the inquisition."

"It *is* kinda fun having a new big brother."

"Well, that big brother probably would have taken a swing at me if his six-year-old daughter hadn't been there."

Rosa chuckled.

The husky sound he'd only heard in his dreams lately drew a smile of his own. "I would've gladly taken the hit."

Her gaze shot up to meet his, a question in her brown eyes.

"I get why they're upset with me." Jeremy lifted a shoulder in a half shrug. "Hell, I'm upset that I didn't take care of you."

"There's no blame here, Jeremy. I can take care of myself."

"I know. But maybe if I would have—"

"We were two consenting adults."

"Okay, but I can't help—"

"Who used protection, mind you." She jabbed the throw-up tray in his direction, emphasizing her point. It was almost comical, except for the anger flashing in her eyes, coloring her neck and cheeks with a dark pink blush. "I see how you might feel some responsibility, but just because I'm pregnant does *not* mean I become your charity case."

"Charity case?" Jeremy choked on the words, floored by her accusation. "Why would you—"

The door opened and a middle-aged, portly woman with a short salt-and-pepper bob stepped into the room. A stethoscope draped her neck and *Dr. Claudia Jiménez* was engraved in navy thread on her white lab coat's right chest pocket. The doctor paused inside the doorway, probably sensing that she'd interrupted more than a pleasant conversation.

Charity case?

Jeremy's mind reeled. Where would Rosa even get that idea?

"Buenos días," the doctor greeted them. "Rosa, is everything okay here?"

Great. The last thing Jeremy wanted was for the doctor to kick him out before they even started.

There was a heavy beat before Rosa answered, "We're good. Jeremy Taylor, meet Dr. Jiménez."

Jeremy rose from his chair, extending his hand to shake. "It's a pleasure meeting you."

Dr. Jiménez narrowed her eyes, appraising him, more like the long-time family friend than the average obstetrician looking out for her patient. Still, the doctor politely shook his hand before turning her attention to Rosa. "¿Estás segura que él puede quedarse?"

He chafed at the switch to Spanish. Equally as unhappy with himself and the Rosetta Stone Spanish language computer program he'd bought, but had only dabbled with.

Rosa flicked a quick glance at him, then back to the doctor. "Yes, I'm fine if he stays."

Jeremy's shoulders relaxed. He tipped his head in thanks to Rosa.

"Bueno, let's take a look." Dr. Jiménez stepped to the sink. She made quick work of washing her hands, then moved back to the exam table. "Based on our phone conversation on Monday and the blood test you took afterwards, I understand we have a new development."

She cut a stern stare Jeremy's way.

He responded with a strained smile.

On the drive over Rosa had mentioned that Dr. Jiménez had been giving the Fernandez sisters their annual check-ups since their teen years, so he completely expected the doc's solicitous attitude. But this parental vibe . . . he swallowed uncomfortably . . . that made him feel like a horny teen caught with his pants down.

He'd been to enough family events and celebrations as a friend of the Fernandezes over the past few years to witness how close knit the Latino community was. How protective they were of each other, in a good way.

Wait until word got out about Rosa's pregnancy. The church ladies and Reynaldo's old music buddies, lovingly known as the girls' tías and tíos—aunts and uncles, though not by blood—would be ready to tar and feather him. Or whatever they did on the Island to punish gringos who disrespected their daughters.

Jeremy might be nervous, but he was also undeterred. They wouldn't run him off. Nope. He was sticking to Rosa like, well, like tar.

"So, you two are together?" Dr. Jiménez asked.

"Not really."

"Kind of," Jeremy answered at the same time as Rosa.

The older woman paused in drying her hands, then reworded her question and continued. "So you two *were* together around . . ."

"Late September," Rosa said.

"September twenty-sixth," Jeremy answered.

The doc shot him an amused glance.

Rosa gawked at him with a look that clearly asked, "What's up with you?"

Jeremy shrugged. So he had a photographic memory. He could actually picture his calendar right now. Including the tiny star he'd added in the upper right-hand corner of the box marked September twenty-sixth.

"Based on our phone conversation earlier this week, it's safe to say you're not doing too well, ha, nena?" Dr. Jiménez asked.

Rosa sighed, her thin shoulders rising and falling under her lavender-colored sweater. "I'm okay."

"What's been going on?"

"I've been feeling a little sick."

"A little? She's been throwing up almost nonstop," Jeremy added when it didn't appear that Rosa planned to elaborate. He knew she didn't generally like to complain, but this could be serious. "She can't keep anything down."

"Hey, I invited you because you said you wanted to be a part of this. But I'll send you to the reception area if you're going to rat me out," Rosa warned him.

"Someone has to tell her the truth," Jeremy argued. He crossed his arms in front of his chest and turned to Dr. Jiménez, hoping she'd get past any negative feelings toward him to listen to his pleas. "I'm worried about her. Her sisters are worried about her. I'm no medical professional, but I can't imagine that not eating and losing so much weight is healthy for her. Or the baby."

"Jeremy, please!" Rosa pushed herself to a seated position on the bed. The quick motion must have set off her nausea again because she immediately bent over and started dry heaving into the throw-up tray.

Remorse swamped over him and he quickly moved closer, reaching to comb her dark hair away from her face. He held her hair out of the way with one hand and gently rubbed her back with his other.

"I didn't mean to upset you," he said, the words gruff with guilt.

The doctor flanked Rosa's other side, holding on to her shoulder. "It's okay, nena. Try not to tense up. Just go with it until it passes."

After several anxious moments, the dry heaving stopped. Rosa flopped back against the table, her face glistening with sweat.

Jeremy grabbed a few paper towels from the sink area, ran some water over them, then hurried back to gently wipe Rosa's forehead.

"I'm sorry," she murmured. Her eyes fluttered open to look at him, the beautiful brown orbs filled with despair.

"Hey, now, none of that. There's nothing you need to apologize for," he assured her, keeping his voice soft as he tried to soothe her.

Rosa's eyes drifted closed again, her entire body going slack as if someone had flipped the circuit breaker cutting off all her energy.

Jeremy shot Dr. Jiménez a pained look. He didn't say anything, but he sure as hell hoped she could read his expression if not his mind. *Please, do something here!*

Dr. Jiménez gave a brisk nod, then moved to sit on the rolling stool in front of the computer.

Worry kept Jeremy by Rosa's side. He finger-combed her hair off her forehead, then pressed the damp paper towel to her clammy skin. The urge to pick her up and cradle her in his arms until she felt better built inside him, barely kept in check.

This intense need to take care of her, to do whatever was needed to help her through this had him antsy and on edge in a way he wasn't used to.

In his everyday life, he dealt with rational entities. Computers, software, hardware, numbers.

With his family, their love for each other went mostly unspoken. Except for his mom, emotions weren't often shared like they were so openly in Rosa's family.

Never before had he felt this compulsion to do and be better with any of the women he'd dated in the past.

This was different. Rosa was different.

But how to convince her of that was a problem he'd yet to solve.

His mind grappling with the intricacies of their situation, Jeremy watched the doctor's fingers flying over her keyboard. The screen changed and she read more, her lips moving.

Rosa's breathing had slowed, and he wondered if she might have dozed off. At least her pinched expression had finally relaxed.

He sank into his chair beside Rosa, quietly watching the doctor. Waiting for her to share her game plan. Because he was counting on the good doctor to have a good one.

Finally, Dr. Jiménez slid the rolling stool across the black and grey speckled linoleum floor toward them. Her face serious, she reached for Rosa's hand, gently rubbing up and down her arm to wake her. "Rosa, perdóname, pero necesitas despertarte."

"I'm awake," Rosa said, her voice groggy.

She stretched lazily, and another image slid through Jeremy's mind: Rosa in the hotel bed, arms raised over her head in a languid stretch. The white hotel sheet slipping lower to reveal the curve of her bare breasts. A dark curtain of her wavy hair falling across her cheek.

Desire curled through him like a wispy, sensuous smoke.

"I didn't mean to nod off," she said over a yawn.

"Your body needs all the rest it can get," Dr. Jiménez answered. "I am fairly certain what's going on here. To be safe, I'm going to order some lab work to rule out anything else. On one hand, morning sickness is actually a sign that your pregnancy is progressing well. But Jeremy's right, this amount of nausea and vomiting, this weight loss, it's not good."

Jeremy's heart stuttered. Damn, if the doctor was concerned, it had to mean it could be something bad.

Rosa's face scrunched in the same pained expression from earlier. The little speck of white as her top teeth worried her bottom lip told him her head whirled with questions and information from the pregnancy books and websites he'd bet anything she'd spent the past week scouring.

"I'll put in a rush order with the lab," Dr. Jiménez continued. "And while we wait, we'll get some IV fluids in your body. You're dehydrated, and that makes things worse. I'm assuming you can stick around for a while?"

The doctor aimed the question at Jeremy.

"Uh, yes, definitely. I'm here for the duration." He hesitated, realizing he may have overstepped with Rosa. "If that's okay with you?"

She gave him a wobbly smile, her tired eyes filled with gratitude. "Yeah, I'd like that."

Warm relief loosened the anxiety knotting his insides, and Jeremy reached out to clasp Rosa's hand. She wanted him to stay. That was good.

She kept insisting that she could do this alone if need be, but damn it, she wasn't alone. They were a team now. An "us."

Sure, there were details to be figured out, but all that mattered now was getting these test results and following the doctor's orders. Doing whatever would keep their baby and Rosa safe.

Rosa watched Jeremy uncross and re-cross his legs, changing positions for the umpteenth time in the uncomfortable plastic clinic chair.

She glanced at her watch again. Only five minutes since she'd last checked. A mere twelve minutes since the previous time. Marking a little over two hours since her various samples had been sent to the lab.

She twisted uncomfortably on the exam table, flipping from her back to lie on her right side, the sanitary paper crinkling underneath her.

Jeremy looked up from whatever he was reading on his cell phone. Concern sharpened his features, darkened his blue eyes. "You doing all right?"

She bit her lip, then nodded.

In reality, it was a toss-up.

Physically she felt better than she had in weeks, thanks to the IV fluids they'd pumped into her.

Mentally, thoughts and fears and worries bounced around her head like popcorn kernels in a pot on high heat.

Emotionally, waterworks were just below the surface. One wrong move, one wrong word, and her tears would blow like Old Faithful.

Jeremy leaned toward the table, propping his arm against the edge. His fingers brushed back and forth along the hem of the hospital gown on her upper thigh sending a flutter of awareness rippling through her.

Her pulse raced. Her skin tingled with the memory of his hands caressing her, coaxing a response from her that she'd never experienced before.

"You need something?" he asked, his voice gentle.

Ha! She needed something all right. The problem was, she couldn't figure out exactly what that something should be.

Part of her wanted him to climb onto the exam table and snuggle with her, forget the outside world and all the problems that awaited them.

Only it wasn't that simple and throwing caution to the wind hadn't exactly ended well for her last time.

The doubts and uncertainty were driving her crazy. Upending her need for organization and structure.

Having a baby meant life-altering, potentially career-altering decisions for her. Those changes scared her more than childhood tales of El Cuco coming to get her in the dark of night.

There were few things she'd wanted more in her life than to say yes to his proposal. But she couldn't.

"You're going to give yourself a fat lip if you keep that up." Jeremy rubbed her lower lip with his thumb. His touch was soft, bittersweet. "What are you thinking about?"

Another million-dollar question. The man was on a roll.

Jeremy stared at her intently. His expression honest, earnest, tinged with doubt.

That doubt fed her fears, kept her from divulging her deep dark thoughts.

"I just want to stop feeling this way," she muttered.

A weighted moment passed before Jeremy gently asked, "What way?"

Conflicted. Disappointed. Uncertain. Scared.

Coward that she was, she went with the safest answer. "I'm ready to be done with this all-day morning sickness. I can't see how it's a 'good sign' that the pregnancy is going well."

She wrinkled her nose at the inanity of the doctor's earlier statement.

Jeremy speared a hand through his dark blond hair and scratched his head. "Yeah, sounds like an oxymoron to me. But I'm willing to do whatever your doctor recommends. Whatever you ne—"

The exam room door opened and Dr. Jiménez walked in. There was no mistaking her serious expression.

Rosa's stomach clenched, the muscles spasming in protest. Instinctively she pressed a hand to her belly.

Dios, proteje a mi bebé, she prayed over and over. God, *please* protect her baby.

An iPad in her hands, Dr. Jiménez pulled the rolling stool closer to the exam table with her foot, then sat down. She tapped on the screen, her eyes scanning whatever she'd brought up, nodding as she went.

Rosa waited, her heart in her throat. Worried she already knew what Dr. Jiménez was going to say.

Jeremy grabbed her hand. Despite her warring emotions where he was concerned, she was relieved to have him at her side.

"The good news is, I was right, so we know what we're dealing with." Dr. Jiménez's sober expression belied her positive words. "Based on your symptoms and lab results, you're suffering from what's known as 'hyperemesis gra—'"

"Gravidarum," Rosa finished, her spirits sinking as low as her potassium levels no doubt were.

Jeremy gave a confused shake of his head. "What does that mean?"

Dr. Jiménez waited a beat. When Rosa didn't elaborate, the doctor explained, "Hyperemisis gravidarum is a condition characterized by severe nausea and vomiting, weight loss and electrolyte disturbance. It's obvious Rosa's been suffering from the first three. The lab results confirmed the latter."

Those Old Faithful tears threatening, Rosa swallowed trying to relieve the knot in her throat. She hoped her fear wasn't noticeable as she added, "My mamá had hyperemesis gravidarum with all three of her pregnancies, but with Yazmine it was the worst."

She shuddered, recalling the horror stories she'd heard over the years when the older women started swapping pregnancy and childbirth cuentos with each other. With Jeremy already in overprotective mode, she did not plan to share those stories with him. "Mami struggled with similar symptoms through the first half or more of her pregnancy. But she was eventually fine."

"Do not trivialize this, Rosa," Dr. Jiménez said, her tone grave. "Marta had to be hospitalized when she was pregnant with Yazmine. *Twice.*"

Jeremy squeezed Rosa's hand, his wide-eyed gaze flying to hers. "Hospitalized?"

"I'm not anywhere near that condition. I'm good. I am!" she asserted at Jeremy's snort of disagreement.

"Nena, everything I have here says differently." Dr. Jiménez tapped her iPad screen. "My job is to make sure you and your little one are healthy."

"Mine too," Jeremy chimed in.

Dr. Jiménez gave him a brisk nod of approval. "My first inclination is to order complete bed rest—"

"What? No way!" Rosa shot up to a seated position on the exam table. Her stomach immediately objected. Her head spun from the sudden movement, and she swayed to the side.

Jeremy's strong arm wrapped around her shoulders, keeping her from falling off the table.

"You were saying?" Dr. Jiménez asked in a bland tone.

Rosa pressed a hand to her temple, waiting for her head to stop spinning. "I need to talk with Principal Meyer first. Even then, I'm sure I can't be off work for an extended period of time. It's only my first semester at Queen of Peace."

"I can provide for you and our baby," Jeremy said. He tightened his hold around her shoulders. "You don't have to worry about how you'll support yourself anymore."

Rather than finding comfort in his words, she felt overwhelmed. More claustrophobic than protected.

His offer, his proposal, the insistence behind them. It was almost like he *had* to take care of her. *Had* to have the answers to solve this unsolvable situation. But he didn't.

Suddenly, the exam room walls and all her problems closed in on her. Suffocating her with the fear of inevitable, uncontrollable change. Just like after Mami had died.

Frantic, she shook Jeremy's arm off her shoulders. "Look, I, I appreciate you saying that, but . . . but I need . . . ay, Dr. Jiménez, necesito . . ."

She held her hands out in supplication, though she had no clear idea exactly what she pleaded for. Tears of exasperation welled to the surface, burning her eyes.

"I need things to slow down. So I can catch up," Rosa whispered, the words ragged and rough in her throat.

Yesterday she'd told her sisters she'd be fine if she had to leave Queen of Peace. Today, confronted with the reality of it happening sooner than she anticipated, she wasn't so sure.

Hot tears spilled down her cheeks. "My students rely on me. I'm just starting to make a difference with some."

She swiped at the tears, but they kept flowing, coming from a place deep inside her that had been aching for so long.

All of this was because of one rash decision on her part. Confirmation that she had no business trying to be someone she wasn't. It was the same lesson life had tried to teach her back in high school the day of Mami's car accident.

Only, this time, the consequences were different. This time she hadn't lost a loved one.

Instead, she'd become a living, breathing example for the importance of abstinence often spouted in sex education lectures in Catholic schools everywhere.

How could this be happening?

Overwhelmed by the ramifications facing her, Rosa dropped her chin to her chest.

"Hey, look at me." Jeremy ducked his head, leaning closer to try and catch her gaze. "It's going to be okay. We'll get through this."

Rosa covered her face with her hands, unable to take the confidence shining in his blue eyes. Confidence, but not love.

She couldn't go through with a loveless marriage built solely on a foundation of responsibility. Talk about soul crushing.

"What about half days?" Jeremy's question halted her Tasmanian devil mental tailspin.

"Or working part of the week?" he added.

When Dr. Jiménez didn't say anything, Rosa peeked through her fingers, anxious to see her doctor's reaction.

The older woman's pensive expression implied she might be weighing the idea.

Por favor, Rosa prayed. Repeating the words over and over in her head.

"Both of you need to understand the severity of the situation." Dr. Jiménez looked pointedly from Rosa to Jeremy and back again.

"We do. I mean, she does, right?" Jeremy nodded at Rosa who returned the gesture.

"There are, what, three weeks before school is out for winter break?" Dr. Jiménez asked her.

"Yes."

"I *might* consider something like Jeremy's idea," the doctor said slowly.

Hope eased the tightness constricting Rosa's chest. There had to be a solution that wouldn't require her to give up her job right away, at least not until the school council decided otherwise.

And she planned to fight for that not to happen.

"We can request moving you to half days for medical reasons until school begins in January." Dr. Jiménez tapped her iPad screen as she spoke. A calendar popped up on the display. "That'll be three weeks to end the semester and two weeks of winter break. Before school begins again we'll re-evaluate."

"Yes!" Rosa fisted her hands in triumph.

"But when you're not at work, I'll want you on bed rest." Dr. Jiménez motioned to Rosa. "That means having someone there with you so you're going up and down the stairs at home as little as possible."

"Está bien," Rosa agreed. "Lilí will be home for winter break in a couple of weeks. She can—"

"I'm not talking about in a couple weeks," Dr. Jiménez cut in sternly. "I'm talking about right now. Ahora mismo. You need help starting the moment you leave this office."

"No worries," Jeremy said. "I'll be at home with her."

"Excuse me?" Rosa drew back in surprise. "Um, that's not necessary."

"Yes, it is," he pressed. "I'm in between projects right now so things are slow. It shouldn't be a problem for me to work remotely most days. Or if need be, I'll take paid time off."

Dios mío, he seemed to think he had everything worked out. Like it was that simple.

But it wasn't. Not for her.

That earlier sense of suffocation squeezed her chest again.

"There's no need for you to go to all that trouble. I don't want you jeopardizing things at work," she said, groping for an excuse that might have him backing off.

Their relationship was too precarious. No way could she allow herself to rely on him. What if the Japan project got the green light again and he headed overseas for six months? What if Cecile or someone else in his social circle, a woman more suitable to his family's lifestyle, drew his attention. She'd die before being a noose around Jeremy's neck because he felt obligated.

"Look, I have the weekend to figure this out. Lilí is home until Sunday afternoon. I'll talk to Principal Meyer on Monday, and Yazmine will be around to help."

"Rosa, why can't I just—"

"Ah-ah-ah!" She held up a hand to stall his argument. "I appreciate your offer. Really. But you playing nursemaid at my house? Nuh-uh." She waggled her pointer finger back and forth in the air. "That's moving too fast. And frankly, doing so is what got us here in the first place."

Dr. Jiménez snorted, then covered it with a cough.

Rosa shot her doctor a scowl before turning her focus back to Jeremy. Just like yesterday when they'd sat together on the couch in her living room, she could almost see the wheels turning inside his head. He wanted to argue. Continue pushing his point.

Instead, gentleman that he was, he gave a slight jerk of his head indicating his agreement, but remained quiet.

Any relief she felt was short-lived though. Based on the determined jut of his chin and the thin line of his lips pressed together, as if he were forcibly trapping his argument inside, she was certain he wouldn't stay silent much longer.

Chapter Seven

"So, what's on your mind?"

Jeremy slid his gaze away from the view of the Chicago skyline and the wispy purple, pink and orange clouds painted by the setting sun. He glanced to his right as his mom sank down onto the sofa beside him in his parents' penthouse.

Dressed in straight-legged black dress slacks with a maroon blouse and a simple strand of Cartier pearls, her blond hair pulled back in a low chignon, Laura Taylor looked the epitome of a prominent lawyer's wife, ready for one of her many charity board meetings or events. While some who read the society pages dismissed many women in her position as vapid shopaholics, his mom's sharp, grey eyes told of her intelligence and keen insight.

Right now, those grey eyes were trained on him with motherly intuition.

"Come on, spit it out," she insisted, giving his knee a gentle pat.

He'd been impatiently waiting for a moment alone with his mom since arriving at his parents' penthouse several hours ago for dinner. Anxious to talk with her about Rosa and the baby, and how scared he was that Rosa would continue pushing him away.

With his younger brother Michael finally off to meet up with friends and his dad on a business call in his office, Jeremy had her undivided attention.

He rubbed his sweaty palms against his thighs, wiping the moisture on his grey slacks.

"What makes you think something's on my mind?" he asked, stalling for time.

Chicken.

His mom smiled, her eyes crinkling with that expression of loving indulgence he'd seen countless times growing up. Even during his moody periods in high school and his difficult years at the end of undergrad when he was mad at everyone, but mostly himself.

She reached out to press her pointer finger in between his brows.

"This little crease makes me ask. And a mother's sixth sense." She took a sip of her favorite after-dinner drink, chilled Limoncello. A habit she'd acquired on her and Sherman's last extended trip to Italy. "Do you want to talk about it?"

Jeremy slouched back against the stiff sofa cushions and balanced his Scotch on the rocks on his thigh. The ice cubes rattled in the glass, mimicking his rattled nerves.

He'd danced around this moment for a week now, trying to figure out how to share the news with his mom. Without dredging up painful memories of her past. Hating the idea that she'd see anything of his birth father in him.

"Sweetheart, you don't have to talk if you don't want to."

Her words soothed the unease twisting his stomach.

That was his mom. Always there, but not hovering unless necessary. For as far back as he could remember, even when it was just the two of them and she was working during the day and taking online classes at night to finish her degree, she'd made sure he knew he could count on her.

There was no one whose opinion he trusted and valued more. Though Sherman had become a close second.

"No, I've been needing to talk with you about this for a few days now." He sat up and turned to face her. Excitement and uncertainty clashed inside him in a cacophony of swords. "I need your advice about something."

"Sounds serious." His mom's cool hand clasped his forearm when he nodded, her diamond solitaire glinting in the fading sunlight. "Whatever this is, we'll get through it. Nothing, *no one*, gets us down."

Jeremy winced at the irony.

Though the name went unspoken, he understood that she referred to his birth dad and the trouble the jerk had tried to cause a few times. Thankfully they hadn't heard from him since his sentencing nearly five years ago.

What gnawed at Jeremy was the fact that his situation with Rosa might bring echoes of Roger Wilson. How the creep had mistreated Jeremy's mom when they'd dated, going into a violent rage when Laura told him that she was pregnant. It hadn't been easy, but Laura had eventually gotten away from Roger. Never looking back.

She hadn't heard from the scumbag again until Sherman Taylor came into the picture when Jeremy was five. Then Roger had shown up, thinking he'd benefit by trying to extort hush money from Sherman. Huge mistake.

Laura Taylor was no longer the scared coed Roger had abused and manipulated. She'd finished her degree and started her career as an office manager before meeting Sherman Taylor at a fundraiser. Together, the new power couple had outwitted Roger. Bringing Laura's story of mental and physical abuse to the press while donating resources and funds to a local women's shelter.

While her situation had been significantly different, if there was anyone Jeremy trusted who could provide some insight into what Rosa might be feeling and thinking when confronted with an unplanned pregnancy, it was his mom.

Only, no way would Jeremy act like the degenerate Roger Wilson had been. Still was. Jeremy had been fighting most of his adult life to prove himself a better man. God forbid this news make his mom see him in the same light.

The very idea sent a shiver across Jeremy's shoulders.

Nervous, but desperate for advice, he laid his cards on the table. "You remember Rosa Fernandez? I've mentioned her to you before."

"Yazmine's sister? The one who was in Champaign while you were there this past spring?"

"Yeah, she graduated and is a librarian in Oakmont now."

"That's nice." His mother's noncommittal tone told him she wondered where he was going with this.

He took a sip of his Scotch, welcoming the slow burn down his throat and into his chest. Kind of like the slow burn he'd been carrying for Rosa in secret for a while now.

"She and I recently reconnected, so to speak. At Yazmine's wedding."

"Wait, I thought you took Cecile as your date." His mom tilted her head to the side in confusion. "You two were giving things another chance, weren't you?"

Cecile.

He hadn't even thought of her in the midst of everything this week. Hell, they hadn't spoken since he'd left for Japan, and that conversation hadn't gone too well.

It'd been wrong to consider reconnecting with her when he moved back home. He'd done so tentatively, thinking he'd give their relationship another try, mainly for Sherman and his mom. For years, they'd hoped for a deeper union between Cecile's family and theirs, as it being partners at the boutique law firm Sherman and Harold Millward had started together wasn't enough.

Her leaving Yazmine's reception early so she could "put in an appearance" at the Millwards' event had been a light bulb moment for him. Bright enough to convince him that breaking things off when he'd taken the job in New York years ago had been the right decision.

"Mom, I told you a while ago, Cecile and I are not going to happen."

A disappointed frown marked his mom's pale brow. "Honey, you haven't been back in town all that long. Maybe if you give it some time. . . ."

Her words drifted off as he shook his head. Dismay stamped his mom's face, giving her high cheekbones and angular nose a sharp look.

"Are you sure?" she pressed.

God, he hated disappointing her. And he hadn't even gotten to the big news he needed to share.

"I'm sorry. I tried." He lifted a shoulder, then let it drop in a listless shrug. "We're better as friends. She and I talked about it over the phone before I left. Honestly, I haven't even thought about calling her since I've been back."

"Because of Rosa."

It was a statement, not a question. Spoken with a hint of resignation.

"No. Or, not only because of her." The sudden negative turn the conversation was taking had Jeremy angling to face his mom on the couch, his drink splashing over the rim in his haste. "Don't blame Rosa. It's me. I moved back home because I missed you guys. But, you know me, I didn't miss the spotlight that shines on us here. That's what Cecile craves."

"And Rosa doesn't." Again with the resignation, now with an added touch of accusation.

"If anything, Rosa seeks the opposite. It's refreshing."

His mom set her aperitif glass on the teakwood coffee table, then crossed her arms. Her gaze assessing, she eyed him like she had when he was a kid, beating around the bush rather than admitting whatever he'd done wrong. "This is why you had reservations about going to Japan, isn't it? You never mentioned anything, but I could tell something had changed right before you left."

"I didn't have—"

She gave him The Look. The one all mothers mastered, that never failed to coerce a confession.

"Okay, there were slight reservations," Jeremy amended. "I can't say I wasn't relieved the project got held up and they decided to bring me back home. In fact, I'm going to ask that they send someone else next time."

"But you're in line for a potential promotion, and this project will benefit that. You can't possibly consider derailing those plans, the prestige that comes with it, because you 'connected'"—her hands finger-quoted around the word— "with a new woman."

"She's not new," Jeremy shot back, his frustration growing at his mom's surprising dismissal of Rosa. "And you of all people should know that prestige isn't something that matters to me."

His mom's chest rose and fell on a heavy sigh, her pursed lips indicative of her frustration over a debate they'd held for ages. A debate that would always end in an unspoken truce.

She wanted him to accept what she thought was his rightful place in their social strata. But he'd never felt fully comfortable there. Especially after his decision to forgo law school.

"Anyway," he said, "it's more than a connection with her, especially since we found out that . . ."

Worry about how his mom would take this news had his voice faltering. Especially since she'd just been championing Cecile's cause.

Not to mention, if there was one thing she'd made clear when she'd sat him down to give him the sex talk when he hit puberty—even though Sherman had volunteered—it was the expectation for him to be responsible. Use protection. Take care of his partner as well as himself.

Hell, he'd done all that. He was still doing everything he could to take care of Rosa. She simply wasn't interested in letting him. The only thing she'd asked for was space.

Other than a few text messages, he hadn't heard from her since dropping her at home after the doctor appointment on Friday. He'd spent the weekend worrying about if she had gotten worse. If she was resting like Dr. Jiménez had ordered. Wondering if Lilí needed any help, maybe someone to run to the store while she stayed with Rosa.

"Found out what, J?" his mom asked.

Jeremy nervously shifted his glass from one hand to the other, then he crooked an elbow on the dark wood framing the couch's deep green brocade.

"We had one night together. An amazing night I doubt I'll, well, you probably don't need the details." He paused, embarrassed.

Her motherly Spidey senses must have picked up on the level of his discomfort because his mom's expression sobered.

Dread tightened his chest.

"We were careful. Honest. But somehow, not careful enough."

He stopped, unable to say more. Waiting for her to connect the dots.

It didn't take her long.

"She's . . ." His mom pressed her fingertips to her lips as if to hold her words back. Her grey eyes filled with shock in the moment before she closed them.

Remorse gutted him.

"Mom, I—"

She shook her head. "Give me a minute."

Dejection tightened his chest as he watched his normally poised mom work to gather herself. She smoothed a shaking hand along her hair to her chignon, then leaned over to grab her glass for a fortifying sip of Limoncello.

Once again, he was disappointing the most important people in his life. The same way he had when he'd finally admitted to his parents that he had no interest in law school and joining Sherman's firm.

He'd come back home this summer confident he could make the Taylor name proud in his own way. This development might not help that cause, but he could never think of Rosa's pregnancy as a negative.

"This is surprising, unexpected news," his mom finally said, more to herself as she stared down at the tiny glass in her hands. "Makes me think about, well, quite a few things."

Guilt slammed through him and he hung his head. "I'm sorry if telling you this dredges up memories of the past, Mom. You've got to know that I don't plan on—I won't be like him, I promise I—"

"Look at me," his mom demanded, her tone sharp.

The twelve-year-old boy in him, ready for the lecture he knew he deserved, obeyed.

One hand fisted in her lap, her face taut with anger, his mom pierced him with a razor-sharp glare. "You are *nothing* like Roger Wilson. Don't ever think that. Do you hear me?"

He gave her a timid nod in answer, but it wasn't until he finally mumbled "yes" that her tension eased and her fist unclenched.

"This situation is not the same," she said, her expression softened with regret. "You care about Rosa. I can see that. Roger . . . he couldn't have cared less about me. You know the story. You know what happened."

Jeremy nodded, unwilling to have her repeat—relive— the terrible details.

"I'm sure whatever the two of you shared was consensual."

"Yes, ma'am," he immediately answered.

"And, how's Rosa?" she asked, her concern far different from the resignation that had tinted Rosa's name when his mom had spoken it earlier. "This has to be difficult for her."

"She's not too good, actually." Jeremy frowned, picturing her sickly green complexion when her nausea hit. "She's lost weight, can't keep anything down. Yesterday her doctor diagnosed her with hyperemesis gravidarum so she's on partial bed rest. At least for the rest of this month."

Before his mom could respond, the maid stepped into the living room area, interrupting their conversation. The middle-aged woman, new to the family since Jeremy had moved away, inquired whether either of them needed anything, then, at his mother's request, began reviewing the next day's dinner menu.

Listening to them discuss an upcoming soiree his parents were hosting at home, Jeremy couldn't help but compare their plans for staff and extra hired help to what Thanksgiving preparation at Rosa's had entailed. How the entire Fernandez family had pitched in, rubbing elbows in the kitchen while cooking the meal. It'd been crowded, sometimes messy, but entertaining. Comfortable. Like pretty much every time he'd visited the Fernandez home.

Rising from the couch, he walked to the glass windows overlooking the outdoor patio, a perk of owning the penthouse. With its potted plants, open pit brick fireplace, and strategically placed comfy chairs and end tables, it was the ideal location for a private cocktail party. The city at dusk and early evening, streetlights casting their beams across Lake Michigan, created a beautiful backdrop. Many lucrative deals and some important networking had taken place out on that patio.

An invite to a Taylor private party wasn't something most people would pass up.

Funny, he couldn't help but wonder what Rosa would think of one. If she came, it wouldn't be because of any deals or networking she hoped to capitalize on.

"Bed rest, huh?" his mom said from behind him.

He turned away from the sliding glass doors to find his mom approaching him. The maid had already cleared their empty glasses and left the room.

"Yeah, and she's not happy about it." He explained about the doctor visit, following up with Rosa's request for space and her absolute refusal, multiple times, to marry him.

His mom flinched with surprise at that last bit of info.

"What?" he asked.

"Marriage? That's your answer?"

"It's the right thing to do."

She spun away and strode a few paces toward the fireplace, her stiff-shouldered gait telegraphing her displeasure.

"Mom—"

"Jeremy, please!" Her arms lifted and fell on a frustrated huff. "Don't sacrifice yourself because you feel the need to atone for Roger's behavior with me."

"I'm not."

"Aren't you?" Her voice was a harsh whisper, even more gut-wrenching than if she'd yelled at him.

Dismay clouded her grey eyes, carved deep grooves that bracketed her mouth.

Her question hit a nerve. Doggedly, he ignored it.

God, he'd known she'd be upset about this news, but he'd never imagined she'd be against him proposing to Rosa. At least not this vehemently.

"J, it is truly admirable that you want to 'do the right thing,' but—" She paused, dug her hands in the pockets of her crisp black slacks, and seemed to weigh her words before speaking again. "In this case, son, you're not the main person who can determine what that is."

"I know."

"I'm not sure you do." She shook her head slowly, her disappointment palpable. "Be careful that you're not so afraid of being Roger, that you err on the other end of the spectrum. Marriage isn't something to jump into, especially given the situation. No good will come of that. For either you or Rosa."

Jeremy turned away to face the glass doors. His mother's warning echoed in his head as he stared blindly at the darkening Chicago skyline. Dusk's waning light sent long shadows creeping across the patio, mimicking the doubt slowly creeping up on him.

He'd been so sure before. Now . . . now, he didn't know anymore.

"So, you're really taking Rosa's side?" he asked.

"This isn't about sides, J."

The gentle reprimand confirmed his complaint sounded as whiny as he'd thought.

"I know," he grudgingly admitted.

"It's about a woman whose life is set to change, drastically. And she probably still needs to come to peace with that, on her own terms. Not yours."

His mom's hand on his shoulder drew his gaze to his left, where she now stood. Her usually calm expression was back in place, the light sheen of tears in her eyes the only sign of her emotional disquiet. "I'm not saying back off completely. Make sure she's aware that you want to be a part of her life. And the baby's. But you cannot push. That's not fair to her."

If there was one thing his mom would demand of him, it's that he be fair. That he treat the mother of his child with respect and compassion. Two things she'd never gotten from Roger Wilson.

Anger flared in Jeremy's gut, fueling the determination to prove himself that had always driven him. "I'm not going to be a deadbeat dad."

"Of course not, I raised you better than that."

Her patronizing tone cooled his anger and had his lips curving in a smirk. His mom's answering smile calmed him even more.

Then her expression sobered. "But a father and a husband are two different relationships. Before you rush things with Rosa, you need to make sure marriage is the right answer. For *both* of you and your child."

Darkness had fallen outside. With a resigned sigh, Jeremy closed his eyes, blocking out his reflection in the glass doors as he contemplated his mother's advice. Which was not the advice he'd expected when he had started this conversation.

As much as he hated to admit it, maybe proposing *had* been a knee-jerk reaction. One that forced Rosa to kick him in the shins and give him the Heisman stiff arm move to make him back off.

Jumping into a quickie marriage could be as rash as jumping

into bed with her. As amazing as that night had been, so far it had backfired on him. Despite their intimacy and her resulting pregnancy, he and Rosa were on shakier ground than before.

His mom was right.

Tomorrow he'd talk to Rosa. Calmly, rationally. Do whatever, say whatever it took to reassure her that their next move was up to her. As long as it didn't involve cutting him out of his child's life.

No way was that an option.

Chapter Eight

"I appreciate you being candid with me," Principal Meyer told Rosa during the last hour of the school day on Monday.

Sitting in a well-used wooden chair across from Principal Agatha Meyer's equally scratched and worn desk, Rosa held her hands clasped in her lap.

Inside her, a tiny voice was down on its knees, praying the older woman would be understanding and agree to speak on her behalf with the diocese council.

Outside, Rosa fought to maintain a calm, professional demeanor.

"It's early still, but with the problems I mentioned, my doctor is fairly adamant about partial bed rest." The principal winced at the last word and Rosa rushed to reassure her. "Just through the month of December. We're anticipating all will be well, and I'll be back full-time after the holiday break."

Principal Meyer's mouth twisted, the lines feathering out from the corners of her eyes deepening with her grimace. "You know, of course, that the diocese council will have to be alerted. While teachers and staff didn't sign a morality clause this year, we did add mention of it in the handbook."

"But it's not currently part of our contract," Rosa stressed.

Principal Meyer's expression remained noncommittal. "You are correct. Not this year. However, the intent was clear that staff and administrators should adhere to the suggestion. There will be some who are not pleased with your situation and may call for your resignation."

Part of her had expected this reaction, but hearing the principal say it out loud made the potential fallout more of a reality.

Closing her eyes, Rosa said a quick prayer, asking for the words that would convince her boss to see her perspective and walk this fine line with her.

"I recognize that you've been a welcome addition to our staff this year," Principal Meyer said. She glanced at her computer screen, but from this side of the desk Rosa couldn't tell what the principal might be reading. "The number of students taking advantage of the tutoring program you started is commendable. And the Poetry Club hasn't seen this many members in years."

Esto era lo que ella siempre quería. The compliment perked her flagging spirit as the thought whispered through her mind. Yes, it was definitely what she'd wanted—to make a difference.

"Working at Queen of Peace has been my goal since Mrs. Patterson shared her retirement plans with me while I was an undergrad. The prospect of earning this position is what drove me to complete my master's studies after my father's death. This is my home." Rosa pressed a hand to her chest, willing the principal to hear the truth behind her words. "It's where I belong."

Dios mío, she still remembered her first day of kindergarten here. The excitement of putting on her white button-down blouse with the Peter Pan collar. Zipping up the blue and green plaid romper. Slipping on her white bobby socks and black buckle shoes. Mami walking Yazmine and her to their respective classrooms. Taking a picture with Sister Magdalena. The thrill of her first visit to the library.

Over the years, from elementary to middle and on to high school, the library had become her second home. Mrs. Patterson had become a surrogate mother figure at school. Rosa had spent many of her lunch periods and countless after-school hours volunteering in the library. The smell of books old and new, the *thump* of the old checkout stamp with the return date in the back of the books, the classical music softly playing over the speakers. They all brought her a sense of comfort and security.

By her last two years of high school, it had even gotten to a point where if Mrs. Patterson was out for some reason, the note left for the substitute typically read, *Rosa Fernandez is my right hand. If you have any questions, she'll know the answer.*

When Mami had died and Rosa struggled with filling her role for the family, Mrs. Patterson had been Rosa's sounding board at school. The Queen of Peace library her safe haven during the day.

That's what she wanted to create for her students now. A place to learn, grow, trust, flourish. Not just a place to hang out when they wanted to get out of class.

One rash decision couldn't curtail Rosa's plan now.

Being at Queen of Peace wasn't just about having a job. It didn't just pay her bills. Refusing Jeremy's offer to take care of her and the baby wasn't just pride on her part. With Papi gone, Yazmine starting her own family, and Lilí in college, Rosa needed this place, the community and balance it signified in her life.

And yet . . .

Ay Dios mío, the push and pull of fighting for her job or accepting the consequences and forging a new path, however scary that might be, was tearing her in two.

Ultimately though, she knew if she didn't fight for herself as hard as she fought for others, she'd regret it.

Whether Principal Meyer and the diocese council agreed with her or not, she'd go down swinging. Probably surprising many in the process. Especially herself.

A new determination driving her, Rosa leaned forward, placing her clasped hands on Principal Meyer's desk.

"I am committed to Queen of Peace. To our students. I recognize that once my news gets out, it will put you in a difficult spot. My hope is that my work here will speak louder than any dissidents. That the good I am doing with our students will be considered."

Principal Meyer reached across to cover Rosa's hands with one of her own. Her older, wrinkled skin was cold, but her grip tight. "Oh, how I wish all my teachers shared your same commitment and drive. I regret that I can't tell you there won't be any problems. Ultimately it's not my decision. But you can count on me to speak highly of the work you've done here so far and remind the council of your family history at Queen of Peace."

She sat back in her desk chair, all business once again. "However, they must be careful of any precedent that could be set. Remember, it is the diocesan council, Father Yosef, and potentially the archbishop himself who will ultimately decide your fate."

Rosa nodded mutely. Any words she might have been able to form were trapped below the knot of fear and dismay clogging in her throat.

"The council doesn't meet again until late January." Principal Meyer flipped a page in her planner. "You have nearly two months. Hopefully you will be off bed rest and back full-time by then so that won't be an issue. For now, let's deal with the approval for your medical time off."

The discussion turned to library coverage over the remaining weeks of the fall semester. Both agreed that Brenda, Rosa's assistant, would be fine managing things in the mornings. Rosa would come in by lunch and stay after school for tutoring and Poetry Club.

"I'll get the paperwork started for your medical half days and schedule a meeting with Father Yosef to explain the situation. He may feel that a special meeting with the council is warranted rather than waiting until January," Principal Meyer said. "I suspect he will want you present when I speak to him. You should be prepared to present your case, so to speak."

The end of the day bell rang, the shrill sound punctuating the principal's warning.

"Yes, of course," Rosa murmured.

Long-ingrained Catholic schoolgirl guilt flooded her chest, rising like the Caribbean sun to heat her face.

She pushed back her chair and stood on shaky legs, hoping her lips were curved in a smile. Not the grimace she fought to hide.

Ave María purísima, the irony. She was the "good" sister. The one who'd never been sent to the principal's office before. Or, as one of her tutoring students with a penchant for colorful, if often inappropriate, phrases dubbed his numerous visits to Principal Meyer's office, "being called up to the big leagues."

Apparently, when she was finally called up to Father Yosef's big league, she hit it out of the park.

By the time Rosa reached the library, the adrenaline that had carried her through the meeting with Principal Meyer had seeped away, leaving her body drained and as limp as a wet noodle.

The anxiety that had built up before their talk, the uncertainty of how Principal Meyer might react, and the guilt of having to face her longtime priest with the news of her pregnancy had pushed her into I've-had-enough territory.

Weary, Rosa tugged open the library door. Her relief at finding her home away from home empty was quickly pushed out of the way by a flash of shame. She should want her library filled, every chair taken. With finals a little over two weeks away, students should be taking advantage of study time or the help she offered. Like she normally encouraged them to do.

Her legs shaky, Rosa made her way toward the checkout desk and her back office along the far left side of the room. She cast a quick glance at the black and white industrial wall clock above the checkout desk. 3:10. School regulations said the library would be open another fifty minutes. Of course, she usually stayed till 4:30 if students were here. When Poetry Club met, they were known to stay longer, especially if one of the members volunteered to practice reciting or, as it was commonly known, spitting something they'd written.

Her stomach rumbled. Whether from hunger or nausea, she'd given up trying to tell. Since her visit with Dr. Jiménez, she'd been surviving on prenatal vitamins and mini bites of pureed chicken soup with a side of her favorite Export Soda crackers. She'd have to ask Tomás to pick up another one of the green tins from the colmado in west Chicago after work.

As much as Rosa hated to admit it, Dr. Jiménez had been right. Working a full day was too much right now.

Gracias a Dios Yazmine had dropped her off this morning and planned to pick her up after the library study hour. Rosa didn't trust herself behind the wheel of a car. Not when all she wanted was to lie down on her office floor and take a nap.

Bypassing the stool behind the library checkout counter, Rosa continued to her office and the small restroom attached. A splash of cold water on her face, maybe a wet paper towel on the back of her neck, might revitalize her.

Moments later, she dabbed her face dry, then trudged back to the stool behind the counter, hoping to get there before her legs gave out. It was important that she be out front to greet any students who might arrive. It was part of her plan to gain her students' trust.

A friendly smile, the brightly colored bienvenidos welcome mat, and the framed snapshots of students and her scattered throughout the library on bookshelves, tabletops, and various nooks and crannies. They were all intended to create a sense of family and belonging. Inviting her students to think of the library as a home away from home, like she did.

Rosa had barely made it to the metal stool before Carlotta Juárez walked into the library. The tall, slender girl with light olive skin and long, straight black hair slowed her steps as she drew closer to the counter. She pushed her thick glasses farther onto her nose and slanted Rosa a tentative glance.

"Hola, Carlotta," Rosa greeted. "How are you doing today?"

"Um, okay. How about—?" Carlotta broke off, her brows arching closer together as she stared more pointedly at Rosa. "Perdóname but, you're not looking too well, Señorita Fernandez."

Rosa chuckled, dabbing her face with the moist paper towel again. "No need to apologize, nena. I saw my reflection in the mirror a few moments ago."

Carlotta blushed, pushing her glasses up again in the nervous gesture Rosa had begun to notice the more time they spent together.

"Does that mean you're heading home early then?" Carlotta asked. Head bowed, she fiddled with Rosa's Shakespeare bust paperweight, moving it away from the counter's edge, then trailing a finger down the back side of the figure. "I can stop by tomorrow if that's better."

It was obvious the girl had something on her mind. That she'd come here to get it off her chest, maybe ask for advice, was like a shot of vitamin B in Rosa's arm.

She scooted to sit up straight on the stool, elated that Carlotta would turn to her. "No, I'm staying. Something isn't agreeing with my stomach, but I'll be fine. Are you planning to study? Or do you maybe need help with something?"

"Yeah."

Rosa dabbed her face again to cover her smile. Carlotta probably didn't even realize she'd replied to both options.

"Okay then," Rosa said. "Make yourself comfortable. Let me know if I can be of assistance. I'm going to send a few emails, but I'll be right here."

The shy teen nodded, then heaved her over-full backpack onto the nearest tabletop with a loud *thud*. She winced, offering Rosa an "I'm sorry" glance as she pulled out one of the plastic chairs and plopped down.

Rosa clicked open her email, intent on drafting a message to her assistant, Brenda. Typically Brenda worked mornings so her hours wouldn't change while Rosa moved to afternoon half days for the next few weeks. They'd overlap for about an hour and could review any particulars then.

Two sentences into her email, Rosa paused, a sense of anticipation tiptoeing across her shoulder blades. Fingers on the keyboard, she looked at Carlotta.

Hunched over a spiral notebook, a mechanical pencil tightly clutched in her left hand, Carlotta peeked through the curtain of black silky hair that draped her shoulder and pooled onto the table. The girl was actually quite beautiful, though too shy to see it. Tall and thin, with beautiful skin and thick brows arching over dark eyes and delicate features, she could easily pass for a model. Add Carlotta's brains and, if you asked Rosa, her student was the "total package," as some kids might say.

Unfortunately, Rosa hadn't heard Carlotta mention many friends. In fact, the teen spent most of her time studying or taking care of her three younger siblings. Based on what she'd shared before, Rosa figured the girl didn't get much chance for socializing.

Dios, Rosa remembered the difficulties of adolescence, the rejection and insecurity. Especially when it came to dating. Like Rosa, Carlotta often kept to herself, attending the Poetry Club meetings, but usually not saying much.

Sensing her student's hesitation and need for reassurance, Rosa infused her smile with every ounce of encouragement in her tired body.

Carlotta dropped her gaze back to her notebook, her shoulders rising and falling on a heavy sigh.

Okay, so she wasn't ready to share. Rosa understood better than most that pushing wasn't always the right answer. Instead, she turned back to the computer to finish her email. Her stomach churned and she pressed a hand to it, hoping to allay the nausea while at the same time wracking her brain for an inconspicuous way to entice Carlotta to open up.

"Señorita Fernandez?"

Carlotta's unexpected inquiry startled Rosa out of her thoughts.

"I was wondering," the girl went on once she had Rosa's attention, "well, if you don't mind, or if you have time, would you look at this poem I've been working on? Maybe give me some feedback?"

Carlotta's left palm pressed down on top of her spiral notebook as if protecting her work. Creating an unconscious connection between her words and herself.

A closet poet who rarely shared her work with others, Rosa understood how difficult, how personal, Carlotta's request might be for her. Ironically, while Rosa considered her poetry more like her private diary, she'd been encouraging her students in the Poetry Club to volunteer for their first open mic night the evening after their last day of finals. It was the perfect way to cap off their semester.

Despite Dr. Jiménez's orders that she not overtax herself, Rosa refused to disappoint her students by postponing or canceling the event.

"I'd be honored to read your piece." Rosa slid off the stool, her stomach roiling in protest. She swallowed, pushing away the discomfort, then circled the length of the checkout counter. "Is this the one you were working on before the Thanksgiving break?"

"A new version actually. I was inspired by one of the spoken-word artists you mentioned at our last Poetry Club meeting."

A thrill lit through Rosa like a July Fourth sparkler. "¡Ay que bueno!"

"Pues, not so good if you ask my mamá." Carlotta scowled, her mouth puckering before she explained. "I was watching one of the performances on YouTube and Mamá walked by my room. My fault for not closing my door."

"¿Por qué?"

"Because she wasn't too thrilled with some of the language."

Rosa's hand stilled on the back of the chair she'd been about to pull out. "Language? What do you mean? I reviewed all the pieces before recommending them. None of them were inappropriate."

"Oh, I know, but I started clicking around and came across the over-eighteen page."

"Por favor, tell me you didn't."

Carlotta winced.

"I—I kinda clicked the link?" The teen's voice hitched up at the end turning her statement into a question. A sure sign she knew she'd messed up.

"Even though you're not over eighteen."

Carlotta had the grace to dip her head in remorse at Rosa's admonishment.

The last thing Rosa wanted was to get one of her students in trouble. Or worse, have a parent call the school with a complaint about her condoning inappropriate material. Not when she was already dreading having to meet with Father Yosef about her pregnancy.

Talk about digging a deeper hole for herself.

When Carlotta tipped her head to peer up at Rosa, her black eyes shone with a feverish light.

"It's just that, this girl, she's not much older than me, and she has such a way with words," Carlotta said, her voice filled with awe. "I wasn't even thinking really. I got so caught up in her verses and her live performances, I couldn't not click on the next one. It's like . . . I don't know."

Carlotta's thumbs rubbed against her fingertips as if she were trying to feel for the right words. "Es—es como que me conoce."

"Like she knows you," Rosa slowly repeated Carlotta's assessment, a sense of kinship worming its way to her poet's soul.

The young girl nodded, her expression earnest. One palm flattened against her chest, the other once again pressed atop her spiral notebook.

Rosa bit her lip, torn between reprimanding the girl for going to an unauthorized website and empathizing with her over the intense experience of having someone speak the words in your head. In your heart.

Dragging out the plastic chair beside Carlotta's, Rosa sank down into it with a heavy sigh.

"You're upset with me, too," Carlotta muttered. She pushed her rectangular glasses higher up the bridge of her nose, her shoulders slumping.

Rosa gathered her thoughts, wanting to bring home the importance of following the rules, yet not discourage one of her favorite students from confiding in her.

"Here's the thing," Rosa started. "I love that you're excited about poetry. That you're challenging yourself by putting your thoughts and ideas on paper." Instinctively she reached out to place a comforting hand on Carlotta's shoulder. "And I'm honored that you'd ask me to read your writing."

"There's a 'but' coming. I can sense it."

Rosa chuckled at Carlotta's disgruntled tone. Smart girl.

"Peeerooo." Rosa drew out the word, teasing a tentative smile from her student. "But you know what your parents think is acceptable and what's not. You know their rules. So, while I am all for diving into the spoken-word arena, I am not okay with anything that will get you in trouble. Or me."

Carlotta's head whipped up, her jaw dropping in a shocked "oh."

"Get you in trouble? Ay que estúpida soy. I didn't even think about that. Perdóname."

"You're not stupid. You're an inquisitive teen. Who also knows better than to break the rules. If you're looking for more poets to study, I can give you a few other names and titles before you go. But stay out of the over-eighteen pages!"

"Gracias, Señorita Fernández." Carlotta flung her arms around Rosa in a tight hug that stole Rosa's breath. "You're the best!"

Rosa tucked Carlotta's declaration into a corner of her memory. The one reserved for special moments she liked to recall whenever she doubted herself, or needed a pick-me-up. This might be her first semester as Queen of Peace's librarian, but little by little she was making progress. With time, patience, determination, and love, she'd make her own place here. Out of her sisters' shadows.

If the diocese let her stay.

As if her brain relayed the troubling thought to Rosa's stomach, it picked that exact moment to complain again. Her stomach spasmed with contractions that had her pushing out of her seat and beelining for her office restroom. Her stomach heaving, she sank onto her knees in front of the toilet.

Long moments later, once the worst had passed, she heard a tentative knock on the door. "¿Señorita Fernandez, está bien?"

"Yes, I'm okay," Rosa answered, her voice weak. "I'll be right out."

It took way too much effort to pick herself up off the floor, rinse her mouth in the sink, and pat the sweat off her face. By the time Rosa finished, lying back down on the tile floor sounded like the best idea she'd had all day.

Time for her to head home, even though it was earlier than normal.

When she opened the door, Carlotta waited on the other side, her face a mask of worry.

"I'm the one who needs to apologize now," Rosa said. She leaned against the door frame for support. "I'm sorry, but I really need to call my sister for a ride home. Any chance I can take a look at your work tomorrow? Maybe during lunch or after school?"

"Sure, that's okay. Here, let me help you." Carlotta stepped to Rosa's side. The girl swung her right arm around Rosa's waist, then hooked Rosa's left arm over her shoulder.

Her legs feeling like they were filled with mango jelly, Rosa leaned on Carlotta as they made their way to the front counter, where she'd left her cell phone.

"Are you sure you're doing okay? You've been sick for a few days now, haven't you?"

"I'm good. This will pass." She hoped.

They reached the stool behind the counter, and Rosa hooked a foot on the rung to support herself as she sat down.

"You kinda look like my mom when she was, um, never mind." Carlotta waved off the words, an embarrassed look crossing her youthful face.

Rosa froze, afraid to respond. Certain she knew where Carlotta had been headed with her observation. Thankful the girl had dropped it because Rosa would not have wanted to lie to her.

Mortified, Rosa reached for her cell next to the computer keyboard so she could call Yazmine. Just as she'd unlocked the phone screen, the library door opened again.

"We're closing up," Carlotta called. "Señorita Fernandez isn't well. Come back tomorrow."

"Looks like I got here just in time. I'm her ride home."

At the sound of Jeremy's deep voice, Rosa dropped her phone. It clattered onto the counter, nearly falling off the edge.

Her gaze shot to the doorway, her mind screaming a silent, *What is he doing here?*

The sight of his broad shoulders cloaked in a navy wool winter coat made her pulse skip. His dirty-blond hair was wind-mussed, his cheeks ruddy from the cold front that had blown in overnight, dropping the temperature to icy twenties. She hadn't seen him since her doctor's appointment on Friday, but out of sight had not meant out of mind.

Not for her anyway.

"You know this guy?" Carlotta leaned toward Rosa and stage whispered.

"Yeah," Rosa answered. "He's my—"

Long-time crush, one-night stand, baby daddy.

Jeremy cocked his head, his blue eyes considering her, waiting for her response.

"Friend," she finished, her voice tripping over the lame description.

Jeremy's eyes flashed with disappointment. Then he blinked and it was gone.

His lips curved with a friendly grin for Carlotta as he strode toward the counter. Confident. Sure. Gorgeous. Totally unexpected.

Rosa's pulse picked up speed with each step that brought him closer.

Her two worlds—school and personal life—were about to collide. Like an eyewitness helpless to stop a train wreck, she watched, stunned into muteness.

"Jeremy Taylor. I'm a *very close* friend of Rosa's, er, Señorita Fernandez." He held out his hand toward Carlotta. "Nice to meet you."

The young girl eyed Jeremy warily before accepting his handshake. "Carlotta Juárez. She's not feeling so hot. You probably wanna get her home right away."

Before Rosa could object, Carlotta morphed from shy schoolgirl to big sister in charge, thanks no doubt to her role at home. The teen made quick work of shutting down the computer, grabbing Rosa's purse and jacket from her desk drawer, and locking the office behind her. Once back out front, Carlotta held the jacket and purse out at Jeremy.

He looked at the black shoulder bag blankly.

Carlotta shook it at him, her bug-eyed expression clearly saying she expected him to take it.

If she wasn't still shell-shocked by his arrival, Rosa might have laughed at Jeremy's confusion.

For someone who tended to be quiet most of the time, Carlotta certainly knew how to take charge when needed. Her whirlwind of activity helped ease the nervousness tingling across Rosa's shoulders at seeing Jeremy again. Especially after the brief text message responses she'd given him all weekend.

He had asked her to let him know how her conversation with Principal Meyer went, so she would have called him later tonight or tomorrow. She just hadn't expected him to show up here.

"Señorita Fernandez is pretty weak. You may need to help her to the car," Carlotta directed Jeremy. "I can lock up behind us if you give me a quick sec."

The teen hurried to the table, where she crammed her spiral notebook and pencil in her backpack.

"I guess she means business," Jeremy mumbled, his wry chuckle softening the words.

He slung Rosa's purse strap over his shoulder, turning to model it for her with a quick wink.

Pleasure washed over her, erasing some of her unease.

This was her old Jeremy. The one who joked easily, smoothing away her shyness. The one who didn't overwhelm her with his intensity. Or his insistence on moving their relationship at warp speed.

"I'm the oldest," Carlotta explained. "Both my parents work two jobs to pay the bills, so I'm always stuck in charge at home when they're out or if my mom's not well."

She slipped her arms into her book bag straps and hefted it up onto her back, then marched for the door. "Let's go. She needs some rest."

Jeremy held on to Rosa's elbow as she slid off the stool.

Still weak from her recent bout of dry heaves, she leaned against the counter while he helped her into her coat. Turning her around to face him, he began fastening the buttons without a word.

Rosa bit her lip, desperate to believe they could go back to the comfortable relationship they'd shared before. Afraid they couldn't.

He dipped his hands into her collar to carefully pull the ends of her hair out of her coat. His warm fingers brushed against her neck, and heat seeped down her body like molten lava.

Her thoughts flashed back to a set of cool white bedsheets, Jeremy's naked body against hers. His big hands caressing her neck, her belly, her bare breasts as he leaned over her to press a kiss to her skin.

The lust she felt only for him sparked, overwhelming her already weakened body, and it finally gave out. Unable to stop herself, Rosa crumpled toward the floor.

"Whoa!" Jeremy yelped, grabbing her under the armpits to stop her fall.

The next thing she knew, he'd bent down to hook one arm under her knees, the other sliding behind her back. He swung her easily up in his arms, cradling her against his hard chest.

"I can walk," she protested, but even to her own ears, her plea sounded wimpy. About as wimpy as her ability to resist him.

Jeremy ignored her, heading to the library entrance, where Carlotta held the door open.

"Nice move, Galahad," Carlotta teased, stepping aside to let them pass by.

Jeremy laughed, a deep, throaty sound that Rosa felt rumbling through his chest.

Embarrassed as she was to have Jeremy carry her out of the building, she smiled along with him. She had to hand it to Carlotta. The girl had sized up Jeremy quickly, correctly pegging him for the gallant knight Rosa knew him to be. Bueno, most of the time anyway.

Carlotta locked up, then dropped the keys into Rosa's purse. "Nice meeting you, Mr. Taylor. Make sure she's okay. Hope you feel better by tomorrow, Señorita Fernandez. Adios."

With a wave good-bye, Carlotta hurried away down the hall.

Rosa recalled the teen's brief observation comparing Rosa's sickness more than likely to her mom's pregnancies. Hopefully Carlotta would forget about it. Certainly not share it with anyone. Not yet, anyway.

"And then there were two," Jeremy said softly.

He gazed down at her, his charming smile crinkling the edges of his blue eyes.

Yesterday, Rosa would have been anxious to keep her distance from him. Too tired to fight. Too scared of what the future held for them with so many uncertainties up in the air.

Right now, it felt so good to be in his arms again. She didn't have it in her to complain.

With his strength supporting her tired body. His smile warming her heart. The scent of his earthy aftershave soothing her roiling stomach. Keeping her distance was the last thing she wanted.

Sí, they still had to work through things. Big things.

Maybe him coming here was a sign she should share with him the pro-con list she had started. The old Jeremy would listen, offer a suggestion.

She hesitated, afraid of the consequences. Of him not agreeing and pushing his own agenda. Namely, a marriage of convenience.

It was time for her to swallow that fear and stand her ground. Have that adult conversation without worrying that she might fall on old habits and go along with the "right thing" everyone expected. She could do it.

Later though. Now she'd assuage her desire to be close to him. Just for a little while.

Wrapping her arms more tightly around his broad shoulders, Rosa laid her head against his shoulder, his wool jacket scratchy against her cheek.

"Take me home, Sir Galahad," she murmured, barely suppressing a sigh of satisfaction. "I'm beat."

Chapter Nine

Jeremy slid a quick, worried glance at Rosa seated beside him in the passenger seat of his BMW.

"Take me home. I'm beat," she had told him back at her school.

He wouldn't argue with that. As soon as he'd walked into the library, he'd noticed how worn out she looked. Even more so than on Friday.

Now, eyes closed, she dozed while he drove, her arms slack at her sides. Her shoulders drooped like they carried a heavy weight. Her face was pale and gaunt, worry lines feathering her brow.

Despite all of that, he still found her beautiful. Like always.

As for her order that he take her home—hell, he wanted nothing more than to whisk her off to his place, where he'd tuck her in his bed and pamper her until she felt better. Take care of her and their baby. Convince her that he was good enough. That she could trust him to be a good husband and father who was worthy of her.

His mom's cautionary words from yesterday whispered in his ear.

Swooping Rosa off to his condo caveman-style was the exact opposite of behaving calmly and rationally and letting her take the lead.

"So how did you get roped into picking me up?"

Rosa's sleepy, husky-voiced question drew his attention as he slowed for a red light. "I called Yazmine to see how you were doing. Figured she'd level with me."

"You could have called me," Rosa mumbled.

"I thought you might not be able to answer if students were in the library. And I wanted more than a one-word text response."

Guilt and exasperation melded in the brown depths of her eyes.

The streetlight turned green and Jeremy eased his car forward, wishing he could move them past this new unease between them.

"I don't want to fight with you, Rosa," he admitted on a tired sigh.

He wanted to kiss her. Comfort her. Hold her in his arms.

Fight? Not so much.

"I don't either. But you have to stop being a bully."

"A what?" Shocked at her description of him, Jeremy barely kept his foot from tapping the brake as his mind tripped over the word.

He'd never been called a bully in his entire life. That was Roger Wilson's calling card, especially with women. It's what had ultimately landed the man in jail.

Jeremy shook his head in exasperation. If he'd done anything to make Rosa feel like he was forcing his will on her. To make her doubt his sincerity or his pledge to be there for her and their baby. He'd never forgive himself.

Frustrated, he clenched his fingers on the steering wheel. She deserved better.

"I'm sorry. I didn't mean to sound so harsh." Rosa laid a hand on his wrist, concern lacing her voice.

Great. He was supposed to be looking out for her, and here she was trying to cheer him up.

"No, you're good." Relaxing his tense grip, he covered her hand with one of his, giving it a gentle pat. "I don't want you to ever think there's something you can't tell me. Especially if I'm being a jerk. We need to be honest with each other, okay?"

She nodded, her face solemn.

"I'm sorry for shutting you out," she said. "I'm a little—bueno, more like a lot—freaked out about all this."

"Me too."

She slid her hand out from under his to scoot herself up in her seat. Silly as it might be, he wanted her to touch him again. Maintain that connection, however small it might be.

"So I talked to Principal Meyer this afternoon."

Based on the way her lips twisted in a grimace, he figured it hadn't gone too well.

"And?" he pressed when Rosa didn't elaborate.

"And, the good news is that she agreed to the half days through December. The diocesan school council won't meet until January, and unless Father Yosef objects, she doesn't see the need to say anything until then."

"Sounds promising." He signaled to make a right turn into her neighborhood before venturing to ask, "What's the bad news?"

"She thinks I'll have to meet with her and Father Yosef to get his approval of the half days. Principal Meyer also mentioned the morality clause. I was right—my pregnancy could be a problem with some of the council members."

"They'd be crazy to make you leave, Rosa." And he'd talk to whomever, even drop the Taylor name if it would help her. Despite how much he shied away from relying on that pull.

"I agree. Muy loco." Rosa's Mona Lisa smile curved her full lips.

Jeremy chuckled, the flash of her shy cheekiness a balm to his lingering worries.

Moments later, they pulled up in front of her house. The two-story brick ranch with its grey shutters and mix of orange and yellow chrysanthemums lining the front walk welcomed visitors. The woven Mi casa es su casa mat Jeremy knew waited at the front door was a testament to their open-door policy for all who knocked.

Intent on carrying Rosa in, Jeremy quickly rounded the hood of his car to her side.

"That's not necessary, really," she insisted when he bent to pick her up. Though she didn't balk at the arm he crooked for her to hold on to.

Her slight weight pressed against him as she leaned her head on his shoulder, her subtle vanilla scent teasing him.

Jeremy shortened his gait to match hers, guiding her up the curved cement walkway connecting the driveway to the front steps. A smattering of red and gold leaves blew across the path, crunching under their footsteps. With the cold front that had blown in, he expected the trees would soon exchange their leaves for a coat of the threatening snow.

Fireplaces would be stocked with wood. The tasty Fernandez hot chocolate would be heating in a pot on the stove. If he had his way, he'd find himself enjoying a mug next to Rosa on her couch.

Rosa unlocked the front door and Jeremy held it open for her. Inside, he hung both of their coats and her purse on the wooden rack in the foyer as she moved gingerly into the living room.

"I appreciate you dropping me off," she said once she'd eased herself down onto the sofa. "I'm just going to rest a bit. Yazmine will probably drop by later to check on me."

Not wanting to crowd her, yet still make it clear he planned on being more than her taxi service, Jeremy sat in the matching ottoman angled next to the sofa. "If you don't mind, I'll stick around for a while."

"I don't want to be a bother."

He scrubbed a hand over his face, searching for the patience that made him so well-respected at his company. IT problem-solving and troubleshooting were often time-consuming tasks. His tenacity and patience paid off.

Unfortunately for him, when it came to Rosa, his ability to practice patience had fled the moment she'd announced her pregnancy. Which was what had probably led to her calling him a bully.

Whether he liked it or not, there was a fine line for him to walk here.

"Rosa," he began, measuring his words to avoid saying the wrong thing. "I don't know how many times I can say this before you believe me, but I'll keep saying it until you do. You're not a bother. This baby is not a bother."

"Oh, but *you* plan to be a bother."

He opened his mouth to argue, then caught the hint of a smirk on her full lips. Her shot of humor, the flash of the snarky side she didn't show everyone, stalled his argument.

"Smart-ass," he deadpanned.

Head leaned back against the sofa cushion, Rosa chuckled. Then winced and pressed a hand to her belly.

Poor thing. She was wiped out.

She needed rest, not verbal sparring with him. As fun as that might be.

For her sake, he hoped this sickness went away once she passed the first trimester. Dr. Jiménez had mentioned it was a possibility.

As for him, he hated feeling powerless to help her, especially since she kept pushing him away.

"It's really okay if you go home," Rosa said, her voice groggy with sleep. "I'll be fine—aaaah."

The word ended on a huge yawn that she covered with her fist.

"Here, let's get you more comfortable." Jeremy slid to his knees on the carpet in front of her, his arm accidentally bumping against the wooden coffee table.

"What are you—" Rosa craned her neck to look down at him. Her mouth formed a little O of surprise when he reached for one of her feet to slide the black low-heeled shoe off, then did the same with the other.

"Come on." Gently grasping her shoulders, he coaxed her to lie down across the sofa. Then he lifted her legs to rest on the other end so she could stretch out.

In a clear testament of the depth of her fatigue, Rosa didn't even argue. Her chest rose and fell on a soft release of air as she relaxed into the cushions.

"I'll just rest for a little while, if you don't mind then."

The words were barely a whisper. Had he not been kneeling beside her, he probably wouldn't even have heard them.

In minutes, her beautiful face relaxed, the tension easing away. The tired lines creasing her mouth and eyes smoothed and her breathing slowed, growing measured.

Unable to resist, Jeremy brushed a hand down her silky hair to cup her cheek. Rosa's lips curved and she burrowed closer to his touch.

Desire arced through him. He pressed a kiss to her forehead, then forced himself to back away. What he really wanted was to spread out beside her, feel the length of her pressed to his side again.

No doubt she'd feel crowded on the cramped sofa and he'd wind up scaring her off even more.

Damn, her bully comment still rankled.

He'd spent his entire life striving to show others that despite being an adopted Taylor, he deserved the name.

Rosa deserved better than Roger Wilson's son. Jeremy vowed to *be* better for her. And their baby.

Thinking she might be hungry or thirsty when she woke up, he headed into the kitchen, where he stopped in front of the fridge. Bemused, he studied the calendar held up by a plastic magnetized clip, a map of Puerto Rico decorating the front. Rosa's neat print marked the days with chores, appointments, special occasions, and other notes. Different colored ink indicated categories in whatever organizational system she'd devised. *Poetry Slam* was written in bright red ink, several exclamation points emphasizing the date in just over two weeks.

Must be the school club event she'd mentioned to Dr. Jiménez. The one she absolutely refused to miss. If it meant that much to her, he'd like to hear more about the slam. Add it to his calendar.

Making a mental note to ask her when she woke up, Jeremy tugged open the fridge. He peered inside, intent on finding something he could easily throw together for Rosa. A plastic container sat center stage on the top shelf next to a gallon of skim milk. He picked up the container and pried off the lid. A quick sniff confirmed the cream-colored mush with orange flecks was probably the pureed chicken soup with vegetables Dr. Jiménez had recommended.

To avoid making more noise than necessary, he nixed using the microwave and quietly dug out a pot from a lower cabinet to heat some of the concoction.

Ten minutes later, he had a dinner tray set with a small bowl, several crackers from the green tin on the counter and a cup of apple juice. With the soup warming on the stovetop, he returned to the living room to wait patiently for Rosa to wake up.

His phone vibrated in his pants pocket and he dug it out to find a message from Yazmine.

Tomás came home with whatever flu bug Maria has. Can you stay with Rosa? I'll see if Pablo's wife Dolores can stop by to check on her in a bit.

Jeremy tapped out a quick response. **I've got it covered. No need to bother Dolores.**

There was a brief pause before Yazmine got back to him. **Too late. She said she'll be over soon.**

Jeremy muttered a soft curse.

When he'd first reached out to Yazmine earlier today, she'd played the protective big sister card. Again. Her lecture had been short and to the point, peppered with a few Spanish words he didn't understand. More than likely choice ones he wouldn't learn via his Spanish language computer software.

Eventually she had run out of steam and quieted enough to listen to him. He knew she'd always stand up for Rosa, but at least she had come around to believing that he had Rosa's best interest at heart. It's the only reason why she'd entrusted him with driving Rosa home today. Now that he was here, he planned to take advantage of this extra time with her.

If she woke up before Pablo's wife arrived.

Though he'd only met the older woman a few times he knew she was a staunch disciplinarian. Lilí often groused about Dolores holding her feet to the fire for some antic or another Lilí had tried to pull growing up. Pablo and Dolores had always been like surrogate parents to the Fernandez girls, even more so since both their parents had passed.

What he didn't know was if Rosa had shared their pregnancy news with the older couple. If so, no telling what kind of reception he'd get from Dolores when she arrived.

Better that he let Rosa take the conversational ball when the time came. No use letting the cat out of the bag before she was ready. That definitely wouldn't add a check in the pro column of the "Say Yes to Jeremy" pro-con list he'd bet she had already drafted.

Jeremy had been lounging on the ottoman answering work emails on his phone for a good forty-five minutes before Rosa stirred.

Like a sultry Latina Sleeping Beauty, she rolled her shoulders, her small breasts pressing against her pale peach sweater. The stretch undulated down her body like a caterpillar's crawl, her black slacks pulling taut over her slender hips as they rose off the couch before she shifted over onto her side.

Her eyes blinked open and she sent him a soft smile that shot directly left of center in his chest.

She looked at peace. Content. And for the first time in the past week he felt the same.

It didn't last long.

He knew the moment she realized they were at her house. Him quietly watching her sleep.

Her body stiffened. Her brown eyes widened with surprise, her face coloring a sweet shade of deep pink.

She pushed herself up, immediately grabbing her head with one hand and her stomach with the other. She swayed to the side, and Jeremy was off the ottoman and on the couch in a flash.

"Take it easy," he said, wrapping his arm around her back.

"I—I just moved too fast." Rosa scratched her temple, confusion puckering her brow. "What are you doing here?"

"I brought you home."

"I know that." The "duh" wasn't said, but definitely implied by her tone. "You've just been sitting there, for—" She glanced at her watch. "Dios mío, almost an hour?"

"You needed rest. And I didn't mind. It's nice being with you."

Her cheeks pinked again, a much better color than her recent pallor.

As if she'd become aware that they sat much closer than they normally would when they'd been mere friends, Rosa scooted to her left. Moving to the farthest cushion.

Jeremy dropped his arm, missing the warm sensation of her tiny frame nestled next to his.

Patience, he reminded himself.

With that mantra on repeat in his head, he stood up and strode to the kitchen.

"I heated some soup for you," he called over his shoulder.

"You didn't have to do that."

"I wanted to. Now sit still. I'm bringing it over there."

He dished up a ladle full of the soup mush, then picked up the dinner tray. On his way back to the living room, he explained about

Maria and Tomás coming down with the flu, and that Dolores had been called in for reinforcement.

"I really don't need a babysitter," Rosa complained.

She took the tray from him, mumbling her thanks, but he caught her frown when she glanced down at it.

"What's wrong?"

"Nothing," she grumbled. "I'm just tired of eating baby food. Not to mention throwing it back up."

He grimaced. That stuff didn't look good in its present state. He didn't want to think about it coming back up. Too bad she'd been doing more than just thinking about it; she'd been living it.

"Sorry, that's probably gross." Rosa wrinkled her nose at him, a cute gesture that reminded him of her niece, Maria.

He couldn't help but wonder if, should he and Rosa have a little girl, she would make that same adorable face.

God, he hoped so.

Rosa picked up the spoon and dipped it along the edge of the bowl. With barely a nibble on the utensil, she brought it to her mouth like she was sampling the food.

Jeremy watched, entranced, as her mouth opened, her lips closing over the spoon before she slowly withdrew it. If he was a betting man, he'd lay his next paycheck down on the fact that Rosa had no idea how incredibly sexy she made eating pureed chicken soup look.

Even wearing plain black slacks and a ribbed pale peach sweater, in her stockinged feet and with her nearly makeup-free face shadowed by the circles under her eyes, she took his breath away.

No use denying that she always had.

There must be a way to get them back to the closeness they'd shared before the night of Yazmine's wedding. Before he'd followed her up to her room and crossed a line they weren't ready to cross. Even though she'd jumped over it first.

That was irrelevant.

What mattered now was regaining her trust.

"Listen." He rubbed a hand along the tension knots in the back of his neck while he chose the right words. Hopefully. "I feel like I've been sticking my foot in my mouth ever since you came to my condo."

Rosa swallowed, then carefully placed the spoon back on top of the napkin he'd folded and left beside the bowl. She lined up the bottom of the utensil with the edge of the napkin, nudging the top to straighten it out.

"I know I came on a little strong before," he said. She arched a brow.

"Maybe more than a little," he added.

She gave him the stern, no-nonsense stare he'd seen her lay on an unruly child at the bookstore where she'd worked during her graduate program.

"Okay, *a lot* strong," he admitted.

Her expression softened. "I'm listening."

"Pushing you to get married might not have been my smartest move."

He could have sworn he saw hurt flare in her eyes, but she ducked her head and reached for her juice. She took a sip, then set the drink back down, the tip of her tongue slipping out to lick a drop of the nectar clinging to her top lip.

Heat pulsed through him.

It took everything he had not to slide over to the couch, take her mouth with his, and sample the juice on her lips himself.

Talk about coming on strong.

Instead, he concentrated on convincing her of his sincerity.

"I care about you, Rosa."

Gross understatement. But he wasn't sure what exact label fit his feelings for her. The talk with his mom had illuminated that.

"I don't want to mess things up between us," he said. "So I promise not to push you into anything. But I need you to understand that I'm not going anywhere. There's no chance that I'm walking away."

Head still bowed, she gave a slight nod. She reached up to rub her nose, but he caught the flick of her knuckle under her left eye.

Holy hell, was she crying? Remorse clenched his gut.

"Rosa?"

"I'm fine," she mumbled. Tucking her wavy curtain of black hair behind her ear, she finally looked up at him. "It's just hormones." She sniffled. "And relief. I hate being mad at you, even when you deserve it."

Her attempt at a playful scowl reassured him, but the tears glistening on her lashes lured him to her like a hummingbird to a flower's sweet nectar.

Thankfully she didn't scoot away again when he joined her on the couch.

He wiped a tear from the edge of her right eye with his thumb. "I don't like you being mad at me either."

They shared a soft smile, and a sense of peace he hadn't felt since their time in Champaign engulfed him.

"I realize this baby affects you, too, Jeremy. But it's my life, my body, that'll have the most drastic changes. Many of which I can't control. And that . . ." Rosa took a shaky breath, her fingers nervously tapping against the metal edges of the dinner tray. "That really, really scares me."

She was a creature of habit, his Rosa. The queen of "everything has a place and everything in its place." With both an online and a hard-copy color-coded planner to keep her "everythings" running smoothly. He'd marveled at her planners the first time he'd seen them.

Her organizational skills were unparalleled. Though he was also aware that her need for order occasionally led to a level of stress when things went awry. Like they had when Reynaldo had died. And like they were now.

The uncertainties their situation created for her—both personally and professionally—had to be playing havoc with her carefully guarded sense of security.

Which brought him back to why she should allow him to be a source of support.

He took Rosa's hand in his, hoping she saw it as the gesture of encouragement he intended.

"That's why I'm here, to relieve you of some of that fear. Any way I can." Cupping his other hand, he caressed her smooth cheek with his knuckles. "Whatever you need. A ride home from work, a chef to cook your dinner, a companion for your doctor appointments, a housemate so you're not alone if you wake up in the middle of the night feeling sick. Someone to hold back your hair when you're puking over the toilet."

She huffed out a laugh and rolled her eyes at his last suggestion.

But she hadn't immediately put the kibosh on his housemate idea. Progress.

"The bottom line is, you're in control here. I'll follow your lead. Even if it's not always easy for me."

Jeremy paused. He wanted to tell her about his own fears, how they drove him to do and be better. But, they'd never spoken about Roger before.

He needed her to keep seeing him for himself. Not Sherman Taylor's money and influence. Certainly not Roger Wilson's selfish behavior. Too many others viewed him from either skewed lens. It would hurt too much if Rosa joined them.

So he kept his secret.

"Just, don't push me away," he went on. "Let's do this together. Whatever 'together' means for us. I won't walk away from you and our baby. I can't."

He stared into the innocent depths of Rosa's eyes, praying like the saint he wasn't that she'd acquiesce. Take him at his word and help them try to get back to the comfortable relationship they'd shared before.

If marriage wasn't the answer for her right now, he'd have to accept friendship and mutual respect. And maybe, if things worked out right, down the road they'd have more.

He could take things slow. Especially if it meant he'd eventually get what he wanted—an active part in Rosa and their child's lives.

She caught her plump bottom lip between her teeth. Her I'm-giving-it-some-thought tell was a relief to see.

After several long, drawn-out beats, Rosa nodded.

"Okay?" he asked, his voice a rough rasp of relief. He needed to hear her say the word. Make sure there was no uncertainty between them.

"Okay," she whispered.

Yes! He gave a silent whoop of joy, mentally high-fiving himself.

"But we need to establish—"

The doorbell rang, interrupting Rosa's caveat.

He didn't know if that was a blessing or a curse. No telling what condition she'd been about to put down. Then again, their visitor was probably Dolores, here to check on Rosa. More than likely cutting his visit short.

She moved to set her food tray on the wooden coffee table, and Jeremy put a hand on her forearm to stop her.

"Bed rest, remember?" he told her as he stood up, then bent to drop a quick kiss on top of her head to cement their new agreement. "Eat a little more dinner. I'll let Dolores in."

"Bossy, bossy," Rosa mumbled.

Jeremy chuckled at her complaint, a lightness finally in his step.

Unfortunately, one look at the suspicious scowl on Dolores Torres's face when he opened the door sent his mood plummeting.

Too late, he realized his miscalculation. He'd forgotten to ask Rosa whether or not her godmother, or madrina as the Fernandez girls referred to the older woman, knew about the pregnancy and his role as the father. If not, no telling how Dolores would react when she found out.

Throw him out. Grab the pair of decorative maracas off the wall and give him a good whack. Set the date for a shotgun wedding.

He'd promised Rosa that he would go along with whatever she wanted. Fingers crossed that Dolores, even in mother-hen mode, would do the same.

Chapter Ten

Rosa forced herself to take another bite of the pureed soup while Jeremy answered the door. She didn't know why Yazmine had called Dolores. As if sending Jeremy to pick her up wasn't enough. Her sister knew she despised being the center of all this attention.

She stirred her soup absently, relieved that she and Jeremy had at least reached some level of understanding. Though things were far from settled, and now with Dolores here there'd be no chance for a private conversation with him, at least the two of them might be able to show a united front.

Because once her madrina found out about the pregnancy, all hell was going to break loose. Telling Dolores would be like confessing to her own mother.

Ave Maria purísima. Rosa made a quick sign of the cross, asking for the confidence and strength to get through the inevitable confrontation.

"¿Ay, nena, qué pasa? ¿No te sientes bien?" Dolores hurried into the living room, her black low-heeled boots tap-tapping on the hardwood floor.

She dropped her shoulder bag on the coffee table and pushed up a sleeve on her black sweater, her gold bangles jangling.

"I'm feeling fine, tía," Rosa answered. "I don't know why Yaz called you."

"Pero, nena, you've had this flu for several weeks now, have you gone to the doctor?" Dolores pressed the inside of her wrist to Rosa's forehead, checking for a fever.

Over her madrina's shoulder, Rosa caught Jeremy's questioning look from the foyer where he still stood, holding on to Dolores's winter coat. She knew what he was asking: *Does Dolores know?*

Rosa gave the tiniest of head shakes.

He frowned back at her, but thankfully turned to hang up the coat without complaint.

Dolores cupped Rosa's cheeks with cool hands, still checking her temperature. "You're not warm. What are you feeling?"

Rosa eased back from her tía's motherly touch. "Some nausea, but I'll be okay. I'm sorry Yazmine bothered you."

"Your sister said you needed someone to take care of you. ¿Por qué?"

Dolores sat down next to Rosa on the couch. She eyed the dinner tray, her eyes narrowing as they moved from the barely touched soup, to the crackers, finally landing on the apple juice.

Dios mío, was her shrewd madrina putting the pieces together?

Rosa's stomach clenched, which of course made the few bites of food she'd managed to swallow decide they wanted to make a reappearance. Immediately.

Pushing herself off the couch, Rosa made a beeline for the hall bathroom.

She raced by Jeremy, shoving the dinner tray at him on her way.

"¿Ay, nena, what's going on?"

Her madrina's cry of surprise didn't stop Rosa as she shoved open the bathroom door.

"Here, take this please, Dolores."

Rosa heard Jeremy, but his words didn't really register until he knelt beside her, his hip bumping up against hers as his large body took up most of the space in the tiny half bath.

He scooped her hair out of the way, clutching it in his fist as her whole body clenched and her stomach convulsed.

"Remember what Dr. Jiménez advised. Don't fight it. Relax as much as you can and go with it," he said softly.

Warmth from his hand on her back seeped through her sweater, like a heating pad soothing her tired muscles. Despite avoiding him for the past week, she was relieved to have him here with her. His touch and deep yet gentle voice soothing.

Eventually, the body-racking spasms slowed to a stop. But they had taken a toll and when she tried to stand, her shaky legs threatened to give out.

"Here, lean on me." Jeremy slid his left arm around her waist to pull her snug against his side.

One-handed, he managed to turn on the faucet, wet part of the hand towel hanging on the rack, then gently press it to her forehead. The cool moisture revived her.

"Thanks," she murmured after he finished wiping her cheeks. Feeling a little less wobbly, she eased a step away. "I'm—I'm good now."

"You sure?" Jeremy gazed down at her, one arm loosely draped along her lower back. His long fingers curved around her hip, causing little pinpricks of awareness to fan out. He tucked her hair behind her ear, his touch lingering to brush her neck.

Part of her wanted to burrow against him. Give in to his Sir Gawain tendencies. Let him be her Knight of the Roundtable, ready to fight her battles. Namely, Tía Dolores waiting in the living room.

But if they were going to be partners in all of this, she had to be equally strong.

If she couldn't stand up to her madrina, how was she going to face the naysayers who would undoubtedly share their opinions, especially once word spread in Jeremy's social circle? Yaz had warned her about that already.

"Yeah, I'm better." She leaned on the wall behind her, locking her knees to steady herself. "Let me freshen up a bit and I'll be right out."

Jeremy eyed her for a few seconds before he backed out of the bathroom, closing the door behind him to give her some privacy.

Resting her forearms on the sink's cool ceramic edge, Rosa cupped some water in her hand and rinsed her mouth. She pushed herself to a shaky stand, then finger-combed her hair out of her face to peer at her reflection in the oval-shaped mirror.

Great. She looked like hell. Dark circles casting a raccoonish appeal, skin a pukey shade of tan, lips chapped. For a second, she had the crazy idea to hang out in the bathroom longer, see if Dolores would tire of waiting and leave.

Ha, right.

And maybe Rosa would find the courage to spit one of her own poems at the Poetry Club's open mic night. Fat chance.

No, hiding out was not an option. Time for her to own up to her choices.

Minutes later, Rosa skulked back to the living room. Jeremy sat on the ottoman, his handsome face marred by an uncomfortable frown.

Her madrina perched on the edge of the sofa, fingers tapping a silent but impatient rhythm on her knees. Dolores stood up when she saw Rosa, her expression grim.

"I take it you have been to visit Dr. Jiménez already, ha, nena?"

Busted.

Rosa paused at the edge of the floral area rug. She met her madrina's stern gaze, reminding herself that her tía's concern came from a loving place. "*Sí,* I had an appointment last week."

"And this gring—young man—has something to do with the situation."

It was more a statement than a question, punctuated by a head tilt and an arched brow in Jeremy's direction. Never mind Dolores's near slip of the tongue.

Gringo. Aka Anglo. Spoken in a derogatory tone that implied he wasn't worthy of her.

The negative connotation of the familiar term, used in conjunction with Jeremy, who'd been a close family friend for several years now, caught Rosa by surprise.

Based on the blue fire lighting his eyes, his rudimentary Spanish was enough for him to catch the dig, too.

Dios mío, Rosa prayed Dolores hadn't said something rude to him while she'd been cowering in the bathroom.

A spurt of protective anger ricocheted around Rosa's chest like one of the fireflies Maria often caught in a glass jar.

When Rosa had needed someone today because Yazmine was busy taking care of her own sick family, Jeremy had stepped in. No questions asked. When she'd needed a connection to family during her last semester after Papi's death, Jeremy had been there. A lifeline that helped her keep putting one foot in front of the other.

Her madrina had no right to treat him so rudely.

"Sí, tía, Jeremy is involved. He's been adamant about staying by my side. And I want him here."

Straightening her shoulders to stand taller, Rosa held a hand out to Jeremy, counting on him to understand the importance of them presenting a united front.

In hindsight, she should have expected this reaction from Dolores. But with her thoughts on her job and being freaked out about Jeremy's proposal, she hadn't even considered how, in the eyes of her community, he might be considered persona non grata. If there was any doubt about his treatment of Rosa, or his commitment to their child, the people in her Latino community would run him out of Oakton. Send him straight back to his fancy penthouse in downtown Chicago. No questions asked.

One thing you could count on, they would stand up to protect their own.

Never mind that Rosa'd been the one with doubts from the very beginning. Not him.

Thankfully, as if he'd received her telepathic unity message, Jeremy rounded the coffee table to clasp Rosa's hand in his. He linked their fingers, a callus on his palm rubbing against her smooth one.

"We're figuring things out. But the baby and I will be fine." Rosa pressed a protective hand to her belly.

In that moment, standing side by side with Jeremy, facing the woman who was like a mother to her, the reality of their situation crystallized in Rosa's mind.

They were having a baby. Together.

Questions she hadn't allowed herself to consider suddenly bombarded her in a firestorm.

Would he or she have Jeremy's blue eyes? Maybe her brown ones? His thick dirty-blond hair or her wavy black locks? She hoped their child possessed Jeremy's sharp mind; math had never been her favorite subject. But without question she'd make sure their little one inherited her love of reading.

A pang of pleasure-pain pierced her heart.

So many things to consider when a child's life was in your hands.

Dolores's dark eyes shifted between Jeremy and Rosa. Considering. No doubt measuring Jeremy's suitability. Questioning Rosa's emotional state.

Rosa made herself maintain eye contact.

This was not the time to let her shyness prevail. She was going to be a mamá. Soon joining the young mothers group at church. A rite of passage.

The silence dragged on and Jeremy squeezed her hand.

She leaned her shoulder against the side of his arm, gaining strength from his presence, hoping her touch did the same for him.

Hands clasped at her chest as if in prayer, Dolores turned toward Rosa. "Bueno, espero que los dos estén—"

"English, please, Tía," Rosa interrupted, mindful to keep her tone respectful. "Jeremy doesn't speak Spanish."

"But I'm learning!" he quickly threw in.

Dolores gifted him with her famous how-you-have-disappointed-me frown. The one Rosa had avoided most of her life. Yazmine and Lili had typically been recipients of Tía Dolores's glass-melting glare because of their antics. Especially Lili.

"Bueno, I hope that you both," Dolores repeated, in English this time, "are prepared for what you are getting into. From the looks of you, Rosita, I would say you are suffering like your mamá did with all three of her pregnancies. ¿Verdad?"

Rosa nodded, tears of regret burning her throat when her madrina called her by the childhood nickname Mami had often used. Oh, how she wished her mamá were here to offer counsel and reassurance.

Jeremy let go of her hand to wrap his arm around her shoulders. "Unfortunately, Rosa hasn't been feeling too well. But we saw Dr. Jiménez last week and she provided some guidance. She put Rosa on half days at work with bed rest at home after."

"So, you will need someone to stay with you. It was right for Yazmine to call me," Dolores said, still not having spoken directly to Jeremy. "Pablo and I were supposed to leave for Puerto Rico on Friday for the holidays. I will change my ticket and leave later so I can take care of you."

"No, please don't!" The last thing Rosa wanted was people making a big deal, throwing their own schedules out of whack because of her.

Her skin itched with the terrible thought of drawing attention to herself. If Dolores changed her flight, people would wonder why. There'd be talk, gossiping. Especially at church, and that wouldn't help her cause with Father Yosef.

Dios mío, her heart raced with anxiety.

She needed to maintain an air of normalcy. For herself, her sanity, not to mention her job security.

"If it makes you feel any better," Jeremy said, "I plan to pick Rosa up after work and spend the evenings with her so she's not alone." He looked down at Rosa. His blue eyes flashed with a question, waiting for her confirmation.

She hesitated. They'd come to a friendly agreement about him not pushing. But they hadn't actually discussed what that meant before Dolores arrived.

"And if she is sick at night? Or in the early mornings? Who will make our special teas to ease her nausea?" Dolores folded her arms across her chest with authority.

Now that she'd finally acknowledged him, she punctuated her questions with her fiery glare. The same one she had perfected while volunteering with the often-rowdy youth group.

"I know my way around a kitchen," Jeremy answered. "And if Rosa needs someone here overnight, or in the mornings, I have no problem staying. In Yazmine's old room," he added when Dolores's glare turned glacial.

"Wait a minute. Let's not get ahead of ourselves," Rosa argued. She held her hands up to stall the conversation before it became train-wrecked. "I doubt—"

"And you would do that?" her madrina interrupted.

"For Rosa and our baby, I'll do anything." A steely resolution wove its way through Jeremy's words. The same implacable expression Rosa had come up against all last week tightened his jaw muscles.

"And what kind of job do you have to provide for your family that would allow you to be here playing nursemaid to my Rosita?"

"¡Tía, por favor!"

Rosa had never raised her voice to Dolores before. Respecting her elders had been drummed into her since birth, but her madrina's questioning was beyond insulting to Jeremy, and embarrassing to her.

"I don't see this as 'playing nursemaid,'" Jeremy answered, admirably calm in the face of Dolores's interrogation. "It's helping someone I care for. Who also happens to be the mother of my child." His arm tightened around Rosa's shoulders again, pressing her more tightly to his side. "As for my job. I have a dam— darn good one that provides flexibility, so it's not a problem for me to be here for Rosa. *If* that's what she wants."

Great, he'd finally gotten the message that she didn't want to be coerced into something they weren't ready for. Only now Dolores had stepped into the role of aggressor.

Somehow, the downhill snowball that had become Rosa's life had gained in speed and size, leaving her few options to stop it.

She rolled her eyes, then quickly blinked to hide the act—smart enough to remember it was one of her tía's pet peeves. Lilí had gotten enough head thumps for the two of them because of a disrespectful eye roll over the years.

"Bueno, nena, the choice is yours then." Fists on her plump hips, Dolores pierced Rosa with a challenging stare. "Am I changing my ticket? Or is this young man staying to help you?"

Jeremy was more than a little surprised by Dolores's ultimatum.

Frankly, he had a hard time believing the older woman would actually agree to him staying overnight with Rosa. They weren't a married couple, so no way would many of the elder members in their community think it proper.

Still, Dolores *had* to know that Rosa would balk at the idea of changing holiday flight plans.

All three of them knew Rosa would bend over backwards before inconveniencing someone else.

He'd watched her do so countless times.

Whether she was letting Lilí get out of some boring chore around the house. Or canceling her own weekend plans to cover for a bookstore coworker with a lame excuse. Or picking up the slack for a classmate who bailed on a group project in one of her graduate classes.

Rosa was the consummate people pleaser. Well, except for recently when she'd had no problem putting her foot down with him.

His arm still around Rosa's shoulders, he felt their rise and fall as she released a deep sigh.

"So, what will it be, nena?" Dolores pressed. "I have three days to help your young man learn what he needs so that I can leave in peace. Or, I can send Pablo to Puerto Rico ahead of me."

Like a little kid in the back of the classroom, jumping up and down in his seat, hand raised high, a voice inside him screamed, "Pick me! Pick me!"

Rosa didn't answer. Instead, she got busy worrying her bottom lip.

Interesting.

A thrill of excitement wormed its way through Jeremy's chest. Maybe he actually had a shot here.

Dolores crossed the living room to one of the bongo drums that flanked either side of the dark cherry entertainment center. She picked up a framed Fernandez family photo that had been taken when Rosa was in early high school, before her mom had died.

Jeremy had eyed the picture many times, captivated by their smiling faces. Reynaldo and Marta stooped down, arms wrapped around all three of their daughters, who stood in front of the couple. Love, pride, and joy shone in the parents' eyes. Hints of the girls' personalities were evident in Lilí's mischievous grin, Yazmine's sultry look, and Rosa's shy expression.

It was that shyness that continuously drew him to reach for the picture when he visited.

Before, he'd wondered what lay behind her gentle smile.

He didn't have to wonder anymore. Not since he'd had the privilege of experiencing the fire and passion Rosa kept hidden from most. That experience had been like a gift he wanted to unwrap again and again.

"I made a promise to Marta that I would care for you and your sisters like you were my own," Dolores said, drawing Jeremy's attention back to the decision at hand. "We are familia."

"I know, Tía. And I'm grateful for the guidance you've given me. Especially in the years since we lost Mami."

The tremor in Rosa's voice had Jeremy tightening his arm around her to offer comfort.

"Familia es importante," Dolores continued, her eyes shining with unshed tears. "We protect one another in difficult times, especialmente when someone comes along who might hurt us."

Jeremy cringed at the underlying subtext.

He was *not* family. He was an interloper. A gringo.

Even worse, he'd come into their circle and taken advantage of the most delicate, most fragile of the sisters.

He already felt blame for getting Rosa into this situation. Hearing the censure in Dolores's voice was sea salt poured over an open wound.

"Señora Torres, if I may . . ."

He broke off when Rosa bent her elbow to link the fingers of her right hand with his where they lay on her shoulder.

"With all due respect, Tía," Rosa said, her fingers tightening around his. "Jeremy *is* familia. You and Tío Pablo go to Puerto Rico, please. Enjoy the Christmas and Three Kings holidays. I'll be fine here. With Jeremy."

Another knuckle-snapping squeeze from Rosa punctuated his name. He didn't know what secret message she might be trying to send him, but her words were a thrill to hear.

"Yazmine will be over to help eventually," Rosa steamrolled on. "And Lili's winter break begins soon. I will have plenty of nursemaids."

Her wry tone made it difficult to tell if Rosa was trying to convince herself or Dolores that everything would be fine.

There was no need for her to worry about convincing him. If Rosa wanted him to stay with her, he'd move in tonight. His gym bag was in the car so he already had a change of clothes and toiletries.

What better way for him to show her that he was ready for this? Words hadn't done the trick, even though she was a woman who valued them.

"If Jeremy is sure . . ." Rosa's fingers slid from his as she turned to face him, his arm dropping from her shoulder. "I'll take his offer."

She gazed up at him, her expression an interesting mix of confidence and vulnerability. The first filled him with pride that she had spoken up for him. The second made him want to wrap her in his arms and promise to make everything better.

"Like I said before," he told her. "I'm all in. One hundred percent."

He watched Rosa's throat move with a swallow. No doubt she was as overwhelmed as him by how fast things were changing between them. In monumental steps.

Two months ago, she wasn't answering his phone calls. Two days ago, she was keeping him at a ten-foot-pole distance. Today she was agreeing to have him stay in her home.

Talk about a head-spinning one-eighty.

Jeremy cupped her shoulders, the simple connection to her both calming and exciting him at the same time. Reminding him of how good they could be together, if they were able to figure things out.

"Are you sure?" Rosa asked, her voice soft but her tone firm. A true reflection of the many facets that drew him to her.

"Whatever you want, I'm game."

Her eyes flashed with . . . was that triumph?

That seemed odd, but before he could think more about it, she lifted up onto her toes to press her soft lips against his.

Her fingers grabbed on to his waist, curling into his sweater. The sweet vanilla scent he would forever associate with her filled his lungs. God, how he wanted to tug her closer. Deepen the kiss to satisfy his hunger for her.

Instead, Rosa lowered back to her stockinged feet, giving him a shy look under her lashes.

Dolores cleared her throat. Like he needed a reminder of her presence.

"Bueno, if he is staying and I am going, we have much work to do." The older woman's no-nonsense voice rang with a challenge.

"Let the games begin," Rosa whispered for his ears only.

"Nena, get me a pen and some paper so I can make a grocery list," Dolores ordered, moving to sit on the couch again. "Your young man can run to the store right now while I am here."

Thank you, Jeremy mouthed as Rosa moved to follow her madrina's request.

She hesitated, guilt flickering across her face before she turned away.

An hour later, Jeremy stood in aisle seven of the local Whole Foods Market, staring blindly at the unbelievable number of shelves weighed down by the insane variety of olives.

He glanced from the paper with Dolores's scrawled list of items back to the shelves.

Holy hell.

Should he get plain green? With or without pimento? Garlic or blue-cheese stuffed? Queen-size? Would Rosa prefer if they were pitted so she wouldn't have to spit something out?

Damn. His first errand for Dolores and he was already stumped.

At least the list specified green olives. That eliminated some options.

Maybe if he tried thinking like a pregnant woman . . .

Jeremy shook off the silly idea and refocused. No way would he call to ask for more guidance. That smacked of incompetence. Failing in Dolores's eyes was not an option. Neither was failing in Rosa's.

All he needed was a strategy.

Bingo!

His hand basket already mostly full with boxes of mint tea, fresh ginger and papaya, a couple of limes, a large bag of white rice, and two bags of salt and vinegar potato chips, Jeremy dashed to the front of the store for a cart.

Dolores asked for olives?

The woman was going to get olives.

Twenty minutes later, Jeremy pushed open the Fernandezes' front door, arms draped with reusable grocery bags filled with the list of ingredients Dolores needed for her special concoctions, along with every green olive option known to man.

Rosa looked up from where she sat on the couch reading a book. Right away, he noticed her red-rimmed eyes and dark pink nose. She'd been crying.

Obviously, she and Dolores had shared a difficult conversation while he'd been out shopping. Guilt speared him with a sharp blade. He should have been here to back her up.

Then she smiled at him. A hopeful smile that ensnared his heart as easily as if she'd swung a lasso around it and pulled tight.

She'd changed from her work clothes into a pair of red fleece sleep pants with a black sweatshirt, the slogan *Reading is Sexy* in red cursive letters across the chest.

Jeremy grinned. Ten bucks said the sweatshirt had been a gift from Lilí.

While Rosa's black fuzzy socks and high ponytail didn't exactly scream sex siren, the whole ensemble encompassed everything about her that appealed to him. She was the comfortable girl next door, the one he could feel at ease and be himself with, and yet, underneath that sweatshirt was a sexy body he hoped she'd want to share with him again.

Setting her book down on the cushion beside her, Rosa pushed off the couch as he strode past her toward the kitchen.

"What did you buy?" she asked. "There were barely five items on Dolores's list."

Jeremy glanced over his shoulder to find Rosa bringing up the rear behind him.

"To be clear, there were six specific items, along with one more that had far too much room for interpretation," he answered.

Rosa's face scrunched with confusion. "Huh?"

"I wanted to make sure I didn't—"

"¿Pero qué es esto?" Dolores's cry brought him to a halt one step into the kitchen.

Arms raised to indicate all his purchases, the older woman gaped at him.

Undeterred, and quite pleased with his problem-solving skills, Jeremy placed two bags on the laminate-topped breakfast table. "*These* are the majority of the groceries you asked for. And *these*"—he set the other three reusable bags beside the first two with a flourish—"are the green olives."

Both women exchanged befuddled looks. Then, in unison, they stepped closer and began rummaging through the items. Rosa pulled out a box of mint tea and sniffed it. Dolores started lining up the olive jars on the table, glass clinking against glass with each new addition.

It wasn't long before two sets of dark eyes framed by puzzled brows turned to stare at him.

A niggling sense of worried doubt wove its way through his head, similar to the sensation he'd experienced the first time he'd read a photo caption in the *Tribune* identifying him as "the adopted son" of Sherman Taylor. As if that made him less than.

"You didn't specify what type of green olive, so I bought one of every option." Shoving his hands in his front pockets he lifted a shoulder, going for nonchalant when he'd actually started wondering if he'd been overzealous in his bid for Dolores's acceptance. "I figured, why not cover my bases."

Arms crossed in front of her, Dolores gave him a solid impression of a stern Mother Superior. Slowly shaking her head from side to side she mumbled, "Increíble. Este hombre está loco."

Rosa's lips twitched. She giggled, then quickly covered her mouth with her hand. Still, her eyes twinkled with a glee that had been missing since she'd come to his place just over a week ago.

Relief at her reaction wiped away all his doubt. Dolores might think he was crazy, but he was okay with that as long as Rosa was happy.

She giggled again and he winked at her, pleased to see the deep pink blush that crept up her cheeks.

"I thought I'd be buying pickles and ice cream." Shrugging out of his jacket, Jeremy slung it over the back of a kitchen chair. "Or is that an old wives' tale and pregnant women really don't crave that combination?"

"Back home, on the Island, it is olives," Dolores answered. She pulled out another box of mint tea along with the ginger root, then crossed to the counter. "Like your pickles here in America, the vinegar helps with the . . . ay, how do you say, Rosa, el malestar? O la mala barriga?"

"The nausea. Or bad, upset stomach," Rosa translated. She sank down into one of the wooden breakfast table chairs. "I guess malestar really means when your whole body doesn't feel well. That pretty much sums things up for me."

"You sit there and relax. I will—*we* will take care of everything, verdad, Jeremy?" Dolores held the ginger root out to him.

It was the first time she had addressed him by name this evening. He liked the way Dolores's heavy Spanish accent softened the syllables.

On his drive back from the store, he'd worried about what might have gone down between Rosa and her godmother while he'd been gone. Whatever had been said, Rosa's red-rimmed eyes told him it had been difficult for her. But somehow, and for some reason he was thankful for, Dolores appeared a hair more accepting of him.

At least she had stopped shooting poison-laced daggers at him with her eyes.

Encouraged, he took the ginger from her with gusto. "Right! No, verdad."

Dolores's lips curved, the faint wrinkles along the edges of her mouth deepening, before she nodded in approval.

And thus began his first Puerto Rican cooking lesson.

While Rosa sat at the kitchen table, Dolores showed him how to peel the ginger, then chop it up to boil in water that was then used to steep the mint tea.

If that didn't do the trick with Rosa's nausea, he was to boil half a cup of rice in a full cup of water for ten minutes. Then he poured the rice water in a coffee mug for Rosa to sip. Not something he'd been excited to sample, but he did.

He'd made himself a promise. Whatever she tried, he tried. It was only fair.

Rosa had balked when he'd poured himself some of the ginger mint tea. She flat-out objected when they got to the rice water. Saying there was no need for both of them to taste the gross stuff.

He'd stood firm.

They were in this together.

After they'd shared a few sips of the water, Rosa declaring a preference for the tea, Dolores moved on with her lesson.

Next up, a quiz on his egg-cooking prowess. Apparently they'd provide sustenance while not aggravating Rosa's stomach.

Did he know how to boil an egg? Dolores had asked.

He'd actually done a double take at that question.

Uh, yes.

Could he fry an egg over easy?

Check. Along with a mental note that it was Rosa's favorite.

Basic scramble?

No problemo.

Dolores gave him another eagle-eyed assessment at his wise crack.

He tried not to laugh, seeing as how she didn't seem to appreciate his humor.

Eventually they moved on to the papaya. It wasn't as difficult as he'd thought when first holding the smooth-skinned fruit. Cut, scoop out the seeds and membrane, peel, slice, enjoy.

Once he'd mastered that task, Jeremy sat down next to Rosa at the table, setting the plastic container of fruit in front of her.

Odds were good that Dolores didn't intend the papaya tasting to be a sensual affair. However, with Rosa's first bite, the sweet juice dripped down her chin and all he could think about was licking the trail of nectar off her skin.

He settled for reaching out to swipe the juice with his thumb, then bringing it to his mouth to sample.

Heat flared in the depths of her eyes.

Her tongue slipped out to lick her lips, the delicate pink tip teasing him. Desire and hunger slammed into him, surging through his body with an electric jolt.

Rosa's gaze moved to his mouth, paused, then slid away. A dull pink blush climbed up her face.

Any doubt that she had wanted him as much as he had craved her that night was erased as deftly as a message written on the shore before a rising tide.

His fear that he'd somehow misread her signals dissipated.

"The bag of papitas can stay closed for now, but give them a try later, okay, nena?"

Her back to them, Dolores put the bag of salt and vinegar potato chips in the pantry next to the basement door. Clueless as to the inappropriate thoughts swarming around Jeremy's head. The same ones sending his blood south in an even more inappropriate response, considering he and Rosa were currently chaperoned.

Dolores moved toward them, pointing at Rosa as she spoke. "Take them to school tomorrow, with one of Jeremy's olive jars?"

The older woman's cackle of laughter, coupled with the at least fifth or sixth olive reference she'd made at his expense, deepened his sense of belonging, especially after the good-natured ribbing she'd given him throughout the impromptu remedy-making lesson.

Dolores had teased him mercilessly for his overindulgent shopping trip. At the same time, she'd patiently taught him the Spanish to English translations for the various ingredients they'd used.

Rosa's good-natured chuckles over his mispronunciations took the sting out of his embarrassment.

He imagined this was what most evenings had been like for her when she was growing up—hanging out in the kitchen with her mom, laughing together. The other two sisters running in and out with their busy schedules, Reynaldo practicing music with his trío, Los Paisanos, in the basement.

Since Dolores's husband, Pablo, had been a Los Paisanos bandmate, she'd probably been a regular here as well.

The music, the revolving welcome door for family and friends, the food and sense of community and belonging . . . this environment was far different from his. He'd grown up in a mix of fancy dinners with Sherman's law firm partners and clients, nights at the orchestra or ballet, and formal charity galas that were more about appearances and networking than relationships and bonding.

Here, life was more laid-back. Comfortably appealing.

In large part due to the enchanting woman beside him.

"I'm guessing Rosa will thank me for my inventive shopping skills when those olives come in handy at the library," he teased back.

Dolores muttered under her breath as she looked toward the heavens, but he caught her smirk before she spun away to wash the few remaining dishes.

Rosa snickered, rubbing at her chin with the back of her hand to wipe the juice.

Jeremy slid a napkin across the table closer to her.

"Finished?" he asked. At her nod, he placed the plastic lid on the papaya container.

He pushed his chair away from the table, moving to put the fruit in the refrigerator. The action was less about helping tidy the kitchen and more about stepping away from temptation. The cool air when he tugged open the door provided a welcome balm to his heated face.

When he turned back around, he caught Rosa covering a wide yawn with both hands.

"Ay, excuse me," she mumbled.

He checked his watch. Just after eight. Not too late, but she'd had a full day, with little of the rest Dr. Jiménez had ordered. "It's a school night, señorita. We should be getting you to bed."

He winced. Damn if the words didn't sound more lecherous than he intended.

If Dolores noticed, she cut him some slack and kept it to herself. "Walk me to the door, Jeremy. Rosita, abrazos."

Rosa stood to give her madrina the requested hug. "Gracias, Tía. I appreciate you coming over."

"Nonsense. Where else would I be?" Dolores cupped Rosa's face in her hands. "And I can stay behind if that makes you feel better. Not only because I promised your parents, but because I would do anything for you and your sisters."

Dolores pressed a kiss to Rosa's forehead.

Out of respect for both women, Jeremy remained silent, allowing them to share their special moment.

Then Dolores glanced at him over her shoulder, her expression now more accepting than assessing. "Though I must admit that I think he might do okay. Not as good as me, but the boy is a fast learner."

He gave her a wink, chuckling at the resigned sigh she answered with.

After another tight hug with Rosa, Dolores motioned for him to follow her to the front of the house. The older woman made quick work of slipping on her winter coat and scarf, then motioned with her head for him to step out on the front porch with her.

"Rosita needs a lot of rest," Dolores said the moment Jeremy closed the door behind him. Worry clouded her eyes and puckered the lines across her forehead. "She has lost much weight. I had noticed at church the past few weeks, but never expected . . . bueno"—she waved off the obvious—"I doubt the two of you did either."

Dolores was the closest Rosa had to a parent. A fact that compelled Jeremy to reassure her of his commitment.

"I'm going to do whatever it takes to help her through this," he asserted. "Whatever Dr. Jiménez recommends. I promise."

"I am trusting you, Jeremy Taylor." Dolores pointed a finger at him, her no-nonsense stare back in place. "No hanky spanky tonight. Rosita needs her sleep."

Hanky spanky?

He gulped at the inadvertent image her idiom mix-up brought to mind.

God help him. The absolute last subject he wanted to discuss with Dolores was whether he and Rosa should have sex tonight—or any night, for that matter.

As it was, if anything could put the kibosh on his libido, it was picturing Dolores's Mother Superior expression as she waggled her finger at him in warning.

"I will be by tomorrow, after Rosa is home from school," Dolores said.

"And I'll be here, making sure she at least eats a little, has plenty of fluids, and gets her rest. I'm not going anywhere," he promised.

The cold wind picked up, making him shiver since he'd left his coat on the kitchen chair.

"You go inside," Dolores ordered. "I do not want you getting sick. But Jeremy—" She grabbed his arm, her fingers tight around his biceps, her face still drawn with worry. "Protéjela."

His rudimentary Spanish didn't fail him this time.

He placed his hand over Dolores's, willing her to feel his sincerity.

"Don't you worry. I will protect Rosa, and our unborn child, with my life. They're my familia now, too."

Dolores may have stood a good half foot shorter than he did, but the shadows cast by the front porch light intensified the fierce expression on her lined face. It would have made many grown men cower.

Jeremy didn't even blink. He meant every single word and it was imperative that she understand that.

"Hmmm," Dolores finally said. "Perhaps you will do after all."

After giving his cheek a quick pat, she hurried down the walk to a silver Camry parked in front of the house.

Shivering against the bitter wind, Jeremy returned her wave good-bye, then stood and watched until she rounded the corner.

Despite the cold, he gazed up at the stars winking at him from the dark blanket of the cloudless midnight sky.

Yesterday, after dinner, he'd told his mom he would slow down with Rosa. Let her make the calls. And quit with the knee-jerk re-actions.

Little had he imagined that twenty-four hours later her play-calling would involve him moving in with her for the next two weeks.

Anticipation pumping his heart faster, Jeremy moved to go back inside the Fernandez home.

Earlier tonight, he'd realized words hadn't been enough to convince Rosa that he was worthy.

Well then, the time had come to take some action.

Chapter Eleven

Upstairs in her room, Rosa heard the click of the front door closing. She paused in the midst of turning down her bed, her fingers clenching the comforter's cushiony cotton material. Indecision paralyzed her.

Maybe climbing into bed was too suggestive. What if Jeremy got the impression she was inviting him to join her?

Embarrassed heat climbed her face.

Suddenly panicked, she flung the comforter back into place, hurrying around to the opposite side to straighten it out. Bending down, she snatched the red and orange decorative pillows off the floor, tossing them willy-nilly onto the bed.

Dios mío, how had things spiraled to this crazy, inconceivable moment?

Agreeing to Jeremy staying over hadn't been the brightest of light bulb ideas, but she'd been cornered.

Tía Dolores mentioned changing her ticket and Rosa had freaked. No way did she want to disrupt Dolores and Pablo's plans. People would find out and wonder why. They'd talk. About her. If word got back to Father Yosef before she spoke with him . . .

No, no, no. That wouldn't be good.

To avoid any problems, she'd opted for disrupting her own life. Like it wasn't disrupted enough already. Not to mention Jeremy's.

He was too nice to complain. Too much of a good guy not to come to her rescue, but this was only for a few days. Tops.

As soon as Dolores got on her flight to PR, Jeremy could go home. Rosa would be fine on her own. Yaz was good backup if needed, and Lilí would be here soon enough.

The stairs creaked. Papi's built-in home "alarm system" for when Lilí or Yaz had tried to sneak in late was still on alert. Now it signaled Jeremy's imminent approach.

Rosa's gaze swept across her room, from her queen bed to the chocolate-stained six-drawer double dresser along the left wall, scurrying over to the matching low bookshelf and comfy reading armchair and ottoman in the right corner—desperate to decide where would be best for him to find her waiting.

"Rosa?" he called out.

"In—" She cleared the scratch from her voice. "In here."

Knees weak, she sank onto the edge of her bed. She grabbed a circular orange pillow, hugging it against her chest like a shield.

This was Jeremy. No need to be nervous. Yeah, right.

It would help if every time she looked at the bed she didn't picture the two of them together. Recalling the intoxicating juxtaposition of his strength and gentleness with her.

Not to mention the number of times she'd lay in this very bed, wishing he were here with her. Relegated to satisfying her lonely heart by composing lines about him in her private poetry journal. He had inspired some of her best work. Though no one would ever read those lines to know it.

To make matters worse, he was not going to be thrilled with her plan to thwart Dolores.

That certainty had Rosa squeezing her pillow shield tighter.

Jeremy poked his head around the open doorway, a tentative smile curving his lips. He moved to lean against the doorjamb. Not quite crossing the threshold.

It occurred to her that he'd probably never been upstairs. If so, it hadn't been to visit her room.

Then again, no guy had ever been in her room before. "You need anything?" he asked.

The rich timbre of his voice plucked an achy chord deep inside her. She needed some sense of normalcy. Some reassurance that she was making the right decisions.

She needed them to be okay. But they were far from it.

Ave Maria purísima, how had her life gotten so complicated, so quickly?

At the start of the year, her plan had been to graduate and come home, take care of Papi, start carving out her place at Queen of Peace.

Not even a month later, Papi was gone. Taken from them much too soon.

He'd been the one person who understood her almost as well as Mami had. The only one who'd recognized the deep void Mami's death had left in her life. Though Rosa had never admitted her guilt to him, to anyone.

With Papi's passing, she'd graduated in May and come home to an empty house.

Alone.

Forced to regroup and find her new footing.

Only tonight, and for the next few days, her home wouldn't be empty.

Jeremy would fill the place with his generous personality and this new commanding presence she'd seen only hints of before. He'd be on the other side of the wall in Yaz's old room.

The thought of him being so close both scared and electrified her.

He'd be close, but still a world away. Still unattainable.

Being pregnant with his child actually made her feel less secure about whether or not she could fit into his social circle. Right or wrong, there would be those who assumed she'd gotten pregnant on purpose to snag the oldest Taylor son.

Dios mío, she could picture the gossip column headline now.

Her heart sputtered, overwhelmed by the swarm of dismay and dread she'd been trying to squash.

The maelstrom of emotion must have shown on her face because

Jeremy pushed away from the door, closing the distance between them.

"Hey, what's going on?" he asked, concern lacing his words. He sat beside her, placing one arm on the bed behind her, the other gently on her forearm.

The mattress sank under his weight, tipping her toward him, and her shoulder bumped his muscular chest.

"Are you feeling sick again? I can help you to the bathroom."

"No, I'm fine," she lied. "I think the day just caught up with me."

The day, the week, the month.

Caramba, the whole freaking year.

"What can I do to help?" Jeremy tucked her hair behind her ear, a new habit of his she found herself enjoying, especially with the faint brush of his fingertips sending heated shivers down her neck.

His nearness confused her though.

She felt too much, wanted too much when she was with him. She couldn't think straight when he was around. And the fear of making another mistake weighed heavily on her.

Dropping the round pillow on top of the others, Rosa got up and crossed to her dresser. Needing even a small measure of distance between them.

"I know this is an inconvenience," she said, leaning her butt against the dresser top. "Commuting in and out of the city for work can be a hassle."

"Like I said, I have plenty of vacation days racked up. It won't be a problem to take the next two weeks off."

"No!"

Jeremy blinked in surprise at her raised voice.

"I'm sorry. I didn't mean to raise my voice."

He fiddled with the band of a two-tone watch wrapped around his left wrist, unsnapping and snapping the clasp several times before he spoke. "I'm just trying to make things easier for you, Rosa. That's all."

"I'm sure you are. And I appreciate it. But this . . ." She waved a hand back and forth between them. "A few hours ago we both agreed to slow things down. You staying here for the next few days? That's not slow—"

"Wait a minute." Jeremy held up a hand to stop her. "Next few days? You said Lilí won't be home for two weeks."

Rosa grabbed onto the dresser edges on either side of her, closing her eyes on a heavy sigh. Paciencia y fuerza, she reminded herself. This conversation was going to take a mix of both patience and strength.

"Working half days I'll be getting more rest than I was before. As soon as Maria and Tomás are better, Yaz can help if I need something. I'll be fine, so you'll be off the hook."

Jeremy crossed his arms in front of his chest, the rolled-up sleeves of his light blue button-down oxford giving her a peek of his muscular forearms. That pugnacious, tightjawed expression she'd never seen until this past week was back on his face.

"What are you playing at, Rosa?" he demanded.

"I'm not 'playing at' anything."

His answering steely glare nearly had her ducking her head. Instead, she jutted out her chin and looked him square in the eyes.

"You can stay until Friday. But once I know Tía Dolores and Tío Pablo are on their way to Puerto Rico, you're free to go."

"If I'm free to go, then I'm also free to stay."

"No, you're not," she insisted. "I'm sure you have plans for the weekend. Some charity event your parents are hosting. Dinner with coworkers or clients."

"No. And if I did, I'd cancel."

"That's not necessary. I don't need a babysitter."

"Don't think of it as babysitting. More like companionship."

"Forced," she muttered.

Jeremy's mouth twisted with a grimace. "That's a little harsh, don't you think?"

His quiet rebuke gave her pause, but her frustration with his obstinacy was exponentially growing.

Lips pursed to stop herself from saying anything she might regret, Rosa gave him her best I'm-not-playing-games-here stare. The one that usually shushed her students or got them back on task.

Jeremy didn't budge.

"Here's the deal," he said, rising from his seat on her bed. He didn't move closer, but his height combined with the palpable anger emanating from him was intimidating enough.

Rosa stood her ground though.

"You might not be worried, but I am. Both Dr. Jiménez and Dolores said this diagnosis isn't something to fool around with. I mean, come on!" His frustration palpable, he jabbed a hand through his hair, leaving it sexily rumpled. "It put your mom in the hospital, for God's sake."

"She was much worse. There's no need for us to overreact."

"Yeah, there is." Jeremy dug his hands in his pants pockets, his expression stony. "Here's the deal. If I'm the one who stays here tonight instead of Dolores, then I'm staying until Lilí is home for the holidays and you have someone with you full-time."

"But that's not—"

"No buts. It's either me"—he jabbed a thumb at his chest—"or Dolores. And don't think you'll be able to kick me out after she's gone to Puerto Rico. I already have her on speed dial, remember? I'll be on the phone with her so fast, ready to buy her a first-class ticket to fly back here if need be. It's your call."

Ay, he was not playing fair.

Brow quirked in an annoying arch, he looked like a sexy corporate pirate challenging the maiden to either accept his terms or walk the plank.

Only she wasn't a damsel in distress.

She refused to be one. Or to have him think of her as one anymore.

Standing to her full five-feet-six-inches, still much shorter than his six-feet-plus, Rosa fisted her hands on her hips. "Fine. Stay then. But I will not be coddled like some china doll you have to handle with kid gloves. I have a ton of stuff to do by the end of the semester, and I won't have you hovering like, like some kind of helicopter parent."

He gave a quick double shake of his head, his confusion evident. "A what?"

"Helicopter parent. It's a relatively new term. Common in recent parenting how-tos." She gestured toward the stack of books on top of her corner bookshelf. The ones she'd ordered online to avoid anyone in Oakton eyeing her purchases at the local bookstore. "Feel free to borrow any if you'd like."

Jeremy's confused expression lingered, though he mumbled his thanks at her offer.

"If you're determined to stay, grab your bag from your car and I'll check Yazmine's room to make sure it's ready."

"Don't go to any trouble."

Halfway to her door already, Rosa spun back around in a huff. Her stomach complained. She ignored it. "You are a guest in my home, Jeremy. Of course I'm going to make sure you're comfortable."

"I'm a big boy. I can take care of myself."

"Ditto. But that doesn't seem to make a difference to you or Tía Dolores. I guess that makes us even."

The corners of Jeremy's mouth twitched like he was biting back a grin.

"What?" she asked, wondering what could possibly be amusing to him.

"How come it seems like I'm the only one you give a hard time?"

A blush of embarrassment crept up her neck and into her cheeks.

"Don't get me wrong. I kinda like it," Jeremy said.

He stepped closer, stopping barely an arm's length away from her.

Ay, how she longed to reach out, lay her palm against his chest, feel his heart beating as she lifted onto her tiptoes for his kiss.

"Makes me feel like you're comfortable enough to tell me what you're really thinking," Jeremy continued. "Even if it's something you might not share with others."

"Well, if you'd just do what I tell you, things would be a heck of a lot easier," she countered.

He threw back his head and laughed, a deep, robust sound that enticed her to join in.

She couldn't resist and she grinned back at him.

Reaching out, Jeremy hooked the fingers of her left hand with his right ones. Their arms swung gently back and forth between them.

Her chest swelled. Desire, uncertainty, and hope for what might be melding together.

"Feeling pretty cheeky all of a sudden, aren't you?" he teased.

"Just telling it like it is."

His chuckle sent a thrill scampering across her shoulders. Little did he know that it was him bringing out her cheeky side.

"Come on." She tugged him toward her bedroom doorway. "Let's get you settled in."

The very idea had her shivering with the possibilities and what-ifs.

For the next couple of weeks until Lilí arrived, Jeremy's room would be right next to hers. Nervous excitement fluttered in Rosa's belly, making her feel like a freshman coed, giddy at the thought of the hunky boy living on her dorm floor.

Only, there was more at stake here than the possibility of sharing a table in the cafeteria. Or maybe a Friday-night date.

They had bigger issues to contend with. She could only hope they'd figure out a positive resolution.

Jeremy rubbed a towel on the bathroom mirror, clearing a circle in the fog so he could see his reflection. He brushed his teeth with the new toothbrush Rosa had pulled out of a drawer for him, then set it in the ceramic holder.

Her pink toothbrush hanging next to his blue one implied a sense of intimacy he'd be foolish to buy into.

Hell, look how hard he'd had to push to stay here until Lilí came home for the holidays. Talk about driving a hard bargain. Rosa was quiet, but headstrong.

His threat about calling Dolores had been a low blow. But at this point, he'd do whatever it took not to lose the chance to spend more time with Rosa.

His gaze caught on a few bottles clustered in the corner of the black-and-light-brown-flecked granite counter. Picking up a bottle of lotion, Jeremy took a whiff of the coconutty-vanilla scent that was pure Rosa.

He closed his eyes and took a deep breath. Let the scent course through him, soothing the insecurities he hid.

Rosa represented goodness. When he was with her, the self-doubt he'd carried since childhood seemed to vanish. Making it seem possible for him to be the man he wanted to be for his family.

When he opened his eyes, his reflection stared back at him, the bottle pressed to his nose. The sappy expression on his face snapped him out of his stupor.

What was he doing standing here in Rosa's bathroom, getting high on the smell of her body lotion?

If that wasn't a little crazy, at the very least it was a little weird.

Shaking off the haze of his coconut-vanilla-induced stupor, Jeremy set the bottle down, making sure he put it back exactly where he'd found it. Rosa was so meticulous, she'd probably notice if it had been moved.

After making quick work of wiping down the sink and hanging up his bath towel, he dropped his gym bag back in Yazmine's room, then hurried down to the kitchen to grab a flavored vitamin-infused water for Rosa. If she got thirsty in the middle of the night, he didn't want her traipsing down the stairs.

Moments later, he was tapping on her door.

"Yes?" she answered.

"Are you still up? I brought you some water."

"Oh, thanks. Come on in."

He turned the knob and opened the door to find her sitting in bed, the cream covers pulled up to her waist. A leather-bound notebook lay on her lap, a mechanical pencil in her right hand. The bedside lamp cast a warm glow around her, giving the room a cozy atmosphere.

She looked like an innocent little girl waiting to be tucked in. Only, the images and ideas that came to his mind when he thought about Rosa in bed were far from innocent.

Waiting for her to invite him in, he stayed hanging out in the doorway.

"Are you working on something for school?" he asked.

She shook her head. "After my nightly prayers, I usually spend a little time working on my poetry. Helps get my thoughts out of my head before sleep."

"May I?" He gestured toward her nightstand with the bottle of water.

"Sure. I appreciate it."

Jeremy set the water down, accidentally knocking off a white envelope.

He bent down to retrieve it, catching the signature and inscription scrawled in cursive across the front.

Para mi Rosa. Con Amor, Papi.

His rusty college Spanish skills worked at translating the words.

For my Rosa. With love, Papi.

Aw, man. The importance of the letter hit Jeremy square in the chest.

Reynaldo had left one for each of his daughters, a private message of encouragement and love. The girls had mentioned the letters, but never shared their contents. This was the first time Jeremy had seen one.

That Rosa kept hers by her bed spoke volumes of how much she loved her dad. How much she still missed him.

She stared up at Jeremy, face scrubbed clean and ready for bed. Her satiny hair fell around her shoulders. The look in her eyes warm, yet subdued.

He couldn't help but wonder how difficult it was for Rosa to live here, in the home where she'd grown up. One that for years had been full of family and bustling with activity, but now remained mostly empty except for her. And Lilí when she was home on school breaks.

"Didn't mean to knock this off," he said, setting the envelope back on the nightstand.

"It's okay. I use it as my bookmark."

Rather than stand and tower over her, or risk making her uncomfortable by copping a seat on the edge of her bed, Jeremy sat on the floor between her bed and the dresser.

"How you holding up?" he asked.

Rosa closed her journal, a finger stuck in between the pages to hold her place. "Nausea's better. One of the teas must have helped."

"Good. What about everything else?"

She frowned. "What do you mean?"

"I figure that wasn't how you wanted to tell Dolores about the baby. What with your mad dash to be sick again." He crooked a knee and propped an elbow on it. "I'm sure the conversation between you two while I was out buying the groceries couldn't have been easy for you."

The sadness on Rosa's face confirmed his suspicions.

"I'm sorry I wasn't here for moral support."

She shook her head. "It was on me to tell her. I should have said something sooner. I just . . ."

Her chest rose and fell on a sigh, the red material of her sleep shirt stretching with the deep breath. *Reading is Sexy*. The words taunted him.

He dropped his gaze to his stockinged feet, away from her temptation.

"It was hard enough talking with Principal Meyer today. But Dolores is like my second mom," Rosa admitted. She picked up Reynaldo's letter. Opening her notebook again, she lay the letter on the page, gently smoothing the envelope with her hands. "I don't like disappointing people, especially my loved ones."

When she looked up, he caught the sheen of tears glistening in her brown eyes.

"With the possibility of losing my job, even though there's no actual policy I'm breaking as a single mom, I can't help but feel I'm letting a lot of people down."

Jeremy's muscles tensed at her "single mom" comment.

He wanted to argue that she had another option. Marriage. To him.

If not for the vulnerability on her beautiful face and the hand pressed to the letter from her dad, Jeremy would have pushed the issue.

Forget the advice his mother had given him. He couldn't stop this compulsion driving his belief that he and Rosa should marry.

They got along well. Usually anyway.

Attraction wasn't an issue between them. Obviously. Hell, the sex had been incredible.

No question that he could provide for her and the baby, even though she didn't seem to have any expectations when it came to his family's financial status.

But if she wanted to continue working at Queen of Peace, marrying him would silence any moral judgments against her being pregnant.

"I can hear the arguments going on inside your head," Rosa said, smoothing the comforter around her legs. "I appreciate you keeping them to yourself."

He lifted a shoulder in a lazy shrug. Though, around her, he felt anything but lazy.

Excited. Frustrated. Hungry. Determined.

Definitely determined.

"I've made it clear what I think we should do," he reminded her. "Say the word and we'll get married."

"Jeremy—"

"Hey, you're the one doing the mind reading. I was keeping quiet."

She wrinkled her nose at him in protest.

Man, even when he wanted to be frustrated at her hardheadedness, he couldn't be. Not when she looked so cute.

"Why?"

"Why what?" he asked, his thoughts meandering through the list of everything about her that he found appealing.

"Why this compulsion for us to get married? Other than," she quickly threw in, stopping him from giving his automatic response, "because it's the right thing to do. I can't help feeling like that's not your only reason."

His pulse skipped a beat, surprise at how well she could read him, robbing him of speech.

"I'm sorry, it just . . . it seems like there's something you're not telling me. Something . . ." She shook her head, rubbing at the frown lines between her brows. "Never mind, I'm probably being silly."

She looked down at her journal, rubbed a finger over Reynaldo's signature, then closed the book and carefully set it on her nightstand.

She wasn't being silly. Her intuition had picked up on his insecurities. He should tell her about Roger. Now was his chance.

If anyone would understand his compulsion to be better, do better, it was Rosa. The Fernandez sister everyone thought of as "the good girl."

He should be able to trust her with the ugly truth of his past. Right?

Taking a deep breath, Jeremy opened his mouth to tell her.

What came out instead was, "So you think the meeting with your principal went okay, then?"

Rosa's shoulders sagged at his question, mirroring his own disappointment with himself. "It could have gone better, could have gone worse. Once I meet with Father Yosef, I'll know more."

Another tough conversation looming on the horizon for her. Damn.

"Summoned to the priest's office. I bet this is a first for you, huh?"

"Of course!" Rosa's *Duh!* expression was classic. "That's Lilí's territory, not mine."

Her surly tone made him chuckle, easing his discomfort at the turn their conversation had nearly taken. And his fear that her view of him might change once she knew about his connection to Roger.

"It's true. Ask Yaz—she'll agree." Rosa tugged her covers higher up her torso with a huff, her signature Mona Lisa grin tinged with a saucy slant.

It was a good sign that she could poke fun at what they both knew wasn't really a laughing matter. Her job was important to her, as was her reputation in her community.

Man, what a mess they'd made of things.

And yet, his only regret in all of this was the distance Rosa had put between them since that night.

Resting the back of his head against the dresser, he watched her adjust the pillow between her and the bed's headboard.

Her face was still a little pale, more a faded tan than green though. Dark shadows and a feather of tiny lines rimmed her eyes, evidence of her fatigue. But she didn't seem as fragile as she had earlier when he'd carried her from the library. Or when she'd gotten sick after Dolores's arrival.

Apparently satisfied with her pillow fluffing, Rosa sank back against it. She rolled her head to the side and shot him a sweet, more than likely unintentionally sexy smile.

Pleasure washed through him.

God, this felt good. Sitting here with her. The house quiet around them. Rosa looking cozy and comfortable, both under her covers and with him. He could almost forget about the difficult conversations they were avoiding. The decisions, his secret.

This was what he'd missed between them. What he wanted to focus on. The sense of ease he felt when he was with her. The way she seemed able to relax and be herself around him, too.

If her getting rest wasn't a priority, he'd stay like this all night.

"I'm not looking forward to meeting with Father Yosef," she admitted.

"I can go with you if you want. For moral support," he added when she started to shake her head no. "The two of us are in this together, Rosa. Good or bad. Whether that's drinking warm rice water or standing at your side when you're sent to the priest's office. It doesn't matter. I'm in."

She stared down at her lap for so long he wondered if she planned to ignore his offer.

"Let me think about it, okay?" she finally said. "Sure."

He wanted to press for more, but he'd promised not to do that. As difficult as it might be for him.

She put a hand over her mouth to cover a yawn.

Time for him to go.

Pushing himself off the floor, Jeremy rose to stand. "You should get to sleep. I'll be right next door."

She craned her neck to look up at him so he sank onto the edge of her bed.

Her thigh pressed against his hip, but she didn't scoot away.

"Call out if you need anything," he reminded her.

"I'll be fi—"

"Fine, I know." He smiled to soften the words. Then found himself getting lost in her eyes. So open, honest.

The tip of her tongue snuck out to run along her bottom lip before she caught it with her teeth. No way did she mean it as an invitation. Still . . .

He leaned toward her, driven by the urge to forget caution and kiss her delectable mouth like he'd wanted to all night. Remind her how good they were together.

Her brown eyes flared, the dark depths brightening with . . . desire? Uncertainty?

The uncertainty had him stretching to press a kiss on her forehead instead. He inhaled her sweet scent, certain he'd dream about it, about her, when he finally fell asleep.

Gently, he caressed her silky hair, amazed by how drawn he was to her. How badly he wanted to protect her, care for her.

"I'm here if you need me, okay?"

He waited for her nod before stepping away.

"Jeremy?"

Her soft voice made him pause as he reached the doorway.

"Thank you," she offered. Her sweet smile had his insides melting faster than a snowman under the midday sun.

"My pleasure," he answered truthfully. "Get some rest."

He pulled her door shut behind him, then strode down the hall to Yazmine's room, thinking that at least one of them should sleep tonight.

As far as he was concerned, he'd be keeping one ear tuned for the slightest sound of distress from Rosa.

Not to mention that, with her nestled all alone in her queen-size bed on the other side of a thin wall, his body would be too keyed up to relax and fall asleep.

Yeah, it was going to be a long night.

Chapter Twelve

Thursday afternoon found Rosa and her Poetry Club regulars spread out at several tables in the library.

"So, you're sayin' we gotta have the open mic poetry slam here? In the library?"

There was no missing the skepticism in Iván's question. The library, with its musty books, plastic chairs, laminate-topped tables and industrial-grade carpeting didn't necessarily scream "young and hip, listen to my words as I tell it like it is"—the underlying vibe of her students' spoken-word pieces.

The beat of their verses, the emotion behind the words . . . they deserved the low lights and intimacy of a coffee shop. Not the harshness of institutional fluorescent lights.

While Iván bemoaned the lack of ambiance, Rosa surreptitiously gauged the reactions of the rest of the students.

On her right, Carlotta sat in silence, busily picking at her nails. Ever since Rosa had gotten sick earlier in the week, the teen had been sticking close to her.

Carlotta had eyed her with worry-tinged suspicion when Rosa had mentioned that she'd be working half days until the holiday break while she dealt with a medical issue. Thankfully, the girl hadn't asked any questions.

At the next table over sat Ricky. With his side-fade-cut hair and peach-fuzz goatee, the senior responded to Iván's complaint with the typical tough-guy, sí compadre approving jerk of his chin. However, she'd seen his eyes bug out when Iván had asked why they weren't using the school's auditorium for their open mic night.

Barbara and Marla sat at another table, their blond heads together, giggling over something one of them had written in a notebook. Their smiles had wavered, worried looks exchanged when Iván first brought up the idea of stepping out onto the auditorium's huge stage all by himself.

Then there was Javier, the last one in the group. Javier sat at her table across from Carlotta, quiet and mellow, per his usual. The clean-shaven and baby-faced junior cut a glance at Carlotta, quickly averting his gaze when she happened to look up at him.

Rosa couldn't help but smile. Those two had been dancing around each other since the first Poetry Club meeting back in September. No telling when one would be brave enough to make the first move.

"The thing is," Rosa answered, carefully measuring her words. She wanted to build their confidence, not feed any insecurities about sharing their poetry. Not that she had room to talk. Oh, she was participating in the slam, but reading one of her favorite pieces written by another poet. Not one of her own. "This is the club's first slam. The first time many of you have performed or even read your work aloud. This"—she opened her arms wide to encompass her home away from home—"has been our safe space, so to speak. It'll always be that, even outside of Poetry Club. Hopefully you know that by now. I think it's the perfect place for us to start."

Carlotta and Javier nodded. The blond besties joined in with their agreement.

"Next semester, if everyone is comfortable, we'll talk about locations where we can venture out," Rosa offered. If she was still working at Queen of Peace.

The thought sobered her. Still, she soldiered on for the kids. "Maybe the coffee shop downtown. They've held open stage nights for musicians in the past. I can touch base with the owner if everyone is up for it."

"Fiiiine," Iván groaned the word. "Guess my big public debut will have to wait."

Ricky barked out a laugh. Carlotta and Javier shared shy smiles.

"Iván, your debut happened the day you walked in here and shook the place up," Rosa teased. "The world has no idea what's in store for it when it comes to you. But I know you'll be great!"

True to his tough-guy reputation, Iván answered with some cocky head bobbing, his lips twisted in a "you know it" smirk as he fist-bumped with Ricky. But she caught the slight shade of embarrassed flush that stained his tan cheeks.

"To recap," Rosa said, "we'll meet—"

The library door opened, and everyone turned to see who was walking in nearly an hour after the last school bell. Their meeting was about to end.

Jeremy stepped inside, his tall, broad-shouldered frame draped in his navy-officer-style cashmere coat, a grey scarf tied around his neck. Dark jeans and a pair of dark brown leather Chukka boots peeked out from underneath the length of his coat. His cheeks were ruddy from the cold, his hair mussed more than likely from the bitter Chicago wind.

"Oiga, Señorita Fernandez, it's your boo," Iván catcalled.

Now it was Rosa's turn to feel the burn of an embarrassed flush.

Jeremy's gaze immediately sought her out. Their eyes met, his lips splitting in his trademark confident grin.

"Don't be so immature. He's just her friend," Carlotta chided Iván.

"Ha, the dude's been here to pick her up every day this week," he shot back. "I seen his fancy wheels out front. If being her ride every day is what you call a friend, then maybe I want you to be mine so you can drive me around. I'm saving up for my own set of wheels."

He waggled his brows at her, laughing at Carlotta's muttered, "Dream on."

"Don't mind me," Jeremy said, pulling out a chair at the table closest to the door. "I'm simply the lady's chauffeur."

He winked at Rosa, completely undermining his claim. Gracias a Dios her students couldn't hear the more than friendly thoughts about him running through her mind. Or see the pulse in her throat racing simply because he'd walked into the room.

This was day three of Jeremy staying at her house. Sleeping in the room next door. Sharing her bathroom and mixing his toiletries with hers. Making breakfast and brewing her mint ginger tea. Driving all the way into Chicago to pick up a few tins of her favorite Export Soda crackers from the mercado. Sitting on the floor or the end of her bed in the evenings while they talked about the latest books they'd read, what drew him to work with computers, a foreign film they'd heard about, or the places they longed to visit.

She could almost fool herself into thinking that they'd fallen back into their old friendship. Yet, she'd be lying if she didn't admit to sensing the ever-present undercurrent of awareness between them.

For her, at least.

Her body knew what it wanted.

Her mind kept getting caught up on what-ifs, buts, and what-abouts.

Those doubts kept her from broaching the topic of how they planned to move forward, co-parenting together. Instead, she'd focused on resting and keeping the nausea at bay.

Jeremy was no longer pressing her for answers, but it was as if a timer slowly, relentlessly ticked away the seconds, minutes, hours of her reprieve. The conversation couldn't be held off much longer.

She still wasn't eating much, but the half days at work, along with having someone handling things around the house, did help. Jeremy took his role as caretaker seriously. He wouldn't even let her lift a pinky finger to do anything. She was either relegated to the couch or in her bed resting. Maybe at the kitchen table while he brewed tea, made a new pot of soup, or washed the dishes.

He'd actually suggested he carry her up the stairs to avoid overexerting herself.

She'd put her foot down over that one.

Not because she was perfectly capable of walking on her own.

More like because she didn't trust herself to let go of him once they got to her room.

"You sure you don't wanna be my chauffeur?" Iván teased Carlotta, drawing Rosa's attention back to her students.

Carlotta rolled her eyes at him.

"Okay, let's wrap things up. Does anyone have a piece they need help with, or have you all decided what you're going to perform? Our poetry slam is two weeks from today. That's the last day of finals so it'll be a super way for us to close out the semester before break. Invite your family and friends. I'll bring drinks and sweets."

"¿De veras?" Carlotta's surprise matched the other kids'.

"Really," Rosa confirmed.

"Oye, tremenda fiesta in the library. We be getting the special treatment, a'right," Iván singsonged.

Leaning over his table, he started thumping a rhythm with his hands. Ricky jumped in, adding a mix of beatbox sounds with his mouth, creating a vocal percussion imitation in sync with Iván's rhythm.

The beat was like a contagious virus infecting them all. Barbara and Marla hopped up to dance by their table. Even normally quiet Carlotta rose and crooked a knee on her seat, her arms and torso moving to the groove.

Rosa's foot tapped, her shoulders shimmying with the beat.

Then Javier surprised them all by chiming in with a freestyle verse. "You think you really know us. That you got us figured out. But listen to our words, and don't you make us shout. Open your ears. Listen to our voice. Don't miss our slam by makin' the wrong choice. Yeah."

He punctuated his last word with an arms-crossed, tough-guy smirk at the other two boys. A pose Rosa had never seen the reserved young man mimic before.

"Oooooh, my boy's been holding out on us!" Iván crowed. He slid out of his chair, racing around to slap Javier on the back.

Ricky reached an arm out to fist-bump Javier, who flashed a wide grin. He glanced at Carlotta, who gazed at him with admiration.

The kids whooped and hollered over Javier's impromptu rap, and Rosa couldn't help but smile, pleased by their camaraderie.

It hadn't been like this three months ago when she'd held their first meeting. Only Marla and Barbara had known each other. Carlotta had seen a flyer; Javier had heard the announcement about it over the school intercom. Iván hadn't been an original member, joining about a month into the school year, and he'd dragged Ricky along a week later.

The Poetry Club, her pet project, had brought together this mix of students who normally wouldn't socialize with each other, helping them find common ground.

This was exactly what she had been hoping for.

An overwhelming sense of peace and rightness sprang through Rosa like a fire hydrant spouting water on a hot summer day. She turned to Jeremy, anxious to include him in this moment.

He smiled at her. A patient, understanding curve of his lips that warmed her soul. Somehow she knew he understood how happy this scene with her students made her.

Kids feeling at home in her library, bonding over spoken and written word. Sharing the experience with each other. With her.

She was delighted that Jeremy had arrived in time to witness this. See why her job was so important to her. Why it would be painful if she lost this.

Though, if it meant standing up for herself and her baby, no matter how hard it would be, she'd step away.

Overcome with the rush of pleasure-pain her thoughts brought, Rosa laid a hand on her stomach and stretched against her chair back.

"Okay, okay, people, let's take this outside," Carlotta called out. "Señorita Fernandez needs to get going."

"Thank you, Carlotta," Jeremy said as he walked over to join Rosa and the group. "Hi guys, I'm Jeremy. A close friend of Señorita Fernandez."

He shot her a teasing wink, as he used the description of himself he'd given Carlotta on Monday when he'd first met her.

Introductions were quickly shared around the tables, Barbara and Marla doing a grand impression of a teenage girl swoon. Then the intros reached the feistiest of their group.

"Iván here." The teen hopped off the corner of his table to stand in front of Jeremy. Shoulders back, feet anchored in a wide stance, chin tilted up, it was as close to a tough-guy impression as Iván could pull off while wearing his Queen of Peace Academy navy sweatshirt over a white polo and khaki pants. "So you're a *close friend*, huh? I see how it is. You treat her right. She's one of the good ones."

Jeremy offered his hand to shake. "No worries with me, pal. I know what a gem she is."

Iván gripped Jeremy's hand, and the two engaged in a man-to-man stare-down.

"On that note—" Rosa pushed back her chair so she could rise, mortified at their mini-standoff over her.

Thankfully Iván took her cue. The teen gave Jeremy one of his signature chin jerks of approval. Then, with a "Let's roll, people," he grabbed his backpack and led the group toward the door.

"Make sure she gets some rest, okay, Galahad?" Carlotta told Jeremy.

Jeremy answered with a two-finger salute to his temple. Carlotta shot him her big-sister stare before turning to Rosa. "Hasta mañana. I hope you feel better."

"Gracias," Rosa answered, slightly embarrassed at all the fuss over her, but amused by Carlotta's use of her nickname for Jeremy.

The kids piled out of the library, chattering on their way out, but not before Rosa noticed that Javier was carrying Carlotta's backpack for her.

Jeremy moved to Rosa's side, and together they waved good-bye to her students.

As soon as the door closed behind them, Rosa let herself fall back into her seat. With her workday at an end, the fatigue she'd been battling could no longer be ignored.

"Sorry about that," she mumbled. "I'm not sure what Iván was thinking with his warning and stare-down."

She'd been surprised, yet sweetly touched, by the teen's protective posturing. As well as Carlotta's.

Jeremy shrugged out of his winter coat and pulled out the chair beside her. His blue and grey plaid crew-neck sweater brightened the color of his eyes and stretched snugly across his broad chest. With his jeans and boots, he looked casual and comfortable. Devastatingly handsome.

Then again, she'd found him equally as handsome in gym shorts and a T-shirt, sweaty after hours of playing basketball at the university gym.

"They're good kids," he answered. "It's clear you have a positive effect on them."

"I try."

"You *do*," he stressed. "Don't brush off the compliment. You deserve it. Rosa, you care. About your job, about your role as a mentor. About them."

Not one to accept praise easily, she ducked her head, pretending to pick at a piece of nonexistent lint from her black skirt.

Jeremy nudged her knee with his own. "Hey, it's not every day I have to defend myself to a scruffy-faced hip-hop poet with a fade cut and a mile-wide attitude."

Rosa smiled, slanting Jeremy a look from under her lashes. "That mile-wide attitude is what brought him to the Poetry Club in the first place."

"How?" Jeremy leaned his forearms on the table, like he was settling in for her story. Actually interested in hearing about her kids.

His obvious interest chipped away at her uncertainty concerning whether he might grow bored with her simple life here in Oakton, with her.

The students' acceptance of him, his ease in venturing into her world this week made her think that their different lives could mesh. Then again, it was far easier for him to go slumming in the suburbs. Jeremy seemed comfortable anywhere.

She, on the other hand, had qualms about fitting into his life in Chicago. Despite what she'd told Yaz about getting used to the spotlight the Taylor family lived under. Rosa liked her quiet life in the suburbs. Jeremy was used to charity events, networking cocktails, and fancy dinners. Could their worlds intertwine? Doubts continued to hound her.

"What do you mean?" Jeremy prodded, reminding her of his question.

"Iván's English teacher and I were in the teacher's lounge about a month into the school year, and she brought up some concerns about him. He wasn't necessarily misbehaving in class, but she knew he wasn't working to his potential either."

Rosa paused, remembering that first conversation. As a new employee, she'd been surprised the older woman had confided in her.

"They'd started a poetry unit. Not a favorite of many students. But for three days in a row he 'accidentally' brought the wrong text-book."

"Classic avoidance move," Jeremy said.

"Exactly." Warming to her story, Rosa swiveled in her seat to face him and her knee wound up pressed up against his under the table.

Jeremy didn't slide away to give her more space.

Sucker that she was, she didn't move either.

Instead, she let herself enjoy the contact, as innocent as it might be.

"He was on the brink of getting a demerit for repeated misbe-havior," she continued. "I suggested a different solution for her to consider. He could either take the demerit, and put himself in a hole before the first nine weeks had barely begun, or attend the Po-etry Club meetings during the weeks they were studying the poetry unit."

Jeremy chuckled, the laugh lines around his eyes deepening. "Oh, that's evil. But smart."

Rosa grinned back at him, enjoying their easy conversation. "It just so happens his first meeting we were discussing Juan Felipe Her-rera."

Jeremy's blank expression led her to elaborate.

"Herrera's the first Latino U.S. Poet Laureate. He was selected in 2015."

"Got it. See, even I learn when I'm around you. It's a given your students are going to as well."

His teasing caused a delighted warmth to spread over her.

"Anyway," she continued, preferring to talk about her students rather than herself, "Javier knew about Herrera so he chimed in with some info. Then I showed a video of a Herrera interview where he mentions his idea that all text, even that found in ads or greeting cards, or used by songwriters and *rappers*, has poetry at its core."

Jeremy's expression brightened as he made the connection. "Great idea to play that video. I'm sure it made an impact on the kids, just like you have."

"Yes, well, apparently I—um—" Flustered by his compliment, Rosa

stumbled with her story. "Apparently something that day really res-
onated with Iván. The next week, he showed up for the meeting
with Ricky in tow."

Jeremy leaned toward her, his knee pressing against hers. "It's
interesting. I read an article recently about how some schools in the
Chicago area are using poetry to help students convey the jumble
of thoughts and feelings they struggle with. Especially when it
comes to what's going on in their lives, in our city's inner-city neigh-
borhoods."

Surprised by his knowledge on a topic so important to her, Rosa
angled closer, placing a hand on his forearm. "I might have read the
same one. I considered finding out more about the schools in our
area, see if there's some way my kids can connect with theirs.
Would you happen to remember the article's title or where you
read it?"

"I can share it with you. My mom emailed it to me, along with
several others. They were part of her wily way of trying to convince me to help with one of her charity events. Actually, she wants
me to . . ."

He broke off, his gaze shifting away from her to stare at his
clasped hands on the laminate tabletop. His jaw muscles clenched as
if he was trying not to say something.

"What is it?" she asked, worried by the pained expression on his
face.

"I have to ask you a question, a favor really, I'm not sure you're
ready for. But my mom insisted I try."

If the dread lacing his voice hadn't grabbed Rosa's attention, his
mention of his mother at the same time definitely did.

"You can say no, and I'll completely understand." He swiveled
in his seat, moving to place his right hand on the edge of her back-
rest, his left arm still leaning on the table, his knees straddling her
chair.

"I already told my mom that I won't allow you to overdo
things," he rushed on. "Not when you're finally feeling a little better. I mean, you seem like you're getting better rest and you look
like you're feeling healthier. It seems like you've had another good
day—have you?"

Bueno, that might be a little optimistic. Her pureed chicken soup from lunch had made an unfortunate reappearance shortly after. But she'd munched on a couple crackers with olives, then a few bites of papaya before Poetry Club, and that had all thankfully stayed down.

But forget her health for a second, there was something else she wanted to get straight.

"First, let's make this clear." Rosa turned in her own seat so she could face him, meeting him eye to eye. "There's pretty much nothing you can or can't 'allow' me to do, okay?"

Jeremy had the good grace to wince at her words. "Point taken."

The flash of chagrin in his baby blues nearly had her reaching out to hug him. Dios, he was such a good guy.

Her heart ached with that knowledge, because it also meant there was no way she could be certain whether he was here with her because he really wanted to be, or out of his sense of duty.

That doubt and her deeply rooted fear of rejection had her fisting her hands in her lap. Resisting the temptation to hug him.

"Now, about this invitation—you aren't selling me very well. I mean, if you're iffy, maybe I should be, too."

"No-no-no!" Jeremy cupped her shoulder in a tight grip. "I'm not iffy. Get that idea out of your head. Please. I just—"

His eyes fluttered closed for a second and he shook his head.

Rosa stilled, growing more and more nervous to hear whatever it was he struggled with.

When Jeremy finally looked at her again, his gaze was earnest, determined. "Without a doubt, there is no 'if' involved here, Rosa. Let's make *that* clear, okay?"

He waited for her response.

She nodded, the mix of his serious intensity and her jumbled nerves leaving her mute.

"I would love for you to join us on Sunday. I'm hoping you say yes. At least to the part about meeting my mom. The rest of it . . ." He shook his head, a befuddled frown tugging his brows together. "Mom's the chair for next year's Literacy Ball. On Sunday, she's having a couple committee members over for tea and updates, not a full-blown meeting. Anyway, she's been trying to sweet-talk me into volunteering since I moved back to Chicago. And, if I'm not mistaken, I believe she thinks you're a surprise ace up her sleeve that could make me fold."

"Me?" Rosa squeaked.

"Yeah, you."

His thumb caressed her shoulder through her sweater, the lazy back-and-forth motion creating waves of desire that lapped her soul.

"She's hoping your interest in books and reading will convince you to join the group, dragging me along with you."

Join the Literacy Ball committee. With Jeremy's mom. And a posse of women she didn't know, and probably would have very little in common with. Women who would think God knows what when they learned about her pregnancy.

Rosa gulped.

Dios mío, she was already worried about what Jeremy's mom would say about her surprise pregnancy.

Laura Taylor was a woman with class, style, and grace. Rosa'd seen her picture in the Chicago papers plenty of times. Read all the articles about her charity work. The Taylor family had connections to people Rosa had never even dreamed of meeting, much less socializing with.

Mortified by the idea that Laura might believe Rosa had intentionally trapped Jeremy with this pregnancy had her stomach flip-flopping, sending her nausea rising.

"Hey, what's going on?" Jeremy tightened his grip on her shoulder, his other hand moving to cup the side of her face. "You feeling okay? Come on, let's head to the restroom."

He moved to stand, but she put a hand on his thigh to stop him. "No, I'm—I'm good. Just, give me a minute."

"Whatever you need."

Jeremy smoothed a hand over her hair. His tenderness drew a pang from her heart.

"Look, forget the committee. I'll tell her to bag that idea. It's crazy for my mom to even bring it up. But she's been involved for so many years it's like her baby."

Baby.

The word had Rosa placing a hand against her belly again, where their child grew.

Jeremy followed her movement. Slowly, gently, he put his hand on top of hers.

The heat from his skin, the intimacy of the gesture brought the prick of tears to her eyes.

"This is real, Rosa. This baby connects us. As friends, as something more, who knows. But I *do* know that I plan to be a part of your lives. And I want you to be a part of mine. So when you're up for it, no pressure if you're not ready and Sunday is too soon, simply understand that I would really, *really* like for you to meet my mom. And the rest of my family."

Fear of the unknown, of the surreal circumstances one simple decision had wrought, was like an evil specter crooking a bony finger and wielding a strange power to suck the breath from her body. Her head spun, but the certainty in Jeremy's voice, the sincerity in his eyes and the secret love for him she held deep in her heart gave her courage.

He'd been so patient with her this week. While she'd been content to play house and avoid any difficult conversation.

Jeremy was doing his part to make their strange situation less awkward. He'd faced her family. All of them, including Tía Dolores.

He'd come to her school. Met her students. Showed an honest interest in what was important to her.

She owed it to him and their unborn child to do her part in making things work. Whatever "things" wound up meaning for them.

"Okay," she whispered. "But, to only meeting your mom, not the committee."

He blinked in surprise, or shock. Maybe both.

"Okay?" he repeated, his voice a whisper of gruff relief.

She nodded, and before she could say anything else, Jeremy leaned in to press a kiss on her lips.

Caught by surprise, she stiffened for a heartbeat. Then the desire building inside her swelled and she gave into it. Grasping his sweater in her fists, she pulled him closer.

Jeremy answered by digging his hands into her hair on either side of her head. His tongue flicked across her lips, and she opened for him, savoring the hint of coffee she tasted.

Their tongues brushed, caressed. Desire chugged through her

veins, heating her body. Giving rise to an ache she knew only he could soothe.

He deepened the kiss and she moaned, wanting more from him. His arms wrapped around her to pull her onto his lap. She went willingly. Matching him kiss for kiss.

Then his lips broke from hers to run a trail along her jaw, over to her ear where he blew a warm breath before moving to press a kiss on the sensitive spot behind her ear.

"You taste so good," he murmured.

She couldn't answer, her senses keenly focused on the heat of his lips against her skin. On how she wanted more.

He continued his trail of kisses along her neck, returning to her jaw, coming closer and closer to her lips.

"I don't want to stop." His words were nothing more than a mumble, but they reminded her of their surroundings.

"But we should," she lamented, because, darn it, she was always the one who did what she should.

Well, almost always.

His lips met her for one last deep, mind-boggling kiss. His tongue teasing hers in a sensual dance. Drunk on the taste of him, she didn't want the moment to end, but ever the gentleman, Jeremy eventually drew back.

Rosa slid off his lap onto her chair, belatedly realizing she still held a death grip on his sweater. She uncurled her fingers, then patted down the bunched-up material. Taking full advantage of the opportunity to feel his muscular chest.

"It seems like we communicate pretty well in this area, don't we?"

Jeremy's words brought heat crawling up her neck, into her face.

He chuckled, brushing the back of a knuckle up and down her cheek. "You're kind of cute when you blush."

Rosa rolled her eyes with a groan. "Dios mío, I wish I could stop it from happening. It's the bane of my existence. The genesis of the high school nickname I detest."

"Rosie Rosa, huh?"

She narrowed her eyes at him. "I can't believe Lilí shared that story with you."

"How about Beautiful Rosy Rosa?"

Angling her head, she gave him one of her younger sister's infamous are-you-kidding-me side-eye glares.

"I'll take that as a 'no' then."

"Smart man."

He laughed, the sound deep and husky, a balm for her lonely life.

"Okay, I'll stick with, 'Beautiful, sweet Rosa, thank you for agreeing to meet my mom. It means a lot to me.'"

"Well, when you put it that way, how can I resist?" she teased, delighted by his words.

"I'll tell her we can stop by for tea with her and my dad. That's all. Sound good?"

She nodded. The intimidating thought of meeting both his parents making her too nervous to say anything else.

With a smile, he stood and extended his hand to her. "Come on, let's get you home."

Rosa clasped her hand with his. The rightness of his palm pressed against hers, the warmth shared between their touch wrapped around her like a force shield. It was so easy to draw courage from his confidence.

While a part of her dreaded Sunday and the idea of stepping into his world to meet Laura Taylor and any preconceived notions the woman might have about her, Rosa refused to be afraid.

Come what may, she'd be strong, holding her head up high. For herself. For Jeremy and their baby. For their future.

Fifteen minutes into their nearly hour-long drive from Oakton to his parents' building on south Michigan Avenue, Jeremy decided it might be best to let sleeping dogs lie. Stop trying to draw Rosa out with small talk. Her one-word answers made it clear she wasn't interested in conversation.

He tuned his satellite radio to a smooth jazz station and drove in silence, hoping music would calm her nerves.

Unfortunately, as he maneuvered from I-90 to West Congress, then onto West Jackson Boulevard, her face remained pale, her lower lip raw and red from her constant gnawing on it.

A winter storm had blown in overnight, turning the day a bitter and frigid barely twenty degrees. Despite the cold, since there hadn't been any snow or ice, the streets were busy with holiday shoppers and traffic.

Pulling up in front of his parents' building, Jeremy handed his BMW keys to the valet and hurried around to Rosa's side of the car. He wrapped an arm around her shoulders, offering his warmth as he ushered her inside.

"Good afternoon, Mr. Taylor. It's good to see you."

"Hi, Charles!" Jeremy returned the greeting, noting the doorman's wind-burned cheeks. "It's pretty bitter out today. Need any of those heated hand warmers? Say the word, I'll go pick some up for you."

The older man shook his head. "You're too kind, but don't worry. This old battle axe can take anything Mother Nature and Chi-town want to throw at me."

Jeremy shook his head at the old line Charles had been giving him since Jeremy was a kid.

A robust, red-haired Irish Catholic with wizened green eyes and a quick smile, Charles had been as much a fixture of Jeremy's youth as summer days on the shore of Lake Michigan with his brother and their friends.

"Rosa, I'd like you to meet Charles O'Riley. Charles, this is Rosa Fernandez." Jeremy glanced down at her, still pressed against his side, shivering with cold. "Charles is a legend here. This man has contacts with contacts with *contacts*. There's nothing about Chicago history he doesn't know. But don't get him started on his beloved Cubs baseball team or we'll be here all afternoon."

Charles's belly laugh tugged a tiny smile from Rosa's until-now frowning lips.

"Welcome, Ms. Fernandez. Don't let this young scamp get away with anything, you hear me? And if you wanna talk Cubs ball, go right ahead."

Rosa pulled her leather glove off her right hand to offer a shake. "It's a pleasure to meet you, Charles. Please, call me Rosa."

"The pleasure's all mine," Charles responded, sidestepping her name request.

She could ask all she wanted. Jeremy had been trying to get Charles to call him by his first name for ages. The older man refused to budge.

"Unfortunately, I'm not the sports fan in our family," Rosa said. "That moniker belongs to my younger sister. But Chicago history"— Rosa leaned toward Charles like she was about to divulge a secret—"now there's a topic I can dive into."

"Ooh, I like her." Charles wagged his finger at Jeremy, a sly grin adding more wrinkles to the older man's ruddy face.

"Me too," Jeremy said. "And I want to keep it that way, so no sharing of adolescent misdeeds, okay?"

Charles laughed in response.

A hand on the small of Rosa's back, Jeremy ushered her through the entry foyer with its brocade-covered settees, gold wall sconces, and Tiffany lamps, toward the burnished metal elevator doors.

"Nice meeting you, Charles." Rosa waved good-bye as Jeremy hit the button to call the elevator.

"He's friendly," she said, pitching her voice so only he could hear.

"Yeah, he's a good guy," Jeremy answered. "Charles helped my brother and me through a few scrapes over the years." The doors opened, and Jeremy waited for Rosa to move in ahead of him. "Who am I kidding, he's still bailing Michael out every now and then."

Jeremy inserted his private keycard into the panel slot and pressed the penthouse button, then moved to stand next to Rosa.

"So, your parents live in the, uh, the penthouse?" Her voice hitched on the last word as the doors closed.

"We moved in here when I was in seventh grade. There's a great view of the city from the patio."

The elevator began its smooth ascent, and it was almost like the ease Rosa had shown with Charles seeped out of her, remaining back on the building's ground level with the doorman.

Her entire body stiffened. Hands clenched, she gripped her leather gloves like a lifeline.

Jeremy playfully bumped her shoulder with his, trying to lighten her mood.

Rosa jumped like he'd poked her with a live electrical wire.

His spirits dipped.

Damn, he'd been so hopeful about today. Looking forward to his mom and Rosa getting a chance to know each other.

Now he wasn't so sure. Other than those few moments in the lobby with Charles, Rosa had been closed off, growing more withdrawn every mile they'd driven farther from her house.

"Hey, if you're not up for this, we can get off on the next floor and take the elevator back down," he offered, forcing a note of calm into his voice even though his stomach twisted with disappointment. "I'm fine with whatever you want to do."

Rosa bowed her head.

"I'm sorry," she whispered. "I'm trying to not . . . I seem to have worked myself up to a . . ." Her voice trailed off, and she sucked in a shaky breath.

When she finally glanced up at him, her soft brown eyes were a tumultuous mix of fear and resignation.

His heart melted a little more for her.

Sure, Rosa typically preferred staying in her comfort zone, but he hadn't expected her to be this nervous about coming here today.

"My mom's not that bad, I promise."

"It's just, I've wanted to meet her for a long time, you know?" she said.

No, he hadn't known. Her admission intrigued him.

"The thing is, I hadn't intended it to be like, well, not like this." Rosa pressed a hand to her stomach.

Shame shadowed her beautifully expressive face.

Aw, man. Guilt for putting her in this awkward position soured his excitement over their visit.

Without thinking twice about it, he stabbed a finger at the red stop button on the panel.

The car jerked to a halt.

"Ay Dios mío!" Rosa stumbled backward and he grasped her elbows to steady her. "Qué estás haciendo?" She shook her head as if realizing she'd spoken in Spanish. "Jeremy, what are you doing?"

"Giving us a minute to get something straight," he said, his voice gruff with frustration. Mostly at himself for not realizing how she felt. "You have nothing to be ashamed of here, Rosa. I care about you. And I'm pretty sure you care about me, right?"

"Um, yes," she murmured, her eyes wide pools of shock.

"We're not coming here to be judged. Not the slightest bit. We're here because you're important to me."

He slid his hands up to cup her face, bending to press a kiss to her forehead, her cheek. And because he couldn't resist, he lightly brushed her lips with his. "We're here because my mom wants to meet the amazing woman who's pregnant with her first grandchild. There's no pressure. No expectations other than I hope you like her as much as I know she's going to love you."

Blinking rapidly, Rosa caught her lower lip between her teeth.

God help him. Every time she did that, he wanted to nibble on that luscious lip for her.

The urge to take her mouth with his, try calming her nerves—hell, his own nerves—by giving in to the undeniable chemistry between them was nearly irresistible.

It took all his willpower to keep his mind on the original reason why he'd stopped the elevator: to calm her down. Convince her there was no reason for her to be nervous.

It definitely hadn't been so he could coax her into engaging in all the hot and heavy activities he'd rather be doing with her in a stopped elevator.

"Look, if you're not ready, say the word," he offered.

He'd leave right now if Rosa asked him to. Though his mom would be disappointed.

Who was he kidding?

He'd be disappointed. Big time.

This was a huge step for him. He hadn't brought a girl home since freshman year of undergrad, and then only once. Cecile, whom he'd dated for a bit before starting his master's degree, didn't really count. Their families had been close for ages so it wasn't out of the norm for her to be around.

With Rosa, it was different. He *felt* different.

"Do you want to go home? It's okay if you do."

Rosa shook her head, tiny side-to-side jerks that weren't too convincing.

"I don't want you to do anything you're not comfortable with."

She stared up at him, her brown eyes big pools of indecision.

He could see the wheels turning in her head. All he could do was hope like hell they'd wind up steering her in the direction he wanted. But he wouldn't push.

"We should stay," she finally said. "I don't want to disappoint your mom."

Jeremy bit back a sigh. Of course she'd think of the other person before herself.

"Come on." She waved her gloves at the control panel. "Push the button again before we get stuck in here and someone has to come get us out. Talk about making a scene."

"Are you sure?"

Her head bobbed agreement; her eyes hinted at the opposite.

Doubt poked at him like a woodpecker tap-tap-tapping on his brain, warning him that there was more bothering Rosa than her pregnancy and meeting his mother. She hadn't said or hinted at what it could be, so he had absolutely nothing to go on other than gut instinct.

Had she done some digging around, discovered his connection to Roger? Worse, was it making her doubt him?

The age-old insecurity that had taken root early in his childhood sprouted another suffocating vine.

He needed to level with her. Stop anxiously waiting for the other shoe to drop.

He was too afraid she'd look at him in an unfavorable light. Wasn't sure how he'd deal with it if she did.

Annoyed with his inability to man up and broach the topic with her, Jeremy jabbed the stop button on the control panel. The elevator made an ear-piercing screech before the car started moving again.

Rosa shot him a worried glance.

God, he hoped bringing her here hadn't been a mistake.

They'd actually made progress this week. Slowly easing back into the camaraderie they'd built over the past few years. Especially when they'd been together on campus.

The past few mornings, they'd fallen into an easy routine. She used their shared bathroom first while he headed downstairs to brew fresh mint tea with ginger for her. Evenings, he took care of a simple meal and the dishes while she stayed off her feet. Friday night, they'd dimmed the living room lights and watched a documentary about the jazz era until she'd fallen asleep, her head nestled on his shoulder. Yesterday, she'd read or written in her poetry journal on the couch for most of the day while he'd taken care of some work on his laptop. After they'd said an early good night, he'd continued working in Yaz's room.

This morning, Yaz had swung by to pick up Rosa for mass. He'd tried not to be hurt when Rosa had told him it was best he not go with her. No need to fan the gossip fires by having him sitting beside her in the pew, she'd said.

He was used to being the subject of gossip columns. Rosa, however, was not.

They were good together, even though they still mostly danced around their attraction. Well, except for that kiss in the school library.

His body pulsed at the memory.

Same as their first night together, Rosa had surprised him, going all in, matching his intensity kiss for kiss. Murmuring her pleasure when he nuzzled her neck, teased her with tiny brushes of his lips.

He wanted more though. Especially because he knew how amazing it would be with her.

The past few nights, leaving her at her bedroom door after they said good night, he'd had to fist his hands and force himself to step away from her. What he really wanted was to follow her inside, start where they'd left off in the hotel room the morning after.

Only, she hadn't given him any sign that she'd welcome him back into her bed. And he wouldn't make any move until she did.

23-24-25. The floor numbers lit up one after the other, drawing closer to his parents' place on the 42nd floor.

Right now was not the time for him to be thinking about how sexy Rosa was, or how easily she turned him on. Or how badly he wanted her in his bed again, moaning with satisfaction.

The need to feel a connection with her drove Jeremy to reach out and cover her hand with his. Hers were ice cold.

She glanced up at him, anxiously gnawing on her lip.

"If it's any consolation, I'm probably more nervous than you are."

Rosa gave him a *what are you talking about?* frown.

"I mean, what if you don't like my mom? Then what? You have nothing to worry about. I'm sure my mom's already half in love with you based on what I've told her," he explained. "I'm betting that, five minutes in, you'll have her eating out of the palm of your hand."

Rosa scoffed, but her lips curved, hinting at her sweet smile and easing his reservations.

"Thank you. I appreciate the pep talk." She twisted her wrist to link her fingers with his.

Lifting their joined hands to his mouth, he kissed the back of hers. Hoping it eased her jitters as much as it did his own.

Because he did have jitters. He realized that now.

This whole time he'd been so worried about her, he'd ignored the tangled mass of knots inside of him. As each floor passed, bringing them closer to the penthouse, Jeremy's heart hammered faster and faster as if he were sprinting toward the Chicago marathon finish line again.

God, how he wanted this to go well. For Rosa to feel comfortable in his childhood home, with his mom and family, though Michael wouldn't be around today.

The clock was ticking. Their baby's due date grew closer with each day. Even if he was no longer pushing Rosa toward marriage, he couldn't let go of the idea. He still thought about the two of them being married and ready to start their family together when their child arrived. Their time together this week had solidified that in his mind.

This afternoon was an important step in making that goal a reality.

Everything had to go right today. So much depended on that.

Finally, the elevator eased to a stop. The doors whooshed open, and Jeremy ushered Rosa out with him.

Chapter Thirteen

Rosa barely contained her gasp of awe when the elevator doors opened to an ornately decorated foyer.

Jeremy led her out with a hand on the small of her back. If not, she might have still been inside when the doors slid shut.

It was like stepping into a picture straight out of Chicago's *Architectural Digest* magazine. White marble floors gleamed, leading into a formal living room lined with glass windows overlooking what appeared to be a sizable outdoor patio. Several dainty, more than likely antique hutches held beautiful statues and delicate vases with fresh flowers. The high ceilings were elaborately accented with intricate crown molding, perfectly framing large pieces of beautiful artwork.

A middle-aged woman dressed in black slacks and a white button-down with a grey cardigan stood off to the side. She greeted them with a polite smile. "Good afternoon, Mr. Taylor."

"Hello, Mrs. Davis, it's nice to see you again. This is Rosa Fernandez." Jeremy shrugged out of his coat and handed it to the maid.

"Hello, miss."

Rosa blinked, still taken aback by the wealth surrounding her, feeling uncomfortably like she'd entered a museum. "Oh, hello. Please, call me Rosa."

"Here, let me help you." Jeremy moved behind her, reaching to slide her jacket off her shoulders.

"Thanks," she murmured.

"Is my mom around?" he asked, as the maid took Rosa's jacket from him. "She should be expecting us."

"Yes, she's in the library with Ms. Millward. If you'll excuse me, I will let them know you've arrived."

"Wait!"

Rosa jumped at his blunt command. Mrs. Davis, who had turned toward a hallway off to the right, looked surprised as well.

"I'm sorry, did you say Ms. Millward?" Jeremy asked, his tone making his displeasure evident.

"She and her father arrived about an hour ago," Mrs. Davis answered. "Mr. Millward and Mr. Taylor have been in the study ever since."

The frown puckering his brow confirmed Rosa's guess that he wasn't too happy about the news that his parents had extra company.

She wasn't too happy about the full house herself. Jeremy had told her his dad had wound up going into the office, so she'd only be meeting his mom today. She'd been happy about that reprieve.

Obviously there'd been a change in plans though.

Her anxiety ratcheted up. If she'd thought meeting Laura Taylor might be intimidating, Jeremy's dad, tough lawyer for Chicago's elite, would be worse.

Rosa took a backward step, coming to halt when she felt Jeremy's hand on the small of her back.

"Thank you, Mrs. Davis. I appreciate the heads-up. We'll be waiting in the living room."

The moment the maid started down the hall, Jeremy moved to stand facing Rosa. He grasped her hands, his expression conciliatory.

"I had no idea Cecile and her dad would be here."

Cecile.

It took a moment for the name to register with Rosa's memory. Cecile Millward had been Jeremy's plus-one at Yazmine's wedding.

The statuesque, aloof blonde who'd ditched him because she'd felt it more important to be seen at some charity event.

If her dad was Harold Millward, Cecile had been more than a simple wedding date or an ex with whom Jeremy had decided to remain friends. Harold was Sherman's law partner, the other half of Taylor & Millward, Chicago's top litigation boutique firm. The two lawyers' careers were intertwined; rarely did you hear about one without mention of the other. The same could be said about their families.

Lilí loved skimming the society pages. Oohing and aahing over some fancy benefit or soiree. Pointing out pictures of a designer dress or a cool pair of heels neither one of them could afford. Since Yaz had introduced them to Jeremy several years ago, Lilí had really keyed in to any mention of his family and the people they were often seen with. That's why Cecile had seemed familiar to Rosa the night of the wedding. She simply hadn't been able to put two and two together until now.

"Rosa? What's wrong? Are you feeling okay?"

Jeremy's concern pulled Rosa out of her thoughts.

He tucked her hair behind her ear, ducking down to make eye contact with her.

"Yeah, I'm fine." She leaned away from his touch, fighting her rising anxiety. "Can we sit down somewhere?"

"Sure, come on." He led her into the formal living room, past another ornate antique hutch, this one displaying what looked like a collection of Fabergé eggs, to a deep green brocade–covered sofa with dark wood accents. It was more decorative than comfortable, its stiff cushions definitely not conducive to napping like the couch at her house, but it would do.

"I'm sorry for the welcome wagon that seems to have assembled," Jeremy said, sitting down next to her.

"Don't worry about it. I'm thinking it can't be as bad as when you had to deal with Tía Dolores."

She hoped so, anyway.

Jeremy chuckled wryly. "She does know how to keep a guy on his toes. Understandably, when it comes to you girls. She's called me to check up on you every day since she and Pablo left for Puerto Rico."

"No way!"

"Yep."

Dios mío, que vergüenza. The embarrassment had Rosa covering her face with a hand. "I had no idea."

"Hey, I get it. I've been worried about you, too." Jeremy grasped her wrist, gently pulling her hand down to the cushion between them. He held on to it, giving her a reassuring squeeze. "Had she been the one staying with you, I would have done the same."

The *tap-tap-tap* of heels on the marble floor echoed from the foyer connecting the living room with the wings off to the right and left of the penthouse.

"Listen, Mom knows about the baby. I'm sure she told Sherman. But I asked them to keep it under wraps until you're ready, so I'm fairly certain Cecile and her dad don't know. Okay?"

"Thank you," Rosa murmured.

At least she didn't have to worry about the socialite having another reason to look down her nose at her. Cecile hadn't been the friendliest at Yazmine's wedding. No telling how Cecile would react to Rosa showing up here, on what the other woman probably considered her own turf.

"Sweetheart, I'm happy you were able to make it today."

Laura Taylor floated into the living room on a pair of conservative heels, her tall, slim figure casually stylish in navy fitted pants and a cream turtleneck sweater. Dark blond hair the same color as Jeremy's was slicked back in a tight chignon any of Yazmine's dance students would admire. A simple pair of gold and diamond studs accented her ears, and a diamond pendant hung from a delicate gold chain.

His mom's simple, understated elegance and friendly welcoming smile reminded Rosa of Jeremy.

"Rosa, it's so wonderful to finally meet you." Laura extended her hand in greeting at the same time Rosa instinctively opened her arms for a hug.

There was a brief moment of awkwardness as Rosa regrouped and stuck out her hand and Laura leaned in for the hug. They ended up with clasped hands squashed between them as they gave each other a one-arm embrace.

Mortified, Rosa drew back, a heated blush seeping into her face. "I appreciate the invitation, Mrs. Taylor."

"Please, call me Laura."

Rosa bobbed her head in response, then turned to the younger woman who had entered with Jeremy's mother. "Hello, Cecile. It's nice to see you again."

The socialite tilted her head in greeting, the highlights in her blond bob catching the light cast by the pair of intricate chandeliers dangling from the high ceilings. A short-sleeved fuchsia sweater dress hit Cecile mid-thigh, hugging her model-slim curves. The pair of black leather over-the-knee boots gave her a trendy, chic vibe that had Rosa tugging at the waist of her plain cable-knit sweater and resisting the urge to frown down at her sensible black skirt and flat-heeled faux suede boots.

This wasn't a competition. Not as far as she was concerned.

Jeremy hugged both women hello. Rosa was unable to help noticing the way Cecile pressed her cheek to Jeremy's, her hand remaining on his forearm slightly longer than necessary.

"This is a surprise. I didn't know you were going to be here," Jeremy said to Cecile.

"A good surprise, I trust."

Dios mío, Rosa hadn't remembered Cecile's voice having that sultry undertone. Apparently neither Jeremy nor his mom, who smiled at Cecile's compliment-seeking remark, seemed to notice. Mrs. Taylor laughed softly, gesturing toward the brocade-covered couch and matching wing chairs.

"Why don't we sit down? I imagine Sherman and Harold will be done in the office and will join us shortly. Apparently there's some type of glitch with Sherman's laptop or a file he tried to send." She waved a hand over her shoulder toward the left wing of the penthouse, where no doubt the office was located.

Jeremy cupped Rosa's elbow and led her back to the couch, leaving his mom and Cecile to take the wing chairs.

"Should you maybe go see if you can help?" Rosa asked him. He was, after all, an IT specialist.

Jeremy shook his head abruptly, exchanging an uncomfortable look with his mother.

Strange.

"Are you . . . sure?" Rosa tried again. The idea that she could help one of her sisters and not do so wasn't something she'd ever entertained.

"I don't really get involved with anything pertaining to the law firm," Jeremy explained. Rosa's surprise must have registered on her face because he went on. "They have an IT specialist. I'm sure he's working on it for them."

"Actually—"

"Jeremy decided ages ago," Cecile said, at the same time Laura had started to speak, "when we were in college together, that he would go his own way professionally. Right, J?"

J?

Rosa had never heard anyone call him by that nickname. Then again, she wasn't privy to his inner circle of friends like Cecile no doubt was.

He nodded, but Rosa caught his uncomfortable gulp. Noticed the tense flutter of his fingers against the cushion between them. Something was off here; she just didn't know what.

"Personally, I find his independent streak admirable. Attractive, really. It's part of what draws us to each other."

Cecile's blatantly flirtatious remark seemed to surprise Jeremy and his mom as much as it did Rosa. An awkward silence filled the room. Cecile crossed her long legs, a satisfied expression on her artfully made-up face.

Over the years, Rosa had been forced to wait for her turn in the bathroom while Yaz took forever doing her makeup. The experience had taught her that a flawless "natural look" like Cecile's took effort, and more products than Rosa cared to deal with. She was fine with her fifteen minute routine.

Rosa knew what the other woman was doing, staking her claim.

Yazmine would have laughed at Cecile's gall.

Lilí would have thrown it back at her, in spades.

Rosa found herself falling on old habits, accepting the rudeness without standing up to it. She despised herself for doing so, but as a visitor in the Taylors' museum-esque home, no way would she risk offending someone who apparently was more than just the "old friend" Jeremy had described Cecile as on the night of the wedding.

Jeremy cleared his throat, breaking the silence. "Yes, well, that was a while ago, Cecile. But I, uh, appreciate your vote of confidence in my career choice."

He angled on the couch toward Rosa, away from his former love interest. But was it former?

Rosa had a sinking feeling that if you asked Cecile, she'd say things between her and Jeremy weren't finished.

"My younger brother, Michael, has taken the legal baton Sherman wanted to pass along to both of us," Jeremy told her. "He'll join the firm when he finishes law school and passes the bar."

It hit Rosa that despite the amount of time they'd spent together last spring, not to mention this past week at her house, Jeremy hadn't revealed much about his family life. Oh, he'd mentioned generalities like how he'd missed them when he lived in New York. He'd shared a few stories about his close relationship with his mom and memories of clowning around with his younger brother, but he had rarely mentioned his connection with Sherman. He praised Sherman as a good father, but Rosa had no idea what type of relationship they shared.

Could there be some problem or rift between the two of them she wasn't aware of?

For someone who'd been unbelievably close with her dad, she found the idea incredibly sad.

"I'm more the black sheep of the family," Jeremy added.

"You are not!" Laura's grey eyes flashed with dismay.

"It's a joke, Mom." Jeremy waved off her concern, but Rosa didn't.

Jeremy might *say* he was kidding. The satisfied smirk on Cecile's bowed lips might imply she agreed with him. But one result of Rosa's keen infatuation for Jeremy was that she had gotten pretty skilled at reading his expressions, clueing her into his moods.

For instance, she knew that when the right side of his mouth turned down the slightest bit, he was annoyed. When the edges of his eyes crinkled, or one of his brows twitched in a slight quirk, his laugh was about to roll from his chest.

When the pupils of his eyes flared, his desire sparked and he wanted to kiss her. Which she usually didn't mind.

Or, like now, when the muscles in his jaw flexed, his anger or frustration simmered and he fought to not let it boil over.

But which was it now. Anger? Or frustration? And why?

Somewhere in the penthouse, a door opened and two male voices could be heard talking.

Laura rose from the wing chair. Her mouth trembled as if she wanted to say something, but she hesitated.

"Drop it, Mom," Jeremy grumbled. "It's all good."

Rosa glanced from him to his mom, ignoring Cecile, who seemed to have set off this underlying tension. Whatever the root cause of it might be. Forget Rosa's nervousness about meeting Jeremy's parents for the first time, or the fear of them thinking she might not be good enough for their oldest son. There was more going on here and apparently she was the only one in the dark about it.

Her discomfort grew as Rosa found herself doubting Jeremy, certain he was keeping something from her. Something his "old family friend/flame" and pot-stirrer Cecile was privy to.

"Before I forget—" Cecile propped an elbow on her armrest and leaned toward Jeremy. "Sharon and Morgan have two extra box seat tickets to the ballet on Thursday. I told them I'd see if you were free. How about it? Dinner and drinks beforehand. The four us, like old times."

The bold woman actually reached out to put her manicured hand on Jeremy's knee.

Rosa wanted to smack Cecile's grubby paw away, stake her own claim on Jeremy. Only, she didn't have a right to do that. Not really.

She may have thought they were growing closer over the course of this past week. Now she wasn't so sure. Not with whatever secrets he was keeping from her.

"I don't think so, Cecile. Rosa and I already have plans. You guys have fun." Jeremy pushed up off the couch, and Cecile's hand dropped away. He combed his fingers through his hair, leaving it mussed. Something Rosa had mostly seen him do when agitated.

Cecile shot Rosa a brittle smile. "Another time, maybe."

"Hello, beautiful. Sorry to keep everyone waiting." Sherman Taylor entered the room with gusto, his vibrant personality like a visible force. One arm outstretched, he curved it around Laura's shoulders, bringing her closer to him so he could kiss her temple.

Jeremy must have gotten his height from his mom because even in her low heels Laura stood even with Sherman, both maybe five-foot-ten or so. Sherman's brown hair was peppered with grey, but with the long sleeves of his buttondown shirt rolled up and his crisp grey slacks, it was evident he was fit for his age.

Behind him trailed a shorter, slightly paunchy older man, his cheeks had large jowls that spread with joy when he spotted his daughter.

Rosa and Cecile stood at the same time, the other woman moving to her father's side.

"Jeremy, good to see you, son," Sherman greeted him.

"You, too, Dad. Harold, it's been a while."

The men shook hands while exchanging pleasantries.

Rosa tried to catch any sign of discomfort between Jeremy and his dad, but she came up empty. Sherman appeared happy Jeremy was here. Jeremy showed no signs of his earlier frustration.

She could almost convince herself that she'd misinterpreted everything. Only, the tiny V marring the area between Laura's thin brows hinted at the woman's lingering worry.

"And this young lady must be Rosa."

This time, Rosa knew to hold out her hand, forgoing the hug that was second nature to her and her family.

"You have a beautiful home, Mr. Taylor. It's a pleasure to meet you."

He winked at her, a habit Jeremy had evidently inherited from his dad. "When the weather is nicer and we can enjoy a meal out on the terrace, you'll have to come for dinner."

"I'd like that, thank you." She could see why Sherman was known for swaying juries. The intensity of his gaze zeroed in on her and made her feel like she was the most important person in the room.

Jeremy stepped closer to place a hand on the small of her back. She angled her head to look at him, catching the barely discernible question in his deep blue eyes.

Before she could consider what he might be trying to ask her, Sherman was introducing her to Harold Millward.

Right away, it became apparent that while his physical appearance could mistakenly lead you to think him soft, Harold Millward's quick wit matched Sherman's. Explaining how the two men had, together, built Taylor & Millward into the most sought-after boutique law firm in the Midwest.

"We're going to head out now," Mr. Millward said after their colorful discussion about the must-see sunset view and the don't-miss gatherings often held on the Taylors' terrace. "I promised my gorgeous daughter an early dinner treat, and I don't like to disappoint her." He held out a crooked elbow, and Cecile slid her arm through it. "Looking forward to the holiday party Wednesday night."

"Oh yes, Rosa, I'm sure Jeremy's mentioned it. We hope you can join us." Laura held out her hands in welcome to Rosa, who had no idea what party they referred to.

"We've both been so busy, I hadn't even thought about the firm's annual party," Jeremy said. "We might, um, have to take a rain check, right?"

He turned to Rosa for confirmation.

Anger sparked in her. She didn't appreciate feeling like a pawn in some game she didn't even know she was playing. Confused, refusing to lie, she answered with a half-hearted shrug.

Disappointment flashed in Laura's eyes.

Sherman's mouth thinned the tiniest bit.

"Well, hopefully things work out and you can make it," Harold answered. "We'll be off now. Sherman, we'll need to have Henderson take a look at your laptop, maybe poke around the ones in the office. Something's off. Or, hell, have Jeremy give it a look over. The kid's got more computer degrees than most folks we know. Probably even more than Henderson."

Jeremy's hand flexed, his fingers pressing into Rosa's back.

"I don't mind giving it a try," he replied, his lazy tone contrary to the tension Rosa sensed in him.

"There you go." Harold gestured at Jeremy. "What good is it having a son who turns down law school and winds up an IT whiz if you don't take advantage of his skills?"

Jeremy's shoulders stiffened. Rosa cut a quick glance at Laura Taylor and could swear the woman's pale skin had blanched a shade lighter.

Despite the friendly smiles on everyone's faces, a strained undercurrent vibrated in the air, snapping at Rosa's already stressed nerves.

"That's okay, son. I won't bother you about it." Sherman pshawed, brushing off Harold's idea. "Henderson can take care of everything tomorrow."

"I'm sure he can." Jeremy's stiff response didn't seem to bother anyone else. But it certainly confused her.

Dios mío, the subtext she couldn't grasp made Rosa's head spin with questions.

Laura offered to walk Harold and Cecile to the door. Thankfully Sherman joined the group, leaving Rosa and Jeremy alone in the living room.

As soon as they were out of sight, Jeremy sank onto the couch with a muffled groan. He gripped his thighs, his pale skin tone in stark contrast to his black jeans.

An inexplicable pain shadowed his blue eyes, twisted his lips in a grimace.

Confused, Rosa battled with anger and betrayal. Jeremy should have given her a heads-up about whatever everyone else was dancing around here.

At the same time, seeing him hurting like this tugged at her heart. She cared for him too much not to want to ease whatever caused his pain.

"I'm so sorry about this," he said, his voice a rough whisper.

"It's okay." Rosa laid a hand on his shoulder. "You don't have to apologize."

He hung his head, shaking it from side to side. "God, Rosa, you're too good. Even when you're dropped in the middle of someone else's family drama, you don't complain. And you should. Hell, I would!"

"Hey!" She joined him on the couch, slipping her hand from his shoulder to wrap around his back to offer comfort. "I'm not saying you don't have some explaining to do. But right now, I feel like you could use a hug more than I need answers."

Jeremy pressed his forehead against hers. "I'm supposed to be taking care of you, not the other way around."

"Uh-uh, if we're doing this—whatever 'this' is—it's fifty-fifty. I won't accept anything else."

They stared deeply into each other's eyes and she caught the flare of his pupils. She knew what was coming and, despite his parents in the nearby foyer, she let her eyes flutter closed.

His lips brushed against hers in a kiss so feather soft she could almost think she'd dreamt it.

He held her face with both palms as he kissed her again.

And again.

Little nips that teased her. Enticed her desire. Leaving her wanting more.

The elevator doors dinged, signaling its arrival. Goodbyes could be heard from the foyer.

Jeremy pulled back with a muttered groan.

Rosa's eyes fluttered open, meeting the chagrined smile in his baby blues.

"Look, my mom knows you haven't been feeling well. Us coming today was tentative, based on how you were doing. Would you mind if we kept this short, then headed home?"

Home.

She liked the sound of that.

Oh, make no mistake about it. They had a major conversation ahead of them. Rosa the quiet dormouse was no longer in residence at casa Fernandez.

Jeremy might think she was okay being kept in the dark and walking into his parents' intimidating home without a clue that there might be a drop of bad blood.

If so, her handsome housemate was going to have to think again.

Chapter Fourteen

Balancing a dinner tray in one hand, Jeremy knocked tentatively on Rosa's bedroom door with the other.

He didn't relish bothering her, but she'd been holed up in there since they'd come back from the awkward visit with his parents. It was past her regular dinnertime. He figured she had to be hungry.

Bringing up her food gave him an excuse to check on her. Find a way to explain what he should have explained before getting to his parents' place.

Right now, his quiet librarian was also an angry librarian. Deservedly so.

She'd barely said a word during their drive home. After abruptly telling him she wasn't ready to talk, she'd sat in the front passenger seat, eyes closed, dozing. Or pretending to anyway.

As soon as they'd gotten inside her house, she'd marched straight upstairs, claiming she was tired.

Talk about disastrous.

He had hoped the visit would reassure her that she was welcome with his family, the same way he always felt with hers.

Of course, he hadn't counted on Harold and Cecile being there. Or that his father's partner would dredge up the uncomfortable reminder of the huge disappointment Jeremy had given Sherman, thumbing his nose at his father's dream of having his sons join his law practice.

Most of the time, Jeremy assumed they had moved past the deep disillusion Sherman had felt and the overwhelming sense of suffocation Jeremy had struggled with before making the decision to go his own way.

His mom claimed he was the only one who hadn't moved past it. But while Sherman asked about his work and career aspirations, Jeremy sensed a difference between the way his father viewed him and his younger brother. As if Michael and their dad now shared a bond beyond that of DNA, something Jeremy and Sherman would never share.

"Come in," Rosa called at his knock.

The disgruntled tone of her voice wasn't quite the welcome he'd wanted, but at least she hadn't told him to go away.

"I thought you might be getting a little hungry," he said as he entered.

She sat on the red upholstered armchair next to her bookshelf, feet propped up on the matching ottoman, her poetry journal lying open on her lap. She glanced between the tray he held and his face, a mix of emotions clashing in her eyes—annoyance, disappointment, and finally resignation.

"I want to tell you to go away. That I'm not ready to argue with you." She narrowed her eyes in a glare that lasted all of a few seconds before her generous, occasionally sassy and always forgiving personality shifted back into place. "But I *am* getting hungry, surprisingly, and I'm not foolish enough to bite the hand that feeds me."

"Whatever reason lets me in, I'll take what I can get," Jeremy answered.

"Wise man."

Marking her place with her father's letter, she closed the journal, then put it on top of the low bookcase. He bent down, and she deftly reached for the cup of apple juice balancing precariously on the wicker tray.

"Here you go." Jeremy laid the food on her lap, noting that she'd changed out of her skirt and sweater into comfy grey sweats with a matching top. Emblazoned on the front of the sweatshirt was an open book. Written in a flourishing font on the book's pages were the words: *It's a truth universally acknowledged, that a single man in possession of a good fortune, must be in want of a wife.*

He smiled as he backed away and sat on the end of her bed.

"What?" she asked, suspicion lacing her question.

"What's the first line of *Pride and Prejudice*."

"Excuse me?"

"I'm playing our version of *Jeopardy* with you."

She sighed. A heavy, put-upon sigh she mostly reserved for Lilí when she was pushing Rosa's buttons.

But she hadn't told him to leave. That was a good sign. He pointed to her sweatshirt. "The answer is: What's the first line of *Pride and Prejudice*. Which I know happens to be your favorite classic novel, right?"

She took a sip of the apple juice, then carefully set the glass next to her Moleskine journal on the bookshelf. Her pensive gaze told him she was either thinking of a way to politely ask him to go, or coming up with her own *Jeopardy* question.

He was hoping against hope that she'd play along. Throw him a rope across the vast distance she'd put between them as soon as they'd gotten in the elevator to leave his parents' house.

"Fiiiiiine," she said on a groan. "You're right."

He clapped his hands in triumph.

"Give me another one," he said, scooting back and making himself comfortable on her bed.

He'd kicked off his shoes in Yazmine's room earlier; now, he tucked his stockinged feet to sit cross-legged. They hadn't played literature *Jeopardy* since they'd lived in Champaign.

He couldn't remember whose idea it'd been, but they'd had fun challenging each other from time to time while walking across campus or eating dinner. Sometimes it was character names, authors, or, like now, first lines.

"It was the best of times, it was the worst of times," Rosa monotoned.

Jeremy rolled his eyes. "Puh-lease. That's too easy. What is *A Tale of Two Cities*?"

Rosa quirked a brow. Still, he caught the faint twitch of her lips. Her Mona Lisa smile trying to sneak onto her face.

He arched a brow right back, daring her to test him with something harder.

Her gaze dropped to the small bowl of pureed chicken soup. Picking up her spoon, she dipped it in the concoction, then brought it up to her mouth.

Watching her lips close over the utensil, Jeremy nearly swallowed his tongue. His body stirred and he shifted, adjusting himself. He could practically see her mind working, searching for a book that might stump him, blissfully unaware of his reaction to her unknowingly sexy eating habits.

"Okay," she said after swallowing her baby bite of soup. "Let's try, 'You don't know about me without you have read a book by the name of . . .'" She broke off, waiting to see if he'd caught it yet.

The glint of mischief in her brown eyes warmed him. It was a far cry better than the hurt-filled anger that had flashed at him earlier.

"You give?" she asked after only a few seconds had passed.

"Wait!" His fingers tapped against his knee. The answer was on the edge of his brain.

"'. . . read a book by the name of *The Adventures of—*'"

"What is *The Adventures of Huckleberry Finn?*" He blurted the words in a quick jumble, pointing his finger at her in triumph.

She laughed, the dinner tray shaking in her lap and making the spoon rattle against the red ceramic bowl. "Right."

"Give me another," he prodded. "C'mon, one more. For old time's sake."

Her smile dimmed, a nostalgic wistfulness covering her features.

Too late, he realized his faux pas. There was no going back to "old times" now, not with the baby and all the changes ahead of them.

"How about, 'We didn't always live on—'"

"Mango Street," he finished, remembering another one of her favorites, this one a young adult novel by a well-known Latina author. He had never read it until Rosa had mentioned how much she'd enjoyed it. High praise he'd never discount. "What is *The House on Mango Street?*"

She nodded, dipping her spoon into the soup again.

"You're going soft on me, Rosa," he chided.

One of her shoulders lifted and fell in a half-shrug. He would rather she yelled at him instead of quietly retreating to seethe. Or worse, push him away.

God forbid the twilight zone visit with his parents made Rosa pull back again, decide single parenting was better than getting mixed up with him and his hang-ups.

The idea gutted him.

For several anxiety-heavy minutes, Jeremy watched Rosa eat in silence. Desperate to reach her, he tried again. "'He was an old man who fished alone in a skiff in the Gulf Stream and he had gone—'"

"'Eighty-four days now without taking a fish,'" she finished. "What is *your* favorite classic novel, *The Old Man and the Sea*? Now you're going easy on me."

"Because I owe you an apology."

He spoke the words with all sincerity, praying that she would accept his apology. Allow him to explain, and not think less of him when he finally admitted his past.

"Yes, you do."

Her matter-of-fact words matched her expression when she finally looked up at him.

Okay, she wasn't going to make this easy. At least she was listening.

"Today didn't really go as I had planned." He paused, figuring she'd have a comment about his candy-coating the obvious.

Lips pursed, Rosa stared blankly back at him as if to say, *And?*

"And it wasn't exactly fair for me not to have prepared you for the potential awkward situation. To be honest, part of why I moved back is because I thought Sherman and I had moved past it. I'm not so sure that's true. But apparently others, people I haven't socialized regularly with for years, don't mind bringing it up."

"It. You keep using that word, but you haven't defined what 'it' really is."

Where to start?

His eyes closed, negative emotions welled up inside of him, most notably fear over her reaction.

He knew where to start. The beginning. The reason why it had taken him so long to admit to Sherman he had no desire to go into law. Because he hadn't wanted to disappoint his father. Because he felt compelled to prove himself worthy of the Taylor name. Instead of just the "adopted" Taylor son. All because of . . .

Anxious, he rubbed his hands together while he worked up the nerve to tell her.

"I don't really talk about this much. At all really. But if you Google and click enough links you'll probably come across several old articles that mention I'm adopted."

Rosa's expressive eyes widened in surprise.

"Yeah, I figured you didn't know. Or else you were being discreet by not asking me about it." He took a deep breath. Now or never. "I don't talk about being adopted because my birth father isn't exactly a model citizen. Hell, let me go ahead and put it out there. He's a scumbag who's in prison now."

Her spoon clattered against the side of the bowl, and a small gasp shaped Rosa's mouth in a little O of surprise.

Uncomfortable yet relieved to finally rid himself of the past's dark cloud, Jeremy rushed through the sordid story. "My mom met Roger Wilson when she was in college. They dated for a while, but he had a temper, and it started to get physical. At times violent. She tried to break it off, but he wasn't happy about it. He showed up at her apartment drunk one night and . . . and things got ugly."

He paused, gulping back the anger that always clawed at him when he thought about what his mom had gone through. "Thankfully the neighbors heard her screams and called the cops. Mom wound up with a broken arm, bruises from his chokehold. She pressed charges, but a couple weeks later, when she found out she was pregnant, she offered him a deal. Sign away parental rights and she'd drop the case against him."

One hand pressed to her chest, Rosa stared back at him, dismay slackening her features.

He floundered with the story for a second. Struggling with the fear that knowing his true parentage could make Rosa think less of him in some way.

That "adopted son" label that cropped up in an article about Sherman's family from time to time still managed to get under his skin.

"Flash forward about five years," he went on. "My mom was working as a legal assistant for a law firm in Chicago. She met Sherman, a young lawyer on the rise, at a charity event. He swept her off her feet and jumped in to take on a fatherly role with me. Mom deserved everything Sherman offered—a healthy relationship, love, a better lifestyle. But she wasn't easy to win over."

Jeremy found himself smiling as he remembered his mom turning down Sherman's first proposal after they'd only been dating a few months. She said she needed to be sure. More importantly, she wanted Jeremy to be sure.

Sherman had wined and dined both Jeremy and his mom. What was even better were the times he'd patiently listened to Jeremy rattle on about this dinosaur or that amazing play in the Cubs game earlier in the day.

Oh man, he hadn't thought about those early years in a long time. Absently, Jeremy picked at the inseam of his jeans, letting the good memories wash away the bad. Far too often lately the negative ones had held sway over him, causing a chronic stress that kept him awake at night.

"I am so sorry about what happened to your mom," Rosa said, her voice thick with tears.

He glanced up to find her eyes glistening with moisture. The good in her must be horrified by the hatefulness of his story.

"My mom says it made her stronger." He cleared his throat, as always, humbled by his mom's perspective. "She'll tell you that she came out the winner, because she got me."

"Sounds like a smart woman who's an amazing mom."

Rosa's sincere words made his eyes sting.

"Yeah, she is."

They shared tentative smiles, and his heart swelled with optimism.

"I'm relieved that you felt comfortable enough to share that with me. But, um, I'm not too sure how that plays into what happened today?" she asked quietly.

The tiny furrow between her brows showed her confusion. Unfortunately, the only way to clear it up was to share more of his ugly story.

"Right after Sherman and my mom got married, he started the official adoption process so there'd be no second-guessing his commitment to the both of us. Even when Michael came along a couple years later, Sherman didn't change how he treated me. The thing is . . ."

Uncomfortable baring his secrets, even to Rosa—or probably especially to Rosa—Jeremy slid his gaze to the framed photos on top of her bookshelf. One showed a young Rosa wearing a white dress, a tiny veil on her head. Her First Communion. She stood sandwiched between her mom and dad, her hands clasped in prayer at her chest. The photo captured their love and joy in one still frame.

The juxtaposition of her happy family photo with the shameful family story he needed to share with her embarrassed him even more. But he owed it to her to explain.

"My sophomore year of high school, Roger Wilson was arrested for manslaughter. He got in a bar fight and a man died. In Chicago, a story like that makes the papers once, then another one takes its place." Jeremy scrubbed his hands over his face, the frustration and shame he'd battled back then sweeping over him again. "But a damn reporter found out about my tie to Roger. The papers had a field day: 'Sherman Taylor's adopted son connected to a killer.'"

He finger-quoted the air as he recited the awful headline the paper had printed.

"Ay Dios mío, that's terrible! Why would they say that about you?" Rosa looked more upset for him than scandalized by Roger's charges.

"Mom and Sherman went on the offensive, and the story got squashed. But kids at school talk. Rumors don't die as easily. It became my mission to prove I'm nothing like that man."

"You aren't. Not in any way." Rosa held out her arm to him.

He grasped her hand, grateful for her acceptance. A bit leery if he deserved it. Skeptical as to if she'd feel the same once she heard the rest of what he had to share.

"I've always tried to make my dad proud," he admitted, forcing himself to continue. "Avoid doing anything that would make him regret adopting me. Or remind anyone of where, *who*, I come from. Before I even started college at Northwestern, Sherman had begun voicing the strong desire to have his sons follow him into the family business. But, when the time came, I just couldn't bring my-self to go to law school. Everyone assumed I'd follow in his foot-steps. Part of me wanted to. I really thought I could."

Frustrated all over again, Jeremy speared a hand through his hair.

"I can't imagine your parents not wanting you to be happy in whatever you chose," Rosa said as she set the dinner tray on the footstool's cushioned top, her soup halfeaten.

"I couldn't see that back then, and I botched things. Afraid of disappointing them, especially my dad, I didn't say anything. I took the LSAT and applied to law schools, at the same time I was taking the GRE and applying to master's programs in computer informa-tion science on the sly. When I got accepted to Harvard Law, they planned a surprise dinner party for me. Only—"

God, he hated remembering the mortified look on his mom's face that night. "Only, I surprised them in the middle of it by an-nouncing my intent to go to University of Illinois for my master of computer science."

"Oh, Jeremy, you didn't?"

Shame filled him at the sadness weighing down Rosa's softly spo-ken words.

"That's the first and only time in my life I've seen my dad at a loss for words. Oh, he recovered quickly. I mean, hell, the man is a master when it comes to speaking in front of a crowd. But I could tell how devastated he felt."

Jeremy shook his head slowly, going back to that spring night. The outdoor terrace lit with lanterns, their family and a few close friends gathered around the brick fire pit to help fight the cool Chicago spring weather. "I knew I had let him down. Big time."

Elbows resting on his knees, Jeremy hunched over. "That was not my finest moment. To my parents' credit, they supported my decision, even if they didn't approve of my behind-the-scenes ma-neuvers."

"No one likes to be kept in the dark."

Her accusation hit left of center in his chest with bull's-eye accu-racy.

His spirit sunk even lower and he slid to the edge of the bed. His feet hit the carpeted floor as he held out his hands in supplication, desperate for her to understand. "I should have told you about

Roger Wilson sooner. I own that. But I assure you, Rosa, I am nothing like him. You know me!"

For several heart-stopping moments, she stared at him in silence. Then a tear slipped from her left eye, leaving a wet trail down her cheek. She swiped at it with one hand; the other reached out to grab his.

Her tight grip punctuated her words. "I *do* believe you're a good man, Jeremy. Nothing could make me doubt that. But"—she let go of him and crossed to her dresser—"but you've lied to me."

"What? No!"

He moved to follow her, but she threw up a hand to ward him off. When she turned away from him he sank down on the bed, feeling rejected.

Her back to him, he caught her reflection in the oval, gilt-framed mirror hanging above the chocolate-stained dresser. She ran a finger over the intricate design carved into the lid of a small wooden box. Moved the treasure holder a touch to the left. Slid a black-handled comb and brush set off to the side. Gently tapped a framed picture of her and her sisters, edging it back the tiniest bit.

The concentration scrunching her face would make you think her task involved intense brain power. He knew the mindless organizing helped her work through whatever was bothering her.

Namely, him. His history with Roger Wilson. Whatever she thought he'd lied to her about.

"Rosa?" he said when he'd started to feel like he was stuck in one interminable silent scream, waiting for whatever would happen next.

"You should have told me all of this sooner. I was worried about what your parents would think of me," she said, still fiddling with the items in front of her. "If I was a gold digger trying to trap you."

"They'd never—"

"I know, it's foolish of me to worry about that." She caught his gaze in the mirror, her mouth a twist of displeasure. With him? With herself? He wasn't sure, but she went on. "And that's my hang-up, not theirs. But if your parents were supportive of your decision to not go to law school like you said, what was all that about today?"

"You're not the only one with hang-ups. Or so my mom says," Jeremy admitted. "Ever since I decided to go for a dual master's in business and computer science, I distanced myself from anything having to do with the law firm. It was easy most of the time. I left for school, was only home for holidays, and right after graduation I moved to New York."

He shrugged, trying to play it off like it hadn't been a problem. In reality, the time away, the distance he'd purposefully put between himself and his parents—and even Michael, unless his kid brother visited—had eaten away at him.

Rosa turned around, leaning her butt up against the dresser's edge. Her red and white candy-cane-striped house socks drew his attention when she crossed her feet, her arms mimicking the same pose over the *Pride and Prejudice* quote on her sweatshirt. The shot of color from her socks next to her nondescript grey sweatpants epitomized the flash of attitude she seemed to like throwing at him every once in a while.

"And today?" she asked.

"Today was me, and probably my dad too, trying to feel things out. I haven't been back that long, and I know he's leaving the ball in my hands. Letting me decide what I'm comfortable with, especially when it comes to the law firm."

"I guess I can see why you may not have wanted to share all that with me before, though some type of warning would have been appreciated."

"You're right."

"But there's something else I want to ask you about." She didn't elaborate, and he followed her gaze to her nightstand. A set of wooden rosary beads pooled next to a sepia-toned photo of her parents when they were younger.

Her top teeth set to work worrying her bottom lip. Something else was on her mind. Or still didn't make sense to her.

He waited, knowing she'd share her thoughts when she was ready.

"What I don't know is," she finally said, her head tilted in question as she stared at him, "where does Cecile fit into this puzzle?"

He gave himself a mental smack upside the head, remembering

the snide ex-girlfriend routine Cecile had put on today. Like he and Rosa didn't have enough problems already without adding an old ex to the mix.

"Your—how did you put it the night of Yazmine's wedding?— oh, yeah, 'family friend' seemed to imply that she was or is more than just a *friend*."

The crazy side of his brain wondered if, based on the finger air quotes she put on the last word, Rosa might be jealous.

The saner side, the one interpreting her pursed lips and tapping foot, told him pissed might be a better description.

Damn. He'd miscalculated. Again.

"Cecile and I dated a long time ago."

"Narrow that time frame down a little more for me, please." Her tone implied that wasn't a request.

He rubbed the back of his neck, the tension headache he'd been fighting off threatening to go nuclear on him.

"We dated at the end of my senior year of undergrad, while we were both at Northwestern. To be honest, I knew it would please my parents and, since I was struggling with the law-school-versus-computer-science indecision, I gave things with Cecile a shot."

"She hardly strikes me as someone you pity date. That's more like—never mind." She swiped a hand through the air. "Were you two serious? I mean, if you moving back to Chicago opens the door for the two of you getting back together, don't let me stop you."

"No!" Jeremy was off the bed in a flash, grasping Rosa's forearm crossed in front of her chest. "There's nothing between me and Cecile."

"I need you to tell me the truth, Jeremy."

The hurt pooling in her brown eyes crushed him.

"We were together for a few months. That's all," he rushed to reassure her. "She figured out that we wanted different things. I needed to get away from the suffocation I felt here, and she craved the lifestyle we'd been raised to expect. When I left to start grad school early in the summer, we broke things off. Mutually. And she went to France to study art history."

Rosa stared at him intently, as if weighing his words.

"Cecile's family and mine are connected through Sherman and Harold. Those two have a history that goes back even before they started the firm together. But I have no plans of getting back together with her. That would be true even if you and the baby weren't in the picture. Though I'm happy you both are. In the picture, that is."

He slid his hands up her forearms to cup her shoulders. Desperation driving him to reach her.

"I am committed to you and our baby, Rosa. You have to believe that."

"I want to," she whispered. "But I'm afraid."

"Don't be."

Her full lips quirked in a poor imitation of her usually gentle smile. "It's not that easy. I know the pressure of doing something for family out of guilt. Only, your answer was to escape, eventually all the way to New York. You still don't have resolution with Sherman. I'm not even sure you're at peace with yourself."

"That doesn't matter," he argued.

"Yes, it does. How can I be confident that you're ready to start a family with me, if you haven't worked things out with your own? My papi always said, familia primero."

Family first.

Jeremy had heard Reynaldo share the motto when the older man and his trío group, Los Paisanos, performed their songs. In fact, the last time had been at an impromptu concert almost a year ago here, in the basement, barely a month before Rey had passed.

Thinking of the older man, who had treated Jeremy like a son in the few years they'd known each other, and wondering how Rey would feel about him now, considering the difficult position he had put Rosa in, brought more shame on Jeremy's already burdened shoulders.

"You told Dolores that I'm familia now too," he argued, his heart pounding with the fear that she might be slipping away from him. "Are you saying that, because of my past, you're going to shut me out?"

"Of course not. We can't undo our mistakes or take the blame for the mistakes others have made." She uncrossed her arms and put her hands on his chest. "You and Sherman are good men, Jeremy. Don't you want to try and make amends with your father before you become one?"

He closed his eyes, the fight draining out of him.

Damn it, he didn't want her to be right.

"You should go to the firm's holiday party on Wednesday," she said.

That got his attention. "Are you sure you're up for it?"

"Oh, I'm not going." She made a wide-eyed are-you-kidding-me face as she shook her head. "No, I'll stay home and rest, but you"—one of her hands patted his chest— "you can make it. Don't you think?"

He frowned, not keen on leaving her alone. Certain she'd gripe again about not needing a babysitter if he said so.

Instead, he settled for leaning down to press his forehead against hers. The faint scent of her coconut-vanilla lotion teased him. "I think I'd rather we just kiss and make up. Doesn't that sound good?"

Her fingers flexed, tugging on his sweater. For a hot second, he thought she might take him up on his suggestion.

"Oh, I wish it were that easy," she said softly. "Unfortunately, doing what feels good is how we got into part of this predicament in the first place. I'm afraid you're solo, my friend."

And with those last two words, she effectively killed all hope that he might get lucky with a good-night kiss.

Disappointed, Jeremy backed up a step. The serious, uncertain expression on her beautiful face let him know that despite her banter, he hadn't quite convinced her that he was worth believing in yet.

Chapter Fifteen

"¡Ay Dios mío, que sinvergüenza!"

Rosa laughed out loud at Yazmine's spot-on description of Cecile's behavior the previous day. Most certainly the socialite had behaved shamelessly.

"Please tell me Jeremy put that woman in her place!" Yaz slowed her car as they approached a red light on their way to Queen of Peace just before noon on Monday.

Jeremy had been called into the office for a meeting, so Yaz had shown up to "Drive Señorita Daisy," as she'd announced when she walked in the door.

"He did, kind of. I think?" Rosa frowned. "Really, the whole visit was surreal and Cecile was only a small part of it."

"Bueno, chica, you need to go to that holiday party with him," Yaz said.

"No, I'm staying home."

"You said you were feeling better. Is that not true?" Her big sister gave her a stern once-over as the light turned green.

"Estoy bien," Rosa reassured her.

"If you're fine, then you need to take your butt to that party. Don't let Cecile get her manicured talons in him again."

"¡Ay!" Rosa huffed in frustration. "We are not adolescents vying for the hot guy's attention."

"You're right, but like I told you on Thanksgiving, if you plan to be a part of Jeremy's life, then people like Cecile, events like this swanky holiday party, are par for the course."

"I know."

"¿Pero?"

"But what?" Rosa really wanted to twist in her seat and glare at her sister. Too bad riding in the car exacerbated her nausea so she had to keep her eyes on the horizon ahead.

"I know you, and when you get petulant like Lilí, you're hiding something."

"¡Ave Maria purísima!"

"Hail Mary nothing. If you want to keep whatever it is to yourself, fine. But take it from me." Yaz pulled up in front of the school and put her blue Ford Focus in park. "Hiding out in Oakton, sending Jeremy on his own to an event I personally don't think he's thrilled about attending, based on off-the-cuff comments he's made in the past, is not the smartest move. ¿Me estás escuchando?"

"Yes, I'm listening to you," Rosa complained. She unbuckled, then reached for the door handle.

"You said you were going to do what's right for you and your baby, and I'm telling you—" Yaz jabbed a finger at Rosa, emphasizing her point. "Staying away from that part of his life is not the right thing. Damn, girl, he's putting up with daily phone calls from Tía Dolores. That says a lot! Jeremy's stood by you. If you're well enough to go with him, don't you think maybe you owe it to him to do the same?"

Rosa slung her messenger-bag purse over her shoulder and pushed open the door. "I'll think about it."

"¡Ay, que cabeza dura eres, chica!"

Hardheaded?

Whatever.

With a grumbled adios, Rosa stepped out of the car.

Rosa scanned the expanse of the private room at the five-star steak and oyster house hosting the Taylor & Millward holiday party in downtown Chicago.

The diverse mix of people on the seventy-five-plus guest list had surprised her. Off to the left, near the open bar, a group of University of Chicago and Northwestern University law students mingled with several local judges and well-known politicians. Professional athletes and local celebrities chatted with legal assistants, secretaries, and interns. Seasoned lawyers from the firm as well as from the district attorney's office networked with up-and-coming younger ones. She'd been impressed with and pleased to meet the president of the local Latina lawyers' alliance, a fellow Puerto Rican who, like Rosa, enjoyed swapping stories of their visits to the Island.

Sure, some women wore elegantly cut cocktail dresses, sparkling jewels, and designer heels Lilí and Yaz would drool over, but Rosa's forest-green lace sheath dress and low heels weren't out of place like she'd worried. Besides, as far as she was concerned, she had the best accessory, the most handsome man in the room. Who just so happened to place his arm around her waist at that exact moment.

Tingles of heat shimmied from her waist, across her hips and lower. She leaned into his side, finding his nearness reassuring, and peeked up at him from under her lashes. ¡Que guapo!

Handsome indeed! Jeremy's dirty-blond hair had grown a little longer in the past couple of weeks. The sides now skimmed the top of his ears. The length made his hair wavier, and her fingers itched to comb through it. His charcoal suit with tiny white pinstripes fit him like it had been tailor made, snugly giving in all the right places. Like his broad shoulders, strong biceps, firm thighs. A-plus effort on the part of his tailor, who certainly knew how to cut a man's suit to draw the eye.

Bueno, hers anyway.

Jeremy smiled down at her while at the same time he acknowledged the older gentleman standing to his left. With the crowd's din, she couldn't hear what the other man said, but she didn't mind. She was more focused on the change she felt in Jeremy.

Earlier, when they'd left his BMW with the valet and turned to head inside, she'd caught the uncertainty in his blue eyes.

Outside on the sidewalk, Jeremy had reached for her hand, drawing them to a halt.

"Are you sure you're up for this?" he'd asked for at least the third time since she'd come downstairs back at her house.

His obvious discomfort had made her long to soothe him, but that wouldn't solve anything. Plus, she refused to let him use her as an excuse to bail on the evening.

"Yes, I'm sure," she'd assured him. "I took a nap after work, and I'm feeling fine right now."

"If you get tired or your stomach gives you trouble, just say the word and we'll be out—"

"Jeremy," she'd interrupted him, knowing exactly what he was going to say because he'd already told her. Twice. "If I need to head home, I'll let you know. But right now, it'd be great if we could get out of the cold. I'm sure your parents are excited to see you."

He'd responded by pressing a warm kiss to the back of her hand, following it up with a whispered thank-you. A gesture that warmed her heart, and took her mind off her own misgivings about being here.

Inside, they had been ushered to the private area as soon as Jeremy gave his name. They'd wound past white linen-draped tables with muted candle lighting attended to by strategically placed waiters in red oxford shirts with thin black ties and dress pants. Touches of the holiday season accented the room. A beautifully decorated Christmas tree stood to the right of the hostess table and poinsettias accented the space. Rosa had spotted a gleaming brass menorah displayed on a decorative side table next to a piano whose ivories were being tickled by a middle-aged man crooning about having a blue Christmas.

Admittedly nervous, she'd hoped the song didn't prove to be prophetic. Especially considering how horribly things had gone at the Taylors' penthouse last Sunday.

Inside the private room, Laura and Sherman had stood by the door, waiting to greet them. There had been a brief male staredown between Jeremy and Sherman. Father weighing son. Son weighing father. Then, to Rosa's relief, with a hearty clasping-of-the-elbows handshake, the two had exchanged relieved smiles and the awkwardness had eased.

Sherman had greeted her with a warm handshake, but Rosa had

been pleasantly caught by surprise when Laura had opened her arms for a hug.

Jeremy's mom had softly whispered, "Thank you *so* much for coming," and her tight hug had touched Rosa, easing her qualms.

Now, an hour and a half later, Rosa had been introduced to so many people the names had become a blur.

The older gentleman standing next to Jeremy shuffled a bit to his left, angling his back to the crowd and stepping closer to include Rosa in their conversation. With his dapper deep cranberry-colored suit, black silk cravat, and wizened eyes, he reminded her of a cool cat time-hopping from Chicago's prohibition era. Only his fedora was missing.

"Jeremy tells me you're a librarian—is that right, young lady?" he asked in a gravelly voice.

"Yes, at a small private school in Oakton," she answered with a polite smile. Her legs were starting to tire from all the standing, but she pushed away the fatigue.

"If I know Laura Taylor, she'll have you volunteering for her Literacy Ball in no time." The old man tipped his Scotch on the rocks at her, the veins in his pale hand visibly pronounced as it shook slightly. His friendly smile deepened the wrinkles in his face. "That woman is a dynamo when it comes to helping causes."

"So I've heard." Rosa took a sip of her water with lemon. "Any cause that benefits reading is certainly something I can get behind."

As Jeremy added his agreement, his hand began drawing a tiny circle on her hip. The motion sent answering swirls through her, distracting her from the conversation.

The crowd around them shifted, and across the room, Laura caught Rosa's eye. Jeremy's mom beamed at her. Then someone touched Laura's elbow to gain her attention, and she turned her attention to them.

Yaz had been right—it was good that Rosa had come.

By sticking to her preconceived notions regarding the snootiness she'd anticipated from many in Jeremy's social circles, she had been behaving just as poorly.

A modern-day *Pride and Prejudice* situation if she'd ever been party to one.

Why not embrace what was, truthfully, her first real "date" with Jeremy?

Once she'd gotten past her nerves, and Jeremy himself had relaxed, she'd focused on the night out with him.

Whether to make her or himself feel more comfortable, Jeremy had remained by her side the entire time. Well, except for one quick trip to order a drink at the bar. Cecile had approached him then, offering her cheek for a kiss hello. Jeremy had obliged, then deftly stepped aside, scooped up his gin and tonic and Rosa's water, and headed back to her. The socialite had yet to say anything to Rosa, but that was fine by her.

There were plenty of others she enjoyed meeting.

Jeremy had smoothed over any awkwardness by introducing her without a specific label—no "girlfriend," "good friend," or "mother of my illegitimate child"—going with a simple "someone special I've known for several years." That worked for her. And hadn't led to any intrusive questions.

A waiter approached, a shiny silver tray of sushi rolls held aloft in his hand. Rosa turned her head away, hoping to discourage him from stopping. She'd caught the smell earlier and her stomach had rolled in protest.

"—the scholarship students are around here somewhere. You might be interested in meeting some."

The matching expectant looks on the older man's and Jeremy's faces alerted her that they were waiting for her to reply.

"I'm sorry—I didn't quite catch your question."

The gentleman leaned closer and looked about to say something when a shiny silver platter with perfect bite-sized rolls of white rice, seaweed, veggies and some type of raw fish appeared right under Rosa's nose.

One whiff of the fishy smell and Rosa's stomach revolted. Nausea rose up her throat and she pressed a hand to her mouth. Jeremy must have clued in to her calamity because he brushed the tray aside, bending down to whisper in her ear.

"Are you okay?"

She shook her head, unwilling to risk a verbal answer at the moment.

"Excuse us, Mr. Douglas," Jeremy quickly said. "We need to take care of something."

Rosa hoped her eyes expressed her apology to the older man as she backed away, then spun and made a beeline for the ladies' room.

Winding her way through the crowd, Jeremy at her side, she prayed she'd get to the restroom in time. They turned the corner into the dimly lit hallway next to the kitchen door, hurrying past framed, autographed pictures of famous athletes and movie stars eating at the restaurant. Normally she might have stopped to take note of a few. Not right now.

Instead, she hit the women's door with a flattened palm and raced into the last of the three stalls, barely registering the unique floor-to-ceiling light wood doors that closed off each stall completely.

"Do you want me to come in with you?" Jeremy called.

"No! Go back to the party," she answered. The last thing she wanted was to draw attention by having him stand watch outside. "I'll be fine."

"I don't—"

"Please. Go. I'll text you if I need anything."

She heard the outer door close seconds before she lost the contents of her stomach in the toilet.

Fifteen minutes later, the worst had passed and the dry heaves slowed. Hands trembling with fatigue, Rosa tore off some toilet paper to dab her face. She sagged back against the thick wood door, waiting for the spasming in her stomach to ease. Her legs heavy, she wanted nothing more than to slide down to the floor in a heap, but even though the ceramic bowl with its gold accents looked clean, and the modern artwork and deep cranberry-painted wall spoke of the restaurant's opulence, no way was she sitting on the floor of a public restroom. Yuck.

The outer door opened and Rosa expected to hear Jeremy calling out to her. Instead, the voice that carried into her stall belonged to a more recent acquaintance.

"She's supposedly related to one of Jeremy's friends from New York," Cecile was saying.

"She flew in just for tonight?" another female voice answered.

"No, she lives somewhere outside of the city. In the burbs of all places." Cecile's scandalized twist of the word "burbs" expressed her sentiments on non-city living. "She works at a small private school as a teacher—no, a librarian."

Rosa realized the two women were talking about her at the same time it became apparent that neither had bothered checking the stalls for occupants. Granted, the wooden doors ran from floor to ceiling, with no gap between the door and the support walls so you couldn't peek in or out.

The sound of water running indicated they were at the sinks directly across from the stalls. Probably touching up their makeup, maybe adjusting their Spanx.

A tiny flicker of guilt flared in Rosa at the catty thought. It was quickly doused when she heard the other woman's nasally voice announce, "Well, she seems rather bland if you ask me. Nothing for him to get excited about. If you want Jeremy for yourself, I'm sure you could win him back."

The snide comment had Rosa pushing off the stall door to stand tall. Yazmine's admonishment rang in her head, warning her not to let Cecile get her talons in Jeremy again. Cautioning Rosa that she had to get used to dealing with women like Cecile and her bosom buddy.

Cowering in the stall was not what her sister had meant.

Nor was it indicative of the strong woman she was determined to be for her child.

Straightening her shoulders, Rosa unlocked the door, jerked it open, and stepped out.

Dios mío, what she wouldn't give for a still photo of the jaw-dropping shock on the socialites' artfully made-up faces. Cecile's red-painted lips opened and closed like those of a fish in distress.

Her partner in crime stood about Rosa's height, her figure a few too many candy bars shy of being slender. The young woman's short, bottle-blond bob curled around her pale face, huge diamond studs flashing from her ears. Her shocked gaze traveled from Rosa's head down to her sensible heels and back up.

Apparently neither woman had the audacity to say anything, much less apologize, so Rosa took the high road.

"Hello," she directed to Cecile's sidekick, proud of the calm evenness in her voice when, inside her, the good girl who didn't like making waves quaked. "If you don't mind. I'd like a word alone with Ms. Millward."

Both women blinked in surprise, their eyelash extensions fanning their cheeks. Cecile recovered first, nudging her friend in the side with her elbow.

"I'll be—I guess I'll head to the bar," the woman stammered, shuffling quickly to the door.

Once they were alone, Rosa moved to the sink next to Cecile's.

"There's no need to be catty about this. You have a history with Jeremy, and you see me as an interloper." Rosa stuck her hands under the tap, activating the sensor. Warm water cascaded over her hands. She glanced up, snagging Cecile's narrowed, suspicious gaze in the mirror spanning the length of the wall above the brick-red-tiled counter.

"The thing is," Rosa continued, "you and I may both want to be with Jeremy, but it's not entirely up to either of us."

"Oh really?" Cecile answered, one of her perfectly plucked and shaded eyebrows arched in defiance. Her skinny right hip jutted to the side in a kiss-my-ass angle reminiscent of a petulant student.

Rosa barely stopped herself from rolling her eyes as she snagged one of the thick, clothlike paper towels from the woven basket in between the two sinks. She noted a second basket beside it with hand lotion, breath mints, and individually wrapped pieces of gum. While she desperately wanted to, no way was she rinsing her mouth out in front of Cecile. Who knew what the woman would make of that. Instead, Rosa grabbed two pieces of spearmint gum and faced her unwelcome nemesis.

"Yes, really," Rosa said. "Whether he wants to be with me or you or someone else, if you care for Jeremy as much as I do, it won't matter. As long as he's happy. That's what's important to me. I hope the same is true for you."

The black-and-white–checkered material of Cecile's off-the-shoulder cocktail dress rose and fell across her chest as she took a deep breath. She eyed Rosa skeptically, her red lips pursed in a pout many men had no doubt found enticing. "You're being too nice. What's the catch?"

"No catch." Rosa tossed the paper towel in the trash hole in between the sinks. "I'm not here to fight, or gossip, or create a scene. I'm here for Jeremy, because he invited me and I think it's important that he support his family and Sherman's firm. You're a part of that. I get it. We can be enemies, or we can be friends. I know which I'd like, but again, that's not entirely up to me either."

Cecile shook her head, a puzzled frown marring the porcelain skin on her brow. "I can't tell whether you're playing a good game, or if you're for real."

"Guess you're going to have to trust me."

Cecile let out an unladylike huff, and Rosa couldn't resist a tiny smile.

"Yeah, well, in this crowd, that's not always easy." The blonde turned to face the mirror. She ran the tip of a pinky along the edge of her lower lip, smoothing her lipstick. "You're right about one thing—Jeremy's a great guy."

Picking up her black clutch purse, Cecile eyed Rosa speculatively. "Be good to him, you hear? I'll see you around."

With a flounce of her full skirt, the socialite spun toward the exit.

"Cecile?" Rosa called, at the same time a voice inside her shouted for her to leave well enough alone.

The statuesque blonde paused, her hand on the twisted gold-plated door handle.

"I'm glad we cleared the air," Rosa said in her best no-nonsense librarian tone.

"Sure." With a "whatever" shrug of a slender shoulder, Cecile pulled the door open. "Oh, hi, Laura!"

At the sight of Jeremy's mom standing in the doorway, Rosa sagged against the bathroom counter. The tile edge dug into her hip, but she barely noticed.

Dios mío, had Laura heard any of the conversation between Rosa and Cecile?

"Good evening, Cecile. I trust you are enjoying yourself?" Laura asked.

"Of course," the blonde answered, all pep and positivity. "Just freshening up a bit."

Cecile slid around Laura and disappeared, the *tap-tap-tap* of her heels echoing down the hall.

Rosa grabbed another cloth paper towel to dab at the beads of sweat dotting her upper lip. Standing up to Cecile had drained her of the little remaining oomph she'd had left after getting sick. It was time for her to head home.

"Are you doing okay?" Concern laced Laura's question. She hurried over, the taffeta material of her ankle-length skirt billowing around her legs. Earlier, Rosa had admired Laura's simple yet elegant navy dress with its long skirt, high waist accented by a knotted bow, and cap-sleeved top that skimmed the edges of her shoulders and hugged her trim torso.

Reaching Rosa's side, Jeremy's mom wet a towel under the faucet and pressed it to Rosa's forehead. "Jeremy got waylaid by one of Sherman's junior partners, so he asked me to come check on you."

Eyes closed, Rosa gratefully accepted Laura's ministrations, the damp cloth cooling her heated face.

"I don't want to be a bother," she murmured.

"Nonsense." Laura's hand stilled on Rosa's cheek. "You're brave for even coming tonight. Though I have a feeling you did so more for my son's sake."

"Family is important to me."

"And soon, you and Jeremy will have a family of your own."

Rosa drew back, praying Laura hadn't come in here planning either to rally behind Jeremy's proposal or to argue against it. "Marriage isn't—I'm not sure—"

"That's okay," Laura said, stalling Rosa's objection. "Whether it's a traditional family or not is up to you, sweetie. It doesn't matter to me. And like you, I only want what's best for my son. I'm sure you'll be the same with your child."

Heat climbed up Rosa's cheeks. Laura *had* heard her conversation with Cecile. Or at least part of it.

Ducking her head, Rosa reached for one of the mints from the basket, unwrapping it and popping it into her mouth.

"I won't lie to you." Laura slid her hands into the hidden pockets on her skirt. In Rosa's estimation, yet another bonus for the outfit, though the price tag probably wasn't. "For a long time, I hoped Jeremy would move back home, reconcile with Cecile, and settle down here in Chicago."

Rosa's heart sputtered, then dive-bombed to her belly.

Here it came, Jeremy's mom letting her know she wasn't good enough for the oldest Taylor son.

She sucked on the hard candy, the mint soothing her nausea, if not her rattled nerves. Her fist closed around the candy wrapper, the plastic crinkling in her grip.

"But, my son smiles with his eyes when he looks at you." A soft smile of her own accompanied Laura's words. "There's a calmness about him when I watch him with you. And I've no doubt he's here tonight because of your doing. For that, I am exceedingly grateful."

"He would have come anyway," Rosa responded, her mind reeling at Laura's admission. "He wants to be a good son."

A wistfulness washed over Laura's face, clouding her grey eyes. "I know he does. But sometimes, what you think is a good thing might not be the right thing."

Ave Maria purísima, wasn't that the truth.

Laura adjusted the ornate silver cuff bracelet on her left wrist, the gesture almost nervous. The worry stamping her features kept Rosa quiet.

"I don't know how much my son has shared with you about my background." The hesitance in Laura's voice, so unlike the woman the papers often described as possessing a commanding presence, had Rosa holding her breath in uneasy anticipation.

"It's no secret that I was a young, unwed, pregnant coed. I understand the shock, fear, uncertainty, and even the joy, you might be feeling."

Laura covered Rosa's closed fist on top of the counter. The empathy evident in the older woman's grey eyes, the earnestness in her expression, had Rosa's own eyes pricking with tears.

"Yes, I want what's best for my son, and my soon-to-be grandchild. But also for you. I've already said this to Jeremy, only I'm not sure he's inclined to listen right now. Maybe you will." Laura's grip squeezed over Rosa's fist. "This is not a time for rash decisions that will affect the rest of your life. Don't let anyone push you or rush you into something you're not ready for. Not now. Not ever. Okay?"

Rosa nodded dumbly, her mind reeling from the unexpected counseling and advice session with Jeremy's mom. With so many others urging her to jump into marriage, hearing the opposite from Laura, in such a compassionate way, made Rosa's heart swell with gratitude.

Chalk it up to fatigue or the rush of relief, whatever it was, Rosa's body finally decided it had had enough. Her legs wobbled, threatening to give out, and she sagged against the counter's edge.

"Easy." Laura grabbed on to Rosa's upper arm to help steady her. "I think it might be time for you to go home so you can lie down and rest. Will you be okay on your own while I go find Jeremy?"

Leaning her forearms on the counter for support, Rosa craned her neck to meet Laura's gaze in the mirror. "Yes, would you mind seeing if he's ready to leave, please?"

"I'll be right back," Laura promised, her hand gently stroking the back of Rosa's head before she turned to go.

As soon as the door closed behind Jeremy's mom, Rosa sank down to her haunches and burst into tears.

Dios mío, her stomach muscles ached. Her heart was heavy with indecision. Her head pounded with what-ifs and why-nots.

The conversation with Jeremy's mom should have been reassuring.

Instead, it confirmed Rosa's misgivings about jumping into marriage with him.

Laura said he hadn't wanted to listen to her advice about not rushing. He wasn't "inclined" was how his mom put it.

Rosa knew why.

That damn drive to prove he wasn't like his birth father. To make Sherman proud but still follow his own path. The same hardheadedness that had taken Jeremy away from Chicago when he wasn't sure how to live up to his own expectations when it came to his family.

What would he do if he felt he'd let her or their child down? If he thought he hadn't lived up to whatever expectations he put for himself when it came to being a father or a husband?

At some point, he was bound to disappoint them. No one was perfect. It was crazy to think that would never happen.

Could she depend on him to stick around when something went

wrong? Especially if he was only with her because he felt responsible.

She knew the heavy weight of taking on a role out of a sense of responsibility and duty. At times, it chafed. It stifled.

That's not what she wanted for Jeremy.

No matter what he said, she refused to go along with a decision he'd eventually come to regret. If she had to push him away to make him see she was right, she'd do so. It would hurt. But she'd do it. For him. For her. Most importantly, for their baby.

Chapter Sixteen

"Good morning!"

Jeremy smiled brightly when he turned from adjusting the heat on the stove burner to find Rosa shuffling into the kitchen Friday morning.

The stiff smile she greeted him with didn't inspire much confidence that today would start better than the night before had ended.

His spirits dipped a notch.

Wrapped in her favorite orange fleece bathrobe, its long sleeves and skirt covering her from her fingertips to her pink-polished toes, with her black hair disheveled, she looked adorably bed rumpled.

It was a true act of willpower to rein in the urge to scoop her in his arms, take the stairs by twos, and not stop 'til they reached her room.

Once there, he'd untie her thick robe and slide it off her shoulders. Taste her sweet lips and get high on her delectable vanilla scent. Slowly peel off her *Reading Is Sexy* pajama shirt and remind her how sexy they could be together.

Unfortunately, while his mind carried the two of them upstairs to start the day how he'd like every morning to begin, Rosa tugged out a chair at the kitchen table and sank into it. Her heavy sigh rivaled a moody teen's, cooling Jeremy's back-to-bed thoughts.

"How's your stomach feeling?" he ventured to ask.

"Ehhhhh," she muttered.

Okay then. Apparently not having coffee to help her wake up was going to be a pregnancy-long problem.

Rather than poke the ornery bear that she was this morning, Jeremy busied himself with pouring hot water from the kettle into a mug he'd already fixed with a mint tea bag and fresh ginger shavings.

Rosa wasn't normally a morning person anyway, but after the catastrophic end to their evening last night, he definitely hadn't expected Peppy Patty to come strolling down the stairs.

The moment he'd stepped into the ladies' room at the restaurant and caught sight of her tear-stained face, he'd been bombarded by regrets for bringing her to the party. It was an idiotic move on his part, especially given Dr. Jiménez's demand that Rosa get as much rest as possible.

He'd apologized repeatedly the entire time he'd led her down the blessedly darkened hallway, through the restaurant's kitchen, and out the back door, where the valet had brought Jeremy's Beemer for them. Thanks to the nice-sized tip he'd offered the kid.

Rosa had barely spoken the entire drive back to Oakton. Only one-word answers. If that.

Eyes closed. Head leaning against the passenger-door window. She'd made it clear she wasn't in the mood to chat. Once home, her horrified glance up the stairs had led him to swing her up in his arms. That she'd actually let him carry her up to her room was evidence of how poorly she'd felt.

Of course, as soon as he'd put her down, she'd shooed him away, her face pinched with fatigue. He'd tried chalking it up to her desire for privacy. Maybe her embarrassment over getting sick and having to sneak out the restaurant's back door.

But her refusal to make eye contact, the arm's distance she kept—hell, she'd even sidestepped a hug—had set alarm bells clanging in his head.

Something more than feeling sick was wrong with her. He had no idea what the hell it might be.

Last night he'd come *thiiiis* close to calling his mom, asking if Rosa had mentioned anything when his mom had checked up on her in the bathroom. Only it had been late and it had made no sense to worry his mom any more than she already was.

Instead, he'd sprawled fully dressed on Yazmine's old bed, listening as Rosa went to wash up, then returned to her room. The house had grown quiet and still he'd lain awake. Wanting to go to her, make sure she was okay. Certain she wouldn't want him hovering.

Eventually he'd washed up, too, then climbed under the sheets, worried thoughts keeping him awake until early morning.

Now, he watched as Rosa pressed the cup of medicinal tea to her lips and breathed deeply. Usually the minty aroma would do the trick. This morning, he hoped the concoction not only calmed her stomach, but also whatever else was bothering her.

Once she'd taken a couple sips, he grabbed the bottle of prenatal vitamins and a small plastic bowl filled with diced papaya from the counter. He joined her at the table, sliding the napkin and fork he had set out earlier closer to her.

"Gracias," she mumbled.

"De nada."

His Spanish skills got her lips to tug slightly in the right direction so he left well enough alone until she'd eaten several bites of fruit.

"Do you want to talk about last night?" he asked.

"Not really." Rosa wiped her mouth with the napkin, then took another sip of her tea.

"I'm sorry I had to send my mom to check on you."

"Don't worry about it."

He did though. Just like her dull responses and listless attitude worried him. Sure, she wasn't a morning person— he'd learned that real quick once he'd moved in. But this was more than simply not liking mornings.

He also knew Rosa didn't like to be pushed. Best for him to say his piece, then let it be. She'd either work through her issue privately or work up the nerve to spit out whatever was bugging her. On her own time frame.

"When you sent me back to the party, I headed for the bartender to get you a glass of 7 Up or ginger ale. It's supposedly good for upset stomachs. At least, that's what my mom always says. And, I figured they wouldn't have mint ginger tea anyway so why bother asking."

He was babbling, but Rosa's Mona Lisa smile had peeked out for a second behind her morning frown so he didn't care.

"I got halfway across the room when one of Dad's junior partners stopped me to ask about identity theft and malware programs. He's dealing with a pretty serious problem right now. Some new guy I hadn't met before happened to be standing nearby. He overheard and chimed in to say he's been having similar issues in the last week."

"Que horrible," Rosa mumbled into her teacup.

"Yeah, it is horrible. Not to mention, it's kind of a strange coincidence." Jeremy tapped his fingers on the wood table, mentally reviewing an idea that had come up when he'd been unable to sleep last night. "I plan to do a little digging into something when I get to the office today. Before our update meeting on the Japan project. If I find anything, I'll pass it along to Mark Henderson."

"Who?"

"The IT guy at Taylor & Millward. I'm wondering if anyone else at the firm has mentioned similar problems recently."

Rosa leaned forward, dangling her fork over the bowl of papaya as she decided which one to spear. Her front teeth set to nibbling on her lower lip, like the decision required rocket science, and Jeremy nearly reached out to rub her plump lips with his thumb.

"Do you know this Henderson guy?" she asked.

She stabbed a large piece of fruit with her fork, then sat back in her chair. Her eyes no longer quite as sleep groggy, she gazed back at him in question.

"Uh." He had a hard time computing what she'd asked, his attention still caught on her lips, now decadently sucking on the sweet papaya.

All he could think about was how delectable the juice would taste on her mouth if he closed the distance between them and kissed her. Or if he dribbled a little on her neck, then slowly licked it off.

"Jeremy?"

"Hmm?"

Rosa's morning frown deepened. "Henderson? Do you know him well?"

"Uh, yeah." Jeremy cleared his throat. Man, he had to stop his mind from meandering into the gutter before he got himself in more trouble here. He shifted in his seat, adjusting his jeans, and continued. "Mark, um, Mark Henderson's been with the firm for ages. I think he almost retired a couple years ago, but changed his mind. I wasn't here, didn't really get the full story. . . . Anyway, I'm not sure why he stayed."

He shrugged, mentally kicking himself for bringing up the fact that he'd left and had avoided anything to do with the law firm for a long time. No need to remind Rosa about that.

Instead, he got up and crossed to the fridge. "Want me to fry you an egg?"

She shook her head. "No thanks. You think you might have figured out something about the identity theft?"

"Maybe. All I have is a theory at the moment."

"It's good you're helping."

"I haven't done anything yet," he qualified, opening the bottom cabinet to the left of the stove to grab a skillet. He turned the burner switch on medium, then added a squirt of cooking spray to the pan.

"Still, you're trying. So," Rosa said, drawing out the word, "I think this is the second time you've mentioned a meeting about the project in Japan. But you haven't said much else."

Jeremy's hand froze as he cracked an egg against the edge of the pan.

Damn, he hadn't intended to bring this up until he had more concrete information. No use worrying her unnecessarily.

He pulled the shell apart with his thumbs, the egg white sizzling as it hit the hot surface. "Nothing's settled yet, but the merger between the two Japanese companies is progressing faster than either of the parties anticipated."

"That's—that's a good thing, isn't it?"

He glanced over his shoulder to catch Rosa tracing the edge of her mug with a finger, her gaze trained on the motion.

Was it a good thing?

He wasn't so sure anymore.

"For the companies involved, yes," he answered.

Once everything was finalized, they'd be ready to move forward with the IT upgrades. That meant someone from his company, presumably him, would head to Japan to lead the project.

The problem was, he didn't know if he wanted to go anymore. Not with Rosa suffering from this hyperemesis gravidarum. Once she got better, because, damn, she *had* to get better, there were a ton of baby preparations she'd need help with.

Nor did he care to be gone once the baby arrived. He wanted to be a part of the baby's firsts. Experiencing them alongside Rosa. Not remotely via Skype or through pictures sent over the phone and email.

"If things progress, you could leave again, right?" Rosa asked.

"The project lead would go. Maybe a few others to round out the team."

"And that's you. The project lead, I mean."

Technically, yes. Though he'd considered asking to be taken off even if passing up project lead might derail a potential promotion down the line.

Others in the company had moved to non-travel status when their wives were expecting or due to family health issues. His situation wasn't any different. Other than the fact that Rosa didn't want to get married.

"There are a few others who'd be interested in taking lead," Jeremy said.

"But they selected you."

"Well, yeah, but—"

"Don't." Rosa pushed back her chair, the wood legs screeching against the linoleum floor. "Think back to how excited you were when they offered you this opportunity. I remember it. I saw it on your face when you told me at Yaz's wedding. Before . . . before this."

She placed a hand over her belly, the long sleeves of her orange robe covering all but her fingertips. "Don't give up something you've worked so hard for, because of me." Her hand made a slow circle on her stomach, an expectant mother's caress. "Because of us."

"It's not that simple."

"I'm serious." That Fernandez stubbornness she rarely exhibited tilted her chin in defiance. Her hair a wild mess of waves framing her don't-mess-with-me glare. "Nothing good can come from regrets. I refuse to be the cause of them. You deserve better. Por favor, don't do anything rash."

"I'm not!"

"Just, slow down. And consider what might be right in the long run. For all of us." As quickly as it flared, Rosa's defiance drained away, leaving disappointment in its place.

Without another word, she stood and left the kitchen.

Jeremy watched her go, stunned by the downward spiral their conversation had taken.

Damn it! Why did everything keep getting so screwed up? Why did it constantly feel like for every one step forward, they wound up taking two steps back?

Anger and frustration flashed through him and he spun back around to the stove. Only then did he register the acrid stench of burnt eggs.

Great, seemed like everything was going up in flames this morning.

Dragging the skillet to the back burner, he twisted the heat off with an annoyed jerk of his wrist.

Rosa was right about regrets. They sucked.

But she was dead wrong if she thought he had any when it came to what they shared together. He'd do whatever it took to prove that to her.

Jeremy strode quickly toward his car in the darkened parking garage near the Taylor & Millward offices, hours past when he was supposed to pick Rosa up after Poetry Club.

The afternoon had completely gotten away from him.

The noon meeting at his office had been brief. With no new progress to report concerning the Japanese company merger. Shortly after, he'd spoken on the phone with Mark Henderson at the law firm. The older man had asked him to consider coming over to the T & M building to discuss Jeremy's theory about the identity theft problems in person.

The request wasn't one Jeremy took lightly. And Mark knew that.

Jeremy hadn't been to the Taylor & Millward building in years. But if he was right, Henderson needed to be aware of the cyber phishing their employees were dealing with and the very real potential that the law firm's system may have been hacked.

After speaking with Henderson and explaining a few diagnostic options, Jeremy found himself confronted with a decision: roll up his sleeves and help, or walk away. Again.

Rosa's advice that he find a way to make peace with the past wormed its way through his thoughts, her voice the sound of reason and encouragement whispering in his ear. So he'd listened to Mark's plea for assistance rather than dismissing it right away.

Jeremy hadn't anticipated that the discussion with Mark would turn into a fact-finding mission. A challenge Jeremy's penchant for problem-solving had pounced on, the same way it had when he was a kid and he'd gotten a new erector set or, later, when he was a member of the U of I Computer Science Department's HackIllinois team.

Once they started digging, time slipped away. Normally, Jeremy didn't mind the hours lost in combing computer files and mining data. Except that, when he finally took a brain break and glanced at his watch, Poetry Club had already started. He'd tried to send Rosa a text message letting her know he was running late leaving the city, only to realize that his phone must have fallen out of his pocket on the drive over. Without his cell, he couldn't send a text. Instead, he'd used an office phone to leave her a voice message, then called Yazmine to see if she could pick up Rosa.

After the way they had left things this morning, he hated not having spoken to Rosa directly. The last thing he wanted her to think was that he'd forgotten about her depending on him for a ride home.

He approached his car and clicked it unlocked. As soon as he opened the driver's side, he spotted his phone wedged between the front seat and the door well. He quickly tugged off a leather glove to tap his screen unlock code. His gut clenched when he noted the number of missed calls and texts from Rosa.

Received word that Father Yosef wants to meet TODAY after Poetry Club. Just wanted to give you a heads-up. 2:05 PM

Tried calling, but got your voice mail. Father Yosef will meet us in the library at 4:30. Didn't want you to be surprised when you arrived. 3:12 PM

Poetry Club is starting. Hope you're okay and I see you at 4:30. 3:29 PM

Father Yosef should be here any minute. No need for you to come now as it'd be worse for you to walk in late. 4:28 PM

6:13 PM shone on the top of his cell screen.

Damn! He smacked the steering wheel with the palm of his hand.

No doubt the difficult meeting with her family priest— the one Jeremy had promised to attend in a show of unity— had finished a while ago. Even worse, she hadn't called or texted to let him know how it had gone.

How in the hell did everything with them keep getting so screwed up? His attempt at doing a good deed for the firm had wound up making him disappoint Rosa.

She had stood by his side last night at the firm's holiday party. Not that he couldn't have gone on his own, but being with her had given him a sense of calm reassurance, as it typically did. He should have been there today, doing his best to help her fight to keep the job she loved.

She had every right to be pissed at him for his no-show.

Frustrated with himself and the situation, Jeremy started his car and peeled out of the parking garage.

As soon as he reached a red light, he listened to her two messages. The first, left shortly after her initial text, repeated the typed message alerting him of the meeting with Father Yosef. By the second voice mail, apparently left as the students arrived because he could hear a couple of the boys in the background, her voice sounded concerned.

Or was that doubt?

Ah man, no telling what she'd been thinking thanks to his incommunicado status.

Hopefully Rosa had noticed his voice message after Poetry Club though based on her last text, it didn't appear so. That meant she'd gone into her meeting with Father Yosef wondering if Jeremy had completely blown her off.

At the next red light, he tried calling, anxious to speak with her. It went straight to voice mail. Either her phone was off or she was avoiding him. Neither option bode well for him.

Evening post-work traffic heading out of the city made the drive to the suburbs miserably slow. By the time he turned onto Rosa's street well over an hour later, he'd passed frustrated and moved on to full-blown aggravation.

He pulled up in front of her house, noting the black Corolla parked in the driveway. Lilí was home for school break.

Disappointment blew through him, and his spirits sank to his toes.

If Lilí was back, Rosa wouldn't need him to stay with her anymore. His temporary roommate status would be revoked. Without him being any closer to convincing her that she could depend on him for the long haul.

Jeremy hurried up the front walk, lowering his head against the bitter winter wind. He searched his key ring for the Fernandez house key, but at the last moment opted to knock instead. With Lilí here, the dynamics changed; it didn't feel right walking in unannounced.

Hunched against the cold, Jeremy waited for someone to answer.

When the door opened, Lilí's gamine features, framed by her pixie haircut, peeked out from behind it. She smiled a greeting, but he couldn't help noticing the dark shadows around her hazel-green eyes.

"Hey, Jer." She beckoned him inside, closing the door behind him. "I'm glad you're here."

"It's good to see you." He wrapped her in a brotherly hug. "I hadn't heard when you were coming. The drive up go well?"

"Yeah, same boring trip up I-57. I meant to call Rosa yesterday, but I've been helping one of my dorm residents with something personal, probably a little beyond regular RA duties. Anyway, between that and finals, I wasn't thinking about much else."

"Everything okay?" He held her at arm's length, noting the absence of her usual mischievous spark.

Lilí dragged a hand through her short hair, leaving her wispy spikes askew. A weighty sigh escaped her as she shook her head. "Not really, but you have your own problems to deal with."

She backed into the living room, eyeing him as he unbuttoned his winter coat and hung it, along with his scarf, on the rack near the door.

"I'm not sure what's been going on down here," Lilí said, "but when I picked up Rosa at Queen of Peace, she had this pinched look on her face. The kind she makes when she's trying not to cry. And when I asked where you were, she gave me an evil eye Tía Dolores would be proud of. We got home and Rosa went straight to her room."

Lilí jerked a thumb toward the stairwell a few feet away in the foyer.

"Did she say anything about Father Yosef?" he asked, edging his way toward the bottom step.

"Nope. But I saw him pulling out of the school parking lot as I was turning in."

"Has she eaten anything? Maybe asked for some mint ginger tea or warm rice water?"

"Mint what?"

"The antinausea drinks I've been brewing for her?"

Lilí did a double take, her brows diving down in a deep frown. "Do I look like a Starbucks barista to you?"

Great. Apparently whatever she'd been dealing with hadn't diminished her smart-ass attitude. Sounded like he'd be giving some cooking lessons in the near future. Dolores would hunt him down if he left without showing Lilí how to make the remedies the girls' madrina had taught him.

On top of that, add the Sears Tower level of worry he'd face once he was home, wondering if Rosa was feeling sick, with Lilí incapable of helping her.

"Look, I'm gonna head up to check on your sister," he told Lilí. "Can you stick around the house for a bit so we can go over a few things?"

"I'm not going anywhere." Lilí pulled her cell from her back jeans pocket and checked the screen. "I told this student I'd be available if she needed to talk."

"Great, I'll be back down in a bit." He started up the stairs, coming to a halt when Lilí called his name.

He looked over his shoulder to find her at the bottom of the stairs.

Maybe it was the lighting in the foyer, but the shadows under her eyes looked more pronounced all of a sudden. Her usually impish grin was more a twisted frown as she stared up at him.

"Don't upset her," Lilí warned, hands on her hips. "If you do, you'll have to answer to me."

It was almost comical, Lilí thinking she could scare him off.

In the past, he would have hit her with a smart-ass comment of his own. Knowing she'd answer with a throaty laugh.

Now, he was afraid he'd already broken that promise, having upset Rosa one too many times.

He only hoped he could convince her to give him another chance. Taking the stairs by twos, he hurried to her room.

"Está bien," Rosa answered when he knocked.

Since she'd answered in Spanish, he figured she thought he was her sister.

"It's Jeremy," he clarified. "Still okay to come in?"

There was a pause, a brief second during which his heart skipped because he thought she might say no.

Her door-muffled "yes" had him turning the knob before she changed her mind.

He entered to find her sitting on top of her bed, legs stretched out, her back against the headboard. Her poetry journal, like a security blanket, rested on her lap.

Dressed in black leggings and a loose-fitting light purple sweater, with her black-stockinged feet and hair up in a ponytail, she looked like a young college coed, home for the holidays along with Lilí.

Her somber expression stopped him a few feet into the room. He took in her puffy, red-rimmed eyes. Noticed the tissue box tilted on its side, lodged between her hip and a round orange throw pillow. The pen wobbled in her hand, and he rushed over to sit on the edge of her bed.

"Rosa, I am so sorry I missed the meeting with Father Yosef. Did you get my voice message?"

She nodded, a tear escaping to trail down her right cheek. She swiped it away, only to have another slip down the other side.

His gut clenched at the sorrow swimming in her brown eyes.

"I stopped at Taylor & Millward thinking I'd just have a conversation with Mark Henderson. Three and a half hours later, I'm elbow deep in the firm's computer system. Digging for clues that might lead to how they were hacked. Time got away—"

Rosa pressed her fingertips to his lips, silencing him.

"Can we . . . would you mind if we didn't talk for a few minutes?"

He shook his head. His mind zeroing in on the warm, gentle pressure of her fingers. His heart torn by the sadness on her face

"Maybe we could just sit here together?"

Surprise at her unexpected request robbed him of his voice so he answered with a jerky nod.

Rosa put her journal and pen on the nightstand, then pushed aside the throw pillows and tissue box and scooted over to make room for him beside her.

Jeremy toed off his brown oxfords and joined her.

The mattress dipped under his weight, Rosa's right hip and thigh pressing against his left side. He figured she'd slide farther away. Instead, she twisted to lay her head on the front of his shoulder.

Instinctively his arms wrapped around her. The need to comfort her, soothe the feelings he'd hurt, overwhelmed him. His fingers combed through the ends of her ponytail and he dropped a kiss on top of her head. She burrowed closer.

The next thing he knew, they were both skooching down until they lay side by side, Rosa's head on his chest, one of her legs crooked over his. He tightened his hold on her, relishing the sensation of her soft curves molding against his body.

She traced a circle around one of his shirt buttons, dragged her finger down to the next one, leaving a trail of heat that he swore seared his skin. His pulse picked up speed, sending blood low in his body.

"Your heartbeat is fast," Rosa murmured, pressing her open palm to his chest.

"Yeah, well, you do that to me."

He felt her soft chuckle, her chest vibrating against his. The weight of her full breasts teased him with the need to touch them, taste them as he had their one night together.

As difficult as it was though, he had to rein in his desire for her. He couldn't risk making another misstep with her.

Then Rosa leaned across him to press a kiss over his heart.

Jeremy reacted without thinking, rolling with her on the bed until she lay on her back. Propped up on his elbows, his lower body lay flush with hers, thighs to thighs, hips pressed to hips. His fast heartbeat no longer the only indication of how she affected him. Aroused him.

She cupped his face, gently caressed his cheeks, sliding her hands behind his head to pull him down for a kiss.

Their lips nipped, nothing more than a gentle brush back and forth. But it wasn't enough. He tasted her lips with a light flick of his tongue and she opened for him.

The kiss deepened, tongues wrestling, brushing, tasting. She was honey and nectar and everything sweet, and he craved more.

Angling onto one elbow, he caressed her hip with his other hand.

Her fingers gently brushed along his neck, traced the shell of his ears with feathery light touches that drove him to the edge. He continued his own delicious exploration, snaking his hand under her sweater, up her trim waist, past her rib cage until he captured one of her breasts in his palm. Her nipple pebbled through her lace bra, and she broke their kiss on a gasp.

She gazed up at him, eyes lust-filled, lips red and swollen from his kisses, chest heaving with each rush of breath.

"You are so beautiful," he whispered. "I can't tell you how badly I want you."

Her eyes fluttered closed, an adorable blush stealing up her cheeks.

"You're pretty easy on the eyes yourself. But I believe this . . ." She arched her pelvis, pressing his arousal oh-so close to the entrance it desperately sought. ". . . gives away your little secret."

Lust coursed through him, and he nearly groaned on the wave of desire that pulled him under.

Her cheeky response and her innocent blush combined to create the unique charm that made her irresistible.

He rocked his erection into her, quickly ducking down to cover her answering moan with an open-mouthed kiss. She devoured him in response. Matching his fevered kiss with her own. Stroke for stroke.

His fingers brushed the soft skin along the top edge of her lace bra, his thumb coming across the front clasp. In seconds, he had it undone. One bare breast spilled out, and he filled his palm with the precious weight, rolling the hardened nipple between his thumb and forefinger.

She moaned deep in her throat and her hands moved to his back, kneading his muscles, before sliding lower to grab his ass. His arousal pulsed between them. Need quickly built, and he knew if they didn't stop soon, he was in danger of exploding.

As much as he wanted to take what she seemed to be offering, a small, still sane part of his brain knew this—no matter how damn good it would be—wasn't the answer to their problems. No matter how badly he wished it could be.

Reluctantly, he tore his lips from hers, twisting to fall onto his back beside her.

Shoulder to shoulder, neither one said a word, their heavy breathing the only sound in the room.

After several minutes had passed, Jeremy broke the silence. "I have to say, that was not the greeting I expected on my race to get here."

"Me either."

He chuckled at her surprised tone.

Their hands touched in between them, and Jeremy clasped hers, pleased when she linked her fingers with his. He raised their joined hands, bringing them to his lips for a chaste kiss.

"I'm really sorry I wasn't there for you this afternoon," he said.

"I know."

"I mean it. I hate that I let you down."

"I know," she repeated.

Jeremy propped up on his elbow to look at her. "How do you—"

"Because I know *you*, Jeremy." She combed the fingers of her other hand through his hair, a gentle yet sad smile curving her lips. "You feel compelled to help others. That's part of what I lo—like about you."

Her smile dimmed. Determination jutted her jaw at the same time sadness filled her eyes.

"I'm happy that what kept you from coming here today is something that could bring you closer to your dad. That's important."

"Yes, it is, but so is this." He squeezed her hand for emphasis. "Us."

"I agree. I also know that we both have personal problems we need to figure out. You might be leaving again, for an extended time. And that's okay," she rushed on when he started to speak. "Like I said this morning, no rash decisions you might regret."

"What makes you think I'll regret anything?" he asked, stymied by her continued use of the word.

Rosa stared up at him intently, as if she was weighing what to say.

"What is it?" he urged.

With a little shake of her head, she rolled away from him and sat up. Her back to him, she reached under her sweater to clasp her bra, then stood and moved a few feet away to her dresser.

Jeremy slid across the bed. He swung his legs over the edge to sit facing her.

"Father Yosef and I had an interesting conversation this afternoon," Rosa said.

Interesting was better than troublesome, which was what Jeremy had expected.

"After talking about the options the school board will consider, termination or wait and evaluate my year-end review, he asked about me." Her gaze met Jeremy's in the mirror's reflection. "About us."

"And I wasn't there." Guilt burned in his chest.

Rosa ducked her head. "Maybe it was for the best."

He didn't like the sound of that. Him not being with her was not "for the best." Not in his mind anyway.

"I mean, Father Yosef's not advocating having children out of wedlock," Rosa continued. "But we talked about the sanctity of marriage. Of two people willingly making a loving commitment to each other. Like my parents did."

Turning around, she motioned to the picture of Rey and Marta on her nightstand.

Jeremy gazed at the candid shot, taken while the couple was dancing. Cheek to cheek, smiles brimming with joy, they exuded happiness.

Man, how he wished he'd had a chance to know Rosa's mom. Her dad had been an amazing person—full of life, his love for his family evident in his words and actions. Jeremy bet the same could be said for Marta Fernandez.

"I'm guessing your parents have that same loving commitment, too," Rosa continued. "Am I right?"

He nodded, remembering how, as a teen, he'd noticed his parents often found little ways to express their love and appreciation for each other. Maybe it was Sherman bringing home fresh flowers because Jeremy's mom liked having them around the house. *Nature's perfume,* she used to say. Sometimes Sherman would even surprise her by special ordering a variety she couldn't find locally. His mom would randomly bake Sherman's favorite dessert, instead of asking the cook to take care of it. Then, she'd bring a piece of warm apple pie to his home office when he was up to his ears prepping for a case. Some nights, Jeremy would find his mom sitting in his dad's office reading on the settee, just so they could be together.

He'd been away from home for so long, he hadn't thought about those times. How they had shaped his view of the type of marriage he wanted. With Rosa.

"I understand the commitment, Rosa. I want to take care of you and the baby."

"The thing is, I don't need a caretaker." Her thin shoulders lifted and fell in a shrug, a pained expression stamping her beautiful features. "I have family and friends who can help with that. But before we can discuss any type of future for us, I think you have to figure things out with Sherman. And your job. For yourself. Not for me. That won't happen if you're driving in and out of the city, stressing about not being here or racing to get somewhere on time."

Jeremy leaned forward, resting his forearms on his thighs. He dangled his hands between his legs and stared down at the cream-colored carpet. The ups and downs of the last twenty-four hours had him feeling like a rookie boxer dodging punches from the left, only to be hammered by one from the right.

"And I need to deal with the situation at Queen of Peace. On my own."

A few minutes ago, they'd been ready to get as up close and personal as a couple could get. Too bad he'd been a gentleman and stopped things from progressing.

Now, she was giving him the stiff arm. Pushing him away, again.

Out of the corner of his eye, he caught sight of his oxfords, one sole-side-up where he'd kicked it in his haste earlier. Anger, rooted in hurt over her emotional about-face, raced through him with wildfire speed. Snagging his shoes with two fingers, he shoved his feet into them and shot to a stand.

"I don't know what you want from me, Rosa. If I walk away, I'm irresponsible. If I push to stay with you, I'm being a selfish prick. You admire that I try to help others. But you want to do things on your own. It's like I'm damned if I do, damned if I don't."

Frustrated, he shoved a hand through his hair.

"That's the thing, I don't want you to feel damned. I don't want that for either one of us." Arms crossed in front of her chest in a defensive pose, Rosa's eyes shone with unshed tears. "Dios mío, we said we were going to take things slow. Then you moved in with me and we started playing house together. In here, it's all good." She waved an arm through the air in a jerky move, indicating the room, her voice rising with anxiety. "I'm not denying there's a strong attraction. But we can't ignore the outside world."

She shook her head, her dark ponytail swinging from side to side. Her full mouth thinned. He watched her swallow hard, pulling herself together at the same time her words were pulling him apart.

"Lili's here now, so I won't be alone." She spoke softly, but firmly. Her mind apparently already made up. "You should head back to the city, take care of things at home."

Subtext: this wasn't his home.

Even having anticipated her words, they still stung.

Suddenly he was tired of trying to be the good guy. Tired of her keeping him at a distance when they both knew how good they were together.

"You're not going to get rid of me that easily, Rosa," he warned, hands shoved in his pants pockets to keep from reaching for her. Frankly, he wasn't sure if he wanted to hug her or shake some sense into her.

"I'm not trying to get rid of you," she answered sullenly.

"Yeah, well, you sure coulda fooled me."

He spun away from her before she saw the hurt he could no longer hide.

"Jeremy, wait!"

He paused in the open doorway, refusing to look back at her. "I'm going downstairs to show your sister how to brew the different teas, explain why the hell there's a trunk-full of olive jars in the pantry, and make sure she knows how to puree the chicken soup I made that's in the fridge. That way, when Dolores calls me to check on you, I can tell her I left you in good hands. Just not mine."

Chapter Seventeen

"So how come Jeremy didn't come tonight?" Yaz asked late Saturday evening when the family had all gathered at her and Tomás's house. "I didn't hear what you said earlier."

Probably because Rosa had purposefully dodged the question.

She didn't want to talk about Jeremy or what their plans might be. It was much easier to keep pretending she was fine when, in reality, a maelstrom of mental what-ifs continually bombarded her.

Besides, tonight was about celebrating together. The annual Hanson Academy of Dance Christmas recital had ended a little over an hour ago and, as was their family tradition since Yaz had been a student at Hanson's, long before she'd become the lead instructor, they were enjoying mugs of homemade hot chocolate. Or in Rosa's case, mint ginger tea.

She flicked a nervous glance at Lilí, hoping her younger sister might be inclined to pick up the conversational hot potato Rosa silently tossed her way.

Sitting cross-legged on the floor in front of the fireplace, Lilí blew into the mug cradled between her hands. She'd made herself comfortable, her brown knee-high boots strewn nearby, the long sleeves of her coral turtleneck sweater pushed up to her elbows.

Maria, already changed into pink princess pajamas, lay sprawled on a blanket beside her tía, playing with two Barbie dolls.

Next to Rosa on the black leather couch, Yaz sat with her feet tucked underneath her. She snuggled against Tomás, casually sipping her drink and awaiting Rosa's response.

Rather than chime in, Lilí scrunched her face at Rosa in a good-luck-with-that expression. She knew it'd been two days since Jeremy had left their house, angry and upset. Two days of Rosa only hearing from him via text. Two *long* days of Rosa, and strangely Lilí too, moping around the house.

Something was up with Lilí. She'd been texting nonstop with someone, taking phone calls in her room for privacy.

Plus, she'd been sticking close to home, quiet and pensive. Two traits no one normally associated with her. Yet every time Rosa asked about it, all she got in reply was a lame, "It's nothing for you to worry about. You've got your own problems."

Too bad Lilí was right.

Father Yosef had emailed yesterday afternoon, before the final bell rang for the weekend, to let Rosa know that he and two other board members planned to attend the open mic poetry night on Thursday. He'd heard positive things about the group and wanted to see for himself.

Rosa couldn't figure out whether the board members showing interest was a good or a bad omen.

She was worried and wanted to share her concerns with Jeremy, get his perspective. Only, he hadn't answered her calls. His brief text messages claimed he was up to his ears helping Mark Henderson. Apparently the cyberattack on the law firm had hit other employees, too. Mark and Jeremy were working on solving this problem and taking measures to prevent future ones.

Her head told her she should be happy for Jeremy. Helping at Taylor & Millward was a huge step.

Her heart, however, hurt every time she remembered their last conversation, when she'd foolishly sent him away.

"Hey, quit ignoring me." Yaz nudged Rosa's knee with her bare foot. "What's going on with Jeremy?"

"Está ocupado," Rosa hedged. She took a sip of her tea, avoiding her older sister's gaze.

"What do you mean, he's busy?" Yaz pressed. "He came to the recital last year. With everything that's going on between you two, I figured he'd want to be with the family tonight."

"He's with *his* family."

"Okay, but—"

"Can we just drop it?" The question came out more curt than she intended. The tense silence that followed her outburst made Rosa feel even worse.

Yaz sat up, her stern frown drawing a deep V in between her brows. She gave Tomás's thigh a double pat, some sign between them he obviously understood because he set his mug on the glass coffee table and rose.

"Vente, Maria, time for bed."

"Aw, Papá, just a little more playtime?" the little girl begged.

Sweetheart that she was, when her father shook his head, Maria scrambled up, quickly giving her tías and mamá good-night hugs.

As soon as her husband and daughter were down the hall out of earshot, Yaz pounced.

"Okay, what gives? Jeremy was here practically twenty-four-seven, living with you like familia. And now, poof!" She made two fists, quickly opening them in jazz hands like a magician. "He's gone?"

"He's not gone. He's simply, not here." Rosa motioned toward Lilí with her tea mug. "Anyway, Lilí's home so I'm not alone like Dr. Jiménez ordered."

"Hey now, I'm happy to be here for you, but don't use me as an excuse to not deal with whatever's going on between you and Jeremy." Lilí set her mug on the brick lining the fireplace, then scooted closer to rest her forearms on the coffee table. "Or, with you."

"I'm fine," Rosa fibbed. "Still worried about my job, but I'm hopeful."

"I'm not talking about work. I'm talking about *you*. And why you keep pushing Jeremy away when I don't really think you want to."

Her little sister's keen perception surprised Rosa. She had tried so hard to keep her doubts hidden.

A log crackled in the fireplace. It toppled to the bottom of the pile, sending sparks into the air behind the grate. Rosa stared at the flames wrapping and dancing around the wood pieces, her thoughts as swirly and chaotic.

"¿Qué pasa?" Yaz asked. She angled on the couch, cross-legged, to face Rosa.

The flickering fire and dim light from the end-table lamp cast the room in shadows, giving an air of privacy ripe for an uneasy confession.

Rosa sucked in a shuddering breath, then nervously admitted, "When I spoke with Father Yosef on Thursday, he was more understanding than I expected. I mean, my job isn't in the clear, but he didn't push for a quick marriage as a solution."

"That's good," Yaz said when Rosa stopped to gather her nerve.

"Yeah, it is. But the conversation also stirred up fears I've been struggling with. For a while now."

"About what?" Lilí asked.

"About . . ." Rosa balanced her mug on her thigh. The heat seeped through her black leggings, warming the edges of the cold angst she'd been hiding. "I've spent most of my life, bueno, since Mami died anyway, often doing the right things for the wrong reason."

"What do you mean?"

Rosa's shoulders sagged at Yaz's simple question, the uneasy guilt she'd carried for so long weighing on her.

Father Yosef had told her she needed to forgive herself for the role she, mistakenly according to him, believed she'd played in Mami's death. One way to go about doing so was to swallow her self-imposed shame and share her secret with her sisters.

"I used to—no, that's a lie. Most of the time, I still do blame myself for Mami's death."

Lilí's shocked gasp matched Yaz's horrified double take.

Rosa took advantage of their stunned silence to rush on before she wimped out. "Mami wouldn't have been on the road that day if I hadn't been acting foolish during lunch at school. Thinking I could be flirty, like you, Yaz, and catch one of the football players' eye. Instead, I tripped and spilled my entire spaghetti tray down the front of my uniform. I was so embarrassed, I called Mami in tears, crying for her to come pick me up so I could go home and hide. It was silly. Dumb of me to try stepping out of my comfort zone to be something I'm not. If I hadn't done that, if Mami had stayed at work, she never would have been in that accident."

"Ay, Rosa, how come you never said anything?" Yaz scrambled over on the couch to pull her into a one-armed hug, nearly knocking Rosa's mug out of her hand. "It wasn't your fault. None of us have ever thought that, right, Lilí?"

"¡Nunca!" Lilí punctuated her "never" with a sharp jerk of her head.

"That's what Father Yosef said," Rosa murmured.

"Well, that's one thing the old man and I agree on."

"Ay, don't be disrespectful!" Rosa admonished her younger sister.

Lilí waved off Rosa's words with a scowl. "Whatever."

"I don't see what this has to do with you and Jeremy." Yaz crooked an elbow on the back of the sofa, resting her head against her fist.

"Stepping in to try and fill Mami's shoes, at first anyway, was like my penance. After a while, it became second nature. Doing for others gave me comfort. But, there were times when I resented the expectation that I would always take care of everything." Rosa leaned forward to set her tea on the coffee table, too stressed to care about finishing it. "I don't want Jeremy to get to a point where he feels a similar resentment toward me, or our baby. You know, because him sticking around is expected. Instead of what he really wants."

"That's jumping to a pretty big conclusion, don't you think?" Yaz asked.

Rosa shrugged listlessly. She was tired of worrying. Tired of being afraid he might not want to be with her. So tired of the mental what-if game. "I don't know. It's just, I need him to be sure this is what he wants. That it's not an obligation."

"What about you? Are you sure?" Yaz's softly spoken question had Rosa's heart swelling with a sort of pleasure pain.

She was sure that she missed being with him. Seeing his smile when she came down first thing in the morning. She missed the comfort of sitting on the couch reading quietly together or watching a show on TV. Their interesting conversations and how he valued her input. The way he took care of her and his determination to be a good person. Both traits she identified with and were important to her.

And she really missed the rush of desire, the heady wantonness that consumed her only in his arms.

Was she sure she wanted to be with him?

Tears clogging her throat, Rosa nodded.

"Then why did you make him leave?" Lilí asked.

"Because, well, I'm not . . ." Overwhelmed by the uncertainty of whether or not she'd made a mistake, Rosa buried her face in her hands.

"What is it?" Yaz combed her fingers through Rosa's hair, the gesture a comfort from her childhood when Mami and Papi would do the same.

Lilí came around to the other side of the couch, pushing Rosa over so she sat sandwiched between her sisters.

"I know I've asked you this before, but I need you to be truthful," Lilí said, her tone oddly firm, no-nonsense. "Did Jeremy do something to hurt you?"

"Estás loca?" Yaz cried.

"No, I'm not crazy, I heard raised voices in Rosa's room. When Jeremy came downstairs he was pissed. Or maybe hurt. Hell, I'm not sure because I raced upstairs to check on Rosa."

"So they had an argument. What couple doesn't?"

"Right, but you never know what goes on behind closed doors."

"Ay, no seas tan exagerada."

"I'm not exaggerating," Lilí insisted.

"Stop," Rosa grumbled. "Enough already."

Their bickering mimicked her own internal wrangling, and she was exhausted by it all. With a bone-weary sigh, she fell back against the leather sofa cushions.

"No, Jeremy did not hurt me. I sent him away because I want him to really think things through. If he isn't sure. If he's only with me because he feels responsible." Shivers of fear and regret shook her shoulders. "I couldn't live with myself. And besides, I told you two already, and I said the same to Father Yosef. I have to prove to myself that I'll be okay as a single parent. Regardless of what others in our community might think."

"Good for you!" Lilí wrapped her arms around Rosa and gave her a tight squeeze. "I haven't said this enough, but I'm proud of you, girl. I love you!"

Rosa gave her little sister a tremulous smile. She placed a protective hand on her belly. "If I can't stand up for myself and my baby, what kind of mamá would I be, right?"

Jeremy washed his hands in the men's restroom near the IT office at Taylor & Millward late Wednesday afternoon. The tired, scruffy-faced reflection staring back at him was a good indication of the long hours and late nights he and Henderson had put in since last week. They'd painstakingly scoured the firm's computer system, searching for the vulnerable point through which the hackers had gained entry.

Initially they had figured out that the HR files had been breached. That's what had led to the identity theft issues the two men from the holiday party had mentioned.

Jeremy and Henderson's concerns had morphed into bigger ones when they'd realized private client information might have been compromised. If that had happened, it would be a huge hit for the firm and their clients' trust in them.

After all his searching, Jeremy felt confident they'd dodged that bullet. Good or bad, only their employee database had been targeted.

He dried his hands, tossing the paper towel into the trash bin across the tile floor in a fairly decent imitation of a basketball star. Scoring the shot wasn't much cause for celebration, but he'd successfully solved the firm's problem and that did warrant one. The thrill of challenging his computer skills and besting the hacker energized his tired body.

Leaving the restroom, he headed down the empty hall toward Henderson's office. This late in the evening, all of the HR and service staff housed on the third floor had left, the hum of chatter and business earlier in the day now silenced.

As he approached the door, he heard Henderson speaking to someone and assumed the older man had received a phone call. Jeremy pivoted into the office and halted when he caught sight of Sherman bending over the glossy black conference table to peer at the computer Jeremy had been using over the past week.

"Uh, hi. Didn't expect to see you," Jeremy said.

It was actually the first time he'd seen his dad since Jeremy had started working with Henderson. Sherman had stayed away, getting updates via phone. A couple of times, Henderson had ventured up to the sixth-floor partner offices, but Jeremy had stayed behind.

Supposedly his dad was trying to give him some space. At least, that's what his mom had said when Jeremy had finally decided to pick up his cell the third or fourth time she'd called.

Sherman straightened at Jeremy's greeting. With his feet set in a wide stance, hands on his hips, he made a commanding figure. Even this late in the day, his light blue button-down shirt remained wrinkle-free and crisp, his navy and yellow striped tie still knotted tightly, as if he'd just arrived at the office instead of having clocked probably twelve hours already.

"Henderson called with the good news," Sherman announced, a satisfied grin spreading his lips. "I figured it warranted a thank-you in person. You've done an incredible job for us."

He held out his hand, and Jeremy shook it, pleased by his father's praise.

"It was good teamwork," Jeremy answered, tilting his head toward Henderson, who stood in front of the window overlooking the darkened city skyline.

The older man's grey hair was rumpled, his shirtsleeves haphazardly rolled up. His tie had been tossed aside around one when they'd ordered Chinese food for lunch.

Now that Jeremy stopped to get a good look at Henderson, he noticed the haggard tiredness emphasizing the older man's craggy features. The last few days had whipped him as hard as they'd whipped Jeremy.

"You're not fooling anyone, kid. I provided some assistance, but *you* identified the problem." Henderson pointed a stubby finger at Jeremy. "I already told Sherman, I wound up behind the eight ball on this."

"Hey, I just happened to be in the right place at the right time to hear the right information." Holding his arms out at his sides, Jeremy gave a little shrug, loath to take all the credit. "I got lucky."

Henderson shook his head, crossing the grey carpeted floor to reach for his phone when it vibrated on his desk. "I'd say *we* got lucky. No question about it, you saved our asses, kid."

"Just doing my job."

The older man exchanged a look with Sherman before pocketing his phone. "Funny you should say that. I'm going to step out, give my wife a quick call to let her know I'm alive while you two gentlemen talk. It would be great to hear good news when I come back."

Sherman nodded at Henderson as the man strode past him on his way out.

Jeremy glanced between the two of them, wondering what he'd missed during his short bathroom break.

"Son—no, scratch that. This is business. I don't want any misunderstandings about where this is coming from." Sherman swiped a hand in the air as if erasing a whiteboard in front of him. "Jeremy, over the weekend while we discussed this fiasco, Henderson shared an idea with me. One that I believe holds strong merit."

Jeremy eyed his father, uncertain where the conversation was headed.

He'd spent the better part of a week holed up in this office, Henderson by his side. They'd discussed their work and Jeremy's double master's in computers and business. Henderson had shared plenty of stories about his wife and two grown kids; Jeremy had sidestepped questions about his personal life, unsure how the hell to explain what was going on between him and Rosa.

As he thought back over his conversations with Henderson, he didn't recall the older man mentioning talking to Sherman about anything other than updates on the hacking.

"I don't think I know what idea you're talking about," he told his dad.

"Well, it's more like a recommendation," Sherman qualified.

He pulled out two of the black leather rolling chairs side by side at the conference table, motioning for Jeremy to join him.

"It's been a while since you've darkened the halls of Taylor & Millward, hasn't it?" Sherman asked.

Since he'd left for grad school eight years ago. Holiday visits didn't really necessitate stopping by the firm, and that's mainly when Jeremy had come back to Chicago.

He nodded in response, uncomfortable with the direction this conversation could take. Even though he knew it was long overdue.

"I'm not going to lie and say I haven't looked back at that time, wondering if I put too much pressure on you in some way." Sherman scratched his chin, his tone contemplative.

"Dad, this is all on me. My hang-ups. Not yours."

"Yeah, it didn't take me long to realize that."

Jeremy huffed out a laugh at his dad's sarcastic tone.

Sherman leaned back in his chair, fingers interlocked at his waist. "Here's the thing. All your mom and I expect from you and your brother is that you work hard, earn the respect of others, and make a positive difference."

Jeremy's chest tightened with the pressure of wanting to live up to Sherman's expectations.

"In *whatever* career you choose," his dad added.

"I know."

And he did. Now.

Time and distance had helped, but in large part his change of perspective was thanks to Rosa.

Missing Chicago and his family had precipitated his decision to request an office transfer a year ago. Even then, though, he'd been deluding himself that simply moving back was enough. Until Rosa had challenged him to figure things out—for himself, not just for her and the baby— he hadn't fully accepted that the onus was on him to take the first step if he wanted to make amends with his dad.

A step like requesting unplanned vacation from work so he could devote all his time to the problem at Taylor & Millward. Helping a place, and the people, he'd distanced himself from all those years ago. All because of foolish pride and embarrassment.

"Am I happy you transferred back to Chicago? Yeah, I am."

Sherman bobbed his head, his office chair moving in tiny bounces with the motion.

"Am I thrilled you're here?" He jabbed his pointer finger onto the conference tabletop, emphasizing his last word. "In our offices, proving outright the value of your skills and expertise? As a founding partner of this firm, you better believe I'm thrilled.

"But as your father . . ." He leaned forward, grabbing Jeremy's knee in a firm grip. Sherman's piercing stare, the one that had famously swayed juries and judges, ensnared Jeremy, refusing to let him look away. "As your father, I am damn proud of you, son."

All the air rushed out of Jeremy, his body going slack as sweet relief flowed over him. It didn't matter that he was almost thirty, he could be seventeen or seventy and he'd still get choked up hearing those words from Sherman.

Resting an elbow on the table, he kneaded the knotted muscles in his neck and swallowed past the baseball-sized lump in his throat. "That . . . that really means a lot to me."

"It's the truth. It's always been the truth."

Only Jeremy had been too young and immature, and then too far away, living halfway across the country, to mend the broken connection with his dad.

They sat in a companionable silence, the weight of guilt finally lifting off Jeremy's shoulders.

After a while, Sherman thumped his fist on Jeremy's knee, then sat back in his chair. "You're probably wondering how that correlates to Henderson's recommendation."

"Well, yeah. I mean, he didn't mention anything to me."

"I asked him not to until this situation had been defused. Truthfully, Mark's had one foot out the door to retirement for several years now."

"It'll be tough to replace him."

"Yes, it will." His expression contemplative, Sherman stared out the expansive window at the city skyline outlined in lights against the dark evening sky. "We convinced him to stay on as a stopgap while starting a search for his successor. The thing is, until a few days ago, there hasn't been anyone he felt comfortable handing the reins over to."

Sherman shot Jeremy a sideways glance.

Jeremy blinked in surprise. No way was his dad implying what Jeremy thought he was.

"Mark's old school, like me," his dad continued, swiveling his chair to face Jeremy. "He recognizes that technology is changing faster than he can. Taylor & Millward doesn't need a head of IT— we need a director of cybersecurity. Someone with his finger on the pulse of what's cutting edge, with proven success and the résumé to back it up. Someone like you."

His head reeling, Jeremy stared back at his dad, unable to form coherent words. Long ago he'd given up on the idea of joining Sherman at the firm. Instead, he'd broken off and gone his own way. Ignoring the hole his decision had created in his life.

Until Rosa had challenged him to deal with it.

"I know you've got a good position with an eye on a promotion in your company. And you stepping in to help us now doesn't mean you're ready to jump on board. So I'm not asking you to give me an answer right away."

Sherman pushed his chair back to stand, then waited for Jeremy to do the same. "Simply, think about it. Talk with Mark. More importantly, talk it over with Rosa. This would be another big change for you, but it would keep you from going overseas."

Which meant he'd stay close to Rosa and the baby. A definite perk.

"I'm . . . surprised," Jeremy admitted, "but intrigued."

More than intrigued.

Excitement hummed like a swarm of bees in his ears.

"That's good to hear." Sherman clasped Jeremy's hand in a firm grip. "There isn't anyone else I'd trust more than you with this role, Jeremy. I say that as a partner, as well as your father."

A lightness he hadn't felt around his dad in years lifted Jeremy's spirit. "I appreciate your vote of confidence."

Sherman tugged him into a back-slapping hug.

"Mark mentioned an early morning tomorrow to wrap up the security audit. Why don't you get out of here for a bit?" his dad said. "Go home and get some rest. Or better yet, take a drive out to the suburbs."

Stepping back from his dad's hug, Jeremy grinned at the subtext in his father's suggestion. They both knew why the suburbs held so much appeal.

Rosa.

Man, he couldn't wait to see her. Tell her about this opportunity that, without her encouragement, probably never would have presented itself.

A drive to the suburbs, to the place and the amazing woman he had come to think of as home, was definitely in order.

Chapter Eighteen

"Rosa's already in bed," Lilí said when she opened the door to the Fernandez house.

Jeremy's elation fizzled like a dud firework as he stepped into the foyer.

Running on adrenaline fumes laced with excitement, he'd driven to Oakton on autopilot. His only thought: get home to Rosa and share the news.

She'd understand why his heart pounded and his hands shook with nervous energy over Sherman's offer. Because she was the only person he had truly confided in.

Right now, all he wanted was to see her brown eyes sparkle with joy, her lips tugging up in her shy smile. He'd even take an "I told you so" if it came from her.

Jeremy pushed up the edge of his winter coat sleeve to find the gold hands on his watch pointing to nine forty-seven. No wonder the upstairs windows were darkened.

When he'd pulled up and noticed the television's flickering light behind the living room curtains, he'd crossed his fingers that it meant Rosa was still up, maybe watching another documentary.

"Did you not try calling her before you drove all the way out here?" Lilí asked.

Jeremy shook his head as he unbuttoned his coat and shrugged out of it. "Thought I'd get here faster and surprise her."

Dumb move on his part.

Surprise! She was already sleeping.

Lilí turned the front lock, then spun on her black furry house slippers to face him. Arms crossed, she leaned back against the door. Sporting fuchsia fleece pajama bottoms and a black long-sleeved top with fuchsia polka dots, her face washed clean of makeup, she looked ready for bed herself.

His adrenaline fading, he suddenly felt a little foolish for racing out here. Especially since he'd left in a burst of anger the last time and had only spoken with Rosa sporadically via text message in the week since then.

"How's she doing?" he asked, ashamed he didn't know himself.

Lilí's mouth pressed into a thin line. Her youthful face was pinched with worry.

"Did something happen with Rosa? Or the baby?"

His pulse skipped, fear flicking it into high gear.

If something had happened and he hadn't been here for her, he'd never forgive himself.

"Not yet," Lilí answered. "But the way she's stressing about this Poetry Club event tomorrow night, who knows. Sounds like the kids are crazy nervous, so Rosa's stayed late every day this week meeting with them. Even though I can tell she's dead tired by the time she calls me to pick her up."

"Is she eating?"

"Some. But whenever I try to fix her a bowl of soup or remind her to rest she complains about me nagging. That why it's about time you got your butt back out here!"

"I've been dealing with—"

"Yeah, I know, some hacker thing," she interrupted, pushing off the door and advancing toward him. "But if you really care about my sister, and damn it, the other night you told me that you do, you don't 'peace out' like that!"

Hands raised, palms facing her, as if to ward off the anger and hurt flashing in Lilí's hazel-green eyes, Jeremy backed up until the heels of his oxfords knocked into the bottom of the stairs.

Guilt seared his chest. He should have checked up on Rosa. Not sulked, upset because it seemed she could so easily push him away.

Disappointed in himself, he sank onto the third step.

"What are you doing?" Lilí came to a stop. Hands on her hips, she scowled down at him.

"I need to sit for a minute."

"Yeah, well, we have a couch, you know." She waved her left arm toward the living room.

Jeremy shook his head at her exasperated tone.

Yes, he knew they owned a couch. He and Rosa had spent plenty of time on it together lately. He opted to keep that comment to himself. Lilí might take it the wrong way and she was already in protective sister mode.

"This is fine." Shoulders hunched, he bent forward to rest his forearms on his knees. "It's been a stressful week."

"Tell me about it." Lilí's furry black house shoes shuffled into his view seconds before she nudged his shoulder for him to move over so she could join him. "Between worrying about Rosa and this . . . *thing* with one of the freshmen on my dorm floor, I've gotten almost zero sleep."

"What's going on at school? You mentioned something the other day. Are you having a problem?"

"Not me. Another girl." Lilí's heavy sigh sounded like she had the weight of the universe on her petite shoulders. He certainly understood how that felt. "I knew being a dorm resident advisor might be difficult sometimes, but this situation she's going through, it's terrible."

Jeremy angled his body, leaning his back against the banister so he could face Lilí.

The poor kid looked like he felt—beat. Her fiery anger from moments ago had given way to weary angst, her brow puckered with a deep frown.

"You wanna talk about it?" he offered.

"Thanks, but I don't think so. It's pretty personal."

"Have you said anything to Rosa?"

"No way, she's got her own stuff to deal with. Plus, this is . . ." Lilí trailed off, her head bowed as she picked at her chipped purple nail polish. "This is life changing, and not in a good way. Rosa's so

softhearted and gentle, I know she'd feel awful for this girl. I do."
Lilí shot him a misery-laden glance. "I don't want Rosa worrying about
something similar happening to me, and I know she would." Lilí shook
her head back and forth in tiny, agitated jerks. "I don't wanna risk
getting her upset."

Sensing the angst building inside her, Jeremy gently put his
hand on Lilí's back, trying to offer a measure of calm. Whatever
had happened, and it didn't sound good, was eating at her. If she
didn't talk to someone about it soon, it could consume her.

"You know, beneath Rosa's shy exterior is a steely determination many don't take the time to see. Your sister's a lot stronger
than you think."

"I don't know," Lilí hedged.

"Here's what I *do* know—that gentle spirit of Rosa's makes her
a great sounding board. Her empathy is boundless because she
cares so much about others. I'll tell you, whether I wanted to or
not, she's helped me see a few things differently lately, for the better. Honestly, meeting her, getting to know and spend time with her
is the best thing that's ever happened to me."

"Pffff." Lilí huffed out a breath, knocking her bent knee against
his. "That's your hormones talking."

He laughed, pleased to see her impish personality peeking out
through her gloom.

"Here's a truth you can take to the bank," Jeremy told her. "If
you ever need to get something off your chest, I'm all ears. You
need help, just let me know."

Jeremy slid his arm around Lilí's shoulders, pulling her in for a
one-armed hug.

"What can I say, you're my favorite kid sister," he teased. "I'd do
anything for you."

For all the Fernandez sisters. Especially the one upstairs, who had
reminded him of the importance of family. And made him realize
how badly he wanted to be a part of hers.

"Thanks, Jer," Lilí said. "You're not so bad yourself."

"From your lips to Rosa's ears." Jeremy craned his neck to glance up
the stairs, where Rosa lay sleeping. Hope for the future burned inside
him. "I'm crossing my fingers and toes that she agrees with you."

* * *

Lilí's raised voice startled Rosa awake.

Sleep muddled, she pushed the covers aside, wondering who could be at the house this late. She slipped on her robe, fumbling to step into her house slippers in the muted shadows cast by the downstairs foyer light. As she pulled her bedroom door open wider, she recognized Jeremy's deep timbre.

He's here! The realization instantly cleared the sleep from her head.

Her heart leapt with delight at the idea of seeing him again after so many days. Excited, she hastened her steps, continuing into the darkened hallway.

Then Lilí said Rosa's name, her voice clearly upset, and Rosa came to an abrupt stop.

Worried about why Lilí and Jeremy would be arguing about her, she tiptoed closer to the banister, straining to hear better. Through the white wooden rails, she saw Jeremy sitting near the bottom of the stairs. Lilí stood in front of him, shooting him an annoyed glare.

He spoke in a soothing tone that apparently calmed her sister because the next thing Rosa knew, the two were seated side by side sharing a heart-to-heart.

She knew it was rude, but couldn't stop herself from eavesdropping. When she overheard Lilí reveal why she hadn't confided in her, dismay pricked her conscience.

Ave María purísima, she'd known something was wrong. If she hadn't been so wrapped up in worrying about Jeremy, she would have tried harder to pry the information out of Lilí.

Her mind tumbling through ways to politely interrupt them, Rosa missed part of Jeremy and her sister's conversation. She keyed in again in time to catch him saying something about her and the best thing that had happened to him.

Sucking in a shocked breath, she stumbled back against the wall, accidentally knocking her elbow on her bedroom door frame. Pain shot down her arm. Her funny bone had that tingle-hurt pain and she rubbed at it.

Dios mío, could he really be speaking the truth?

Rosa pressed a hand to her chest as if she could calm her pounding heart. Ay, she was afraid to hope. So afraid of getting hurt.

Lost in the swirl of doubts, she didn't notice Jeremy and Lilí had moved to the foyer until she heard the *click* of the front door bolt unlocking.

"Wait!"

The word slipped out as she lunged toward the banister, leaning over the wood railing.

His navy cashmere winter coat in hand, Jeremy came back into view at the bottom of the stairs. "Rosa? Are you awake?"

Embarrassed that they might think she'd been listening, she tugged the lapels on her robe tighter and skirted gingerly around the banister to the top step.

"Hi," she said softly.

"How are you feeling?" He raised a foot as if to move up the steps, then hesitated. Uncertainty crossed his face, and he stayed where he was.

Ay, how she'd missed him.

The long hours his texts had mentioned were evident. He looked tired, his hair mussed like he'd shoved a hand through it a few too many times. His grey suit pants and white dress shirt were rumpled, and several days of scruff shadowed his handsome face. Still, through his obvious fatigue, his blue eyes gazed up at her expectantly.

"I'm fine. The nausea's a little better," she answered. "I heard voices out here and wanted to check on Lilí."

"We didn't mean to wake you. I was just heading out."

He slipped his arms into his jacket sleeves, and she hurried down, desperate for him not to go yet. She hadn't seen him in days. These few moments weren't enough.

"Is everything okay?" she asked. "You didn't—didn't call or anything to say you were coming over. I would have waited up."

She reached the foyer, breathless with unease over what would bring him all the way out here this late.

"Bueno, if you two don't mind"—Lilí wagged a finger between Rosa and Jeremy—"this third wheel is going up to her room. Rosa, remember you need to get your rest. Tomorrow's going to be a long day. And you . . ." Lilí narrowed her eyes at Jeremy in warning. "Be nice to my sister, got it?"

"Got it." Jeremy gave her a thumbs up, punctuating his words.

"Smart aleck," Lilí grumbled. She edged around them, rubbing Rosa's arm in a loving gesture. "Estoy arriba si me necesitas."

"Gracias," Rosa murmured, touched by her sister's reassurance that she was upstairs if need be. Usually Rosa was the one taking care of others. The role reversal felt strange, but in a good way.

She watched Lilí head up the stairs, past the years of family pictures hanging on the wall. Her sister paused, kissed her fingertips, and gently pressed them to a candid photo of Mami and Papi laughing together at their twenty-fifth wedding anniversary.

The touching gesture sent a pang of longing through Rosa. Her parents' love for each other, and for all three of their daughters, had been powerful. Like a living essence, it still connected them.

That's what she wanted to create for her child, hopefully with Jeremy.

Once Lilí had disappeared down the upstairs hall toward her room at the back end of the house, Rosa turned to him.

An instinctive need to be close to him urged her to grab a hold of the unbuttoned edges of his coat and pull him in for a hug. But, despite what she'd overheard earlier, the unpleasant way he'd left last week and the short text messages he'd sent since then made her leery.

"How are things with the firm?" she asked.

He lifted one shoulder in a half shrug, like he was too tired to shrug them both. "There's one last security audit to complete, but if I'm right, we've finally got it under control."

"That's good, isn't it?"

He nodded in response and she racked her brain, desperately thinking of how to prolong their conversation.

Jeremy stared at her, his gaze pensive, his face unreadable.

Rosa ducked her head, her fingers nervously fiddling with the knot tying the sash on her fleece robe.

He covered her hands with one of his, stilling her motions. The warmth of his palm seeped into her, and she peeked at him from under her lashes.

"Yeah, it's a good thing," he said.

"And you drove out here because . . ."

"Because I missed you. And I wanted to see you."

His raspy admission had Rosa twisting her wrist so her palm met his. Their fingers interlocked.

"I missed you, too," she whispered.

Jeremy's lips curved, his smile shining in his tired eyes. "I got some surprising news a little while ago, and the first person I wanted to tell was you."

"Really?"

"Uh-huh." He lifted his free hand to tuck her hair behind her ear, his fingers continuing down to gently caress her jaw.

She leaned into his touch, craving more.

"But it's late, and I know how you need your beauty sleep or you're a grouch in the morning."

"What? I'm not—"

His arched brow halted her complaint.

An embarrassed flush crept up Rosa's face.

"Bueno, not always," she qualified.

"Uh-huh. I don't want Lilí blaming me when you bite off her head tomorrow."

"Whatever." Rosa wrinkled her nose in feigned displeasure as she gave his chest a little push.

His strong arms wrapped around her, and she welcomed his embrace, winding her arms along his waist. She laid her head against his shoulder, his coat's thick cashmere cushioning her cheek. Breathing deeply, she caught the faint hint of his musky aftershave and basked in the deliciousness of being near him again.

"Seriously," he said, his voice a low rumble. "I should have paid attention to the time. Lilí's right, with the open mic night tomorrow, you'll be on your feet more than Dr. Jiménez would probably like."

"She doesn't have to know."

"But I will."

Rosa bit back a resigned grumble. When had everyone else around her become such rule followers? That was her domain.

"So you drove all the way out here to say you have some surprising news, but it's now too late for you to tell me?"

She arched back to make sure he caught her are-you-kidding-me scowl.

Jeremy responded by bending down to press his warm lips to her forehead.

Her frown instantly dissolved. She closed her eyes, savoring the tingles swirling through her, even at this chaste kiss. If only he had aimed a little lower.

Far too soon, he released her and stepped back, bumping into the oak hutch nestled along the foyer wall. Their discarded key rings rattled, and the tall glass candle with the Virgin Mary's picture wobbled from side to side. Jeremy deftly reached out to steady it.

When he turned back around to face her, he pushed his open jacket aside and dug his hands in his pants pockets. "Fine, I'll spill the news. Do you remember me telling you that Mark Henderson almost retired a few years ago, but wound up changing his mind?"

Rosa nodded.

"Turns out, it wasn't a change of mind, but more like he stuck around while searching for a suitable replacement." Jeremy paused, rubbing at the back of his neck while he seemed to consider his next words. "According to my dad, Henderson's found the right guy. Someone Dad, as a founding partner, feels he can get behind and trust."

"That's nice." Jeremy's ambivalent expression didn't lend itself to her assessment of the news, and she frowned in question. "Isn't it?"

"It could be. I want to think it is." His head bobbed yes, but his broad shoulders shrugged a confusing maybe. "If I decide to accept."

Rosa gasped. She blinked several times, processing his words, completely stunned.

Him? Working at Taylor & Millward?

"Yeah, that's how I felt, too, when I first heard Henderson's recommendation." Jeremy chuckled wryly. He gently tapped her chin with his knuckle, and she realized her jaw had dropped open at his news.

"I-I'm surprised. The idea never occurred to me. I know you said you didn't want to work for the firm before. But a position in IT would be different."

"Actually, it's more than basic IT. They're asking me to be the new director of cybersecurity."

Wow! Rosa barely kept her jaw from dropping open again. The magnitude of what it would mean to him to work with his dad. The pride he would feel. More importantly, the wound it would heal within him. How she wanted that for Jeremy.

Yet, taking a position at Taylor & Millward was a huge step for someone who hadn't even taken a baby step into the firm's offices for such a long time.

"What do you think about the offer?" she asked softly.

"I'm not sure," he admitted. "It's definitely unexpected, and I need more details."

"Of course."

Jeremy rubbed at the scruff on his cheeks, his gaze unsure.

Up close, she could see the tiny lines of fatigue around his blue eyes, now clouded with indecision. Seeking to offer him solace, she brushed his coat lapels, smoothing the soft cashmere between her thumb and fingers.

"Working at the firm is an idea I gave up on years ago," he said, his voice raspy with emotion. "I figured Michael was a true Taylor, he'd follow in Dad's footsteps."

He winced, as if the thought pained him.

"Oh, Jeremy, you can't still think like that." Rosa's fingers tightened on his lapel. It was unbelievable that this man who exuded confidence, and often made her feel confident in herself, could harbor a doubt of such magnitude. "You're just as much deserving of Sherman's name as your brother."

His hesitant smile of thanks warmed her.

"It's taken me a while, but I'm getting it," he answered. "Working there this week, I don't know, maybe it was just the project and the challenge it gave me, but I found myself walking into that building every day invigorated. Even when I'd only gotten a few hours of sleep."

"That's a great sign," Rosa said. "Definitely something to put in the 'pro' column if you're making a list of the pros and cons about the job offer."

Jeremy laughed, the husky sound drawing a smile from her.

"What's so funny?"

He shook his head. "Not funny, more like charming."

Before she could decide if he was complimenting or teasing her, Jeremy cupped her shoulders with both hands, his face serious.

"One really important pro is that if I leave my current job to work at Taylor & Millward, I won't have to go to Japan. No more worrying about turning down that project, potentially torpedoing my promotion, so I can be here for you and the baby."

"Wait a minute." She frowned, replaying his words in her head and zeroing in on one key point. "What do you mean, 'torpedoing'? You said it wouldn't be an issue if you requested to be taken off the project, even though I told you not to do it for the wrong reasons."

Unease wormed its way through her, quickly growing in intensity.

"You can't make this decision, whether it's moving to the firm or staying where you are and vying for that promotion, based on what you think *I* need. This is *your* career. Something you've worked hard for."

"Yes, but you're part of the equation now. I have to consider what's right—"

"Don't!" she cried.

Horrified by what she was sure he'd say next, Rosa shook off his hands and edged away. Her worst fear sprawled between them like Lake Michigan separating its various shores.

Words like "have to" and "what's right" were nothing close to the terms of endearment she wanted, needed, from him. She refused to accept anything less.

At the bottom of the stairs, she took the first one, adding a measure of height to better meet him eye to eye.

"I appreciate you wanting to do the right thing, Jeremy. But let me assure you, the 'right thing' is for you to consider what will fulfill you."

She shook her head at him when he took a step toward her. It was difficult, but she forced herself to continue, determined not to show her devastation.

"You were right. It's late. We're both tired, and we've been under a lot of stress. Tomorrow's a big night for my students and me. Not to mention, with Father Yosef and two board members planning to attend, I need to focus on making a good impression. And you—"

She grabbed onto the railing, when what she really wanted was to grab on to him, beg him to see her as more than a responsibility. "You have a big decision of your own to make. An exciting one. And I'm so thrilled for you, whatever you decide. All I want is for you to be happy, Jeremy. If you are, then I will be, too."

Her voice shook the slightest bit on the last word, and she cleared her throat to cover the tremor.

She expected Jeremy to argue, like he'd done last week. Instead, he stared back at her, his expression contemplative.

He bobbed his head up and down in tiny nods. But she had no idea what he agreed with.

"Okay, I'll go," he finally replied, his matter-of-fact tone making her heart ache. "Know that, whatever happens, I won't make my decision lightly. And I definitely won't make it for the wrong reasons."

He snagged his keys off the oak hutch and pocketed them. "Get some rest. I'll see you at the open mic night tomorrow."

The door closed quietly behind him and Rosa sank onto the stairs. Tucking her feet under her, she laid her forehead on her knees and let the tears of disappointment flow.

Chapter Nineteen

"Thank you for coming. The students and I appreciate your support." Rosa hugged Father Yosef, then shook hands with the two school board members who had arrived at Queen of Peace's library with him.

"I'm Frank Walker. Thank you for the invitation." The middle-aged gentleman gave her a polite smile as he introduced himself, the room's fluorescent lights shining off his bald head. His khaki pants and plaid Ralph Lauren sweater vest over a button-down shirt and tie spoke of his conservative bent. One he undoubtedly shared with many others on the board.

She hoped witnessing the good she was doing with her students would sway him in her favor.

"Part of our duties include attending student activities," Mr. Walker went on. "I am quite a fan of American poetry. Indeed, I was intrigued when I recently learned about the club's formation."

"Oh, I've been hearing about this event for weeks now. Hi, I'm Debra Hall, thrilled to join you." The young mom's exuberance eased Rosa's nervousness. Debra's curly, black bob bounced as she surveyed the room, waving to Marla and her parents seated at a table off to the right.

"Marla's our babysitter," Debra explained. "As soon as she joined the club, she told us about it. She's even gotten our eight-year-old writing poetry verses. Her latest bedtime must-read is *Where the Sidewalk Ends*, so thank you."

"That's wonderful," Rosa answered, relieved by the positive endorsement. "Marla's a great addition to the group. All the students have been rehearsing in preparation for tonight. Some are a little more nervous than others. But they're excited to share their pieces."

"We are looking forward to it. As it seems many others are, too," Father Yosef said, smiling as he took in the number of people filling the library tables.

After handing each of them a program listing the individual students and the titles of their poems, she gestured toward the card table set up at the end of the checkout counter. A Christmas-y tablecloth covered the table laden with two liters of soda, water bottles, cups with ice, and a tasty mix of pan dulce, her niece's favorite Florecitas cookies, brownies, and other desserts.

"Please, enjoy the refreshments and find yourself a seat. We'll get started in"—Rosa glanced at her slender gold watch—"less than twenty minutes."

The group moved farther into the open space, but Rosa remained by the door, taking in the scene before her.

All her students had arrived early as requested, so there were no worries about tardiness or no-shows.

The boys looked dapper in dress shirts and slacks. Iván and Ricky had balked at her suggestion of wearing a tie. Unlike Javier, who sported a skinny black tie paired with black dress pants and a cranberry shirt.

The girls had jumped at the opportunity to leave their school uniforms at home, especially Marla and Barbara. Those two constantly chattered about the latest fashion trends, bemoaning their uniforms. Thankfully they'd remembered that even night functions were held to school dress codes. Barbara's red suede skirt barely hit below her fingertips, but her brown leggings did the trick.

Across the room, Ricky laughed at something his younger brother said, and Rosa smiled along with them.

A sense of satisfaction filled her, calming her nervous jitters.

They had a really great turnout.

Family and friends had come in support of each student, filling most of the six-person tables. Carlotta's entire family was here, along with Iván's abuela and Sherry Robinson, the English teacher who'd given him the ultimatum that had led to his joining the club in the first place. It pleased Rosa to see her coworker supporting him. Javier's parents and older brother sat at another table. His younger sister made her way toward them with two pieces of pan dulce and a cup of soda, her dark pigtails bouncing with each step. Barbara and Marla's group took up three whole tables. Their parents, their siblings, a few girlfriends, and now Debra Hall gathered around chatting.

Lilí and Yaz were seated to the left of the podium on the opposite side of the room. Maria and Tomás had wandered off to the children's section, but a napkin holding a brownie and a pile of Florecitas marked her niece's spot.

The only person missing was Jeremy, who'd sent a text earlier letting her know he was leaving work and on his way. Traffic could be difficult heading out of the city this time of day. She prayed he'd make it on time.

Confident that everyone else was taken care of, Rosa headed to her office to gather her notes and center her thoughts before they started.

She closed the door behind her, shutting out the din not commonly allowed in her library. Tonight, she was grateful to hear it.

A nervous flutter tickled her belly. She pressed a hand to her stomach, rubbing it through the material of her sweater dress. The combination of nerves and nausea had kept her from eating all but a few bites of papaya and pureed soup most of the day until dinner, which had consisted of several Export Soda crackers and warm rice water.

With Father Yosef, the two board members, and all the parents in attendance, tonight needed to go well. A trip to the bathroom to be sick was not how she wanted to start things off. Not if her goal was that, this time next year, she'd be in this same office, getting ready for the second annual Poetry Club fall open mic night.

Stepping to the front of her desk, Rosa gathered up her notes along with her Moleskine poetry journal, which she'd brought to show during her welcome. It was a testament to the value and importance of the written word in her life, though the words within it would remain private, like always. Performing in front of a crowd had never come easy for her, and her poems were too personal to share in front of a crowd.

The office door opened behind her, the noise in the library filtering in, and she glanced over her shoulder. Relief coursed through her as Jeremy stepped inside, then shut the door. Dressed in a classic dark blue suit, the two-button jacket perfectly fitted across his broad shoulders, he looked devastatingly handsome. But it was the light shining in his blue eyes, the tentative smile directed right at her that stole her heart.

"You made it!"

His grin widened at her excited words. "Wouldn't have missed this for anything."

He drew his left arm from behind his back to hold out a bouquet of beautiful red roses with white touches of baby's breath and greenery intermixed.

"For me?" She dropped her notes and poetry journal on her desk and buried her nose in the flowers, breathing in their rich aroma.

"A little token to say break a leg."

"I'm not performing, you know." She eyed him above the edge of the gold cellophane wrapped around the bouquet.

"I know." He quirked his head to the side, eyeing her with a considering stare. "But this is your show. One you've been working toward as much as your kids have. It means a lot to you. So, it means a lot to me."

"Thank you," she murmured, touched that he recognized the importance of tonight for her.

Jeremy checked his cell phone, then slid it back in his pants pocket. "Look, I know you don't have much time, so I'll try to be brief. If tonight is like the dance school's holiday recital, I might not get a chance to speak to you alone if your family plans their usual celebratory hot chocolate extravaganza."

"You know you're welcome to join us," she invited.

"Thanks." He tugged at his shirt collar, a frown crossing his brow momentarily before clearing away. "The thing is, I've been doing a lot of thinking. And talking—with my dad and Mark Henderson. I was up at the crack of dawn this morning. Sitting on my balcony, watching the sunrise over the city, and all I wanted to do was be here, in Oakton. With you."

His unexpected admission had Rosa's heart skipping a few beats. Her arms going slack at her sides. The bouquet nearly slipped from her fingers, her mind registering the flowers sliding out of her grasp seconds before they dropped to the floor.

In a few long strides, Jeremy stood right in front of her. The seriousness of his gaze, the intensity in his strong jaw took her breath away. His hands encircled her forearms below the edge of her three-quarter-length sleeves, and the heat from his touch sent sparks smoldering through her.

"I know my timing is crappy," he said, desperation tingeing his voice. "But I've waited too long to say this already. I don't want to wait another day."

"You're kinda scaring me, Jeremy," she whispered. Pero Dios, she hoped it was scary for a good reason.

"I'm sorry." He cupped her cheeks with both hands, his touch gentle. "I understand that tonight is important. And you're nervous. I'm hoping what I have to say will reassure you in some way. Last night, you told me that all you want is for me to be happy. Is that true?"

Not trusting her voice, Rosa nodded mutely.

"Good. First, I said yes to the job at the law firm. Working alongside my dad and brother is what I've always wanted. I know that'll make me happy. But not completely. What I *really need* in order to be happy is you. For us to live here, in Oakton, starting our family together. Not because it's the right thing to do, but because there's no other place I want to be. No other person I want to be with. Not just because you're having our child. But because you're the woman who has taught me the value and importance of family. You are my familia."

Tears burned in Rosa's eyes. She bit her lip, wanting to believe him. Afraid to do so.

Jeremy brushed his thumbs across her bottom lip, prying it loose from her bite. He bent down to drop the lightest of kisses on her lips.

"If you need time to figure things out, to be sure, I'll wait. Just know, I'm not going anywhere. Not out of a misguided sense of responsibility. But because *this* is where I want to be. Are we clear?"

Again, she nodded dumbly. Shocked by his heartfelt declaration.

"I love you, Rosa Fernandez. So get used to me being in your corner."

Jeremy dropped another quick kiss on her mouth, then quietly left her office.

As soon as the door closed behind him, Rosa fell back onto the edge of her desk. Her heart pounded in her chest, the sound a loud echo in her ears. His words played over and over in her head like a recording stuck on repeat.

I love you, Rosa Fernandez.

I love you, Rosa Fernandez.

Elation bubbled up into a giggle, and Rosa slapped a hand over her mouth in shock.

Ave Maria purísima. Jeremy loved her.

Her mind raced over the past few weeks, everything he'd done to show her. The realities about himself he'd faced. The decisions he'd made. All proof of his love and commitment to her.

And here she sat vacillating. Afraid to trust. To believe.

Why?

Hadn't she told her sisters that she was determined to be stronger? To not doubt herself?

Hadn't this all started because the night of Yazmine's wedding she'd decided to take a leap and go for what she desired? Namely him.

How could she ask Jeremy to soul search, if she herself wasn't willing to do the same? Willing to take a chance.

Suddenly, an idea sparked. A scary one. But still . . . she knew what she had to do.

Dios mío, the very idea terrified her, which meant it was exactly the right thing.

Rosa stepped to the podium on trembling legs amid the sound of fingers snapping in appreciation of Javier's spoken-word performance. The kid had wowed the audience with his wit, keen play on words, and intellectual view of the world and his place in it.

All of her students had done well. The chorus of snaps and proud smiles from family and friends throughout the night had filled her with pride for her kids.

Adjusting the mic with one hand, Rosa held a death grip on her journal with the other. Sweat slicked her palms, trickled down her spine. A nervous shiver shimmied across her shoulder blades and she adjusted the cowl neckline of her grey sweater dress, flush with heat.

"How about another round of snaps for all our students and their amazing job tonight?" she said.

She waited several seconds, allowing the kids to soak in the audience's appreciation. They deserved it.

"Now, I know the program lists Javier as our final performer. But if you will indulge me. It seems as if my students"—she let her gaze travel the room, pausing on each one of her kids—"along with one other special person"—she looked at Jeremy, the surprise in his baby blues giving her enough of a confidence boost to continue—"have given me a heavy dose of courage and there's a short piece I'd like to share."

Carlotta clapped with glee, the young girl's obvious pleasure tugging a nervous smile from Rosa.

She chanced a quick look at her sisters, both of whom stared at her with wide bug eyes. They knew sharing her work was something Rosa never—not rarely, but never—did.

As she opened her journal, Papi's letter marking her place, Rosa closed her eyes. She didn't need to see the letter to know what it said.

Papi's voice spoke to her, as if he stood beside her whispering the words in her ear.

Es hora de que escribas tu historia. Sé que va a ser una maravilla.

He was right. The time had come for her to write her own story. And yes, it was going to be marvelous.

"This piece is untitled. Because, well . . ." She cleared her throat, gripped the edges of the podium to keep her hands from shaking.

"Because I, um, I actually finished it moments before we started this evening. So, um, here we go."

Eyes glued to the words she'd carefully written on the page, she took a deep breath, offered up a prayer for courage, and began reading aloud:

Untitled

It ebbs; it flows.
It takes you down paths undiscovered.

It warms you. Scares you.
Makes a person bare her deepest soul.

It hurts. Empowers.
Confuses, elates,
Excites, alarms,
Overwhelms and takes your breath away.

It comforts in the darkest of times,
Challenges you to rise up and fight
For good, for what's right, for each other.

And when Love beckons,
When he asks you to trust,
To believe,
To take that leap together, till death do you part . . .

The answer, para siempre, *for always, is Yes.*

When she reached the last word, not a single snap sounded in the library, as if somehow everyone knew the importance of this moment.

Rosa raised her head to meet Jeremy's gaze. He stood next to his chair, his expression a sweet mix of questioning wonder.

Yes, she mouthed the word to him. Wanting her message to be clear.

He stepped toward her, and Rosa moved out from behind the podium, meeting him halfway.

"Does this mean what I hope it means?" He reached for her hands, clutched them tightly between his.

"Yes," she repeated, her pulse racing with hopeful anticipation.

A huge grin split Jeremy's face seconds before he wrapped her in his strong embrace.

The library erupted with the sound of snaps intermixed with loud clapping.

"You don't know how badly I want to kiss you," Jeremy growled in her ear.

Rosa pressed her cheek against his. "There'll be plenty of that happening later tonight if I have anything to say about it. And in case you haven't figured it out yet, I love you, too, Jeremy Taylor."

He squeezed her tighter, and Rosa snaked her arms around his waist to do the same.

"Now that I've got you, I'm never letting you go," Jeremy told her.

She gazed up at him, marveling at the love shining in his eyes. "That's a promise I'm going to hold you to."

"I'm a better man because of you, Rosa." He pressed his forehead to hers. "Thank you for giving us a chance."

"This isn't a chance—it's a commitment. For today, and always."

"Para siempre." He repeated the line from her poem and her heart swelled with love.

For always.

If you enjoyed *Her Perfect Affair*,
be sure not to miss the first book in
Priscilla Oliveras's Matched to Perfection series,

HIS PERFECT PARTNER

Ad executive Tomás Garcia shouldn't even be thinking about
his daughter's alluring dance teacher, Yazmine Fernandez.
Burned by a shattering divorce, he's laser-focused on his
career—and giving his young daughter, Maria, the secure home
she deserves. Plus, he's certain that with her talent, Yaz will be
leaving Chicago and heading back to Broadway as soon as she
can. But Yaz's generous spirit and caring concern are sparking a
desire Tomás can't resist—and doesn't want to let go . . .

For Yaz, good-looking workaholics like Tomás simply can't be
part of her life ever again. She owes it to herself to get back her
confidence and fulfill the dreams her papá could not. She's glad
to spend time with Maria—and taste the family life she feels she
can never have. And she's sure that she and Tomás can keep
their attraction under control because there's so much at stake.
But each unexpected intimacy, each self-revelation, makes the
fire between them grow hotter with every step—and every risk
to their hearts . . .

Keep reading for a special look!

Available wherever books are sold.

The hottest guy to ever hit Oakton, Illinois, lingered outside her dance studio doorway, bringing Yazmine Fernandez to a stutter-step stop.

Seriously, the guy was like manna-from-heaven Latino *GQ*—from the top of his closely cropped jet-black hair, down his six-foot muscular frame, to the soles of his shiny wing-tip shoes.

Behind her, seven pairs of dancers scrambled to remember the next step in the preschool father-daughter Christmas dance. But Yazmine couldn't look away.

"Hey, a little help here?" One of the dads waved at her from the back row.

"Sorry." Yaz listened to the music for several beats, then fell back into step with their "I Saw Mommy Kissing Santa Claus" routine.

In the studio's mirror-lined wall she caught the stranger's flustered scowl. Even frowning, he still made her heart hop-skip in her chest.

Dios mío, she'd obviously neglected her social life for too long. Sure, her dance card had been pretty full with other obligations for nearly eighteen months now, but her lack of partner-dance practice shouldn't account for the heat prickling her insides. In her line of work, hunky guys were always on the cast list.

Then again, drop an attention-grabbing, well-built man into a room full of suburban soccer dads, and a woman's thoughts naturally wandered down a road better left untraveled.

Untraveled by her, anyway.

The newcomer's gaze skimmed across the people in her studio.

Yaz brightened her smile, but he turned away without even noticing her. Disappointed, and strangely selfconscious, she tugged at the bodice of her camisole leotard as she led the group into a jazz square.

The song's second verse transitioned to the chorus repetition, and Yaz wove through the front line to get a better look at the back row. "Left hand, Mr. Johnson—your other left."

The dad groaned, his daughter giggling at his exaggerated grimace.

"Don't worry, you'll get it." Yaz peeked over the child's shoulder to the studio doorway again.

The hunk glared down at his phone, flicking through something on the screen. His mouth thinned as he slid the cell into the pocket of his suit jacket. Yaz's stomach executed a jittery little sashay.

This guy had to be in the wrong place. No way she'd forget meeting him before at the dance studio.

Yaz dropped her gaze to his left ring finger. Bare.

Not that it should matter to her. She'd learned the hard way it was much better to look than to touch. Especially if a girl didn't want to get her fingers singed, or her heart flambéed.

Besides, as soon as Papi's oncologist gave him the all clear, she'd be on the first direct flight out of Chicago, headed back to New York and Broadway. Nothing would stand in her way this time.

The holiday song drew to a close. Fathers bowed. Daughters curtsied. GQ stepped into her studio.

Anticipation fluttered a million, spastic butterfly wings in her chest. He probably needed directions to another business close by.

Yaz hurried toward him. "Excuse me, do you need some help?"

Or, better yet, a no-strings-attached date for a night out in nearby Chicago?

"Papá!"

Maria Garcia jumped up from her seat on the floor along the back wall, running to fling her arms around the man's thighs. Everyone else in the class turned at the commotion.

Increíble. Apparently the hunk *did* belong here. To the usually subdued, adorable five-year-old who'd joined the class in mid-September.

At his daughter's screech of delight, the worried scowl vanished from the man's features. Relief and joy surged in. For a moment Yaz bought into his pleasure, savoring the smile that softened his chiseled face with boyish charm.

Then, with the stinging slap of a bitter Chicago wind, Yaz recalled the number of practices Maria's father had skipped over the past two months—the number of classes when the child had sat alone in the back and the number of times she'd had to partner with Mrs. Buckley, her grandmotherly nanny, because her father had failed to show up as promised. Again.

The attraction searing through Yaz's body cooled as fast as if she'd dunked herself into an ice bath after a marathon day of rehearsal.

Bendito sea Dios, the prodigal father, more focused on his advertising career than his child, had finally arrived—tardy, of course. Blessed be God, indeed.

"You made it!" Surprise heightened Maria's high pitched cry.

"I sure did, chiquita." Mr. Garcia scooped up his daughter and spun her around, the picture of familial bliss.

Maria grinned with pleasure.

Still, Yaz couldn't stop remembering the hurt in the little girl's eyes over the past weeks because of her father's absences. Legs shaking, she strode to the corner table at the front of the room and jabbed the stop button on her iPod speakers. "Everyone, let's take a five-minute water break."

Mr. Garcia and Maria stepped to the side of the room so the other class members could head to the lobby area.

Anger over the weeks of disappointment he'd brought on his daughter pulsed a heavy, deep bass beat in Yaz's chest. She sucked in what was supposed to be a calming breath and counted to ten. Then twenty.

So much for her brief fantasy of a friendly night out with a hunky stranger. Her first since long before she'd left New York to come home. That definitely wasn't going to happen. Not with this man.

Visit our website at
KensingtonBooks.com
to sign up for our newsletters, read
more from your favorite authors, see
books by series, view reading group
guides, and more!

Become a Part of Our
Between the Chapters Book Club
Community and Join the Conversation

Betweenthechapters.net

Submit your book review for a chance to win exclusive
Between the Chapters swag you can't get anywhere else!
https://www.kensingtonbooks.com/pages/review/